THE FIRE

A Love in O'Leary Novel

MAY ARCHER

Cover Art: Cate Ashwood
Editing: Sandra, One Love Editing
Professional Beta Reader: Leslie Copeland

All the good bits are theirs, and any mistakes are my own!

The Fire

Jameson Burke is the most arrogant, infuriating human on the planet. He's also taller, broader, and impossibly *hotter* than he was before I left town.

For ten years, I dreamed of coming back to O'Leary to open my own bar. Safe to say the reality hasn't lived up to my expectations. Even though the town's the same as it ever was — same beautiful scenery, same wonderful, ridiculous residents — it's hard to feel welcome when your first love and childhood best friend makes it clear you're public enemy number one. And then, *oh yeah*, when your *bar burns to the ground* and you're stuck begging for a place to stay.

But just when I'm ready to give up on the dream entirely, Jamie and I are thrown together in a blizzard and everything changes. One single, scorching night is enough to prove the spark between us never really died, and suddenly I'm dreaming a new dream — one where Jamie lets go of the past and we build something entirely new... *together*.

Prologue

PARKER

Circa 2002

I STEPPED out the double doors of the school into the playground and squinted my eyes against the glare of the sun. All around me, kids were yelling their heads off, running around like a swarm of ants, dangling from monkey bars like we were still first graders, shoving at each other and screaming obscenities that would get them in trouble once Mrs. Simms came out to supervise.

If she bothered coming out to supervise.

I'd overheard my mom telling my dad that Mrs. Simms was overpaid and overfed. She said Mrs. Simms was a glorified babysitter. She also said Mrs. Simms only had the job because her husband was a coach at the high school and people felt sorry for her.

My mom was on the town council, so she knew all kinds of things.

I'd learned over the years to keep these things to myself.

I carried my lunch—in a paper bag, just like everyone else, since I'd managed to "lose" three of the high-end thermal bags my mom liked, and she'd decided to "punish" me by not buying me a new one, thank God—over to the picnic table in the far corner under the trees. It had rained last night, and the sun hadn't penetrated the shade enough to dry this table, but I didn't care. It meant no one was likely to bug me.

I knew I was pretty much the only person in the world who hated springtime. Everyone else in school was all about summer coming and outdoor lunch periods, an end to the everlasting snow. My mom was all about her garden. My dad was all about signing me up for the town baseball league, because hope sprang eternal that I was gonna be a sports prodigy, even though most of the un-talented kids like me had dropped out way before seventh grade.

But me? I'd take snow days forever, thank you very much. Winter meant staying indoors and books, which were way more interesting than people—at least, any of the people I knew. Someday, when I got away from O'Leary, I was gonna go someplace even snowier and more isolated. Moscow seemed promising.

Possibly Mongolia.

I emptied my lunch bag onto the table and glanced around to see how likely it was that someone would hassle me, but everyone seemed occupied. The eighth and ninth grade boys had claimed the jungle gym as their own kingdom, as usual. Sixth and seventh grade girls were clustered on the swings. Dex Albright and the other kids my mom called "*Bernley Estates trailer trash*" were nowhere in sight. I figured it was safe enough to pull out my book.

And that's why I didn't notice when someone approached.

"Hey. Um. Parker, can I sit with you?"

I glanced up to find Molly Burke standing awkwardly next to my table, twisting her hair around her finger. I frowned.

Molly was quiet but in a kind of fairy princess way that made her *more* popular instead of less. We'd been in the same school for the past six years, but she was a year older than me, and I wasn't sure she'd ever talked to me voluntarily before.

"Sit with me? What for?"

So smooth with the manners, Parker.

Molly blushed. "Uh, because I don't have anywhere else to sit?"

She darted a look at a table of eighth grade girls nearby, and they collapsed into giggles when they saw her looking.

I shuddered. Individually, girls were lovely. But in a pack, they sorta reminded me of hyenas. *Hungry* ones.

"Sure," I told Molly, nodding at the empty side of the table. "If you want to."

Molly set her bag down across from me and took out her lunch. I noticed that *she* carried a thermal lunch bag and nobody seemed to give *her* shit about it. Or maybe they did, for all I knew. But when she unzipped it, I also saw that the inside was badly torn and had been mended with duct tape, and that the entire contents of the bag were a water bottle, a tiny orange, and a peanut butter sandwich.

I looked away.

The Burkes weren't Bernley Estates trailer trash—for one thing, they lived in a cute little house over on Lobelia —but I also knew they weren't the kind of people my mom wanted me associating with. Mr. Burke laughed a little too hard and a little too long, and I was pretty sure he'd held a variety of jobs, none for very long. Mrs. Burke looked like she didn't laugh at all. They never volunteered for town committees or festivals like my parents did.

But Molly had really kind eyes and she was… peaceful. Sweet. Interesting.

I slid my book back into my backpack.

Molly noticed.

"I loved that book," she said. "But I like the latest one in the series better. Have you read it?"

"Of course." I nodded. "Bunches of times." Then something compelled me to add, "But they're little kid books. I read other stuff too."

"Well, I don't think they're kid books," Molly said, unwrapping her sandwich. "And neither does my brother."

I paused in the act of opening my juice box. "Your brother? Jamie?"

She tilted her head to one side. "I only have one brother."

"Oh." I shook my head. "I know. I just meant I didn't think he liked to read. Especially *Harry Potter*."

Molly frowned. "Why would you say that?"

"Well, because he's, you know…" I waved my hand, trying to encompass all that Jamie Burke was. Freakishly tall. Smiley. Popular with guys and girls alike. "Good at baseball."

Molly laughed, and her eyes crinkled up at the sides, just like Jamie's did. "And people can only be good at one thing? Or like one thing?"

"No." My face flamed, and I squeezed my juice box so hard it shot fruit punch all over my brand-new polo shirt.

I darted a glance toward the older boys. Jamie was as easy to pick out of the crowd as a tree in a meadow. He had a mop of wiry, red-brown hair, eyes that were nearly the same warm, cinnamon color, and a kind of red-gold tinge to his skin, no matter the season. Plus, he was nearly a head taller than everyone else on the playground, which meant he was like five heads taller than *me*. My dad, who always insisted on us staying and watching the older kids' baseball games after my game was over because it was supposed to inspire me or something, had said Jamie Burke had "filled out early" and that "his stature combined with his natural talent meant he was gonna do great things someday."

I hated Jamie Burke a little.

"I mean, you play baseball too, right?" Molly continued, like this proved her point.

I turned away from Jamie to look at her. "Oh, I play. I'm not any good though. Mostly, I stand in one spot and pray the ball never comes in my direction." Dex said I threw like a girl, but that was bullshit because Grace and Mariely threw better than I ever had.

I opened my potato chips and offered them to Molly.

She smiled as she took one. "You could ask Jamie for help, I bet. He'd, like, coach you or whatever. He's really patient." She leaned across the table confidingly and added, "Pretty sure he's a Hufflepuff."

I laughed out loud. I *read* fantasy, but I didn't *believe* in it. There was no realm in which I would consider asking Jamie Burke—the best ball player in ninth grade—to help my scrawny self, even if he was a *Harry Potter* fan.

Death first.

"You're sweet, Molly," I began.

"Well, shit, Parkie!" said a voice from behind me. "Look at you flirting with a girl. I didn't think you knew how."

I rolled my eyes and sat up straighter.

"Go away, Dexter," Molly said. "Nobody was talking to you."

Dexter sat down beside Molly, forcing her to scoot over.

Pete Daley, the shortest kid in school, took a seat on her other side so she was stuck in place, and grabbed my chips from the center of the table. "Oooh, fancy chips." He stuffed a handful in his mouth. "Parkie's mom buys the good shit."

Mike Morris, the third member of their troupe, sat down next to me and grinned.

I gritted my teeth.

Don't engage with the bullies, and they'll leave you alone, Parker, my mom always said but that was bullshit. I wondered if there were a point in human history when that strategy had ever really worked or if it was just some line they taught in a parenting book. Either way, I'd never once *engaged* with Dex, but he'd still picked on me constantly for years, just because my hair was too tidy, or my grades were too good, or my jackets were too expensive or, well, because I couldn't throw a baseball for shit.

Though maybe I deserved that last one.

"Come on, Molly," I said, grabbing my backpack and pushing to my feet. "It's getting crowded here."

Molly tried to get up, but Dex draped an arm over her shoulders.

"You go on, loser," he said. "Molly would rather hang with us."

Molly attempted to shrug off his arm. "Actually, I wouldn't."

"But we've got lots to talk about," Dex said. "You remember Sandy's cousin Danielle lives in Rushton."

Molly turned red. "So?"

"Soooo. Did you think we wouldn't hear what you did last weekend?" Dex grinned, and Mike and Pete laughed.

Mike bumped his shoulder into mine so hard I almost fell off the bench. "Molly let some guy named Jason get to second base," he explained, mostly just to watch Molly squirm. Then he added with fake seriousness. "Oh, shit. You probably don't even know what that means, do you? It means she let him touch her—"

"I *know* what it means," I interrupted, feeling my face flame. I mean, I only knew what it meant in a *hypothetical* sort of way. I'd never actually experienced it, and honestly, I hadn't wanted to. No matter how many times my mom pestered my dad into asking me if there were any "special" girls at school or if I needed any advice, and no matter how seriously I wanted to please them both, I couldn't seem to muster much enthusiasm for girls. My Nana Mary said I was a late bloomer. I wasn't so sure.

Judging by the mortified look on Molly's face and the way she stared at her sandwich like she couldn't decide whether to cry or commit murder, I didn't think I was missing much.

"Get your hand off her," I said. "Whatever she did or didn't do is none of your fucking business."

Pete snorted. "Will you listen to the mouth on him?" he demanded of no one in particular. "S'not your business to decide our business, Parkie-poo. You can shut right the fuck up before I *make you*."

"Dexter, you're such an idiot. My brother is *right there*." Molly nodded her head toward Jamie. "Move your arm, or I'll call him over."

"You want Jamie to come over here and hear how his *fourteen-year-old sister* has been spending her time, be my guest," Dexter retorted with a grin. "Rumors usually come from somewhere, Molls."

Molly bit her lip and looked up at me like she was torn between suffering embarrassment or suffering *Dexter*. And *she* hadn't done a damn thing to engage him or to bring this bullying on herself any more than I ever had. Molly's eyes filled with tears, and that was *unacceptable.* So I did what any red-blooded man in my position would do.

I grabbed my fruit punch and squirted it in Dexter's face.

It got in his hair. It dripped all over his t-shirt. It formed a puddle on the tabletop. Meanwhile, Dexter's mouth opened, and he gaped like a fish, completely unable to comprehend what had just happened.

It was possibly the greatest moment of my entire life.

Then, all hell broke loose.

I mean, as expected, right?

Dexter jumped up and grabbed me by the hair, which was kind of humiliating, then threw me on the ground, which was painful. He landed on top of me with a knee to the stomach that stole my breath and a knee on my left arm that was gonna bruise like heck, while someone else— probably Pete or Mike—held my other arm down. Dex lifted his arm back to hit me, and you know what? I didn't even care. I was *glad*. Because *fuck him.*

And then suddenly, Dex wasn't there anymore. He was lifted clean off me so I could breathe again. I sat up and saw Dexter bent over the picnic table, with his hands held behind his back, while Jamie Burke mashed his face into the puddle of juice.

"What the hell are you doing, Dexter?" Jamie demanded. "Why's my sister screaming her head off?"

No lie, Jamie didn't look angry. He wasn't even winded. He'd just picked Dexter up, bodily thrown him over the table, and was holding him in place while he wriggled like prey in the paws of a hunter. It was… impressive.

So impressive, I was having trouble catching my own breath, and my stomach was tying itself into knots and…

Oh. *Ohhhhhhh.* So many things became so very clear in that moment.

Could a late bloomer bloom all at once? I was pretty sure he could. I was pretty sure I *did.*

I rolled over, feeling wet mud seep through the knees of my jeans, and tried to stand, but my stomach was aching and my arm *killed,* so I knelt and watched the show while my heart beat furiously.

"Get off me, man!" Dexter screeched.

I didn't scream at all, I thought, perhaps a bit too smugly for a guy who was still on his knees in the mud. *Who's the loser now, Dex?*

"Parker was saying shit about Molly," Dexter lied. "I was defending her."

"What?" I gasped.

"Wasn't I, Molly?" Dexter insisted.

My eyes tracked left to where Molly was standing, arms folded over her chest. She looked at Dexter in disgust, but her throat was working like she couldn't quite force herself to speak up.

Jamie looked over his shoulder at me, and I thought maybe it was the first time he'd ever actually looked *directly* at me, because his eyes narrowed like he wasn't quite sure what to make of me.

"That true?" he demanded.

I shook my head silently, my eyes still locked on his.

He seemed to be waiting for something, though. Some kind of vocal denial or explanation. Molly didn't seem capable of speech, and Dexter sure as hell wasn't capable of speaking *truth,* so I opened my mouth and what came out was…

"I'm a *Gryffindor* for God's sake."

Oh, sweet Jesus, kill me now.

Jamie frowned for a second, like I was speaking a

language he didn't know, and I knew without a doubt that I was going to vomit—literally vomit, right there and then—from the shame.

Then his lips twitched, and his eyes got brighter, like something had lit them up from behind, and I felt some part of myself leave my body and go flying off forever, even before Jamie looked me up and down and said, "Figures. Gryffindors are a bunch of troublemakers."

"Jameson Burke!" Mrs. Simms called out shrilly. Figured she'd finally arrive on the scene at the worst possible moment. "Let go of Mr. Albright at once!"

With a sigh that maybe only I noticed, since I was watching *him* while everyone else was watching Mrs. Simms, Jamie took a step back and let Dexter go.

Like he could feel the weight of my stare on him, Jamie turned in my direction and noticed me still on the ground. "Oh, shoot. Here, lemme help." He reached out a hand and I grabbed it with my good arm, letting him haul me to my feet, and I maybe tried to memorize exactly what his hand felt like and what his eyes looked like up close, just in case I never got to see them again.

"What in heaven's name is happening here?" Mrs. Simms demanded.

"I was trying to—" Dex began.

"Jamie was helping me, Mrs. Simms," I said. "Dexter and I were… roughhousing, and I'm pretty sure he hurt my arm." I nodded at my left arm, which was curled against my chest.

"Roughhousing," she repeated, eyes narrowed. She looked at all five feet of me, and all five-something of Dexter, did some fast calculus, and came to the obvious conclusion. "Voluntarily?"

"Erm. It's all a blur?" I offered, unwilling to give Dexter a chance to defend himself that might embarrass

Molly. "The injury was accidental, of course. But, like, I think maybe I also have internal bleeding? Sooo… possibly we could discuss details later and you could get me some medical care now?"

Mrs. Simms's eyes narrowed farther. "Internal bleeding?"

"Knee to the gut," I explained, hunching over slightly. I didn't have to fake my wince. "Liver. Spleen. Stomach. *Vital organs.*" She still seemed suspicious, so I invoked the name that was bound to get the most action. "I'm thinking *my mother* would be pretty horrified if I wasn't seen immediately. We should call her."

Mrs. Simms's head went back. "Your mother. Oh! Yes. Of course." She threw out her hands in a flapping motion. "Everyone back to what you were doing. Jameson, help Parker to the office while I call Mrs. Hoffstraeder." She said this like she was preparing to do battle against a five-star general, because she *was.*

She made her way back to the school, leaving me to limp along behind her.

Jamie caught up to me a second later, my backpack slung over his right shoulder.

"Oh," I said. "Thanks. I didn't even notice I dropped it."

"It's a little muddy, but it'll be fine once you wash it."

The guy didn't know my mother *at all.* I'd have a brand new one by Monday. One Jamie had never touched. Unless I washed it myself and made sure she didn't see…

I was totally gonna wash it myself.

"Whoa. He really got you good, huh?" Jamie stepped into me and slid his hand around my waist. "You look all confused. Think you're okay to walk?"

"Yeah. I mean, *yes.* My legs are working fine," I told him. But I didn't protest too much because my stomach was all nauseous and excited, and because Jamie Burke smelled like he'd been eating oranges, and that suddenly seemed like the most crucial, intensely personal information I'd ever possessed about another human being.

"I'm not exactly sure what happened back there, but Molly looks pissed and Dexter was covered in fruit punch, so… I'm guessing I owe you one?" Jamie said, completely unaware that I was committing to memory every cell of his skin that came into contact with my own.

I forced myself to laugh, even though it made my stomach hurt. "It's fine. I like Molly." I stopped walking suddenly. "I mean, as a person. Not, like I… you know… *like* her or… anything?"

Jamie snorted and half-dragged me back into motion. "I get it. You're a good kid." He paused, then added, "For a Gryffindor."

I groaned. "I need you to never speak of that to me again."

He laughed. "It was hilarious."

"It was awful."

"Awfully *hilarious*, you mean. But fine. I won't mention it."

"Pinkie swear?" I demanded, as we approached the school.

Jamie opened the heavy fire door for me and ushered me into the cool darkness of the back hallway. Then he obediently held out his hand and linked his pinkie with mine.

"That doesn't mean I've forgotten it, though," Jamie warned. "Memories don't turn off just because you want them to. Not even for *the* Parker Hoffstraeder."

Then Jameson Burke—the baseball prodigy, the popular kid, the guy I'd just realized was the hottest person in all of O'Leary or possibly the world—winked at me, dorky Parker Hoffstraeder—all five late-blooming feet of me—like we were friends.

And I was really fucking glad that memories worked that way, and there were some things you could never forget because I was never going to want to forget a single second of my friendship with Jamie Burke.

Chapter One

"Oᴏ, my God, Ricky! Yes! Yes! *Yesssss!*" a woman screeched as the pounding from the other side of the wall picked up pace for the second time that night.

My eyes flew open in the darkness. "Oh, sweet baby Jesus," I whispered, though I was fairly confident nobody up there listened to me anymore. "No, no, *no.* Doesn't anybody *sleep* around here anymore?"

The clock radio on the nightstand, an ancient relic that had probably been the bee's knees back in the eighties when I was *born*, read 12:22 a.m., and I whimpered. I'd been out for less than an hour after the last round of sexcapades next door, and I was fucking *tired.*

Tired of ten days stuck in this tiny room with its lumpy mattress and shitty internet.

Tired of trying to smile and pretend to be strong and patient when I was actually *neither.*

Tired of not being able to sleep for more than two hours at a stretch before bolting upright with the scent of smoke in my nose and the absolute conviction that something, somewhere was on fire.

And above all, tired of the fact that nothing in my life was under my control.

You'd think the one good thing about returning to my hometown—the tiniest, sleepiest town in all the land, where even the grocery store closed promptly at seven—after over a decade in Boston would be the ability to actually *sleep*, right?

You'd be wrong.

"Ricky! Love me forever. Don't ever stop!"

Please, Ricky. Please make it stop.

I grabbed my pillow and pulled it over my face.

"You're incredible, Ricky! So *fucking* incredible!"

Ricky indeed seemed fucking incredible. Or at least incredible at fucking. So incredible, in fact, that I'd been exposed to more explicit content over the past two evenings at the Crabapple Bed and Breakfast than I'd ever heard on an N.W.A album or in a low-budget porn. (Not that I'd know anything about that, since I had very specific taste in porn. I had *standards*, okay?) And, not to sound like my mom or whatever, but hadn't these two ever heard of discretion? This was a family-friendly establishment. Wasn't *someone* thinking of the *children*?

I was sure Ricky and his lady were a lovely couple, really. You'd better believe I'd checked them out this morning from across the breakfast room, expecting them to look like... I didn't know what, exactly. "Porn star" tattooed across their foreheads? Skin-tight leather? Horns and pitchforks, because only the morally bankrupt could have fulfilling sex lives?

Okay, so I *was* possibly becoming my mother.

But in any case, Ricky and Mrs. Ricky had seemed sweet. A typical thirty-something suburban soccer mom and dad who'd chosen to celebrate their ten-year anniversary in exciting, cosmopolitan O'Leary, of all places. Not remotely the kind of folks you'd think would be given to shouting, "I wanna fuck you against the window so everyone can watch!" and making noises like they were mutated dolphins stranded in Upstate New York attempting to locate the rest of their pod. Honestly, not the kind of people you'd imagine had the *stamina* to attempt to knock through the wall using the headboard as a battering ram not once but four times a night. But it just went to show that you could never judge based on appearances, right?

And good for them. Glad someone was getting some action since I sure as hell was *not*. I just wished their action didn't have to take place inches from my head when I really, really, no-but-*really* needed to sleep before I killed myself or someone else.

Oh, *sleep*. We used to be such good friends. Where did it all go wrong?

I groaned into the pillowcase, and the muffled sound blended into the high-pitched keening and the strangled shout from next door, like we were attempting some kind of three-part orgasmic harmony—though I knew one of us was definitely faking it—and the whole thing, my whole *life* right at that moment, was so ridiculous I couldn't help but simultaneously laugh and sob into the blessed silence as round two ended and Ricky likely took a hydration break.

It wasn't funny, but it also *was*. The humor of the situation was *right there* waiting for me to seize it, but I couldn't seem to get there. I'd realized over the past month that the secret to finding the humor, or the silver lining, or basically *anything* good in the incessant shitstorm of life, was having a person you could roll your eyes with about it. These days the proportion of shit life threw at me to people I could share it with was indecently high.

I mean, there was Caelan James, O'Leary's town baker.

Cal had been maybe my closest friend since I'd moved back to O'Leary last spring, and he was literally just down the street. He'd answer if I called, no doubt, with a growled, "*What?*" And just like he had last month when I'd called him and stammered that, holy shit, my fucking bar —my life's dream—was fucking on fucking *fire*, he'd haul his ass out of the bed where he was probably curled up tight around his boyfriend, Ash, and stand by me for as long as I needed. But I wouldn't call him.

Or there was Ethan Scott, my old roommate, the guy who'd moved from O'Leary to Boston with me back when we were dorky, barely legal freshmen at BU, and stuck with me when we were dorky, barely financially solvent twenty-somethings living in a tiny apartment over a bar in Allston. Ethan was in Bangkok now—or Bangladesh, or Banga-lore? I'd have to check his Insta again to be sure where he'd landed this week—but he'd take my call whether he was sleeping in a yurt or having some fancy foodie dinner with his crazy-rich entrepreneur boyfriend, Taika. And yet, I couldn't make myself call him either.

The sad, pathetic, disgusting, hopeless truth was that there was only one person I really wanted to talk to—only one person whose presence shined so brightly in my life that no substitute would do, even though we hadn't been friends since I'd left O'Leary for college. And if I called Jameson Burke right now, even though he was only two streets away, he'd probably block my number.

"*What we were is dead and buried, Parkie,*" he'd said, one of the many, *many* times I'd tried to talk to him since I'd moved back. "*Can't bring back the dead. So just leave me the hell alone.*"

The motherfucker *knew* how much I hated being called Parkie.

And worse than that, Jamie was probably cuddled up with *his* cute little boyfriend, Brian, while I was stuck in a hotel room across the street from the empty lot where my bar used to be, listening to *live heterosexual porn*.

Because life was nauseating like that.

"Ugh!"

I rolled over, pushed the pillow back under my head, closed my eyes resolutely, and took one of those deep, calming breaths I'd heard about. This was going to be *okay*. It was going to be *fine*. I just needed to relax and get some sleep and—

When the thumping started again, my eyes popped open. I was honest-to-God ready to channel my mother, storm next door, and tell Ricky, in my best Beatrice Hoffstraeder voice, to *consider his neighbors, for heaven's sake*… and also maybe ask him what kind of vitamins and supplements he was taking, because *seriously*… when I realized the noise wasn't coming from behind my head but from the hallway door.

"Parks? Yoo hoo! Parker!" Dana Cobb called.

Oh. Shit.

Dana was the manager of the Crabapple, and her voice was muffled but urgent, so I threw off my covers, rubbed a quick hand over my eyes, and strode across the room in two-point-five seconds to flick on the light and open the door, wondering what the hell had gone wrong *now*.

Dana looked exactly the same as she always did, no matter the season or, apparently, the hour of the day or night. Button-down shirt, chinos, relentlessly blonde hair tied back in a high, cheerleader ponytail. She opened her mouth to speak, took one look at me, and turned beet red, staring over my shoulder and blinking like she'd looked directly into the sun despite the dimness of the hallway. It was a sign of just how tired I was that it took me a full thirty seconds to realize she wasn't having some kind of stroke; she was reacting to the sight of my undies.

My tiny, zebra-printed, thong undies.

"Oh. Damn. Sorry, Dana," I said, backing into the room and pulling on the jeans I'd thrown over the desk chair. "I haven't done laundry and these were kind of a joke from… well." I cleared my throat. "Long story."

"I bet," Dana drawled. "Listen, sorry to interrupt, Parks, but, ah, folks on the second floor called down with a noise complaint."

"Yeah? Thank God." I buttoned and zipped my jeans into place before turning to face her again. "I wasn't gonna narc on Ricky and the missus, but they're getting a little ridiculous. I've barely slept in two nights."

"They?" Dana stepped into the room cautiously and looked around with her hands on her hips like she thought someone else might jump out at her. When no one did, she frowned. "You're… alone?"

"Duh. Who else would be in here?" I refrained from telling her I'd been living like a monk for months. "Just me and my succulents, and they hardly say a word." I waved a hand toward the little table by the window where my precious little houseplants waited for morning sunlight.

"Your… succulents." Dana took a step toward the table and peered down at the array of plants, then back up at me. "Parker, sweetness, I'm worried about you."

"Me?" I braced my hands on my hips and puffed my chest out. "I'm fine. Never better."

"Uh-huh." Her gaze didn't falter, and her skepticism was unmistakable.

"I mean, I'm tired," I admitted, my shoulders slumping

a bit. "Very tired. Those two have been scrumping like bunnies." I hooked a thumb at the connecting wall. "It's loud. I can't sleep."

"Uh-huh."

"And earlier in the week, I was going a little stir-crazy with no work to do every day. And no customers telling me their problems." I cleared my throat. "And limited cable television."

"Uh-huh."

"But otherwise, I'm great." I put a hand to my face. "Why? Do I *look* sick or something?"

"Where to begin…" She pursed her lips. "Precious, why do your plants have colored name tags painted on their pots? Maud, Lucille—" She glanced down again.

"Vera," I supplied. "As in, *aloe* vera. Because… because it's an *aloe* plant. *Heh*. Get it?"

"Yes, honey," she said with a kind of wide-eyed solemnity that suggested I was very naïve or possibly very insane. "I get it."

"It's a *pun*. A *cactus-based pun*."

"I know." She tilted her head and nodded slowly, sadly. "I know. And the name tags?"

I scrubbed at my hair. "Well, see, I inherited the girls when I moved into my old apartment over on Dunkirk Road because the last tenant left them behind. And I don't know the first thing about plants. Or *didn't*. So I just kept watering them a ton for a week, and then ignoring them for like ten weeks after that, because who has time to bother with plants, right?"

"Uh-huh."

"But then the other day. Or last week maybe?" I shrugged. "The days kinda blend together, huh? Anyway, I realized that I *did* have free time. Like, a *ton* of free time.

Epic amounts of free time. So I started researching them. On the internet."

"Uh-huh." Dana clasped her hands behind her back and gave me her patient, solemn look again. "And… the internet told you to make them tiny pots with names on them?"

"No, no, no. See, it turns out Vera and Maud *look* similar but actually have very different watering requirements." I snorted at my own naivety. "I was basically murdering them and didn't know it. So I had to get them new pots, obviously. And, like, why not paint names on there so I can tell them apart?"

"Uh-huh. Why not?" Dana tilted her head in the opposite direction, and her ponytail swished with the motion.

"And then I didn't want Lucille to feel left out if her sisters got new things and she didn't." I tweaked one of her green spines. "Lucille looks tough, but she's sensitive. Can't show favoritism."

"To… your plants."

"Yes." I stood marginally straighter. "Studies have shown that speaking to your plants and raising them in a positive environment helps them grow."

"Uh-huh."

"I mean, they're clearly living creatures, even if they can't act on their own. Although, you know, some schools of thought differ about that because on a cellular level, they do actually, uh… move." I cleared my throat as I realized just how many words I'd been saying and that Dana was looking at me with concern.

"That on the internet too?"

"Yes," I whispered.

"So, you talk to them *positively*."

"I… well, mostly, yes." Positivity wasn't thick on the ground these days.

"Uh-huh. And you named them."

"I… yes." If she said *uh-huh* one more time I was gonna lose my mind.

"Do…" Dana hesitated, then blinked at me. "Do they talk back, love?"

I straightened farther and folded my arms over my bare chest. "Is any of this relevant to the noise complaint, Dana?"

"Oh, I think it's definitely relevant to something."

I rolled my eyes and huffed.

"How long since you left this room, honey?"

"Come on. I was at breakfast just this morning. Remember? I sat at the table in the corner." I scowled.

"Alone."

"Pssht. *Hardly*. The room was packed."

"And did you eat lunch? Dinner? Pop over to Goode's Diner for a snack and a chat?"

"No. *As you know*, I find the chicken at Goode's seriously subpar."

"Uh-huh. You avoid it because of the chicken."

"*Subpar* chicken." I lifted my chin. "Yes."

Goode's Diner was where Jamie worked as a cook, and I'd avoided the place for a while now, but I hardcore refused to go there after Brian and Jamie had gotten back together. The *last* thing I needed was to see the two of them all happy and *together*.

I mean, not because I was jealous of Brian or anything. I was *not*. The geopolitical landscape of the world had changed a dozen times since Jamie and I had been a *thing*. Cities had literally risen and others had fallen. I'd only wanted for the two of us to be friends. To be able to hang out together. To see him smile at me. To have him answer the damn phone when I called. To maybe *finally* have him explain why he'd needed to remove me from his life entirely after he broke up with me all those years ago. To show him that I'd changed—that I wasn't the same needy, weak little nerd I'd been back then.

And sure, he was possibly better looking than he'd been when we dated before, with his broad shoulders and heavy auburn beard, but I wouldn't want him now if he was delivered to me with chocolate sauce and a cherry on top. Not if he was covered in butter and cinnamon sugar. Not if he was arranged on a bed of lettuce with an apple in his…

Uh. *Never mind.*

"Did you eat at all?" Dana asked, and I had to blink to remind myself that she was talking about *dinner.*

"Yeah. Yeah, I went over to Lyons Imperial to grab a sandwich."

Dana tightened her ponytail like she was preparing for battle. "So, by your estimation, how long has it been since you've talked to a real person? Someone besides Vera and Laverne?"

"Her name is *Lucille,*" I snapped.

Then I winced.

Okay, it was possible Dana had a point.

"Have you seen that Tom Hanks movie with the bloody volleyball, Parkie?"

I sat down hard on the edge of my bed. "This is not the same thing at all."

"Except, it kind of is. Plants need the right water. Humans need… other humans."

Or one particular human. *Fuck my life.*

"I'm fine. I just don't feel much like going out these days!" I told her brightly. "Dennis Rodman's stalking my every move."

Dana's eyes widened like I'd confirmed my insanity. "The basketball player?"

"Dana!" I scowled. "The insurance investigator! You know, the one Unity Financial sent out to re-investigate the fire at Hoff's?" I waved a hand toward the window and the ashes of my bar across the street. "The guy you're providing room and board to *right this very minute*?" The betrayal cut deep.

"Oh, right." Dana grinned sheepishly. "Him."

"Yeah, well. The dude has *zero* humor about his name. Ask me how I know." I rolled my eyes. "I had no idea I was so fascinating, but the guy watches me when I eat breakfast, then he follows me to the library and the bakery, like maybe I'm googling 'How to cover your arson-related crime' or dropping confessions about fire-starting over coffee at Fanaille. I suddenly know how Chris Hemsworth must feel."

Dana nodded. "Sure, honey. You're just like Thor." Then she paused and added, "But if Mr. Rodman can figure out who set fire to the place, wouldn't that be worth it?"

"Maybe? Assuming someone *was* responsible. People were tossing around theories the night of the fire and… I mean, I think we all wanted someone to blame. But after reading the actual firefighters' report, I don't know that anyone did anything criminal. There were dozens of repair people working upstairs, leaving flammable shit all over the place and working on the electrical and the sprinklers."

I spared a passing thought for the apartment I'd been having constructed in the loft area over the bar and felt my heart twist a tiny bit at the memory of the beautiful, wide pine floors that had just been installed the day before the fire, then I shrugged.

"The report says no cause could be determined, and I'm not interested in blaming anyone anymore. I just want to get *paid* so I can figure out what comes next." I crossed to the desk and retrieved a letter that I handed to Dana. "Looks like it's gonna take a while, though."

"What's this?"

"Letter from Unity Financial. Read it."

"I don't have my readers on, but I'll give it a go." Dana frowned, then squinted down. "Dear Mr. Hoffstraeder. We have determined that the circumstances of the above-described event—" She looked up at me.

"From the header at the top of the paper," I explained. "See? The date and location of the fire? That's '*the event*.' The destruction of the bar that represented the sum total of my hopes and dreams is '*the above-described event*.' Really captures all the emotions involved, doesn't it?" My eyebrow twitched, and I forced myself to smile like the whole thing was a joke.

A very sick, extended joke.

Dana grimaced and looked back down at the paper. "The circumstances of the above-described event are suffi-ciently undetermined… as to warrant further investigation. No claims will be paid under the above-referenced policy until our investigation is completed." She glanced back up at me. "No payment?"

I nodded and took back the letter. "Unity Financial and I are both very, deeply concerned about *the event*. But only one of us is equally concerned about how I'm going to exist if I don't get paid in the next couple weeks." I patted my flat stomach. "Have you heard of the ramen noodle diet? Because if it works, I'm gonna write a book about it. Make millions."

Dana sighed sympathetically. "I'm sorry, Parks. It's been a really nasty few weeks, hasn't it?"

I fucking *hated* being pitied. "There are silver linings," I assured her. "Finally have free time for, you know, sleeping.

Relaxing. Meditation. All the stuff I kept putting off because I was too busy."

Dana glanced around the nearly empty room and then back at the plants. "Uh-huh," she said again.

Back to that, huh?

Whatever.

Dana hesitated, just a little. "So. Um. I was chatting with your mom the other day."

"Oh, God, Dana…" I shook my head. "Please tell me you told her *no comment* when she asked about me."

"Your mom and I are friendly!" Dana said reprovingly. "I'm not gonna lie to her. She's really hoping you're gonna come down for a visit, and it seems like a darn good idea to me. I love O'Leary, but Arizona sounds real nice about now." She cast a glance out the window, where the darkness beyond her reflection hid a thick coating of ice and a chilly winter wind. "Palm trees? Condo on the golf course? Sipping margaritas in the hot tub? Those pictures your mom sent when they first moved down last winter were pretty spectacular. If my Rena weren't a martyr to prickly heat, I'd have dragged her off to Paradise Valley in a heartbeat."

"Yeah, they seem happy," I agreed with zero enthusiasm. "The pictures are gorgeous."

"So why not go?"

"I've thought about it." Hell, I'd thought about a lot of things. I just hadn't decided on any damn thing yet, because I had to wait for other people—like Dennis Rodman, for example—to make their decisions first. "My mom keeps trying to hook me up with my dad's podiatrist."

"Well, there you go! Date lined up already! Do you guys have a lot in common?"

"Besides being gay? Not a damn thing, that I know of. I

think he's, like, fifty and spends his days looking at people's feet." I shuddered.

Dana's lips twitched and I felt my face heat. Dana had to be at least fifty. Her wife was even older.

"Not that there's anything wrong with being fifty. O-or feet," I added in a rush. "Many of my favorite people have them."

"Nice save." Dana laughed. "And what does your dad say about her setting you up?"

"Eh. He turns up whatever conservative pundit is on TV and pretends he can't hear her."

She laughed again, ruefully this time. "Yup. Sounds like Lance, alright."

"Doesn't it? And then she tells me that he's losing his hearing, and going senile, and having daily heart palpitations because he's missing his *only son* so much."

"Lance?" Dana asked. "But he plays golf all day every day."

"Oh, I know. And he's never missed me a day in his life either." I rolled my eyes. "My mother eats drama for breakfast, Dana. You know this."

It was no coincidence that I'd moved back to O'Leary *after* my parents had moved to Arizona. We loved each other better from two thousand miles away.

I sighed. "I'm just... not sure I'm ready to leave O'Leary for good."

"No!" Dana said, laying a hand on my bare arm before quickly pulling it away. "No, honey, don't misunderstand. I'd never want you to leave *permanently*. This is your home! Just, you know, maybe go for a visit. Until things settle down around here."

I sighed and dropped back down on the end of the bed.

The thing was, I knew it wouldn't *be* just a visit. I

wouldn't stay in Paradise Valley with the golf lovers, that was for damn sure, but if I left O'Leary again, with no bar, and no money, and no dream to come back for, there'd be nothing tethering me *here* any longer either. There'd be nothing tethering me *anywhere*. And that was scary as fuck.

"I'll think about it again," I promised. "Maybe in a couple weeks, once I hear something from the insurance company."

"Uh." Dana licked her lips. "So, in the meantime, have you thought of finding a more permanent place here in town. A new apartment? Or a, um, friend you could stay with? Maybe contacting your old landlady and seeing if she's got room?"

I frowned. "Nooo. I mean, I told you when I moved in here that I've looked for another place, but there's nothing available in the whole area. Doesn't look like there will be for a couple months."

"Seems like Lilah could've done something for you," Dana grumbled. "I know you handed in your notice 'cause you thought your new place over the bar'd be ready and all, but when the place *burned down*, seems to me like she coulda been a little more friendly about letting you keep your apartment."

"She'd already re-rented my old apartment for last week," I reminded Dana. "Lilah felt terrible, but she couldn't change things any more than I could. Besides, I didn't exactly love the place. It was tiny. And it smelled like tuna fish."

She looked at me strangely, then sighed. "It would've been better than *nothing*. That's all I'm saying."

"Well, I don't have *nothing*!" I said with a chipper smile. "I mean, I have my plants. And I hadn't moved my mementos or most of my winter clothes to the new place, so I've still got them." I pointed at the suitcase in the corner and a slightly rusty red tin perched on the desk chair. "So, I've got all my really important stuff still and a decent place to stay, right here at the Crabapple. At least once you ask Ricky next door to—"

"What about Caelan James?" Dana demanded a little desperately. "You're friends, right? He's got a spare room?"

I shook my head at the conversational whiplash. "I… I mean, yeah, he has a spare room he uses as an office. But his apartment over the bakery is tiny and already has two people in it. I'd never impose on him and Ash." The only thing worse than hearing strangers having sex next door would be hearing my friend the baker and his ex-SEAL boyfriend going at it. "What's this about?" I demanded, ducking my head to catch her eye.

She wouldn't look at me. "There's Julian Ross!" she said, rubbing her palm against the side of her pants. "I heard from Angela that he's moving out to Daniel's place in the woods soon. She says they spend all their time there as it is."

"Yeah? That's great for them." I liked Jules a lot and was glad he'd worked things out with his big, blond boyfriend, though, honest to God, it was starting to feel like this whole fucking town was shacked up. "What's that got to do with *me*, Dana?"

"I'm thinking maybe he'll be renting out the apartment over the vet clinic! You should call him and let him know you're interested." Dana bit her lip. "*Tomorrow*."

I blinked. "Tomorrow? But if he's still living there now, why in the world would I—"

"Or! Or, or, or… and just hear me out here," Dana worried her lip more and continued in a rush, "you could always ask *Jamie*."

I frowned. "Ask Jamie what?"

"If he has a spare room. It makes sense!" she insisted

as I shook my head. "Jamie's been rattling around in that house all by his lonesome, ever since his dad died—"

"No."

"A-and you two were thick as thieves back in the day, Parks. Everyone knew—"

"*Nope.*"

"But if you could just—"

"Let me be clear: there is no way in hell I am moving in with Jamie Burke, Dana. Are you out of your mind? He's got a boyfriend, *and* he can't stand to look at me!"

"Aw, but Parker, why do you have to be so stubborn about—"

"*Me?* Stubborn? No. Nooope. *No. I* am not the one being stubborn. *I* have *tried.* Short of investing in duct tape and a cattle prod and committing several felonious acts, I cannot *make* him spend time with me."

"He cares about you, you know. Deep down."

"Yeah?" I snorted. "It's gotta be buried *way* deep." The air in the room felt chilled suddenly, and I stood up to grab a flannel shirt from the closet. "Jamie would have run me out of town himself if he thought I'd stay gone. He has no feelings whatsoever for me anymore."

"That's not true, Parker. It's *not,*" she insisted as I jammed my arms into the sleeves and opened my mouth to protest. "I was here twelve, thirteen years back. I remember how you were."

"That was *then.*"

"And I was here last spring when you moved back to town and opened the bar. Whole town was watching."

I gritted my teeth. There were many things I had *not* missed about O'Leary. My life being a source of entertainment was one of them.

"If you were watching, then you'll recall the man has not said a civil word to me. In fact, he made his opinion of me *very* clear on *multiple* occasions," I reminded her, bracing a shoulder against the wall.

Dana's lips turned up at one corner. "By coming into your bar and having way too many beers?"

"Exactly."

"Just like his daddy used to?"

"I… Well, yes. Exactly." I frowned. *That* had pissed me off more than anything else. Jamie knew better. Back in the day, watching Jamie watch his dad self-destruct, I never would have believed Jamie could ever—

"And running his mouth about how terrible your place was? How the beer in his glass was too warm and the chicken was too…"

"Over-sauced," I said, just a little bitterly. "Yes."

"Throwing shit around," she continued relentlessly. "Breaking chairs and having a temper tantrum. Also like his daddy used to?"

"Yes." I rolled my eyes. "Clearly you recall it all as well as I do."

"That sound like the boy you were friends with, once upon a time, Parker?"

That brought me up short. "No," I admitted.

"Doesn't sound like the man I've known all these years either. And a man like Jameson Burke doesn't go Doctor Jekyll and Mr. Hyde over a person he's got *no feelings whatsoever* for."

I gave her a noncommittal shrug.

"What happened between you two?" Dana asked gently. "Ten years ago."

"Eleven," I corrected. I cleared my suddenly dry throat. "Eleven years and… a bit." No one needed to know I kept track with the accuracy of a fucking atomic clock. "And nothing happened, exactly. We broke up when I left for school."

I'd told that version of events so many times, the lie tripped right off my tongue, even as it made my stomach clench.

"Why?"

"Why what? Why'd we break up?" I shrugged. "Just seemed like the thing to do. Or do you mean why'd I go to college?" I paced to the closet and back again as Dana watched. "So I could have a chance at a decent future, get a good job, and make a solid income to support myself and any family I chose to have. The usual reasons."

Dana blinked. "You've never sounded more like Lance Hoffstraeder than you just did."

I snorted. That made sense since he'd fed me that line a dozen times, at increasing volumes, when I'd suggested that I actually wanted something different.

"And Jamie? He wasn't part of the plan? You were fine with leaving him behind?" she demanded, head tilted to the side in patent disbelief.

My mouth opened, then I shut it again. I shrugged.

It was funny, but no one in my life had ever questioned my story. Not my parents, not my college friends, not the one guy I'd tried to date seriously, not even Ethan—at least not to my face, though he'd heard my drunken ramblings about Jamie often enough that he probably knew there was more to the story than I'd ever discussed when sober.

When I'd mentioned Jamie, which wasn't often, I'd called him my high school boyfriend, and let them fill in the details for themselves. *Aw shucks, we were kids, there was never any future in it.*

Except there had been a time when Jamie was my *entire* plan for the future. And breaking up had not been my choice.

I stared at my own reflection in the darkened window and remembered an afternoon eleven summers ago like it was happening right now. "In the end, he wanted me to go," I said softly. "He dared me to. And I got it. I *get* it. If you can't be a hundred percent into something, you've gotta cut bait." I smiled, just a little. "Just kinda sucks when you're the bait, that's all."

"Hmm." Dana's eyes looked troubled. "If it was his idea, then how come he—"

"I don't *know*. And anyway, it doesn't matter," I said, forcing a laugh. "I mean, God, that was over a decade ago. Practically ancient times."

Dana didn't reply.

"When I came back to town, I hoped Jamie and I could get past it and be friends even though the romance ship had sailed a long time ago. But he's not interested in being my friend." I grinned broadly. "Crazy, right? I can hardly believe it myself."

"Park—"

"It doesn't matter," I repeated, praying it would sink into my brain if I just said it often enough.

"Sometimes things that shouldn't matter seem to matter a whole heck of a lot," Dana said sagely. "You two need an intervention."

I chuckled at that, genuinely amused. "Look, please don't play Dr. Phil with us, okay? I'm not gonna attempt to move in with Jamie and hope things work themselves out. I'm happy to enjoy the Crabapple's hospitality for as long as the investigation takes." *Please, God, let that not be long.*

Dana grimaced and made a strangled little noise.

"What?" I demanded.

"Parker. *Ugh.*" She rubbed her palms together nervously.

"Are you okay?" I demanded. "Because if this is about me and Jamie, I am really done with the subject, and I should try to get to sleep before—"

"We're booked up," she blurted.

"Uh." I stared at her blankly. "Come again?"

"The Crabapple," she explained, knitting her fingers together. "We're full. Starting this weekend."

"But… but…" I shook my head. That was impossible. "When I rented this room, you said I could stay until I found somewhere else."

"I know," she said miserably. "I just… didn't think it'd take this long. You said it'd be a week. Ten days at most."

"That was before the insurance company—"

"I *know*," she said again. She sucked on one side of her lip, then the other. "But what can I do? We've got overflow for a couple weddings at the Scarlet Maple, and if we can't take them, they'll stop sending business our way and our occupancy is gonna plummet! It wasn't my decision. Or, not entirely. I don't own the place. I just manage it."

"But you're kicking *me* out? Not Tricky Ricky and his bride, who're waking up the whole damn zoo?" I pointed at the wall again. Then my mouth dropped open as I realized, "And not *Dennis Rodman*, the insurance dude? You know, he turned up his nose at the french toast this morning," I informed her. "You *really* want that kind of negativity here at the Crabapple?"

"They both made their reservations before you did, Parks! It's not personal. Last reservation made is the first to get bumped if… you know… there's a problem." She swallowed, then whispered, "Which there is."

I sat down again and squeezed my thighs hard, trying to ground myself. Or wake myself from the nightmare. Either one.

"If I can find a place for the weekend, maybe next week I could—" I began, but Dana shook her head.

"We're booked solid Thursdays through Mondays for a month."

"Even the insurance guy's room?" I demanded, wide-eyed. "For a *month*?"

Dana nodded sadly, and my dreams of a quick resolution evaporated.

Still, I took a deep breath and attempted to pull my shit together when I saw the devastated expression on Dana's face. "Hey, it's not your fault," I told her. "I get it! It's not a problem. More like an, um… inconvenience, you know? I'll figure something out."

"Look, if you need a place to stay for a few nights while you're *figuring*, you can come bunk with Rena and me! We've got a pull-out in the den!"

"Oh. Uh. That's sweet, Dana, but—"

"It'll be great! They're predicting a big whopper of a storm this weekend, and it's real pretty out at the farm in the snow! Wouldn't be the first time we've let a friend stay over. My Rena loves guests." Her eyes got all sappy and fond the second she mentioned her wife, which was really cute considering Rena was a pint-sized, gray-haired misanthrope who lived to shock O'Learians—basically the anti-Dana.

Then Dana had to go and ruin it by continuing. "Rena nearly *always* remembers to wear a robe around the house when we have people staying over. And with my work schedule, we're pretty committed to nooners instead of nighttime hanky-panky, so you wouldn't even lose sleep if we got loud, which means it'll be even *better* than your room here, since the folks next door will be staying for another week and a half! Plus, I can tell you from experience that our couch is *very* well sprung and comfy." She winked.

Okay, correction. I'd thought hearing Ricky and company have sex was bad, and listening to Cal and Ash fucking would be worse, but nothing touched the pure horror that the idea of being stuck in Rena and Dana's farmhouse while they had nooners in a snowstorm inspired.

I really didn't want to know how Dana had tested the springs on their sofa.

I took another breath and let it out slowly, absorbing this latest blow. The score currently stood at Parker, 0; Universe, 920,394,203, and here I was, standing around like a dumbass, begging for a sign. *What's coming next? I need to plan for it!*

How many times did I need to be whacked by the universe's fuckery stick before I got the message that it was time to leave town?

"You're sweet," I repeated. "Really. But have you ever felt like someone was trying to deliver a message you refused to hear?" I laughed, just a little. "Pretty sure that's what's happening here."

"A message? What kind of message?" Dana frowned like she was back to wondering about my sanity.

Maybe I didn't blame her.

I took a deep breath. "I don't belong in O'Leary anymore." I rubbed a hand over my chest to ease the ache that came with those words. "Time to move on."

"Aw, Parks, that's not true at all!"

I shrugged, suddenly exhausted in a way that wasn't just physical or mental but soul-deep. "It's fine. Moving back wasn't how I imagined it would be anyway."

Dana sat on the opposite corner of the bed, pulling one leg up so she could face me. "Yeah? What did you imagine it'd be like?"

Satisfying.

The click of puzzle pieces connecting.

A whisper of *"ahhhh, that's what's been missing"* across my soul.

A bone-deep knowledge that I was where I belonged.

"Well, the bar not burning down, for a start." I attempted a smile, and Dana patted my knee. "No, I mean… You know, my dad always said a man isn't finished when he's defeated, he's finished when he quits."

"Oh, I remember," Dana said dryly. "Not a lot of folks around here ever quoted Richard Nixon at me."

I laughed. "But maybe leaving's not quitting. Maybe it's just realizing that I've been going after the wrong things the wrong way." I took a deep, cleansing breath and let it out. "All these years, I've thought there was an O'Leary shaped hole in my heart, and I couldn't be happy until I came back here. But it turns out, there's no Parker-shaped hole in O'Leary."

Dana shook her head. "Honey, you're looking at this wrong. You fit here. This is your home, and—"

"Dana," I interrupted. "Home's where you make it. And it's not here. Not for me."

"So, then… you're headed south?"

"Guess so. For now anyway," I said, making a decision on the spot. "I'll leave in a couple days."

I fingered the hem of my flannel shirt. I wondered how my all-winter wardrobe would look on the back nine or better yet, in the hot tub.

"Aw, Parks—"

"*Oh, Ricky! Tie me to the headboard! Use your necktie just like last night!*"

Dana's eyes widened, and her hand fluttered to her chest. "Good gracious."

I summoned a smile. "Oh, just wait. They haven't even gotten to the good part yet."

"I should maybe run and have a word." She bit her lip like she'd rather do just about anything but interrupt them, and I didn't blame her, but I was tired. All kinds of tired.

"Maybe that'd be good," I agreed.

"Remember the offer of the sofa is open indefinitely, okay?" she said, standing and moving toward the door. She paused with her hand on the knob. "And Parker, remember that everything works out exactly the way it's supposed to."

Was there a worse expression in all of existence? I doubted it.

But I grinned and gave her a salute anyway, and her answering smile flared bright and true as she let herself out.

I snorted and let myself collapse back on the bed.

My whole life I'd had an idea in my head about how I'd react in the face of real adversity. Katniss Everdeen, volunteering as tribute. Batman, owning the night and meting out justice. The brave soldier, picking up the banner when the rest of his company had been shot down. A man of *action*, goddamn it, just as Lance Hoffstraeder had raised me to be.

I believed, more than anything, that you had to be a hundred percent into something—no wishy-washy bullshit. You didn't get to open a bar by thinking about it and talking about it; you *did* it.

And here I'd spent a year waiting for Jamie Burke to talk to me. I'd waited weeks for Dennis Rodman and Unity fucking Financial to get their acts together. If my dad were around, he'd roll his eyes back so far they'd get stuck, and I wouldn't blame him.

I sat up and nodded at the empty room and my few scattered possessions.

This was going to be *okay*. It was going to be *fine*.

I'd wanted to know what came next, well, now I knew. It wasn't gonna be fun, but I could handle it.

I addressed the plants on the table. "Couple more days,

Lucille. Then we'll head to Arizona. And it won't work out for the *best*, but it *will* work out. Because it has to."

Lucille didn't argue, which I took as a tacit sign of agreement.

Then I pulled the pillow over my head and groaned again. I was starting to think I really *was* going insane. And I blamed O'Leary, New York.

Chapter Two

JAMIE

"*Fuck. Fuckity fuckity fuck.*" I pulled open the door to my truck and hauled myself inside, shivering against the cold, before pulling my phone from my pocket.

Three missed calls and two missed texts glared up at me accusingly, along with the time. Seven thirty-four. As in, two hours after my shift at the diner was supposed to end. As in, two hours after I was *one-hundred-percent-definitely, pinkie-promise, super-swear* gonna call Brian so we could get together tonight. As in, two hours after I had failed to call, text, or even send up a smoke signal to let my boyfriend know I remembered his existence.

I hit Call Back and waited for him to pick up… but literally one second later, the call clicked over to voicemail.

I was pretty sure my boyfriend had just rejected my call.

But as Brian's voice reminded me to leave a message at the beep, I couldn't seem to make myself feel guilty, or worried, or even really sad. The overwhelming emotion I felt was *relief*, even though it meant I'd be going home and climbing into bed alone. Again.

"Hey, Brian. I'm so sorry I missed your calls. I know you wanted to have a serious talk tonight, and I was *totally* here for it," I lied, "but I got caught up at the diner. Diane was gonna have to work the grill *alone* since Fran hasn't been doing too well, and we're still shorthanded since everything with, ah, Shane last fall. And Thursday evenings are always crazy once the town council meeting gets out, but this week Daniel Michaelson was doing a reading from his new book at the library too. Plus, you know there's that big snowstorm coming for the weekend, and people were eating pancakes and chicken wings like they might never get another chance, so I stayed to help her out, and… I'm sorry," I said, cutting my rambling short. "Just… sorry. So, uh, stay safe in the snow, I guess. And, um… call me if you want to. Okie dokie… Later."

So suave, Burke. I hit End and threw the phone onto the center console of my truck, then thunked my head back against the headrest repeatedly. Had I actually just ended a message with the words *okie dokie*?

Why did I do the shit I did?

Why did my own mind actively work against me?

In one corner of my brain, I'd known I had plans. Hell, I had those plans stored in the calendar on my phone, *with* a reminder. But, pro tip, calendars only worked if you remembered to check them, and reminders were only helpful when you hadn't put your phone on silent, so essentially, you had to remember there was something you wanted to remember. I seemed fucking incapable of that.

The worst part was, I was really good at remembering other things. Possibly *too* good. I never forgot a work shift. I remembered to celebrate the birthdays of every member of my family—parents, sister, grandparents—even though all but my mom were long gone now. I remembered the exact tone of Coach Simms's voice when he told me I was an All-Section pitcher my junior year of high school, and the way my heart had skipped a beat when the coach from Meridia College had told me he wanted me to play for his team. I remembered every excruciating second of my cocky, stupid, career-ending attempt to block the asshole from Erlington from running for home plate during the final game of my senior year, and the painful pointlessness of the surgeries that followed, once my athletic scholarship had fallen through. I remembered the night Mitch Turner came to the house to tell us Molly had died. And I remembered finding out, last fall, that her car accident hadn't been accidental, because she'd been driven off the road.

In fact, I remembered all *that* stuff so well, I'd had to create a little bunker in my mind where I could store the memories, only taking them out on holidays and special occasions—meaning, the rare times when I got drunk off my ass—because otherwise the remembering would drive me batshit crazy.

So why did I have this fucking mental block where Brian was concerned?

The guy was *cute*, with brown hair and brown eyes and tan skin. He was fit as hell from working a variety of construction jobs. He was smart. And had good teeth. And nice, symmetrical ears. He was generally patient. And a decent driver. And he was forever making me try new restaurants, which was a *good thing* and not annoying, even though he insisted on making me re-try foods I already knew I disliked, just in case.

And yes, okay, he was a little dramatic at times.

Or maybe a lot dramatic.

And he might, possibly, also be just the tiniest bit needy too.

But everyone had quirks, right?

Bottom line, the guy was really, truly interested in me.

And given that I was an all-you-can-eat-buffet of issues—space issues, commitment issues, trust issues, you name it—that was a miracle in and of itself.

When we'd dated for the first time, a couple of years back, we'd broken up because Brian wanted more than I could give him. More commitment, more time, more… love. But this time around, things were different. We were going slowly. We were on the same page…

At least, we would be. If I could get my shit together. If I could figure out a way to care for someone who cared about *me*.

My phone clattered against the hard plastic of the console, and I took a deep breath before hitting the button on the dashboard to put the call on speaker.

"Hey, I'm *really* sorry. I'm aware of all the ways I suck as a human," I said in my best groveling voice.

"Oh, thank God!" Everett Maior said without missing a beat. "Saves me from having to list them all again."

"Ev?" I belatedly grabbed my phone from the cup holder and saw Everett's profile photo, all clear eyes and sardonic smile, grinning up at me before I set it back down. "Shit. I, ah… wasn't paying attention. Thought you were someone else."

"Clearly. Who?"

"Doesn't matter."

I shifted in my seat and hissed when the motion made my bicep ache. Half a lifetime later, my stupid arm still got twinge-y at times. I could predict a storm coming in like I was a human barometer.

"Ah. So it's *Brian*." Ev's voice carried a particular drawl, like Brian's name was sour on his tongue.

"He's a good guy, Ev," I said, for what felt like the seven billionth time, which was kind of impressive when you considered that Brian and I had only been back together for a couple of weeks, and Ev and I didn't talk all that often.

"Who said he wasn't?"

"He's patient. And kind. And cheerful."

"Mmm. Like a human cocker spaniel. A true delight."

"Everett, come *on*."

"Do you notice," he said conversationally, "that whenever I say a negative word about Brian, you make a noise like I've asked you to remove your own spleen without anesthesia?"

"You're ridiculous."

"It's one of my best qualities," he agreed. "So what did you do to piss him off?"

I rolled my eyes and watched the tiny white lights strung up under the diner's awning sway as the wind picked up force.

"I forgot we had a date tonight," I admitted with a sigh. "I worked late."

"Jameson, that's the third time you've done that."

"I know."

"In a month."

"Not *even* a month. I know."

"Pretty sure it *has* been a month. And you are not a forgetful person."

"I *know*," I said again, more forcefully, pushing my fingers through my hair. "I suck. It's like I have some mental block about this. Self-sabotage or something. I need to get past it. He deserves better."

"*You* deserve better."

Everett and I were an unlikely pair of friends—the short, dark-haired, art-obsessed teacher who did crossword puzzles for *fun*, and the overgrown oaf of a diner cook who wouldn't know an Impressionist if he tripped over one—

but we'd bonded a few months back, and our friendship had stuck, against all odds.

We both spoke the language of grief and loss like a native tongue—Everett, from losing his husband, Adrian, to cancer just a couple of years before, and me from losing my sister Molly a dozen years ago—and recognized each other as a member of a club neither of us would have willingly joined.

Connection was weird like that.

"Did you call to give me shit about my boyfriend?" I demanded.

"No," Ev sighed. Then he admitted, "Okay, possibly. I'm looking for distraction."

"Why? Everything okay with you and Si?"

Everett had been happily shacked up with his boyfriend, Silas Sloane, one of O'Leary's finest, for a few months, and they'd always seemed happy together—disgustingly, irritatingly in love, finishing each other's sentences and giving each other looks hot enough to make me worry that spontaneous combustion might occur—but I figured it was only a matter of time before things went south. Love that burned that hot didn't last. *Couldn't*, in fact.

"Everything's fine," Ev said, sounding confused. "Why wouldn't it be?"

"No reason." Unlike Everett, *I* didn't like to give my friends shit over their romantic choices. "Just figured you usually paint something when you need distraction, or you get Si to, you know, *distract* you." I tucked my tongue into my cheek. "Did you fuck him into a coma already, Ev? It's not even eight o'clock. What will the neighbors say?"

"Same thing they usually say. '*Thanks for the show, boys. Same time tomorrow night?*'"

I snorted.

"Nah, Si got called in. It's all hands on deck down at the station, coordinating with the OEM, getting their ducks in a row. They're gonna be opening an emergency shelter tonight at Garnett."

I frowned. "At the elementary school? Why?"

"Because it's a good, central location, and they have a generator."

"A generator?"

"For the snow storm, Jamie." The *duh* was unspoken but very much there. "We're gonna get seventy billion feet and almost definitely lose power. Don't tell me you've missed the weather when literally everyone has talked about it incessantly for a week?"

"Yeah, of course I heard, but I thought it was coming later. Tomorrow, maybe. Or the next day." I leaned forward, searching the sky for flakes. "You sure it's tonight?"

"Very sure. Forecast changed, and the *storm of the century*'s starting any minute now." He paused. "You notice how they call every storm the storm of the century? Why is that?"

I laughed. "Dude. Who knows?"

"I personally think the weather people have a collaboration with the egg and dairy farmers of America to get us to stock up."

"A french toast conspiracy. Sounds legit. Note to self: Get Everett a tinfoil hat for his birthday."

"You're a fool if you think I don't already have *several*," Ev deadpanned, and I laughed again, despite myself.

"*Any*way," he said. "They've already canceled school tomorrow, making this a three-day weekend for O'Leary's hardworking educators, including yours truly. And no way will you be opening the diner in the morning. State of emergency, starting at midnight." He huffed out a laugh. "I swear, Silas hasn't looked this happy since the day I agreed to move in with him. The man *loves* a good state of emergency."

"But that means you're all alone?" I frowned at the thermostat on the dashboard that said the temperature was well below freezing already.

"Yeah. Just me and this motherfucking painting that will never, never, never be done because I can't fucking figure out what's missing." He sighed.

"You could start over," I suggested.

"And waste all this work?"

"Or keep going, see if it works out."

"And put more work into it, when I'm doomed to failure?"

"Ah. Now I understand." Ev did the tortured artist thing so well. "So, why don't you come over to my place? I've got a generator and a fridge full of food. Not a single piece of decent artwork in sight to taunt you."

"Please. Your whole house is like a still life. *Sorry*," he said immediately. "Sorry. That was shitty. But it goes to show the kind of headspace I'm in. Probably best if I stay home. Otherwise I'll be tempted to drop little tidbits of Brian-related wisdom on you all night."

I rolled my eyes. "I wish you'd just try to like him."

"I think you try hard enough for both of us," Ev said dryly. "Besides, I don't *dis*like him. Brian might be a lovely person. I barely know the guy. Maybe he'd be a brilliant boyfriend for someone else. But for you? Eh. He's parsley."

"Parsley. Like the herb? I think you've been breathing in paint fumes too long."

"Parsley," Ev repeated. "Like the wilty green garnish that sits on the side of the plate taking up space. Like the shit that's supposed to distract you from how very little entree is in front of you. How there's absolutely nothing on your plate that nourishes you. *That* kind of parsley."

Wow.

"That's bullshit. Brian is a great guy. He's…"

"I like to think I'm not a particularly violent person, but if you tell me again that he's good and kind and patient, I'm going to find you and smack you because that's totally beside the point." Ev paused. "Speaking of, where are you?"

"In my truck," I sighed. "Parked outside the diner. I got out of work a few minutes ago."

"And why aren't you on your way to Camden to apologize to Brian and beg his forgiveness?"

A good question.

Through the windshield, I watched the lights inside the diner go dark, followed half a minute later by Diane Perkins and Henry Lattimer, Ev's grandfather, shuffling out the door hand in hand. Diane paused to lock up while Hen stood on the sidewalk, keeping a narrow-eyed lookout for any hoodlums or vigilantes who might be wandering O'Leary's mean streets ready to attack his ladylove, just as he did every night Diane worked.

I lifted a hand in a wave, and Henry nodded seriously in return, which was kind of amusing, really. Diane, who'd taught me to cook back when I started working at Goode's as a busboy in high school and still ran the place six days a week, was hardly a delicate maiden. And Hen, who was pushing eighty and was still a bit unsteady on his feet after hurting his leg last summer, wasn't *precisely* the bodyguard type. But when Diane turned and threaded her arm through his, she gave him a brilliant smile that made her look way younger than her sixty-whatever years, and Henry's bushy mustache twitched up in an answering grin right before he pressed a kiss to the top of her flame-red hair and led her down the street to their apartment.

And all of a sudden, it didn't seem amusing at all anymore.

In fact? I was fucking jealous.

Of an octogenarian.

This day got worse and worse.

I put the truck in reverse, backing out of the parking spot and driving down Weaver Street, which was nearly empty except for the lightly falling snow. Toward *home*. Away from Brian.

"I don't know, Ev," I finally admitted. "I should be on my way to his place. I *should*. I just… I don't know, okay. Happy now?"

"Not really. I want *you* to be happy," Ev said, so gently I couldn't even be mad at him for being so ridiculous and… right. "I don't want you wasting time trying to force this relationship to work when there's something that's *meant* for you out there, just waiting for you to wise up."

"I don't believe in fate."

"Doesn't matter, as long as fate believes in you," Ev said with mock cheer.

"Gross. And I *am* happy with Brian. I'm thinking maybe this is just an adjustment period, you know? Having a boyfriend is time-consuming, and I haven't really tried to have a relationship since… well, since the last time I was with Brian. It's gonna take me a minute to settle in, for things to feel natural. Right?" I asked hopefully.

"Time-consuming," Ev repeated. "Why, you hopeless romantic, you."

"You know what I mean," I insisted. "Remembering plans. Calling all the time. Figuring out what to eat. Keeping things on schedule. All the stuff you need to do for a boyfriend."

Ev snorted. "You make Brian sound like an exotic pet you inherited! Where's the excitement? Where's the enthusiasm? Those things aren't hard when you *want* to do them."

I rubbed a hand over my forehead. "Not every relationship is a great romance. Some of us just aren't built for that. Companionship and stability are way more important in the end." I wasn't sure who I was trying to convince.

"Sometimes you can have both."

"And sometimes you can't. But that guy would do *anything* for me. It's really—"

"Off-putting?"

"Loving," I returned. "Sacrificing. That's what people in a relationship *do*. They stick around, even when it's not exciting anymore."

"Jameson, I think we've found your problem."

"Oh, thank goodness."

"You really want to date someone who's gonna lie down in the street and wait to be run over, if you get a wild hair and ask him to? That's not love, friend, that's a total lack of self-preservation. It's *too* easy. You need someone who challenges you, who shares your hopes and dreams. Not someone who clings to you like a sucker fish and says, 'Yes, Jamie. Sure, Jamie. Whatever you say, Jamie.' You need someone you *can't* forget, even if you try to."

I huffed out an annoyed laugh. I should have known this was where the conversation was heading. "Do tell, Everett. Who might you be thinking of?"

"Me? I'm not thinking of *anyone*," Ev said innocently. "Who did you think I was thinking of?"

I rolled my eyes. There wasn't a soul in O'Leary who wouldn't know who he was talking about: The boy with the gray-green eyes and the light hair who'd been my first best friend and first boyfriend, the first person I'd come out to, and the one who'd held me when I cried for my sister. The only man I'd ever said "I love you" to. The guy who'd left O'Leary—and *me*—in his rearview mirror eleven years and almost five months ago and then moved back last year on a whim and expected me to throw a goddamn parade because he'd decided to reappear.

It reminded me of vacation Bible school, back when I was a kid, and that stupid prodigal son story they'd tried to indoctrinate us with. The parable remained as incomprehensible to me today as it had been back then. Why the hell would you slaughter a fatted calf for the son who went off and had his adventures? Save the fucking calves for the ones who *stayed* and *worked*.

"Hear me now, Everett," I warned. "Parker Hoffstraeder and I are *done*. We haven't been *anything* to each other for over eleven years. So if you're thinking... *whatever* you're thinking... just stop thinking it."

"Pfft. I'm not thinking anything," Ev retorted. "Except that you don't talk about Parker. *Ever*. It's telling."

"Yeah? What it should tell you is that I don't have a damn thing to say. I barely remember him," I lied.

"It's like negative space," he persisted. "In a painting. Sometimes, the negative space highlights the subject. Sometimes it *is* the subject."

"Hmm. Can we go back to parsley?" I knew I was being obnoxious. I was beyond caring. "I *understood* the parsley thing. More or less."

"You're a cretin," Ev said. "But sure. Have it your way. Parker's not parsley."

"Brilliant. Concise. Incomprehensible. You're three for three."

"So stubborn."

"I am not! Do you remember every guy you dated for a

hot minute a decade ago, Everett? Should we talk about all of your past loves?" I demanded.

"I only had the one before Silas," Everett said quietly. "And I used to make a point of not talking about him. But it wasn't because I didn't care or didn't remember him. It was because it hurt too fucking much."

Ugh. I took a deep breath and let it out in a sigh. *Awesome job, Jameson. Bring up his dead husband. Let's see who else you can piss off tonight.*

And the thing was, Ev was right. About this part, anyway. Because buried beneath the bunker in my mind where I kept the memories of my parents and Molly, there was a secret vault—a serious, hard-core, bomb-proof chamber, like the ones on TV where they kept the most dangerous prisoners and the biological weapons—and that was where I kept my thoughts and memories of Parker from back when we had been Parker-and-Jamie. Parker's light hair glinting in the sun. Parker's green eyes hot on mine. Parker's smile, lighting up all the dark and lonely places inside me. Those were not memories I took out and looked at, even when I was drunk. Some things were just too painful to fuck around with.

"Look," Ev said after a moment of silence, "if you're not hung up on Parker, that's a good thing. A great thing, under the circumstances, right? But it doesn't mean you have to be with *Brian*. Get it? It's not Brian or Parker or nothing. There are other options, you know? A whole world of options."

I opened my mouth to disagree with him when my mind caught on the first part of what he'd said.

"Wait, what circumstances?" I demanded. I put on my blinker and took the left turn onto Lobelia.

"Uh. Parker's circumstances? Obvs."

"What are you talking about?"

"Ohhh," Ev drawled. "I figured you knew. Parker left town."

I hit the brake so hard the truck jolted to a stop in the middle of my street just a few doors down from my house. For one brief second, it wasn't winter but late summer; it wasn't pitch-dark but bright and sunny; I wasn't an adult but an angry idiot teenager, and I was hearing those words in Beatrice Hoffstraeder's voice, a little smug and a little defiant, as she informed me that her son had gone to Boston for college and wouldn't be back because Parker had seen the error of his ways.

My pulse pounded in my ears. "He what?"

"He's gone to Arizona. He went by the bakery this afternoon to say his goodbyes, and it didn't sound like he'd be back. I mean, what for? Poor guy's lost everything. The fire at Hoff's was… devastating."

"I know," I said thickly. "I was there, remember?"

I'd been finishing up my shift at the diner, thinking about Christmas, when Ruthann Kelley had run in, all breathless and wide-eyed, yelling, "Parker's place is on fire! Everyone's still inside!" The whole diner had cleared out in an instant as everyone—including me—ran down the street to stand behind the police barrier and gawk at the bar patrons who emerged from the building, coughing and stumbling, just before the whole place went up in flames.

I hadn't gone to gawk, though. I'd gone because my heart had stopped beating and the breath had frozen in my lungs the second I thought that Parker might be in danger, and they hadn't resumed normal function until I'd seen him standing shell-shocked in the cold and wrapped my arms around him. Because friend or not, history or not, there was some part of me that couldn't help it.

"I remember," Ev said. "And I remember that he said some stuff the night of the fire too. Stupid shit about—"

"Me causing the fire to get him to leave town. Yeah." I resumed my drive down the street. "That was super fun. Fortunately for me, I had an alibi."

I could practically hear Ev's wince. "People say dumb stuff when they're under stress like that," he offered. "I was a total shit to Silas a few months back, and I didn't mean it."

"I know." And I *did* know. But yeah, it had fucking stung that there was any part of Parker, any tiny corner of his brain, that thought I'd be capable of doing something like that, no matter how much time had passed since we were friends.

And the fact that he *could* hurt me, even after all these years? That made me realize that my super-secure memory vault wasn't nearly as secure as I wanted it to be… and probably never had been.

Which meant it was a good thing he was gone. Better for both of us.

I'd known from the minute he moved back that he wouldn't stay here permanently. Julian Ross had rolled his eyes when I'd told him that, probably thinking it was just more of me mouthing off about Parker, but I'd meant it. Parker came back—prodigal son returning, local boy made good—but O'Leary wouldn't hold him. Some people shined too bright to stay in a small town for long, and Parker Hoffstraeder was one of them. I'd fooled myself about that once before, but I wouldn't make the same mistake again.

"Parker looked like he'd been hit by a truck," Ev continued.

"Yeah, well," I said as I pulled into my driveway and parked, "If you expect me to feel bad, you're barking up the wrong tree. Parker makes his own choices. He always has."

But I was lying to both of us about not being sympathetic, and I was pretty sure Everett knew it. The image of Parker from the night of the fire had been recalled to the forefront of my brain, this time wearing his kicked-puppy look, all huge green eyes and furrowed brow. I felt my heart squeeze against my will. That look was pure kryptonite, and even though I was no Superman, I couldn't resist it. Not ten years ago. Not now.

I'd learned a long, long time ago that life wasn't fair. Molly died, and Parker left town, and my dad had been… whatever. But I swear to God, the most *unjust thing* in this whole *goddamn unfair world* was the way my heart still hurt when Parker Hoffstraeder was hurting. The way every cell of my body yearned to *fix it*. The way I instantly forgot all the shit that had happened, all the things he'd said, all the years and lifetimes that had passed since we were together, and wanted to gather him in my arms.

"We all make choices, Jamie," Ev said softly. "Sometimes we just make the wrong ones. Sometimes life gives us a do-over."

"And sometimes it doesn't," I said, watching the flakes fall and melt on the windshield. No do-over for my dad. Or for my sister. Or for me.

"So true. And you still shouldn't be with Brian."

I sighed. "You're insufferable."

"You asked my opinion about Brian—"

"Did I? Did you receive that communication telepathically? Because you might wanna get your receiver checked."

"You haven't seemed happy since you started dating him again," Ev said, ignoring me. "Not even whatever passes for happy in Jamie Burke's world. You're stressed constantly. You're clinging to Brian like he's a human shield. And what I want to know is, what the hell are you protecting yourself from? Living half a life *sucks*, Jameson. Take it from me."

"I'm writing these tidbits of wisdom down," I assured him. "Compiling a book of Everett quotes. I'm thinking *Parsley and Negative Space: The Important Thoughts of Everett Maior.*"

"Total. *Cretin.* I hope the snowpocalypse blankets your house and you're stuck for days."

"Harsh. Remind me again why we're friends?"

"Because I'm a little ray of sunshine in your cold, dark life?"

"Mmm. Try again."

"Because I'm the only person in town who'll put up with your cranky ass?"

"That sounds more like it. Since I'm the only person crankier than you."

"Just think about what I said, okay?" Ev asked. "If you're really happy with Brian, fuck the haters, including me. Not sure how the hell I became a great dispenser of wisdom anyway. I'm two fruits shy of a salad over here."

"And Silas doesn't seem to mind."

"No," Ev said warmly. "In fact, I think he kinda likes it. Which is *proof* that there's someone out there for everyone. Sometimes multiple someones."

And sometimes not.

"Stay safe, okay? During the storm. Don't let the fumes get to you."

"I won't. And you be safe too, Jamie. Safe, but... not too safe."

Whatever the fuck *that* meant.

Before I could ask, Ev hung up and left me staring out the window at my front yard.

Talking to Ev and, yeah, thinking about Parker, had made me all melancholy, and suddenly there were ghosts popping out all over the place, against my will. There was Molly, lying on the grass in the summer, looking at the stars and telling me the stories of the constellations while mosquitos ate us alive. There was my dad, starting a snowball fight with my mom, back when they'd gotten along, before his accident and his drinking had taken him from us, before my mom had left. And Parker was there too. Of course he was. Leaning against the hood of the ancient, bright green, barely roadworthy Dodge I'd just had towed to the house, his mouth giving me shit while his green eyes shined like I was the largest star in his personal universe.

I swallowed.

I'd told Ev that Parker and I weren't anything to each other, and I'd meant it. He was firmly in the past. But sometimes... sometimes it felt like the past still haunted me.

I checked my phone as white flakes started to accumulate on my windshield. No new messages. Clearly, Brian was *really* annoyed. But for the first time, I kind of admitted to myself that I wasn't sure I *could* make everything better between us... and I wasn't sure I wanted to.

The overwhelming relief of this was probably a clue I was on the right track.

We'd gotten back together because we were both hoping I'd finally be able to commit to him, but apparently, I just wasn't built for that.

I let myself out of the truck into a chaos of falling flakes and collected my winter coat from the back seat before shrugging it on. The neighborhood was silent except for the branches of the giant oak tree in my backyard, which tap-tap-tapped against the house in the wind, like a not-so-subtle Morse code reminder that I'd forgotten to prune the trees last fall.

Even after six years of living here alone, six years of

having my name on the title, it was still weird to think of the place as *mine*. It had been my family's and then my dad's after the divorce. But now there was no one left but me to take care of the trees and the rotting ponytail fence. I'd inherited my dad's dusty gym equipment, and the photographs that lined Molly's bedroom walls, and the couch in the basement, where Parker and I used to sit and plan our future. I owned the collection of colorful glass bottles my mom had left on the kitchen windowsill when she went to Portland to *be happy*, that even now glowed in the light spilling from the window and sent ripples of color across the snow-covered grass.

I stared at the colorful glow for a minute, then I frowned.

The light spilling out of the window? There should absolutely not be a light spilling out of the window.

I froze in my slow walk toward the house.

The kitchen light had *not* been on this morning when I left for work, I was positive. And no one else in the world had a key to my house—a fact worth noting, in a place like O'Leary where neighbors routinely had keys to every house on the block in case of an emergency.

But this is O'Leary, I reminded myself. *And the wildest thing to happen on this block is old Mr. Bale getting lit on the Fourth of July and attempting to show the ladies of the neighborhood his shrapnel scars.*

Then again, the number of kidnappings, murders, and thefts that had plagued this town the past six months were more than all the crimes in the thirty years before put together. And I'd learned the hard way last fall that sometimes the people you least suspected, even a person you considered a friend, could betray you.

For a single second, I debated calling the police station, but Jesus, I refused to be this week's ridiculous callout in the police blotter. *Local mystery reader calls cops in snowstorm after leaving kitchen light on. Assumed thieves were targeting his old baseball trophies.*

Still, I ran back to the truck and grabbed the long-handled ice scraper from the bed, just in case, brandishing it like a weapon as I approached the breezeway between the garage and the kitchen.

I was still maybe ten feet away from the house when I heard the music—some kind of nineties ballad, I was pretty sure—and I got even more freaked out, because I didn't *own* a stereo, so there was definitely someone in there, and what kind of fucked up thief brought their own tunes to the scene of the crime?

I opened the door to the kitchen and immediately heard movement off to the left, in the dining room. The clink of the plates from my mom's china cabinet, the scrape of a chair against the hardwood.

Fuck. Someone *was* robbing me.

Without pausing to give the thief a chance to run away or fight back, I charged into the room and hurled my ice scraper like a javelin.

Brian screamed and threw himself onto the ground, while the scraper sailed harmlessly past his head and lodged in the dark red wall.

Holy shit.

"*Holy shit!*" Brian said from his knees on the floor. He stared up at me with wide, fearful eyes. "Jamie, what the hell are you doing?"

I blinked, then shook my head and blinked again, like somehow that would make the vision in front of me clearer. "Me?" I demanded. "What are *you* doing? *Christ*, Brian. Why are you naked, man?"

"I brought us dinner, obviously." He pushed himself to his feet, folded his arms over his chest—his very bare chest

—and stuck out one hip, which made his dick—his very naked dick—sway. I looked away, feeling my cheeks get hot —and not in a good way.

"But… Why?" I took a step farther into the room and rested my hand on the carved wooden back of a chair, confusion and adrenaline mixing in my brain. Belatedly, I noticed the table was set with my mom's old tablecloth and china. In the center was a bouquet of lilies in a vase, flanked by a pair of white taper candles that flickered merrily. A bottle of wine sat on the sideboard. "This wasn't our plan. Was it?"

"It's our four-week date-iversary!" he fumed, like that was an actual occasion. And, props to Everett, because apparently it *had* been a month. "No, it wasn't *planned*. I thought I'd surprise my boyfriend. Instead, *he* shocked *twenty years* off my life."

"Shit." I sighed, sinking into the closest chair as my heart rate began to slow and the adrenaline fled. I stated the obvious. "I had no idea you'd be here. I thought you were a thief."

"A thief?" Brian's eyebrows arched so hard they nearly met in the middle. "Honey, what would anyone steal? The VCR in the basement? Your collection of Precious Moments?"

"That's not the point. How are you here?"

But Brian didn't seem to hear me. "We were going to celebrate with veal medallions in red wine reduction from Marcio! Your favorite!"

"We are?" I hated veal.

"*Werrrrre*," he repeated, pursing his lips. "Veal medallions don't exactly keep, you know. Especially not for two hours. They're probably all dried out."

"Right." I rubbed my shoulder, which was aching like a bitch. "Sorry about that."

"And now, on top of my complete *waste of effort*, we're going to have to spend the weekend fixing Sheetrock too! It's a good thing you're cute, Jamie." Brian shook his head, and his anger morphed into a fond smile. "But you're still gonna owe me so many sexual favors."

"Sexual… Wait, for what?"

"It's fine," he said, waving a hand. "This is going to make a hell of a funny story one day. Besides, I've never really been a fan of the red walls in here. They're *so* dated. This is an opportunity to do it over. Maybe then you'll consider making over the rest of the place." He glanced around the room thoughtfully. "How do you feel about navy blue? It's bold, but with the right curtains, it could be iconic."

"Navy blue?" I found myself looking around the room too, before shaking my head. "*No.*"

"No, you're right. We'd have to refinish the table then," he mused. "We *could*, though. And redo the floor too. Make it more *ours*."

And just like that, everything Everett had been saying clicked.

I could try and try and try for a hundred years, and Brian would never fit into my life or into my house. I would never look at him the way Diane looked at Hen or talk about him with a smile in my voice the way Everett did with Silas. I thought being with Brian was better, easier, than being alone. Safer, even. But it wasn't. And we *both* deserved better.

"Brian," I said sharply. "You don't need to fix up the walls. You don't live here."

He blinked at me, brown eyes filled with hurt. "You don't have to take that tone. I'm well aware! As if you hadn't told me a hundred times that you hate having people *in your space*. As if you didn't *freak out* when I so much as left a *toothbrush* in your bathroom." He set his jaw. "I happen to work for a construction company, Jameson. I just wanted to help."

I tried to rotate my shoulder to ease the pain. "Look, it's just—"

"I'm trying to be *helpful*," he said. "I'm trying to show you that I care. That I'm ready to take things to the next level whenever you are." He ruffled my hair and gave me a tentative smile.

I stood up, dislodging his hand, and slid the chair back along the floor with a loud scrape. "I thought we said no pressure."

"I'm not *pressuring* you. I—"

"Brian, how'd you get in here?"

He frowned. "With a *key*, obviously. Unlike some people, I don't go around breaking walls and—"

"Which key?"

Brian sighed deeply. "The spare key from the drawer by the fridge. I grabbed it last time I was here. And don't *stress*, okay? I already put it back." He rolled his eyes. "I know you go crazy about that kind of thing."

"Uh, yeah. You might say that. Considering last fall, a guy I *worked with* confessed to killing three people, *including my own sister* twelve years ago."

"Right. That." Brian's mouth twisted to the side for a second before he recovered his smile. "But I also knew you wouldn't mind once you saw the surprise." He stepped closer so all five hundred acres of his nakedness and arousal were pressed against me, and I was so horribly and thoroughly *not interested* I could have wept. "You *don't* mind, do you?"

"Uh." I took a step back, putting some distance between us. "Actually, yes."

"What?"

"Yes," I said again, more firmly this time. "I do mind. Brian, we need to talk. That's what you wanted to do tonight, right? Talk?"

Brian's eyes narrowed so quickly I almost wondered if I'd imagined it. He blinked innocently. "I *did* say that," he agreed, stepping close once again. "But then I realized it's been two weeks since we made love. So you might say I… *realigned my priorities.*" He wiggled his eyebrows and took a step closer again.

I took another step back, feeling my cock shrivel in my pants.

It made me shudder when he called it that. *Making love* sounded so damn hokey. But it hadn't sunk in that he used it as anything but a stupid turn of phrase until now.

My error. *Again.* I'd kinda lost count of them at this point.

"Let's align them back. Brian—" I began. But honest to God, I couldn't keep going while he was standing there naked and clearly getting *very* happy to see me. What about this situation could possibly be arousing? "Would you put some clothes on? Please?"

"Why?" He ran a hand up his chest to tweak his own nipple. "You've seen it all before. *Lots* of times." He smiled slyly and stepped closer. "In fact, you've done more than look."

Which did *not* mean that I wanted to see it now, but whatever. I took another step away, until I was brushing up alongside the ice scraper that was still sticking out of the wall at an odd angle. I realized I'd basically let the man chase me halfway around my own dining table.

Jesus.

I stood up a little straighter and set my shoulders back. I was bigger than Brian—by a lot—and while I generally made a point not to use my size to intimidate people, I wasn't going to be forced into a game of ring-around-the-rosy with my naked, soon-to-be ex-boyfriend either.

I clenched my hands into fists and took a deep breath. "Brian, this thing isn't working out."

"I know! Dinner is *ruined*. And we know whose fault that is. But it's okay. I've already forgiven you for the veal. I'll make us some pasta later." He wiggled his eyebrows. "After-sex pasta is my favorite."

Wow. *No.*

"Not the dinner, I mean the… *us*. You and me. It's not… *good*. It's not *healthy*." Big words eluded me. "And I don't think either of us are really happy."

"What?" Brian whispered, the smile falling from his face. "Of course I'm happy! I'm *ecstatic*. You're everything I want in a lover, Jamie. You're easygoing, and hard-working, and… just… just… really *good*."

It sounded exactly like my description of him.

Except I *wasn't* good. Seemed like once I'd boarded the realization train—thank you so much, Everett—I couldn't disembark, and I saw in a flash that I *wasn't* good to Brian and never really had been.

You couldn't be good to parsley.

I'd been tolerant. I'd been patient. I'd let him steamroll me on things I didn't care about—which were most things, if I was being honest. I'd eaten a lot of veal in the past few weeks because it was easier than arguing, and we'd seen the movies he wanted to see because we had wildly different tastes, but I hadn't cared enough to convert him. None of that had been motivated by real affection, though. More like a need for distraction. A need to not see the glaring absence of an entree in the middle of my plate.

"Brian, you are a great guy," I began slowly, sadly.

"Oh my *God*! No. *No*, Jameson Burke, you are *not* doing this on our one-month date-iversary! Can't it wait until tomorrow? Or the next day? Why do you have to ruin *tonight?*" he wailed, throwing out his hands like he could somehow ward off my words, and my heart hurt a little because leave it to me to find the one guy in the greater O'Leary area who was even more deluded than me. His big eyes widened farther. "Should I have gone for the chicken?"

"No," I said gently. "This was... a nice thought. And I mean, yes, I really wish you hadn't, you know, *broken in* to deliver it. But you deserve better than... this. We're just not meant to be."

"Of *course* we are," Brian said, sounding slightly horrified. "Relationships are work, always! They don't just *happen*. You *have* to make an effort. Maybe we could try couples therapy, or—"

"Oh, no," I said firmly. "No. That's never going to happen."

"Right. God forbid you should have to talk about something, Jameson."

"Hey, I talk!" I said. "I talk!"

Brian shook his head, threw his hands in the air dramatically, and stalked down the hall to my bedroom.

I trailed behind him, trying not to look at his ass shaking.

"Years from now, when we look back on this day, you're going to feel like shit," he said over his shoulder.

"Probably," I agreed, leaning against the doorframe. I felt like shit already. "I'm sorry. I really wish..." *I could be normal and like a guy who likes me. That I'd had this realization before we got back together.* I shook my head uselessly.

Brian ignored me. He grabbed his jeans from his neatly folded stack of clothing at the end of my bed and dragged them on commando, then stood up again. "You. Are. Emotionally. Stunted." He punctuated each word with a jab of his finger into my chest. "You live in a fucking mausoleum." *Jab*. "And you don't know how to be happy or to enjoy a fucking *moment* without thinking about what happened ten years ago or what's happening ten minutes from now. Before you come crawling back to me, you'd better be ready for therapy, understand? You have some *serious* work to do. You'll be lucky if I take your call *at all*," he finished. Then he turned with a flounce to grab his shirt.

I wanted to tell him that I seriously doubted hell was going to freeze over anytime soon, but the last thing I wanted was to prolong this conversation.

"I'll help you out to your car with the—" I frowned. "Wait, where *is* your car? It wasn't in the driveway."

"It's at home." Brian sniffed. "In Camden. I took a taxi. Otherwise, it would have spoiled the surprise."

"Of course it would." I cast my eyes to the ceiling, hoping for divine intervention. It didn't come.

You deserve this, Burke. You deserve to drive the mostly naked, deluded man home to Camden. In the snow. And remember this next time you try to force things.

"Grab your veal medallions while I put away the dishes," I said tiredly. "I'll meet you outside."

Chapter Three

PARKER

"Joe!" I nearly sobbed into the phone. "Thank you, sweet Tom Brady and all the other angels, you finally answered!"

Joe Cross, O'Leary's local tow truck driver and self-proclaimed world's biggest Patriots fan, laughed. "Well, if you're prayin' to Tom Brady, I'm always gonna answer. What's shakin', Parks?"

"I'm stuck," I told him succinctly.

"Literally or metaphorically?"

"What? I mean my car, Joe." The snow was blinding, so there was no one around to see me roll my eyes, but I did it anyway. "How often do people call a tow truck for metaphorical reasons?"

"You'd be surprised. Life has a way of turning the metaphorical into the literal," he said sagely.

Right. "Sure, okay. Look, I was headed to Syracuse for the night so I could catch a plane tomorrow, and the snow got worse out of nowhere." I sounded a little panicked because I was. "I lost control on a slick patch and ended up on the side of the road."

"You alright? You hit anything?" Joe asked sharply.

"No, I'm fine. Only thing I hit was a snowbank. Thing is, when I try to turn the wheel and hit the gas, the whole thing whines like nails on a chalkboard, and it doesn't move. I might have damaged a tire or something."

Joe made a skeptical noise. "Sounds like you damaged the axle, kiddo."

I closed my eyes and grimaced, though no one could see that either. "I'm… guessing that's not the kind of thing you could run out here and fix real quick so I could get on my way?"

He laughed out loud. "Not unless you've got a magic wand and know how to use it. Besides," he added ruefully, "won't be anybody going anywhere 'cept plows and emergency vehicles once the state of emergency goes into effect."

"The… state of emergency," I repeated, watching the snowflakes swirl in the glow of my headlights. My wipers could hardly keep up with the onslaught, and the snow had started to build up on the edges of the windshield. "As in, no cars allowed on the road?"

"As in," he agreed. "You didn't know?"

Mother. *Fucker*. "No. I've been listening to a podcast. And, um, when does that go into effect?" I asked with just a shade more panic. I remembered this from years past—times when the entire world seemed to shut down for a day or two or three or…

"Governor announced it a couple hours ago. Takes effect at midnight and goes until eight o'clock tomorrow morning, but the boys and I are pretty sure it's gonna last longer," he said cheerfully. "We're out plowing right now. Rocco's at the wheel, and we're taking turns."

"Ah. Of course." I cleared my throat. "Alrighty then."

Eight o'clock tomorrow morning was, interestingly enough, when I needed to be at the airport in Syracuse, just in case my ten o'clock flight to Arizona happened to take off on time. Or ever.

"Listen, here's what you do. You hang up with me and call the police," Joe advised. "I know the Staties've been hoppin' with stranded motorists left and right, and I'm guessing the local guys have gotten their fair share too, so you're not alone. Everybody knew the storm was coming, but nobody expected it to come this early or hit this hard. The cops'll get you home, and I promise, soon as I'm allowed, I'll go out and get your car for ya on the flatbed. Then we'll see what's what. 'Kay?"

"Yeah, okay," I agreed, stifling a sigh. "That'd be… great."

Except, of course, for the fact that I didn't have a home for them to bring me to. Or even a hotel room. I was going to have to throw myself on Caelan's mercy after all.

I was *such* an idiot.

I'd known I was going for days, but I'd avoided saying goodbye to anyone until just this afternoon. And even then, I'd spent way too long sitting at Fanaille, watching people drink coffee and eat pastries like the end times were coming, feeling kinda sad and fond and heartbroken because I was gonna miss them, and maybe a little bit terrified too, because I was going to stay with my parents for a while, but I had no clue what came after that.

And yeah, I'd sat there hoping against hope that the universe would send Jamie Burke wandering in so I'd have a chance to say goodbye properly this time, even if he wouldn't say it back, because maybe then my dumbass heart could finally draw a thick line through Jamie's name.

But it figured the second I was reconciled to the fact that he wasn't going to come and I'd be leaving town for good—after I'd given Cal the keys to the little storage unit in Rushton where I was keeping a few pieces of furniture and the spare key to my car so he could retrieve it from the airport for me—*now* the universe was getting wishy-washy. Either that or it was my destiny to be buried under a mountain of snow and not seen again until the spring thaw.

"There's irony in this, Lucille," I said to the cardboard box on the seat next to me, where my plants were safely tucked in bubble wrap and tissue paper along with my other prized possessions. "Maybe only the Alanis Morissette kind, though."

I dialed the number for the O'Leary police department, and Marci, the dispatcher, answered on the third ring.

"Yep. Stay in your vehicle, Parker," she told me once I'd explained my problem and Joe's proposed solution. "Someone'll come out and getcha."

"Yeah. Okay." The wind kicked up in an enormous gust that rocked my car. "Any idea how long?"

"Nope! Anything I told you at this point would be a lie," she said way too cheerfully. "Wind knocked down a tree at the corner of Waterford and Crescent that hit a power line before falling smack onto the back of Quinn Tierney's car. Nearly killed Emmylou Harris."

"The singer?"

"No, honey. Quinn's dog. But that means we've got a couple hundred folks without power already, mostly elderly folks. Plus, poor Quinn's still stuck in his car until the power company can get out here. Snow's piling up, even though the weather folks say the brunt of the storm won't hit for hours yet. We're setting up an emergency shelter over at the school, and right now we've got all our guys and gals out doing evacuations. Could be ten minutes, could be a few hours."

A few hours. I looked at my gas gauge which I swear had been way higher just a couple minutes ago.

"Sure," I agreed. "I'll be fine for a few hours."

"And you've got an emergency kit in your car, right? Food, water, blankets? All that stuff they teach O'Learians in driver's ed?"

"Pfft. What do you take me for?" I scoffed.

Spoiler: I had no such thing. Clearly my decade in Boston, relying on public transportation, had made me soft.

Marci chuckled once, like maybe she knew. "You hang in there, Parks."

"I will," I said, because what else was there to do? Hoffstraeders didn't panic.

But it wasn't that long—only maybe thirty minutes, just long enough for me to work my way from resignation to terror and back again—before I saw headlights coming down the road toward me, oh-so-slowly.

"Thank *fuck*," I breathed, flashing my lights frantically. For once, something was going right.

The huge truck rolled to a stop in the center of the road and I shut off my car, shoving the keys and my phone in my pocket. I twisted to grab my backpack from the floor behind me and dragged the cardboard box from the passenger's seat into my lap.

"Rescue is at hand, lovelies," I whispered to my plants, nearly giddy with relief. Then I pushed open my door, stepped into the blizzard… and fell to my knees because the snow was nearly a foot deep over here. No wonder my car wouldn't get back on the road.

I heard the door of the truck slam as I tried to regain my feet without dropping the box or my backpack. My sneakers slid on the fresh powder while tiny weaponized snowflakes whipped against my face, stinging my cheeks and making my eyes run. I wasn't wearing a hat or gloves —let's pretend those were in my non-existent driver's emergency kit—and the snow began to seep through the knees of my jeans as I fumbled.

"Hey! You okay?" the driver called, making his way through the howling snow. "Hang on. Lemme help." I caught a glimpse of giant boots before his gloved hand reached out to pull me up.

I grabbed it and let him tow me to my feet. "Dude, I'm great now that you're here!" I grinned at my rescuer. "I was on my way to the airport, and I spun out. You're my knight in… in…"

Oh. Fudge.

His auburn hair was covered with a hat, and the semi-darkness threw his bearded face into relief, but I would know those brown eyes and broad shoulders anywhere.

"Parker?" Jamie demanded. "What the ever-loving fuck are you doing out here?"

I had this weird sense of déjà vu as I stood there holding Jamie's hand. It was like we'd been transported back to the playground at school a billion years ago, and suddenly, Jamie was rescuing me again, except back in the day his eyes had been a lot kinder, less filled with murderous outrage and shock. Funny how shit changed.

I pulled my hand away and wiped the snow from my eyes.

"Sightseeing. Obvs."

"You were supposed to have left town." His voice was accusing. Angry. Like I'd lied to him or something. Like it was *my* fault I was stuck on the side of the road.

"Well, I was *trying* to leave," I informed him.

"*Trying?* How hard is it to drive away? God knows you've done it before." He swiveled his head back and forth, his eyes taking in the empty road, the weird, pink sky, and my car, which was tilting at a very odd angle, before finally coming back to me. "I mean, how the *hell* does this shit even happen?"

"Be more specific," I yelled over the wind. "What shit? Snowstorms? Car accidents?"

"*You*," he said. "Being *here. Now.*"

"Physics, idiot. I hit a slick spot and slid."

"Uh, *yeah*. Because you drive a fucking *sled* with no traction whatsoever. And why the hell did you wait until it started snowing before you *left?*"

"It's not a sled; it's a Prius. Because global warming is *everyone's concern*." I hugged my box to my chest. "It's not my fault that—"

"Oh, Jesus. Of course it's not your fault." He rolled his eyes. "Please, tell me how someone else is to blame for this single-vehicle collision. Were you held at gunpoint?"

"What?"

"Did someone steal all your timekeeping devices? Lock you in a closet? Tie your shoes together? Grease your wheels?"

"What the hell are you *talking* about?"

"Tell me." His fingers opened and closed in a *gimme* gesture. "How is it someone else's fault that you're out here wearing sneakers, with no gloves, in a Prius, during the storm they've been predicting all week? I'm waiting."

There was snow dripping down my face and clinging to Jamie's eyelashes, and we were arguing in the middle of the fucking road, while more snow fell around us. It was beyond ridiculous. And yet I felt some part of me—some mad, familiar little spark—flaring to life.

"I didn't say it was anyone's fault! I just said it wasn't *mine*. I was heading for my flight to Arizona—"

"Family reunion? How touching." His voice was saccharine sweet but sharp as steel. "Bea must be over the moon that her little boy is coming home at last. Is she baking cookies? Those cinnamon ones you love?"

I narrowed my eyes. Snickerdoodles *had* been mentioned, which only made me more annoyed. It wasn't like it was my idea, for God's sake.

I straightened to my full height. "Jealousy is not a good look on you, Jameson," I said primly. "If you want someone to bake you cookies, I'm sure *Brian* would."

Jamie's mouth got impossibly tighter, like he didn't appreciate me bringing his boyfriend into our argument. *Too bad, so sad.*

"Some of us are capable of making our *own* goddamn cookies, Parker. We don't *need* anyone else to do it *for* us."

"Oh, right. *Right.* I bet that brave, lone-wolf thing still brings all the boys running, doesn't it? Does Brian—"

"Enough." Jamie's eyes went hot. "Brian's a decent guy. You leave him out of this."

"I'm just saying—"

"*I'm* just saying, shut your fucking mouth for once and answer my goddamn question."

"Shut my mouth *and* answer your question? Through interpretive dance?"

He looked ready to throttle me, and it was some symptom of my madness that I kinda wished he'd try.

In the snow.

On the Camden Road.

Yeah, I was definitely going crazy.

Jamie, meanwhile, folded his arms over his chest like he was getting comfortable, as though the snow pellets weren't whipping against his face and clinging to his eyelashes.

I started to wonder if maybe he was crazy too.

Maybe it was just something we brought out in each other. Jamie and I were like sodium and water—two perfectly ordinary, stable beings on our own that exploded into brilliant fire when we were together. It had always been that way, even when we were kids, and it used to scare me sometimes, the way we fed off one another. At this moment, I welcomed the heat of it. I think I was colder than I'd realized.

"Still waiting," he said.

"Christ Almighty. For *what*?"

"To know whose fault it is that your idiot ass is here on the side of the road waiting for a rescue instead of sunning itself in the desert. Were you forced into last-minute shopping?" He nodded at the box in my hands. "Grindr hookup you couldn't miss?"

"Yes," I shot back. "Yes, you caught me. There's something so thrilling about a roadside blizzard hookup I couldn't resist, but I've been waiting for hours and the only person who's shown up is… Oh! Hey, wait! Are *you* OldFatCreeper87? Because I've gotta say, you looked way cuter in your picture, otherwise I probably wouldn't have wasted my time."

Jamie rolled his eyes. "Would it kill you to admit that you spent too much time eating baked goods and didn't bother listening to the weather?"

I gaped at him. That was eerily accurate. But, "How did you know I was at the bakery?"

"Parker, this is O'Leary. Everything's news."

Which was possibly true, but… "Why do you need me to say this is my fault?"

Jamie stood a little taller and shrugged one broad shoulder. "Just wondering if you've changed since we were kids, that's all."

"What's *that* supposed to mean?" I demanded.

Jamie rolled his eyes. "If you don't know, I'm not gonna tell you."

"You're infuriating."

"And *you* have never taken responsibility for your *shit*."

"How dare you!"

"Me?"

"You don't even know me anymore! We haven't spoken in—"

"In over a *decade*," Jamie said. "And not a damn thing has changed. You still need—"

"In *eleven years, four months*," I corrected. "It'll be five months. On Sunday."

Jamie's eyes narrowed. His nostrils flared. He stared at me across the foot of snowy ground that separated us, and the weight of that stare was almost palpable.

I wrapped my hands more tightly around the box since I wanted to wrap them around his neck. Either that or... or...

I huffed out a breath that fogged the air between us. "Fuck it. You know what? I don't even know why I bothered trying to talk to you for so long. There's really nothing left between us, is there? *Trot along*, Jameson." I made a shooing motion toward town. "Thanks for giving me closure. *Finally*. Eleven years too late."

"Give *you* closure? Fuck that. Your memory is faulty, Parks. I'm not the one who left town."

"No, *you* were the one who practically booted me down the road! *Your parents want you to go to college, and they're so sad you're not? Boo hoo. Why the hell are you whining to me about it?*" I growled in my best Jamie impression. "*I have better things to do than listen to your needy ass bitching about how hard your life is. Don't plan your future around me, because as far as I can see, we don't* have *a future together. This isn't love, Parker, it's something to pass the time. Grow up. Make a decision on your own for once.*"

It felt like another lifetime, and yet it still squeezed my heart remembering it.

"And you did!" Jamie countered. "Didn't take you too

long to come to your senses. You were gone *the next fucking day*."

"What the hell would I have stayed for?" I yelled.

"Why the hell did you come *back*?"

We stood there staring at each other for a ridiculous amount of time. Hours and minutes and years. Jamie's jaw was working like he was trying to swallow, and I had lost all feeling from the knees down thanks to my wet jeans. The snow kept falling, unrelenting in the oddly pink night sky, and I wondered which of us would break first.

But it was me. It had always been me.

"I said, *trot along*, Jameson," I said tiredly. "You don't want to have to explain to Brian why you're late."

Jamie still didn't move. At least, not toward his truck. The muscles in his face were twitching, though—his eyes narrowing and widening, his nostrils flaring and contracting, his mouth pinching and relaxing, and he kept rolling his shoulder like his old injury still hurt when it couldn't possibly.

"Are you suffering a demonic possession?" I demanded. "Blink twice if you're in there."

But Jamie *still* didn't move except to breathe faster, little puffs of smoke that mixed with the air and hung around his head.

This was the last time I was going to see this man. The very last time, I would make sure of it. Because the big, dumb asshole was standing there in his boots and his parka, ten feet tall and three feet wide, staring at me like he was trying to look *through* me, and part of me, this big huge part of me, just wanted to hurl myself at his feet and cry.

But I wouldn't.

Because I did *so* take responsibility for my life, and *fuck him sideways*.

"Fucking *go*!" I shouted to the big, white, empty world.

"Jesus." But he stood there like his feet had been frozen in place, and finally I said, "Fine. Then I will."

I turned back toward my car—which suddenly seemed superior shelter to any involving *Jameson Burke*—but before I'd taken a single step, Jamie's hand shot out to grab my wrist.

I nearly dropped the box.

"Hey! *Watch it!*" I yelled, clutching it more firmly and noticing that the cardboard was beginning to get soggy from the wetness. Was the universe out to ruin *everything* I cared about? "Leave me alone."

"Get in the truck, Parker."

The words were said in approximately the same tone in which some great emperor conceded his kingdom to a conquering lord, all horrified reluctance, like he was hoping the words would wake him from a nightmare.

Spoiler: I was the nightmare.

"Fuck off," I said succinctly, stepping away from him. "As you so thoughtfully reminded me, this is my problem. Not yours."

"It *is* your problem, and now it's mine too. I'm not leaving you on the side of the road."

"Uh, yeah, ya are. Because I'm not going—"

"Get in the truck." Reluctant still, but indignant now, like how dare I refuse? It would have been funny if I hadn't been soaking wet and freezing cold.

Actually, I'm lying. It was still funny.

"No." The look on his face, the heat in his eyes, was enough to keep a guy warm in a blizzard. Possibly.

"You're being ridiculous. *Get in the fucking truck.*" The words were a low rumble that made my stomach flip with something that wasn't fear and was uncomfortably like arousal.

Ack. God. *Unacceptable.* I refused to be turned on by the guy who'd broken my heart, no matter how good he looked.

"I would not get in your truck if there were half-naked dancers doing the conga in there. Not if Daenerys Targaryen and every one of her dragons was coming for me. Not if it was the last truck on the face of the planet! Because if it's my responsibility, it's also my *choice*, and I *choose* to stay right here."

There was a terrible pause, like the whole world was hanging on a precipice, and then Jamie smiled so grimly it wasn't really a smile at all.

"Maybe I'm fucking tired of everything in the universe being *your choice*, Parker. Because you choose *wrong*." He grabbed the box out of my hands. "And it's eleven years five months on *Saturday*. Dumbass." He spun in the snow and stalked to his truck.

I gaped after him for half a beat, so stunned by his words that I could hardly process his actions. Then I turned, too, and ran after him, following in the footprints he'd created. I tugged at the back of his jacket. "Give that back!"

Jamie had always seemed enormous to me. I'd been small, once upon a time—a bookish little kid with long, thin spider limbs, and more head than body. But that was years ago, goddammit. I'd grown taller since high school. I'd filled out. It should have been physically impossible for him to keep right on walking, to make my sneakers *slide* in the snow like he was the world's largest sled dog and I was the sled.

And yet, here we were.

I yanked harder on the tail of his coat and jumped against his back, but my wet shoes had no purchase, and I ended up flailing and grabbing his waist before I fell to my knees again. My backpack, which I'd half forgotten, whacked against my side, throwing me further off balance.

Jamie stumbled forward two paces, holding the box in one hand and catching himself against the driver's side door with the other.

"Will you quit it?" he yelled over his shoulder. "You're like a child."

"Me? You! *You* are a child. Give me my box!" I demanded as I scrambled to my feet. I could feel my pulse behind my eyelids. "This is a crime."

"Report it to the police." Jamie made to throw the box in the bed of the truck.

"No!" I yelled, truly panicked and not just pissed. "Stop, Jamie, please!"

And, miracle of miracles, he did, pausing with the box raised above the edge of the bed. "Why? What's in here?"

"My *things*. My plants," I added, when he didn't look impressed. "Fragile stuff."

He took a deep, slow breath and looked at me. I wasn't sure what he saw—actually, yes, I was. He saw a bedraggled, soggy idiot, that's what—but something about his posture seemed to soften in a way that was visible even through his bulky jacket and the blinding snow.

"You getting in now?" he asked.

"I..." I sucked in a breath and let it out in a cloud. There were not a lot of not-shitty choices here, so... "Yeah. I guess."

He nodded once. "Climb in this door. Snow's drifted on the sides of the road." He threw his door open and ushered me inside.

"I'm gonna get your seat all wet," I warned as I stepped closer, close enough to feel the blessed heat from inside pouring out.

"Like it makes a difference at this point? Go on."

I looked him up and down. His jeans were as wet as mine now, and his waterproof parka looked soaked through. He was watching me with a kind of wary resignation, like I was the brussels sprouts left on his plate and he just *had* to deal with me.

I hated that.

But the truck was warm, and I was too tired to keep fighting. So, I threw my backpack in, then climbed up and over the driver's seat, trying to slide around the center console without putting my feet on anything.

I felt decidedly *drippy*. It was not a good look on anyone.

I hated that too.

Jamie waited until I was situated and had pulled my belt on before handing me my box.

"You need anything from your trunk?" he asked.

I hesitated, then dug out my keys with numb fingers and handed them over. "Blue suitcase. I'm thinking I'll need a change of clothes."

Jamie didn't say a word, just nodded once and closed the door before heading over to my car. Through the snow, I saw the headlights flash as he disengaged the locks, then flash again a moment later as he re-engaged them. A minute passed, and then the suitcase landed in the bed of the truck. I winced, wondering if any of the clothes inside it would be dry by the time I got to the shelter at the elementary school, but whatever. Beggars couldn't be choosers, and I was definitely a beggar right now.

I hated that, most of all.

Jamie opened the door and pulled himself in. He took his hat off and threw it on the center console before turning up the blower for the heat. Without a word, he put the truck in Drive, and we began the longest, most monumentally uncomfortable ride to O'Leary that two people have ever endured.

No, but seriously, though.

Even Jamie's heavy truck could only *crawl* through the snow, it was falling so hard and deep. Plus, once the heat kicked in, the little cab started to feel like a sauna—the insides of the windows were coated with condensation, and my head started to sweat. In the meantime, my feet were rotting inside my sneakers, and I couldn't seem to get my fingers warm, despite putting them in front of the blower.

And all the while? Dead radio silence. Like, *literally*. Jamie had the volume turned all the way down, as if he could concentrate on driving better without music or something, so the only sounds in the whole world were the swish of the wipers, the *whoosh* of air through the vents, and the horrible squeaking noise every time my damp thighs moved against the seat, which was more and more often as the level of awkwardness grew.

This was Alanis-Morisette-level irony, right here. For months and months, I would have paid money to have Jamie Burke as a captive audience because I'd been *so* convinced that if he'd just listen to me, just *look* at me, the part of him that had once liked a part of me would peek out from beneath all his anger, and we could somehow, maybe, be friends.

Now, I just wished I were somewhere—anywhere —else.

A flash of purple speared the sky and I gasped.

"The fuck was that?"

Jamie turned his head slightly to look at me. "It's called lightning, Parker. It's a strange phenomenon—"

"Lightning? In winter?" Some memory from another time and another place surfaced in my brain and I whispered, "Wait. Is this what they call… thunder snow?"

Jamie's eyes cut to me again, wide and horrified, but his lips twitched. "Say that again?"

"*Thunder snow*! Is it?"

"One more time."

"Is. This. Thunder. Snow?"

"That Boston accent is wicked cool, Pahkah. '*Is that thunnnndah snow?*'" He snorted.

"I do *not* sound like that."

Jamie made a noise of disagreement.

"Whatever. I *don't*."

"*Whatevah*."

I took a deep breath and let it out slowly through my nose. "As they say in Boston, 'Shut the fuck up, you giant, gaping asshole.'" I sat back in my seat and folded my arms on top of the box in my lap. "I hope your truck stays wet until September. I hope black mold grows on the seat right where my damp ass was."

Jamie rubbed a hand over his mouth, and I could almost swear he was wiping away his smile, which did *not* make me want to smile in response. That would have been ridiculous.

"Anyone ever tell you that you remind them of Everett Maior?" Jamie demanded.

"Uh. *No*. Why? Does he make threats against your person and your truck?"

"Actually… yes."

"Huh. I always knew I liked that guy."

Silence fell again, but different this time. Less awkward. More charged. Like laughing together had made it even harder to ignore each other. I cast around for something to say, but my brain remained stubbornly blank.

"So, the box," Jamie said after a couple of nearly silent minutes. "What's so important in there that you were willing to get dropped into a snowbank over it?"

I narrowed my eyes. "Who said *I* would be the one getting dropped into the snow?"

Jamie raised one red-brown eyebrow.

"I've filled out," I informed him. "I've got moves now."

Jamie didn't dignify this with a response.

I sighed. "I told you. My plants. A couple DVDs." I shrugged uncomfortably. "Mementos."

"All your baseball trophies in there? Felt a little light."

"My junior varsity participation trophies, you mean?" I snorted. "No, slugger. Unlike some people, my high school baseball career was nothing I care to remember. It'd be pretty sad if I'd kept them all this time."

Jamie huffed in amusement, but I was serious. *Jamie* had been the baseball champion of the two of us—All-State centerfielder, hottest jock in school—at least until he'd hurt his arm.

"My mom went through everything I left behind when I went off to school," I continued. "I only saved the good shit. I let her dispose of the rest."

"Dispose? Please. Bet your mom still has those trophies down in Arizona," he teased. "Bet she's got a whole shrine to her little *Parkie-kins*."

"Shut up." But I honestly didn't know what she'd done with the trophies, and that only made me pissier. "Can we turn on the radio?"

"What, and miss this final opportunity to talk before you leave O'Leary?" Jamie clasped a hand to his chest. "Miss your shot for *closure*?"

"Why, God?" I demanded, casting my eyes to the roof of the cab. "Why me?"

Jamie grinned. "So what's the good shit?" He nodded at the box. "What makes Parker Hoffstraeder's *cut* these days?"

"None of your beeswax."

"Wow! I'm hurt, Parks. I thought we'd gotten past this. Remember that little red treasure box you used to have back when you were a kid? You showed me *that* back when you were thirteen. All your Magic cards and stuff." He chuckled to himself. "Wonder if that thing got *disposed* too."

I made a noncommittal noise. "Can we not—?"

"You still have that orange blanket your Nana Mary made you? The one you thought was lucky?"

It was a total throwaway comment. A tease, even. But it hit me funny and made me draw in a breath. There were a limited number of people in the world who knew I possessed an orange blanket my grandmother had made me, and even fewer—as in, *one*—who understood the significance of it. And it was so wrong that this guy who hated me should have a key to every lock inside my brain.

"Yeah," I admitted grudgingly. "That's in here."

Jamie grunted a little, like maybe the shared memory thing was getting to him too. He cleared his throat.

"What else? Pull something out," he demanded.

"Uhhhh, how about *no*?"

"We've got a ways left to go, Parker, and there are limited things we can talk about."

"Oh, please." I snorted. "There is a whole host of things we can talk about. Which *Pride and Prejudice* adaptation did *you* like best? How are the Patriots doing in the playoffs? I just *cannot* keep up with those Kardashians! You just want me to tell you something so you can mock me for it. Sorry, not interested in contributing to my own demise."

Jamie refused to be diverted. "Not like you've got state secrets in there."

"That's what you think."

Jamie snorted. "Whatever. I bet I can guess."

"Bet you can't."

Jamie gave me a sideways grin, and I rolled my eyes. "Your college diploma, obviously."

"Obviously," I lied.

"Seashells. From the beach. Boston Beach."

"Boston Beach. Your knowledge of geography astounds."

"Whatever they call it." He waved his hand in the air like it didn't matter in the slightest.

"Mmm. It's like you're psychic."

"The picture of you with Mark Wahlberg."

"The what?" I turned my head to stare at Jamie's profile.

"I dunno. Doesn't everyone in Boston have to get a picture with him at least once? It's, like, a requirement?"

"Ohhhh. You mean the photo we're required to have as proof of residency for our state ID? Of course *that's* in there. I thought you meant the other pics of me and Marky Mark." I grinned. "I sold *those* to the tabloids."

He laughed again. "Naturally. Gotta pad that retirement."

"Retirement? Dude, you have no idea how expensive Boston was compared to O'Leary. I could barely afford to live, let alone retire." I shook my head ruefully. "Boston rents are something I don't miss."

"You managed to save enough to open a bar, *Parkie*." The teasing was gone from Jamie's voice now. "Couldn't have been all that bad."

"I didn't say it was all bad—"

"And it's not like you did it alone."

I frowned. "What's *that* supposed to mean?"

Jamie shrugged.

"Okay, let's get something straight. I worked my *ass* off to get a down payment to open Hoff's. *Two* jobs, Jamie, for six straight years. No vacations. Ethan and I used to make these plans of places we were gonna go, but it was all bull-shit. Neither of us left the *state* let alone the country. At least, Ethan didn't until he started dating his boyfriend." I shook my head, feeling my own temper rise. "We weren't exactly living high, you know? And everything I had, I *earned*."

"M'kay," he said, his tone laced with disbelief.

I set my teeth. It didn't matter if he believed me. It didn't matter if he still thought I was weak and dependent. It didn't matter, it didn't matter, it didn't— "Can you drive any faster?"

"Nope," Jamie said with maddening calm. "Otherwise I'd end up in a snowbank. Like an idiot."

"You are the most… *Ugh.* Were we actually friends at some point? Jesus Christ. I feel like I should have gotten a medal. Or maybe therapy for the Stockholm syndrome."

"I'm just saying—"

"Nuh uh!" I held up a hand, palm out. "Stop talking."

"My point was—"

"La, la, la, la." I put my cold fingers in my ears. "Don't wanna know. Not another word."

"Your parents had to be bankrolling you." He shrugged. "At least during college."

"Bank—? *My* parents?" I pulled my hands away from my ears and laughed out loud. "Oh my God. Are you joking? You do remember Lance Hoffstraeder, yes? Does he seem like the kind of guy who'd bankroll his son?"

"Your mom—"

"My mom wanted me out of O'Leary," I agreed. "But she didn't want me working at a bar! She wanted me to be a doctor or a senator. Something she could brag about to her friends. There was no bankrolling, Jamie. *Jesus.* Where'd you come up with this shit?"

Jamie frowned at the road in front of us.

"They paid for my first year of college," I admitted. "I decided to go to BU so suddenly and so late in the summer that there was no financial aid available." *And you know why it was so sudden*, I thought but didn't add. "After that, though? No. My parents aren't *that* well off. So I took out student loans—tons of them—and got scholarships." I shook my head. "Honestly, it's none of your fucking business in the first place, so why do you care?"

"I don't," he bit off. "I don't care at all."

"Whatever." I dug in my pocket for my phone. "I'm gonna call Marci and tell her you found me."

"Don't bother."

"But I'd hate for them to send—"

"Cell signal is shitty on this stretch of the Camden Road," he reminded me. "You can call from my house."

"But what if— Wait. *Your* house?" I shook my head. "No. You can drop me at the school. They have an emergency shelter-thing happening."

Jamie snorted. "I heard. And I'm not bringing you to the shelter."

"Why the hell not?"

"Because you'll be stuck there for days."

"Better stuck there than at your house!" *With you.*

"There are no showers at the school, and the cafeteria always smells like tomato soup and hotdogs." He side-eyed me. "You hate it when rooms smell like food and there's no food."

I blinked. I *did* hate that. It was why I'd been in such a hurry to move out of my last apartment. I had no clue how the fuck he remembered. Or why.

"You bitched about it often enough," Jamie said, like he could read my mind. "Thought it was a pretty fucked up quirk for a guy who claimed he wanted to open a restaurant, but I found it cute. Guess that should've been my first clue, huh?"

Jamie took a right turn onto Lobelia—toward his house, away from the center of town and the emergency shelter—and I let it happen.

Guess that should've been my first clue.

"First clue of what?" I demanded.

Jamie didn't reply. He pulled into his driveway just as another flash of lightning streaked across the sky.

"First clue of *what?*" A hot little ball was lodged in my chest and seemed to be making its way up into my throat, choking me.

Jamie ignored me. "Good thing we weren't a few minutes later," he said as he cut the engine. He pushed open his door. "Storm's getting worse. Grab your stuff and—"

I twisted in my seat and grabbed his arm with both hands, stopping him. "For the love of all that's holy in the *universe,* Jameson Burke, *first clue of what?*"

"That I have shit judgment when it comes to you! For fuck's sake, Parker. Isn't it obvious?" He pushed a hand through his thick, red-brown hair, and in the glow of the little dome light, his cheeks were flushed from some combination of cold and anger. "Listen. You don't wanna be here? I get it! I don't fucking *want* you here. If I could drive you to Arizona myself, *I would.* But we're stuck with each other for at least a day, maybe longer. And I honest to Christ cannot handle this… *thing.*" He motioned between us. "The fighting and the… fucking *remembering.*"

"You make it sound like *I* am the one who's forcing you to—"

He glanced pointedly down at my hands on his arm, and I let go immediately.

"Here's how this is gonna work, Parker. For the entire

time that we are stuck in this house, we are not going to wander down memory lane. We are not going to have deep, painful conversations. In fact, it'd be great if we could go on the way we have been for the past eleven years and five months. Polite strangers."

"If that's your idea of polite," I began.

Jamie cut me a look and I snapped my teeth together.

"Fine," I agreed.

"Fine."

"Super."

"Excellent. Can we leave the truck now?"

"The sooner the better." I shot him a smile and a death glare.

"I'll get your suitcase."

"So kind." *Despite your shriveled little heart.*

"Can you manage the box?"

"With one hand free!" *To throttle you.*

"Be careful jumping down," he called as I opened the door.

"So thoughtful of you to warn me!" *Like I'm an idiot who can't—*

Okay, in retrospect, I maybe should have paid more attention to the descent, but I was a tiny bit distracted.

Jamie came around the side of the truck a moment later and found me lying flat on my back with the box on the ground beside me.

"Seriously?" he demanded.

I sighed. There was no way I was gonna come out of this looking like anything other than a giant dork. And I hated fighting. "The view is really nice," I told him.

Jamie shook his head. "Did you hurt yourself?"

"Only my pride. Again." I thought about it. "Possibly my ass."

"Did you ever wonder if maybe you had too much pride to start with?"

I looked up at him through the falling snow. "Me? *No.* And I'm pretty sure that's not the kind of thing you say to a polite stranger."

Jamie snorted. "I think we need to have a truce," he said. "Before one of us gets hurt."

That one of us being *me*. Well, fine. I could be decent if he could. And besides which, I'd never been able to stay mad at Jamie too long. I simply liked the man too much.

So when Jamie held out a hand to me, I took it. And for the second time that day, I let him put me back on my feet.

Chapter Four

JAMIE

"You can have the first shower," I said, as I hauled Parker's suitcase into the kitchen. "Warm yourself up."

"'Kay." Parker sounded meek as he walked in behind me, and I almost wanted to turn and look at him, but I didn't. I'd been looking at him way too much already and it was giving me a head rush, kinda the way alcohol goes to your brain when you haven't had any in a while. The supposedly impenetrable fortress in my mind where I kept my memories of Parker-and-Jamie was falling fast.

But how the hell was I supposed to stay angry at the man when he persisted in being so fucking cute and vulnerable and… *Parker*.

I put the suitcase down on the floor by the oven, toed off my wet boots, and pulled open the fridge to peer inside. "Have you eaten anything? I've got eggs. Ham and turkey for sandwiches. I could cook up some chicken. Or risotto, if you wanna be fancy." I pulled open the crisper. "And I have salad fixings, if you're into that." I glanced over my shoulder when he didn't respond. "Parker?"

He still didn't reply, so I turned all the way around and

saw him standing stock-still in the open doorway, still holding that stupid box, dripping all over the Spanish tiles. He was looking around the room with wide eyes.

"What?" I demanded, following his gaze. Everything looked okay to me. Normal. Same sunny yellow walls, red-brown floor, and dark wood cabinets I saw every day. And the cleaners had come the weekend before so nothing was particularly dirty. Even the dishes were done. "What's wrong?"

Parker shook his head like he was coming out of a dream. "No. Nothing's wrong. It's just… it looks the same as the last time I was here."

"Oh." I frowned. "Yeah. I've never bothered redecorating."

"No, but I mean *exactly* the same, Jame. Like, I walked in here and expected your dad to be sitting right there"—he nodded at one of the chairs—"drinking beer and reading the newspaper." He set his box on the table. "And your mom should be standing at the sink smoking a cigarette with the window open. And Molly should be sitting here"—he trailed a hand over one of the chairs and smiled—"giving her shit about secondhand smoke. It's just… weird that they're not here. Especially Molly." He blinked at me. "Isn't it?"

There were a *lot* of responses that occurred to me.

Fuck you was first and foremost.

You couldn't last five fucking minutes without trotting out the memories, huh? came second.

But because he was right—because what he saw was exactly what I saw when I walked into this room, and *holy shit*, I hadn't realized just how badly I needed someone to see the same ghosts I saw until *right that minute*—what I said was, "Moll's been gone a long time, Parker. All of them have."

"Yeah." He nodded but frowned at the same time. "Not for me, though. Last time I was in this room, she hadn't been gone a year."

Parker's light hair was plastered to his head, his cheeks were bright red, his nose was runny, and I had to look away because he was staring at me with tears in his eyes and… I wanted to kiss the shit out of him.

Fucking stupid brain.

There'd been a naked man in my dining room maybe two hours before, offering me sex and companionship on *my* terms, and all I'd been able to think was *go away*. But this soggy lump of human who'd *literally* had me fighting in the middle of the street in a blizzard and who threatened my sanity with every word out of his mouth? *He* got me hard.

I'd never really understood why people wanted to jump out of airplanes or stick their heads in lions' mouths, but I was pretty sure I'd somehow gotten infected with the same strain of crazy.

I turned and shut the refrigerator but kept staring at it like the selection of magnets arrayed on the door was fascinating. "You know, if my mother were here, she'd be bitching because you were making a puddle on her kitchen floor. And if you die of hypothermia, *your* mom's gonna have me arrested. So go shower. If you need any clothes, grab some from my room."

"Your room?" Parker sniffed like he was trying to get control of himself, and I pretended not to notice. "You still sleep in your old—"

"Yes," I said shortly, inviting no more questions. "I still do. Just easier that way. And towels are still in the—"

"I know," he said. He grabbed the handle of his suitcase and dragged it down the hall without another word.

I let my forehead fall against the cool black surface of the fridge.

Was I actually insane? Why the hell had I invited Parker into my house? Why had I insisted that he stay? For fucking *days*. During a *blizzard*. I had to be mental to think I could handle this without one of us killing the other or the two of us fucking.

I kinda wasn't sure which would be worse.

So I did what I usually did when I was stressed. I pulled out chicken, put a pot of water on to boil, and started cooking.

Parker padded back to the kitchen a few minutes later. If not for the fact that I'd gotten really used to living alone, I might not have heard him. He wore socks on his feet and carried himself like he belonged here. But because I wasn't used to *any* noise anymore, I turned away from the stove and stared at him like he was another one of my ghosts.

He was wearing green and red flannel pajama pants and an oversized red and white BU hoodie, complete with a bulldog. His hair was wet and neatly combed, his cheeks were pink, and there was this sweet, hopeful expression in his green eyes that made him look younger and more inno-cent than he ever had even when we *were* young and innocent.

I cleared my throat and turned back to the stove. "Making chicken scampi," I said. "Chicken's nearly done. Just waiting for the water to boil."

Parker stepped closer and peered over my arm. "Looks good," he said. "Smells even better."

My gut clenched. My cock stirred. I didn't know if it was the words he'd said or the damp, delicious, fresh-scrubbed scent of him as he leaned into me that did it, but I had to grasp the wooden spoon tightly to stop myself from touching him.

Down, boy. He's complimenting your chicken, not offering to suck your cock.

And I wouldn't want him to, even if he was, I tried to convince myself. *Nothing has changed.*

Except as I inhaled a deep breath and tried to calm down, I realized what I was smelling. *My* body wash. On Parker's skin. *That* was a change. And now that there was so little distance between us, I suddenly—*shocker!*—craved *no* distance. It was fucking terrifying. It was also why I'd avoided having Parker within arm's length for months.

The first time he'd left, it had killed me, but I'd had my dad to take care of. I'd put one foot in front of the other, gotten out of bed in the morning because I had to, gone to work because someone needed to keep the electricity on. If the same shit happened again...

But it wouldn't. It would not.

I stepped away from the stove, away from him, and leaned against the sink.

"So, um. You managed to figure out the shower? It's a little tricky with the diverter, and I forgot to mention—"

Parker smiled. "Not my first rodeo, cowboy."

"Right." I went to fold my arms over my chest and realized I was still holding my spoon like it would fend Parker off. I set it on the little spoon rest by the stove. "That's good. You look better."

Parker's eyes followed the motion of my hand and he studied the spoon rest—a wooden thing I'd made years ago in shop class—with a small smile playing across his lips. Then he looked down at his socks and stuck both his hands in the front pocket of his sweatshirt.

"Yeah. Yeah, I feel way better. My clothes were dry too, by some miracle."

I frowned. "Why wouldn't they be?"

He glanced up. "Uh, because my suitcase was riding in the back of your truck. In the blizzard. *Duh*."

"I covered it with a tarp, Parks."

He blinked at me.

"I keep one back there," I explained. "Just in case."

"Oh." He ran a hand over his mouth. "That was… nice. Thoughtful."

I snorted. "That's me alright."

"Considering you were about to make off with my most precious belongings at the time—"

"Please," I scoffed. "What would I want with your plants and your memories of Boston?"

Parker opened his mouth like he was going to argue, then he shut it and shook his head. "Go shower, Jamie."

"I'm cooking—"

He lifted one eyebrow. "I'm capable of stirring the chicken and boiling pasta, Jameson."

I couldn't resist.

"I don't know," I said slowly. "I mean, I've tasted your chicken wings." I wrinkled my nose in an exaggerated way.

"Okay, first," Parker said stepping closer, his eyes narrowed. "I thought we were supposed to be polite strangers for as long as we're stuck here. And we might not be able to handle the *strangers* part." He looked around the room again, then back at me. "But do you need me to explain *polite* to you?"

I had to bite my tongue to keep from smiling. Parker wasn't really pissed, and we both knew I was teasing. It was… nice. Good. Normal. As normal as me interacting with Parker could be.

Which was to say, really fucking weird.

"I beg your pardon," I said solemnly.

Parker nodded, once, and gave me a cheeky grin. "Now go shower. "

I went without another word, mostly because that smile was fucking dangerous, and I couldn't trust myself to stay another minute.

Unfortunately, being in the bathroom didn't help. Parker's damp clothes were hanging over an unused towel bar, and the room was still humid from his shower, which made it really fucking hard to forget that just a couple minutes ago, he'd been naked and standing under the water exactly where I was standing.

And yeah, that thought made *other things* really fucking hard. But I'd be damned if I jacked off over Parker Hoffstraeder. Not *now* while the man was standing in my kitchen, smelling like my soap, and making me feel...

I pushed at the knob viciously, shutting off the water.

I needed him gone, but that wasn't gonna happen. So, I had to find a Plan B. *Fast.*

The problem was, part of me really wanted him here. He was fucking hilarious when he wasn't being provoking... and okay, maybe even then. It felt *right* having him in my space. He fit here. As much as I desperately did *not* want to have some giant conversation where we rehashed all the shit that happened eleven years ago, I wanted to revel in his presence and that easy banter I'd only ever had with *him.*

And the other problem, I thought as I toweled myself off, was that my mind couldn't draw a line between being friends with Parker and being attracted to Parker. Every joke, every fight, every second I fucking *breathed* around him increased the chances that I was gonna want him.

But okay. That wasn't a catastrophe, right? I could want and want all day long—fuck, *I had*—but that didn't mean Parker was gonna jump into my arms. In fact, the odds of that were about the same as lightning striking twice...

And just like that, I was remembering Parker saying *thundah* snow.

I was a goner.

Whatever.

Parker was literally leaving town as soon as the storm was over. Our time together would be measured in hours. I could control myself for a few fucking hours. And my self-sabotaging brain needed to shut the fuck up. Hadn't even *Brian* said something about not overthinking everything? There was some irony there.

I stepped into a pair of sweatpants and pulled a t-shirt over my head before heading back down the hall to the kitchen.

"Parker?"

I found him standing in the doorway to the dining room, holding his phone. He looked… puzzled, I decided.

"Problem?"

"I'm not sure." He glanced back at me and rolled his eyes. "I, uh, called Marci and told her I was safe. Then I texted my mom. Beatrice is *very* displeased that I won't be arriving tomorrow."

"Ah."

"Apparently, my father has been feeling light-headed since he heard about the bad weather. Also, he has a dry, hacking cough which she agreed *might* be caused by the common cold, but was more likely due to the blizzard in Upstate New York that's delaying my visit."

"No doubt. It's like the weather gods weren't even *thinking* of your parents when they planned this storm. Your mom is going to write them a *very* strongly worded letter."

Parker grinned. "She's going to demand to speak to the blizzard's manager."

"Does she have a priest on speed dial?" I wondered.

"Knowing her? Probably the pope, a couple rabbis, an imam or two."

"A wizard, maybe? She's calling Dumbledore right now." I smiled smugly.

Parker's smile tilted and got warmer, even as he shook his head. "You mention your childhood *Harry Potter* obsession to a guy *once* and he *neeeever* lets you forget it."

"Once?" I scoffed.

"Fine, fine. Two or three times," he allowed.

"Two or three *hundred*. Also, can we accurately call it a childhood obsession when it lasts into adulthood?" I mused.

"It did *not!*"

"Are you forgetting that we drove *allll* the way to Rochester when the last book came out because they had an all-night bookstore and you *needed* to get the book at midnight?"

Parker leaned back against one side of the doorframe. "I might possibly remember something about that," he allowed. "Vaguely."

"Uh-huh. Remember we got a hotel room? '*Jamie, we can be alone all night for the first time since our parents found out we were more than friends.*' That ringing any bells?" I leaned against the other side of the frame.

Parker shifted his weight from one foot to the other. "Maybe," he said, impatiently this time.

"*Jamie, we can finally take things to the next level!*"

"Okay, first of all, why does your Parker-voice make me sound like a long-lost Muppet?" Parker glanced at the ceiling. "And second… in my defense, I *had* imagined—"

"*It'll be an unforgettable night, Jamie!*" I quoted in the same high-pitched voice.

"Are you saying it wasn't?" Parker shot back.

I laughed out loud. "Not at all. I will admit, sitting

together on the bed, reading a children's book over your shoulder until dawn was not the way I'd pictured that night working out. Not after we'd taken the time to buy condoms and lube."

"You didn't complain at the time," Parker said, staring at me levelly. "Not once."

"Of course not." I shrugged and rubbed my hand over my t-shirt. I swear I could feel the heat of his body cuddled against me, his back against my chest in that little bed, like it was happening right this minute. "You were so freakin' happy."

"I was," he agreed softly, a little line between his eyebrows. "I don't think I'd ever been that purely happy."

And that had been enough to make *me* happy, even after Parker's mom had found out where we were. Even though we'd never gotten to use those condoms at all that summer. Or ever.

I cleared my throat and took a giant step away from him, away from all the emotional shit he stirred up inside me.

My plan B was dead in the water. And I didn't have a plan C.

"So. Uh. Is your dad really sick?"

"No." Parker snorted. "He's gonna outlive all of us. My mom just keeps hoping I'll fall for her guilt trip."

"Wonder why."

He looked up at me. "I used to fall for them. But then, I used to believe a lot of things." He shrugged. "That was a long time ago."

I cleared my throat. "So. Dinner?"

"Yeah," Parker agreed. "But first." He threw out a hand toward the dining room. "Mind explaining why there's an ice scraper hanging out of your wall?"

"Oh. That." I peered over his shoulder, opened my mouth to explain, and shook my head. "I need food first."

I dished up the pasta, Parker poured us glasses of water from the pitcher in the fridge without being told, and I carried our food to the living room so I wouldn't have to look at the destroyed wall while we ate. After swallowing my first bite of pasta, I explained about Brian.

Sort of.

"I don't get it," Parker said. He'd plopped on the far end of the brown leather sofa and drawn his legs up pretzel-style. "The guy brought you a nice surprise dinner and you broke up with him? What do you do to door-to-door salesmen? Summary execution?"

"He let himself into my house without telling me," I corrected. "Then I launched an ice scraper at his head thinking he was an intruder, and *then* we broke up."

"Still."

"Still?" I rolled my eyes. "Still *what*?"

"I dunno. I mean, if you're not a hundred percent into him, it's good that you broke it off. But it seems excessive for one little mistake." Parker twirled pasta on his fork and shoveled it in his mouth. His eyes closed, and he hummed in pleasure. "Especially when it wasn't a big deal."

I had to clear my throat as I tried to remember what we'd been discussing. "It wasn't just the dinner. There was other stuff."

"Yeah?" Parker was unimpressed. "Like what?"

"Like, I dunno. We wanted different things, I guess." I pushed my hair off my forehead. "I didn't want a serious relationship. I didn't want..." *Brian.*

"Was he needy?" Parker demanded, his eyes just a little too heated. "Too attached?"

"Huh?"

Parker waved a fork in the air dismissively. He shoveled

more pasta into his mouth and talked around it. "Just sayin', you have a track record for being an asshole during breakups."

"Excuse me? How the hell would—"

He lifted one eyebrow, and my chest constricted.

"We're *not* talking about that," I reminded him through gritted teeth.

Parker snorted. "You notice that you enforce the polite strangers rule only when it's convenient? Because apparently it's *fine* for you to bring up the time we didn't have *sex*, but I try to establish a pattern of behavior, and suddenly—"

"Parks? You've got tomato on your chin."

"Shit." He stuck his tongue out of his mouth and swiped at his chin. "Better?"

My mouth went dry, just like that. "Yeah."

"So, what happened next?" Parker demanded, scooping up more chicken. "After you were all, '*How dare you come into my home and bring me sustenance without an engraved invitation, Brian! How dare you like me more than I like you!*'"

"It was *not* like that!" I insisted, even though it sort of was.

"Patterns of behavior," Parker sang.

"There is no pattern! You're making this shit up."

"Mmmkay," Parker said, patently humoring me and making me want to grab him by the shoulders and shake him… or something. "So, what happened after you broke up with him for totally different reasons that are not connected in any way to any patterns of behavior?"

"I hate you," I said. "Just so you know."

Parker laughed, and it made his eyes crinkle. "The feeling is *so* mutual," he said, and I swear, just that smile had a shiver dancing up my spine and cold sweat popping out on my neck.

I cleared my throat. "I said I wanted to break up, and I drove him home to Camden since he hadn't brought his car. Which is how I happened to be out on the road."

"Hmm." Parker chewed meditatively. "So, does that mean I have Brian to thank for my rescue?"

"You haven't even thanked *me* for your rescue," I reminded him, maybe a little crossly. "Instead, you threatened to have me arrested and then tried to injure me." I rolled my shoulder, which was actually feeling somewhat better, probably thanks to the shower.

Parker ran his tongue over his teeth. "I'm sorry. I didn't mean to injure you."

"Oh, you didn't," I said cheerfully. "I just said you *tried*. Which was rude."

His eyes narrowed.

"And while you're at it, you could thank me for making you a delicious dinner," I added, pushing my luck.

"A *mostly edible* dinner that *I* helped prepare." He snorted.

"Mostly edible enough that you scarfed that whole bowl while I've only eaten half," I pointed out. "And I'll accept you cleaning the dishes in lieu of verbal thanks." I smiled. "I'm easy like that."

Parker pursed his lips thoughtfully, then nodded. "You know, that *is* only fair."

He stood up, grabbed the half-finished bowl from my left hand and the fork from my right, and stalked toward the kitchen.

I sat there for another full minute, staring at my lap and my empty hands, feeling a dopey grin on my face, and wondering how the hell confrontation with Parker made me happier than I'd been in years.

Then, because Parker was apparently a magnet and I was as powerless as an iron filing to resist him, *goddammit*, I heaved myself off the couch and trailed him down the hall.

Parker was standing at the sink with his back to the living room, and I took a moment to study him when he couldn't see me. He'd taken off his sweatshirt and thrown it on the counter, leaving him in a thin t-shirt and those flannel pants that were *so* not sexy, but nevertheless made me lean against the wall for a moment, trying to make out the curve of his ass beneath the fabric.

Parker in the kitchen was… a revelation. His movements were competent. Confident. Practiced. He knew his way around—and not just cooking but cleaning too. Which, yeah, should have been completely obvious—the guy had owned his own place, and you couldn't do that without getting your hands dirty—but I guess I hadn't really let myself picture him doing the dirty work. Watching him squeeze soap into the sink basin was oddly attractive.

What about Parker is not *attractive to you right now, dumbass?*

My eyes strayed to his cardboard box, which was still sitting on the table where he'd left it, and mostly for the sake of distraction, I strolled toward it and paused with my hand on one flap of the cardboard. "Don't your plants need oxygen?"

He lifted his gaze from the sink, and he hesitated. "I guess you can take them out," he allowed. "Although, you know, it's not really oxygen they need. They take in carbon dioxide and give off oxygen."

I shot him an amused glance. "Not *just* a pretty face, ladies and gentlemen, he's an amateur botanist too!"

Parker's cheeks flushed pink. "Shut up. I just had a lot of free time on my hands the past couple weeks."

I pulled the flap back and found three little plants, their pots tucked up in an orange blanket. I moved the box down onto a chair and placed each one on the table in a neat row.

"It's symbiosis," Parker continued as he washed the dishes. I wasn't sure if he was talking to me or to himself. "Plants and animals. It's, um… a mutually beneficial relationship. Have you ever heard of fig wasps? Because I was reading an article, and—"

"Your plants have names?" I said, looking up at him.

"Oh. Yeah, I… Yeah." He blushed harder. "Free time, remember? Weird things happen when you're in a hotel room alone for days on end. You need to have *something* to care about, right? Even if it's stupid?"

My heart shifted a little bit at the idea that Parker didn't have anything in O'Leary to care about besides these little plants. But I reminded myself that was why he was *leaving*. That was why he'd always leave.

"It's cute," I said. "They're adorable."

Parker bit his lip. "Thanks," he whispered. Then he looked away and resumed scrubbing dishes.

Since he didn't tell me *not* to, I lifted the orange blanket from the box and held it up to the light. Parker's superhero afghan had a bright blue shield in the middle with an orange letter *P* inside it, and his grandmother had insisted that since she'd knitted it with love, it would always protect him. It was in amazing shape, considering its age, but it was a little damp from the snow, so I draped it over the back of the chair, tracing the *P* with my fingers.

Then I hesitated.

At the bottom of the box were a bunch of DVDs and a large, red, metal cookie tin with the words PARKER'S STUFF spelled out in tipsy painted capital letters. I lifted it out and ran a hand over the top.

When he'd said he had mementos in the box, I imagined… well, shit from his life in Boston. Surely those were the times he'd want to remember. College, living with Ethan in the big city, partying with friends, making a success of himself. Seeing this old memory box was disorienting. It made me wonder whether there was anything from his old life left inside it. Any memories of *us* inside it.

After that day on the junior high playground when we'd become tentative friends, I'd made a point of walking home with Parker after school pretty much daily. I hadn't expected him to be *grateful* for my friendship, exactly, but I also hadn't expected him to be so totally unenthusiastic. To have to basically wear him down and twist his arm. If I hadn't been a stubborn, cocky little shit back then, I probably would have given up. Instead, I'd been intrigued enough to be persistent.

The first time he'd invited me to his house, I'd felt at least as victorious and excited as I had the first time I'd pitched a no-hitter, and not just because the snacks he'd snagged us from the pantry were the name-brand Oreos my mom never bothered to buy. I'd roamed around his room, stuffing my face with chocolate cookies, peering at all his stuff—books and figurines and recipe magazines—trying to figure out what made him tick and why I liked it so much. I'd found this tin, and without thinking, I'd grabbed it off his bookcase.

"Hey! Is your name on that?" Parker said now from across the kitchen, in the exact tone of voice he'd used to say those same words back in the day.

I put the tin back in the box.

"I wasn't going to open it," I said now, just as petulantly as I'd said it then.

Parker gave me a small smile. "You promised me you wouldn't, like…" He stared into space for a minute. "Eighteen years ago now, I guess? Damn. We're old." He shut off the water and wrung out the dishcloth, laying it neatly over the edge of the sink.

"*You* promised me that someday you'd show me what was in it," I reminded him. "Once you knew you could trust me."

"And I did. You saw all my Magic cards and Aunt Betty's cookie recipe. I wouldn't even show them to my *mom*."

"So why not now?"

Parker busied himself wiping his hands on a dry towel. "I'd never show that tin to a polite stranger."

I didn't want to touch *that* with a ten-foot pole, so I pushed the box a few inches away and said, "Thought you told me your mom threw away all your shit when you left for school."

"Everything I didn't take with me," he confirmed.

"But what—"

"I thought we weren't talking about the past," Parker interrupted. "Or is this another of those cases where it's only okay when *you* do it?"

For half a second I thought about taking it all back, the whole polite strangers bullshit, because I was insanely curious, but in the end I shook my head. "You're right."

"Polite strangers still? You sure?"

"*Still* would imply that we've managed to act like that for even one minute of the last two hours. But yes." I stretched my arms up behind my head, trying not to read anything into the way Parker's eyes tracked the movement, then I blew out a breath and took a step toward the living room. What the fuck would polite strangers do at this moment? "Wanna turn on the TV and see what the weather predictions look like?"

"No." Parker was looking at me strangely. Not mad,

exactly, but his eyes were hot in a way that made my breath catch.

"You sure? It's fun when they send hapless reporters out into the storm to remind us what snow looks like, just in case we're too lazy to look out the window."

"I'm positive." Parker pushed away from the counter. His pants were loose and hung low on his hips, and the t-shirt was flecked with little drops of water from the sink.

I had to look away. "A movie, then. I'll even watch one of your DVDs." I poked through the box and pulled one out at random. "Though God knows I don't think *Death Comes to Pemberley* is gonna be a rollicking—"

"Jamie?" Parker's voice was low, serious, and tentative all at once, and when I looked back at him, our gazes locked. "If we really *were* strangers—if we met on the road for the first time tonight and were stranded here together for just one night before we said goodbye forever—what would you want to do?"

His answer was right there in his eyes, in the tilt of his hip, in the way his teeth were sunk into his bottom lip like...

"*Fuck*, Parker," I breathed.

Parker smiled again, teasing and wanting and focused on me. It was more dangerous than a blizzard and everything I'd been missing for eleven years and *almost* five months. "Seems like a pretty good answer to me."

Chapter Five

"Uн, no," Jamie said, though his eyes said something else entirely. "No. That would be a terrible idea. The worst idea in the history of ideas."

"You think?" I took a half step in his direction—more of a *lean*, really—and Jamie swallowed hard, proving that he was no more immune to me than I was to him.

"Worse than all those guys who invaded Russia in the winter," Jamie assured me. "Worse than anything any Darwin Award winner has ever done."

"Hmm. Even the guy who ran toward the train after he got stuck on the tracks so he could save his car?"

"Worse."

The thing of it was, I couldn't really argue. This *was* a terrible idea. The kind of thing a smart man would only agree to when he was drunk off his ass so he could blame Jose Cuervo in the morning. But Jamie was *right there*, standing closer to me than he'd been in forever, and I wanted him—fuck, I *yearned* for him—not because we were polite strangers but because I *knew* him. Under all the anger, under all the tiny cuts and mortal wounds we'd dealt each other, he was still my Jamie. Touching my lucky blanket, taking care of the things that mattered to me simply because they mattered to me. He knew me better than anyone else ever would. And this was maybe my last chance to be with him. Ever.

You didn't get anything in life by being wishy-washy, right?

"You're definitely not with Brian anymore," I said. "It's definitely over."

It was a statement not a question, but Jamie shook his head anyway.

"It never really began. But Parker…"

"Do you know," I said conversationally, while taking another tiny step toward him, "that it took me two years before I could kiss another guy without feeling like I was cheating on you? Two years. And even then… hell, even *now*… I can't stop comparing."

Jamie inhaled sharply and his nostrils flared just like they had out on the road earlier. He said nothing, but his eyes tracked my movement.

"You remember the first time we kissed? Down in your basement? I'd been hanging out with you in the diner after school when you finished your shift. And someone asked who I was taking to Homecoming—"

"Gracie," Jamie all but growled.

"Right." I smiled, just a tiny bit, remembering. "That's right. And I said I wasn't sure." I moved a step closer. Jamie didn't budge.

"You blushed ten shades of red."

"Probably," I agreed.

"Definitely."

"And when we walked back here afterward. You wouldn't say a word to me. I didn't know if you were mad at me, or if you were thinking about Molly…"

"Both," he snapped. "Both."

"But when we walked in the back door, you pushed me up against the basement wall and you said…" I paused. "You said you were tired of waiting."

Our chests were nearly touching and I had to tilt my neck back to look at him. His eyes were brown and so damn deep that my stomach hitched in trepidation. You could get lost in darkness like that and never find your way back out again.

In the epic fight before I left, Jamie had implied that I was too weak. Too passive. Well, fuck that. I wasn't being passive now.

"My sister had only died a couple weeks before," Jamie whispered. "I'd wanted to kiss you for months. Years, maybe. And I'd finally figured out that life was short and unpredictable." His eyes looked lost.

"It's still short. And still really fucking unpredictable."

Jamie closed his eyes and inhaled. "But we're not kids anymore."

"I'm well aware of that. All the more reason why—"

"Actions have consequences, Parker."

I shook my head, just once. "I'm aware of that." I narrowed my eyes and took a step back so I could see him better. "Is this part two of the lecture you started out on the Camden Road?"

Jamie swallowed and said nothing.

"Oh my God, it *is*. Jesus Christ, Jameson!" I spread my arms, then let them flop uselessly to my sides. "What the hell makes you think *I* need a lecture about this? Hmm? *Me*, of all people?"

"I'm just reminding you, reminding *both of us*, that—"

"That actions have consequences? No shit, son! I have spent the last fucking *year* doing nothing but dealing with consequences. The last fucking *eleven years and five months.*

And every time I think I have gotten to the end, that the last domino has fallen, that there are no more fucking *shoes* waiting to fall on my head, life says *hold my beer*."

"Parker, I didn't mean—"

"Oh, no. *No*. Don't you dare backtrack," I fumed. "You said exactly what you meant, and I know because you said it earlier today, and you've been fucking saying it ever since we first set eyes on each other again last spring. You've treated me like shit for months and I haven't deserved *any* of it. And guess what, buddy? If actions have consequences, then this is yours. You can just stand right fucking *there* and listen to me for once."

My chest was heaving, and I couldn't remember the last time I'd been so angry.

"I've had *one dream*, Jamie. One dream my whole life. And that was to open a restaurant in O'Leary. My father thought I was an idiot to want a *menial job*. My mother thought I was an idiot to want to live in O'Leary. I didn't care. I went off to college, I got my degree, but that dream never died. And finally, *finally*, after years of working, of living as modestly as I could, taking no handouts from anyone," I added pointedly, "I had the money, and I moved back home to open the bar with *my name on it*. It was going to be beautiful. Everything I wanted. The *consequence* of all the fucking *actions* I'd put into it."

"It *was* beaut—"

"It *would* have been, Jamie," I said bitterly. "It *could* have been. Except I'd kinda hoped that my once-upon-a-time best friend would be happy to see my face when I got back, and instead, I found out that he hated me with the burning passion of a thousand fiery suns. I mean, one would think eleven years would be the fucking statute of limitations on you hating my guts, right? On you being illogically and non-specifically angry about my very existence? Especially considering you'd done everything but stick me in a FedEx box and *ship me to Boston*, so I've never understood why you seem to be so pissed and betrayed that I actually went."

"We're not talking about—"

"Oh, fuck you," I said, pushing him just a little. He didn't move. "You say *I* have to have everything my way, but *you*, Jameson…" I shook my head. "And you know what? That's not even the worst of it. Not by a long shot. Because then, the fucking bar burned to the ground and came *this close* to actually *killing people*, and all of a sudden, my income, my savings, my future home, and my entire plan for the future were *gone*, and I sometimes have these nightmares that just—" I swallowed. "What the hell did I do to deserve *that* consequence, Jamie?"

He shook his head mutely.

"And then my landlady, who I'd already given notice to since I was tired of paying an arm and a leg for a studio apartment that smelled like tuna fish sandwiches, told me she'd already re-rented my unit, which maybe smelled like tuna but was still *mine*, goddamn it, and I had to move my shit into a storage unit since there's not another fucking apartment in all of O'Leary, and I ended up at the Crabapple, until they got overbooked and kicked me out too, and my choices were homelessness, visiting my parents in Arizona, or listening to Rena Cobb *orgasm*, and for a minute there, *I considered homelessness!*"

I slapped my palm against his chest to illustrate my point, but Jamie didn't seem deterred. In fact, he moved closer, wrapping his arms around my waist.

"*Shhh*. It's okay. Calm down, Parker," Jamie began in a placating voice, like he didn't know that was the conversational equivalent of throwing gasoline on a fire.

I sucked in a ragged breath. My heart was beating so

hard I could feel it in my temples. "Do not *even* 'Calm down, Parker' *me* right now, Jameson. I'm nowhere *near* calming down. I'm just getting warmed up! Because then the *insurance company*, which I'd naïvely thought was meant to actually *insure me* against catastrophic damage like a giant fucking fire, decided that, no matter what the official fire department report said, the fire wasn't just tragic but *suspiciously tragic*, and sent out a little asshole with a twig up his butt who looks unironically like the insane brother from *Peaky Blinders*!"

"You mean Cillian Murphy?"

"No!" I shouted. "The *other* insane one! And stop interrupting!"

Jamie held up his hands in apology.

"I have tried to make the best of things, Jamie! I have smiled, I have kept a stiff upper lip, and I have employed so much positive thinking that by rights I should have my own goddamn horde of innocent woodland animals traipsing along behind me while I walk through town. I should be Cinder-*fucking*-ella, spinning around a ballroom while sparkles fill the air. I should be fending off unicorns with a *stick* because my heart is *just that fucking pure. That* should be the consequence for my actions! And instead?" I threw out my hands. "Instead, I find myself stranded on the side of the road, in a blizzard, and who comes along to rescue me when I'm at the lowest point in my life, when I have not even one tiny scrap of dignity left to my name, but *you*, the one person I... I..."

"Parks," Jamie breathed. He wrapped his arms around me again so tightly that my face was mashed against the softness of his cotton t-shirt and the steady beat of his heart filled my ears.

And it was *everything*.

I felt his shirt get damp under my cheek and realized I

was crying. I tried to pull away, because *Jesus*, of all the people I didn't want to see me weak, Jamie and my father were tied right at the tippy-top… but Jamie wouldn't let me go.

"You're alright," he whispered. "You're alright, I promise."

"But I'm not," I told his sternum, beyond caring that my words were all garbled. "I'm really not. Because I just threw myself at you, practically begged you to have one night of no-strings sex, and you don't even want me for *that*. And it's so trivial, but it's one more straw and I… I am a very tired and fucking overloaded *camel*, Jamie." I tried to catch my breath, and it came out halfway between a sob and a laugh. "Damn. And if my dad saw me crying right now, he'd be *pissed*. Hoffstraeder men don't cry."

"Hoffstraeder men do whatever the hell they want," Jamie whispered. His arms squeezed me even harder, holding me against him so tightly there wasn't a molecule of available space between our bodies. It was painful. Breathing was almost impossible. And yet that strong comfort was exactly what I needed, and I hadn't realized it until that moment. Plants could keep their oxygen so long as I had Jamie.

Danger, danger, danger.

But Jamie stroked his big hand up and down my back over and over, his fingers surprisingly gentle as they tapped out a rhythm on my spine, and I didn't fucking care that this was going to end badly. Enough shit in my world had ended badly no matter what I did, so why deny myself this?

"Do you know what I thought that day, Parker? The day we kissed for the first time?" Jamie whispered roughly, like the words were being pulled from him involuntarily. "I thought, 'Holy shit, he's so beautiful.' I thought, 'In my whole life, there will never be anyone I want as much as I want him right now.'"

I drew a shuddering breath. "So you're saying you were insane that day? Is that it?"

Jamie slid both hands up to my shoulders and then farther, until he was cupping my jaw. He forced my head back a few inches, and I opened my eyes, blinking against the brightness of the room and then again at the expression on his face—open, intense, and entirely focused on me. He slid his thumbs over my cheekbones, wiping away the wetness there.

"Not insane." His lips quirked up in a ghost of a smile. "Prophetic, maybe. There hasn't been a single moment since then that I haven't wanted you just as much. I don't hate you. I never have."

"But then—" Why did you push me away back then? And just now? Why did you say what we had was dead? Why, why, why?

"Parker?"

Jamie's voice interrupted my fragmented thoughts, and I focused on him again, which was possibly the easiest thing in the world anyway. "Yeah?"

His hands dropped to my waist, and suddenly, I was pinned against the kitchen wall by Jamie's hard body.

"I'm tired of waiting," he whispered. His breath ghosted over my face, warm and sweet and *real*, and then his lips were on mine for the first time in forever.

Holy shit.

I'd spent a lot of the past eleven years pondering the way Jamie kissed—the press of his full lips against mine, the tingling rasp of the scruff that reappeared ten minutes after he shaved, the way his tongue slid against mine that was like... *Jesus Christ*... like dancing, even though I would never share that lame-ass metaphor with *anyone*.

At first, I'd remembered every kiss with regret, because I missed them, missed *him*, so fucking much. And then later, I'd remembered with anger, because *of course* no one else's kiss could compare to a stupid, idealized, rose-colored memory that couldn't possibly be accurate.

I could say with confidence that I had not remembered it accurately. No one could. My memories had been half-assed at best—a glorious ghost, a phantom pain—compared to the electric fucking *burn* of this kiss that set every single nerve ending on fire and made me feel like I was floating.

I moaned into Jamie's mouth and my hands, which had been clutching at the fabric of his t-shirt by his shoulders drifted up of their own accord and tangled into Jamie's thick auburn hair. Jamie braced his forearms on the wall by my head and let the weight of his body rest against mine, grounding me as he owned my mouth.

Perfection.

I broke away with a gasp a long moment later—apparently oxygen was *kind of* important after all—and I was half afraid that would be it, the spell would be broken, but Jamie didn't move away. His lips cruised down to nip at the hinge of my jaw and suck at a spot on the side of my neck. I inhaled sharply and my knees trembled.

"You still like that, hmm?"

I nodded, half-dazed.

"I used to fantasize about this spot," he whispered, his breath ghosting over my damp skin. "The way it made you melt every time I kissed you there."

"So… you're a neck man, then?" I teased in a strangled voice.

Jamie's gentle laughter made my breath hitch.

"Only with you, Parker. Only with you."

He pulled away just long enough to strip off my t-shirt,

followed by his own, and then he was back, the warm hair of his chest pressed to mine.

He kissed me again in the same spot, and I couldn't help the way my back arched and my hips bucked against him. Control was a concept I only had a passing acquaintance with at best, and right now the fucker had entirely left the building. All I could do was feel… and want.

One of Jamie's hands ghosted down my side, the backs of his fingers ghosting down my abs and catching on the drawstring of my pants like they were asking a silent question, but I had a very vocal answer.

"Yes! Jesus, yes."

"The name is *Jamie*," the fucker said, voice warm with amusement. "Just in case you forgot who's taking you apart right now."

I tugged at his hair in punishment, but Jamie didn't seem to find it very discouraging if the way he rubbed himself against my thigh was any indication.

"That's right, Parks. Get a good grip. You'll need it, baby."

Before I could figure out what the hell he was talking about, he lowered his head to bite at my collarbone before sliding lower to lick my nipple.

"*Motherfucker!*" I shouted, yanking his hair again.

"Once again, it's Jamie," he laughed, lifting his head just enough so I could see his eyes dance. "So embarrassing, Parkie. Do you often have this problem?"

No. No, I did not. I'd hooked up plenty in Boston, after those first few lonely years, but there had usually been tequila involved, and other than one ill-fated attempt at a relationship a couple years ago, neither party had ever been concerned with remembering names. Now, though? There was no way I could forget who I was with. And I had no idea what was happening, but I most definitely didn't want it to stop.

I changed my grip on Jamie's head, forcing his mouth back to my chest, and I was rewarded with a puff of laughter against my skin.

"Getting impatient, Parker?"

"Maybe," I tried to say, but the word ended on a yelp as Jamie replaced his lips with his teeth and at that exact moment tugged the drawstring of my pants.

Fuck.

"That's fine," Jamie said, falling to his knees. "I'm not feeling too patient either."

He slid his hands down over the curve of my ass to my thighs, pushing my legs apart, and I whimpered. His hands gripped the fabric and tugged so the pants slid down an inch, then two, and I leaned my head back against the wall to catch my breath because the anticipation was *killlllling* me.

It took me a second to process that Jamie's movements had stopped, and I opened my eyes with a frown.

"J-jame?"

But Jamie didn't answer. His hands were still resting against my legs, gripping the sides of my pajama pants, but he was staring at my erection with absolute fascination... which would have been a lot more exciting if I weren't still wearing my underwear.

"What's wrong?" I whispered.

"Parker," Jamie said warily. "I think... I think there are unicorns on your boxers." He blinked up at me. "Unicorns with... little dogs riding them?"

Shit.

"I can explain!" I said quickly.

Jamie pressed his lips together like he was trying his hardest not to comment.

"See, a couple months ago, I started having this problem where I'd bring my stuff to the laundromat and leave it there while I went to go get coffee because, you know, it's O'Leary, and Spinning Jenny's is like two doors down from the bakery, right?"

Jamie nodded slowly, staring up at me with wide eyes. I started talking faster.

"But my clothes kept disappearing! It was fucking *weird*. Everyone around town was having the same thing happen, and it wasn't a *huge* deal, so I just ignored it. But I was bitching to Ethan on the phone one time—Ethan Scott, my old roommate—"

"I remember Ethan, Parker," Jamie said abruptly. "We all went to school together."

"R-right. Obviously. Anyway, I was bitching, because who the hell takes a man's *undies*? And Ethan cracked up because, well, I mean, it *was* pretty funny, I guess. But then the next day, I got a package *overnighted* to me from Ethan with three pairs of replacement underwear inside." I shook my head. "Dating a bajillionaire has its perks, I guess."

"And he picked these because…"

I rolled my eyes. "Because he said if *these* got stolen, it'd be easier for the police to prosecute the suspect if they were caught wearing shorts with pugs riding unicorns."

I chanced a glance down at Jamie, but he wasn't looking at me anymore. He'd pressed his forehead to my hip, and his shoulders shook with silent laughter.

I carded my fingers through his hair. "If you like these, I also have a pair with kittens riding narwhals," I offered. "Zebra print, dancing reindeer, furry cheetah print. Those itch like the devil, though."

Jamie's shoulders shook harder, and I took a second to appreciate the long, muscled line of his back, before yanking on one thick strand of hair.

"You done mocking me?" I demanded. "Because if you want I…"

Jamie looked up and the words died in my throat. His hair was a mess from my hands, his eyes were crinkled at the corners and sparkling with tears of laughter, and his mouth was smiling wider than I'd maybe ever seen it. *Shit.* Anyone would fall for that face, and I realized with a sick feeling in my stomach that I was already halfway there.

I traced his smile with my fingertips, and the look in his eyes got so intense I had to slide my own eyes shut before I gave too much away.

"Parker?"

I took a deep breath and opened my eyes cautiously.

"Thank you," he said simply and incomprehensibly. And then, while I watched, he stripped my boxers down to my knees and licked the head of my cock, which had flagged a little, what with the unicorns and all.

It took about two point four licks for me to go from half-hard to *oh-my-god-painfully erect*. It could've been embarrassing, honestly, under other circumstances, but my embarrassment reflex had already been exhausted today, and the rough hand Jamie wrapped around my base said that he was really fucking excited by how easily I responded anyway.

Jamie ducked his head and licked again, over and over, getting my entire length *and* his fist positively messy with saliva, then he jerked me deliberately, hard and fast, exactly the way he knew I liked it.

"Jamie!" I moaned, slapping one open palm against the wall behind me while keeping the other firmly buried in his hair. "*Fuck.*"

Jamie responded by pushing my legs farther apart and bending down to lick a stripe over my balls that I swear I felt in my *toes*.

"Fuck," he breathed. "You smell like my soap *everywhere*, Parker. Do you have any idea how hot that is?"

"Show me," I said, staring down at him. His eyes lifted to mine, questioning. "Show me," I repeated.

Jamie got the message and pulled back so he could push his sweatpants down. No unicorn boxers on him, I noticed. No fucking underwear at all, and *holy hell*, I was never gonna be able to see him in those pants again without—

"*Yes!*"

Jamie wrapped his hand around me again. The other hand, he lifted to my mouth. "Lick it, Parker."

Who knew those particular words, out of the hundreds of thousands in the English language, were my own personal *abracadabra*? My own *alohomora*?

Jamie did, apparently. Because I could no more have disobeyed him than I could have sprouted wings.

I licked his hand, taking my time, sucking each finger into my mouth with exactly the same care and attention I wanted to give his cock, running my tongue along all the grooves of his palm. His eyes were on *fire* by the time I was done, and I was glad. I wanted him to burn.

Jamie moved his wet hand down to grip himself, jerking both our cocks with the same sure and steady rhythm, and I swear to God, it was the most erotic thing I'd ever seen. Teenaged Parker would've come all over himself at the sight.

Hell, adult Parker was pretty fucking close.

I closed my eyes again, trying to hang on… until I felt the heat of Jamie's mouth envelop me again, and I knew I was a goner.

"Jamie! I can't—" I said, bucking my hips against his face. "I have to—"

Jamie moaned in encouragement, his head moving

faster, his lips gripping me harder, and I could hear the *slap slap slap* of his spit-slick hand picking up pace as he worked himself.

I knew this man. I trusted him. He made me insane, and he made me angry, but Jesus God, no one had ever, ever made me feel like I was flying half outside my body the way Jamie did. And I might never have this feeling again, but I had it now, and I gave myself over to it entirely.

"Fuck!" I screamed as I came, and then I whimpered Jamie's name as I felt him swallowing me down.

My knees pretty much gave out after that, and I ended up half kneeling, with one leg kicked out between the wall and Jamie's body. Jamie licked his lips, like he was savoring the taste. His glazed eyes never left mine, and his left hand never slowed down.

So damn hot.

I pushed at his good shoulder once and then again, until he finally sprawled on his back, yelping as his back hit the floor.

"Problem?" I demanded, pulling his pants down farther so I could kneel between his bent knees.

"Yeah! Tile is fucking *cold*."

I braced one hand on the floor by his hip and looked up at him. "Poor baby," I said with saccharine sympathy. "Let me make it better?"

I drew a single fingertip up the hard, ruddy length of him.

"Holy God," Jamie breathed, bucking up as I licked my lips and stared at his cock.

I couldn't help but laugh, and *shit*, when was the last time I'd laughed this much during sex? Had I ever?

"Actually, I usually go by *Parker*," I informed him. "But

unlike some people, I'm willing to respond to appropriate nicknames."

Then I sucked him down with a smile on my face until he was spilling, salty, and sweet, in my mouth.

"Come here," Jamie said, the instant I'd pulled off. "Come here. Come *right* here." He grabbed me under the arms and yanked, settling me on top of him.

I looked at him strangely. "I'm kinda heavy, He-Man," I reminded him. "And sticky too."

"Floor's still cold," he said, by way of explanation, then he kissed me, all slow and gentle, while we both caught our breaths.

"We might have a problem," I said a few minutes later.

Beneath my cheek, Jamie snorted. "Yeah? Just the one?"

"I lack the energy to stand, and yet my ass is ice-cold." I lifted my head, propping my chin on my hand so I could look at him.

Jamie chuckled. "That is, indeed, a serious problem."

"It is! And meanwhile, *your* ass is freezing to the floor."

"Accurate."

"Well, *one* of us has to do something," I informed him. "Otherwise they'll find us here, frozen in this exact position, after the snow ends."

"Oh, right. It's snowing." Jamie shifted his head to look at the window, but the only thing visible was a reflection of the kitchen. "I kinda forgot for a minute there."

"Same." I huffed out a laugh. "Pretty sure we're the only people in O'Leary who've forgotten."

"Guess that makes us the lucky ones, hmm? Cold asses and all?"

And I had to smile as I laid my cheek back against Jamie's chest because for once, he was absolutely right.

Chapter Six

JAMIE

I woke up alone and really, really cold.

As a rule, I didn't *get* cold, which was possibly the one benefit of being half-Sasquatch—extra-tall, extra-stocky, and extra-hairy—so this was unusual enough to have me popping my eyes open and blinking in the grey light streaming through the window behind my bed and looking for the blanket I'd kicked off.

Everything looked as it always did—same wood-paneled walls lined with bookcases filled with baseball trophies, same plaid comforter—but there was something in the air, some niggling idea in the back of my mind, that something was supposed to be different today.

When I heard a pan clatter and a familiar voice yell, "Fuck!" somewhere down the hall, last night came rushing back to me, bringing with it a buzz of excitement I couldn't contain.

Parker was here.

Parker had *slept in my bed last night.*

I sat up, taking in the dented pillow where his head had been and the giant pile of covers he'd clearly stolen from me before pushing them off to get out of bed. Then I buried my head in my hands and groaned.

Parker had slept in my bed last night.

In fact, after we'd stumbled our way in here from the kitchen, giggling like a pair of drunken lunatics, I'd spent the night wrapped around him like a blanket.

Seriously, why did my brain do the things it did?

Then again, maybe it wasn't fair to blame my *brain* for last night at all.

I swung my legs off the bed and winced as my feet hit the cold floor. I reached over and tried to turn on the light, but nothing happened. No power.

This morning kept getting better and better.

I threw on some sweats, a thick pair of socks, and a t-shirt. I was pretty sure the ones I'd been wearing yesterday were still lying on the kitchen floor where I'd left them, but I refused to do a naked walk of shame in my own house to get them.

Actually, I refused to be ashamed or overthink this at all. Parker had been exhausted last night. He'd needed comforting, and I... Well, I was Pavlov's fucking dog. I couldn't see Parker hurting and not step in. The look on his face, the hurt in his voice, the stupid plants in their labeled pots... It was all too much. And yeah, the fact that he was hot as fuck and I'd wanted him since I was old enough to know what *wanting* was had played a definite role. When hugging had turned to kissing and then to the best blowjob of my entire life, I'd had zero interest in holding back.

And it had been... fucking amazing. Better than anything I'd ever fantasized about... and worse too. If I'd managed to convince myself in any tiny way that I could resist my attraction to Parker, that idea had exploded in an epic, pug-and-unicorn patterned explosion.

It didn't have to mean anything, though. Nothing serious. Nothing more than basic human need, and forced proximity, and… memories. Memories that had sprung free from my mental vault—which seemed to have the structural integrity of wet Kleenex when I was anywhere close to Parker.

Once Parker left town, though, everything would go back to the way it was. I'd rebuild the vault—expanded to hold a few more memories from this new chapter of our complex, fucked-up history—and this overwhelming desire for him would melt away like the snow.

It *would*.

And in the meantime, I'd just have to be cautious. Attraction was fine. Comfort was… necessary. But I wasn't gonna fuck up and fall for him.

I snorted. *That* would be suicide.

I padded down the hall to the kitchen, following the smell of coffee, and heard Parker before I saw him.

"Yes, Mom. No, I'm fine. Yeah. That's why I texted you last night and… Yes, I *do* think a text message is adequate communication. I let you know that I was safe, which is… No, Mom, it honestly never occurred to me that a serial killer could have taken my phone and pretended to be me. How very imaginative of you." He paused with one hand holding the phone and the other jiggling a frying pan. "I'm very sorry to hear that Dad's cough is worse. A sore tooth too? That's… No, Mom, I don't know any disease that gives you a toothache and a cough. Have you considered talking to an actual… Uh-huh. No, I see. You think he'll perk up the second I arrive, huh? Well, see if he can just hang on a couple more days."

I leaned against the wall outside the kitchen, just as I had last night, to watch Parker work without him knowing I was there. He was standing at our old gas stove, scooping bacon from a frying pan onto a plate lined with paper towels one handed, wearing the same flannel pants he'd worn last night. I could honestly say that seeing what was under them hadn't dulled my interest in the sight of his ass in those pajamas. Not in the slightest. Especially when he reached up to scrub a frustrated hand over his short hair and it did interesting things to the muscles under his t-shirt.

"No, I didn't make it to Syracuse. I told you, I got stuck on the Camden Road. I never made it out of O'Leary." Parker sighed. "Yes, I know. It was *very foolhardy*. Believe me, I've already been read the riot act about my failure to consider consequences."

I smothered a smile.

"I'm perfectly fine, and I'm staying with a friend. Who? Oh, it's…" Parker did an accurate impression of a blender, hissing and clacking into the phone. "Wow! Mom? Mom? Shoot. I think the connection is going. Maybe the weather's knocked out a tower! Mom? Moooom? Nope. I can't hear a thing. *Gosh darn it all to heck*! And I was dying to hear more about Dad's podiatrist too! Welp, if you can hear me, Mom, I'll call you in a few days once I've rescheduled my flight. Love you! *Byeee*!" He pushed the button and threw the phone on the counter with a clatter.

"Wow," I said, walking into the room. "That was a five out of ten for performance, *maybe* two out of ten for originality. And I'm grading on a curve."

Parker whirled around, brandishing a bowl scraper, then straightened when he saw me. "Jesus Christ! Warn a guy."

"Parker!" I mock shouted. "Warning! I'm entering the kitchen!"

"Little late. *Asshole*."

"Parker!" I said, opening the cabinet near his head. "Warning! I'm going to get a cup of coffee!"

"Alright, alright," Parker grumbled, turning back to the counter. "You've made your point. And the coffee is in your mom's old French press." He nodded at the carafe on the counter. "Because there's no power and I had to heat the water on the stove. *You're welcome.*"

I grabbed the pot. "Jeez. Someone woke up on the wrong side of the bed. Were *all the covers* not enough to keep you comfy, crankypuss? Or do evening orgasms provoke this response?"

From the side, I saw him push his lips together for a second. "No. And actually, I woke up in a remarkably good mood. I, uh, slept better than I have in a long time. Hardly any nightmares. So thanks for that."

I tried not to let that remark mean much, but something in my chest loosened at the quiet words.

"And then?" I prompted.

"And then I checked my phone and found I had four missed calls from my mother." Parker moved to the stove and turned on the gas, then expertly lit the flame with a long-handled grill lighter.

"I see you're making yourself right at home," I commented. It should have been annoying, having him in my space. It was, kinda. But with Parker, it was mostly annoying because it shouldn't have felt so normal for him to waltz back into my life. The way I felt about him cooking in my kitchen was way more frightening than my overwhelming desire to throw him to the floor and see if he still smelled like my body wash.

"Yeah, sorry. I guess I am," Parker admitted, putting a second frying pan on to heat. "Confrontation makes me cook. Bacon?" He pointed to a plate of food beside the stove. Parker cooked when he was stressed too. *Interesting.*

I hefted my ass up onto the counter in the corner where I could study Parker's face, and I grabbed a slice.

"I notice you didn't tell your mom exactly where you were."

The bacon was perfectly cooked—crispy and delicious—and my estimation of Parker's skills rose another notch.

Parker snorted. "Yeah, no. I did *not* feel like explaining… *this*." He twirled his spatula in the air as if to encompass the snow, the house, and *us* in one tiny pronoun.

"Good call. Safe to say your mom never liked me anyway."

"What? She liked you!"

"Please. You're either lying or oblivious. Your dad liked me well enough because I played varsity baseball for a minute there."

"More than a minute," he grumbled. "Four epic seasons before you became a human speed bump and tore up your shoulder."

"Epic," I repeated. "You trying to feed my ego?"

"*Please*. It's plenty big enough."

I snorted. "Anyway. I don't think there was much about me your mom appreciated."

Parker huffed and melted a pat of butter in the hot pan. "It wasn't you personally. She just didn't like that we were so serious. Or that *I* was serious, anyway. About you. '*There are a lot of fish in the sea, Parker! Why not date a lot of boys?*'"

"She wanted you to be a playboy," I said, waggling my eyebrows.

"She wanted me to save my focus for other stuff."

Other stuff that wasn't me or in O'Leary. I was very, very aware of what his mother had wanted him to care about.

"She wanted you to have a good future," I said instead. "She wanted you to realize there were other opportunities waiting for you. Ones that didn't exist in

O'Leary. Isn't that what every parent wants for their kids?"

Parker glanced up from the pan where he'd been pouring pancake batter and frowned. "I guess." He looked around the kitchen, at twenty-year-old decor and the family pictures that still lined the walls, and darted a glance at me.

He visibly hesitated, and I rolled my eyes. "You're suddenly shy? I had your dick in my mouth last night, you know."

His green eyes flew to mine and he turned beet red. "I recall."

"So if you have a question, ask it."

"Is that how it works? One blowjob, one question? This is the workaround for your stupid rule?"

"Try it and find out." I gave him a lascivious grin and his blush deepened. It was really adorable. "You know, I don't remember you being this blush-y."

Parker blew out a breath. "I don't remember you being this mouthy either. It's almost like we both *changed*. Imagine that."

I grinned. "If you're telling me that being mouthy is a bad thing, I—"

"What happened to your mom?" Parker blurted. "That… that was my question."

I felt my grin fall away. "She left." I shoved the rest of the bacon I was holding in my mouth and licked my fingers, pointedly not looking at him. "Surely you've heard this, the O'Leary gossip mill being what it is."

"I've heard some. I wanna hear it from you."

I glanced at him warily. This tread perilously close to the things I didn't want to think about, let alone discuss, but I'd started this, so… fine. I could talk about it. It was only a collection of facts, after all.

"Not sure there's much to add beyond the basics. My dad self-destructed after Molly died." I shrugged. "Too much demon liquor. You were here for that part. Well, the start of it, anyway."

"And your mom wasn't happy," he prompted. "I remember that too. They fought constantly."

"The strain of losing a child," I intoned in the overly serious voice of the family therapist we'd been to see once or twice, back in the day, "takes a toll on a marriage." I watched Parker flip the golden-brown pancakes expertly.

"And?"

"And *what*?" I demanded. "You left. He got worse. Two unrelated events," I added with a tight smile. "He didn't miss you that much."

But I had. Dear God, I had.

Parker made an impatient noise, and I rolled my eyes as I continued. "Pretty sure the story writes itself from this point, Parkie. My mom was fed up. Said she deserved to have a little happiness in her life, which she did. So she filed for divorce and moved to Portland, Maine, where one of her sorority sisters lived, to start fresh."

"She just left you?" Parker sounded incredulous, and I didn't get it.

"She's an adult, Parker, and so was I. Being here in this house reminded her of everything she'd lost. Why would she stick around? Hey, I have bananas," I offered, pointing to a bowl on the counter, "if you wanna put them in the next batch."

Parker looked at me like I had three heads. "Bananas go *on* the pancakes, Jameson. Not *in* them."

"What? Of course they do. They get all caramelized that way!"

"But they get *cooked*." Parker shook his head, disgusted,

as he put the first set of pancakes on a plate. "And don't you think for a minute that you can distract me with thoughts of your weird eating habits. We were talking about your mom."

"I think we've exhausted the topic," I disagreed. "Mom's doing well. Lives in Portland still, in a cute Victorian with a stone mason named Bruce. He's a nice guy. I've driven up to visit a couple times, but she doesn't come back here."

"Ever?"

I lifted one eyebrow. "Yeah, imagine that. Leaving O'Leary and not coming back for years and years."

Parker pursed his lips. "So you just… stayed? By yourself?"

"Didn't have a whole lot of choice. Well, I mean, I *did*. But my dad was here. My job was here. The house. It was easier to stay."

"Even after he…" Parker paused with his spatula poised above the pan.

"Died? Drank himself to death?" I said impatiently. "Yes. Not all of us need to leave O'Leary, Parker."

I really hoped he wouldn't ask me if I'd ever *wanted* to, though, because I'd thought about that a *lot*. But where would I have gone? To Boston, only to see how well Parker had moved on and how thoroughly he'd forgotten me? No fucking way.

"Yeah, but…" he began.

And just like that, I was done. "Parker, the coffee is really good, and the bacon is even better, but I think we're done here. Rules exist for a reason," I teased.

Parker frowned. "*Please.* Like you're the rule follower of the two of us. Besides, I thought the fact that you had my dick in your mouth last night meant I was allowed to ask questions."

"You've used up your quota. It was a good blowjob, but not *that* good, if you know what I mean."

"This rule gets more ridiculous by the moment."

I knew it, but I still didn't want to talk about this shit, so I pushed myself off the counter and went to grab a plate and some silverware without saying a word.

Parker sighed like he was disappointed, and I tried to tell myself I didn't care. He dished up the pancakes, I got out the syrup, and we sat down at the kitchen table to eat next to his plants.

"Still howling out there," Parker observed before I'd taken my first bite. "Wonder how long the power will be out."

"Doesn't matter. I have a generator in the garage. Not enough to power the house, but enough that we can charge our phones."

Parker grimaced. "Did you have to tell me that? Now I feel like I have to keep the damn thing charged."

I snorted. "This way you'll be able to check in with all your friends. I'm sure they'll be worried about you."

Parker raised an eyebrow. "You think Cal's losing sleep over me? Bet he and Ash are fucking on a bed of leftover cupcakes."

"Wow. That's… oddly specific."

He chuckled.

"I was thinking more of your friends in Boston." I cut into my pancakes. "If they're following the weather they're gonna be wondering if you made it to Arizona."

"Uh. No. They definitely aren't. No one there even knows I—" He shook his head. "You really have the strangest idea of what my life in Boston was like, you know that?"

I shoveled pancakes into my mouth so I didn't have to

answer, and when the flavor hit my tongue, I moaned. "Holy shit, Parker."

Parker grinned. "Good?"

"Holy *shit*," I repeated, taking another bite. "What'd you put in these?"

"The usual. Flour. Vanilla. Milk. Sugar. Vinegar."

My jaw dropped. "Vinegar?"

"Mmm hmm." His eyes met mine over the top of his coffee cup. "Don't knock vinegar. I use it in everything." He smiled slyly as he set his cup down. "Including my chicken wings. Which is why they're so popular."

"Hmm." I shoveled in another huge chunk of pancakes and took my time chewing before I replied. "Popular doesn't mean a thing is *good*. Know what else is popular? Nickelback."

Parker gaped at me. "I… that… was *low*. You fucking *know* how I feel about Nickelback."

"Do I?" I gave him my most innocent smile.

"For your information, my chicken wings *are* popular because they're good."

"I know," I said placatingly, then added after a pause, "… that you believe that."

Parker sucked in a breath through his nose, and holy shit, why did I find him even hotter when he was pissed off? I was demented, I really was.

"Better than *yours*," Parker said, folding his arms across his chest. "Any day."

"You're throwing down with me?" I demanded. "You sure you wanna do that? Over *chicken wings*? I mean, your pancakes would be a no-brainer, even though I do make a damn good pancake. Stick to pancakes, Parkie."

Parker pushed his plate away, braced his hands on the table, and got to his feet so he was looming over me. The light filtering in through the window picked out the gold flecks in his eyes, and I temporarily lost the ability to swallow.

"My name is *Parker*." He smirked. "I also answer to *God* and *Jesus* under certain circumstances. And *you*, Jameson, need to be taken down a peg or two."

"By *you*?"

He deliberately glanced right and left. "Don't see anyone else around to do it, so yeah."

"Hilarious. How?"

"Cookoff, obviously. Your chicken wings against mine."

"Right now?"

"You got other pressing things to do?" He straightened and glanced out the window, where the snow was still falling steadily. "Planning to wash your truck or something?"

I tilted my head to one side, fighting the desperate urge to laugh. "I had a Grindr blizzard hookup scheduled. OldFatCreeper87 has *needs*, Parkie. But for this, I'll clear my calendar."

"You have the ingredients?" he demanded, the way someone else might have demanded pistols or swords.

"Of course."

"Then it's on. Chicken Wing Death Match."

I leaned back in my chair, sucking on a tooth. "And who's gonna judge this death match?"

Parker frowned just a little, like he hadn't considered this. "We will," he decided.

I snorted.

"What? I can be impartial."

"Sure you can. That idea has about as much merit as the idea of your chicken being better than mine."

"So, you're saying it's totally believable and *chock-full of merit*, then? Excellent. Decided."

I opened my mouth to argue when Parker leaned

toward me again. "Unless you're *scared*," he whispered. "You can forfeit. I won't judge."

"You would *so* judge."

Parker grinned, totally happy, totally kissable. "Yeah, I totally would."

I shook my head as Parker winked and sashayed off to clean up the breakfast dishes. How was I here right now? What fucking confluence of events had led me to share my kitchen with *Parker Hoffstraeder*?

Somehow, despite all the years and all the shit that had passed between us, the man was even more attractive than he'd been before, just as I'd sort of known he'd be.

It's casual and temporary, I reminded myself as I pushed to my feet. *Everything good is.*

This time I was just gonna be smart enough to really enjoy it before it became another memory in the vault.

Chapter Seven

PARKER

"You cheated," I said, leaning back against the sofa and licking sauce off my finger. The sauce was spicy and sweet, tangy and delicious, and I was possibly a little bit pissed and a little bit impressed by this fact. "Your wings never tasted this good before."

Jamie, who was sprawled next to me, shirtless and stomach-down on the living room rug, in front of a crackling fire in the fireplace that made the whole room cozy, grinned lazily. "Same recipe I've used for years. Besides, how could I possibly have cheated when you've been watching me the whole afternoon?"

"Snow's mostly stopped," I reminded him, leaning forward to throw the bone on the plate on the coffee table. "Maybe you ordered them in."

"From where? And did I have them delivered by carrier pigeon? That would be wrong on so many levels." Jamie rubbed a hand through his hair, dislodging a cloud of white dust.

I sat back again and narrowed my eyes. "You're getting flour all over the rug."

Jamie slowly turned his head to look up at me like a lazy, freckled housecat. "And whose fault would that be? Hmm? *Speaking* of cheating behavior."

I pursed my lips. "I told you. The flour incident was an accident," I lied. "I tripped."

"Over nothing." Jamie scooted closer so his head was by my knee. "While standing still."

"Yup."

"Really? Because you upended like three cups worth on my head. And I'm considerably taller than you."

"*Considerably*," I scoffed. "You mean *barely*. Like, half a millimeter or something."

"Like half a foot."

"And it was a few tablespoons," I said, ignoring him. "At most."

"My t-shirt was covered!"

"Are you calling me a liar?" I demanded in mock outrage. "Besides, who decided to retaliate for my *perfectly innocent mistake* by getting sugar all over me?"

"That was every bit as accidental, Parker!" Jamie blinked his brown eyes guilelessly. "I was just so *startled* by the flour attack. Blinded, if you will. And in the ensuing confusion… casualties occurred."

"Casualties. Is that what we call dumping a bowl of brown sugar down a man's pants?"

"Hey, you had another pair!" Jamie pushed his lips together but couldn't restrain his laughter. "Besides, you should thank me. People pay shit-tons of money for fancy brown sugar scrubs. You got one for free."

"I have *sugar* in places where *sugar* should never be."

"Bet you taste sweet," Jamie said suggestively.

"*You'll* never know," I assured him, even as those places started to tingle way more from his words than they had from the sugar.

Jamie grinned and leaned up to grab another wing off the table—one from the tray *I* had prepared—and sighed happily as he chewed.

"I'll admit, your wings are also significantly better than I remembered." He took another bite. "You've finally figured out the sauce-to-wing ratio."

"Oh, please. Same ratio I always use. Could be that this is the first time you've eaten them *sober*." I rolled my eyes.

Jamie chewed silently, but a moment later, serious brown eyes met mine and he shocked the shit out of me. "Guess I should apologize, huh?"

My eyebrows went up. "For?"

He huffed out a breath. "You know for what. For all the times I went into your place last summer and…"

"Made a scene?"

Jamie ran his tongue over his front teeth and nodded. "Not my proudest moment." He winced. "Moments."

He was staring down at the chicken in his hand, so I studied him for a moment, considering how to respond. Part of me wanted to wave a hand and blow it off. *No harm done, Jamie.* Because there hadn't been, really. Not to me. And I didn't want him to think I was whining when I was *not*. But something about the mood—the fire and the laughter—made me say *fuck it* and tell him the truth.

"You scared me, a little."

"Scared you?" He looked up and frowned. "You know I'd never hurt you, Parker."

"Not on purpose," I agreed.

"Not even by accident."

It was on the tip of my tongue to say, "*But you did. It killed me when you didn't want me anymore,*" but I managed to keep from saying it. *That* much honesty wouldn't help anyone.

And before I could say anything, Jamie continued. "That's why it pissed me off that you thought I had something to do with the fire at Hoff's. I wouldn't do that, Parker."

His voice was a deep growl and his eyes were on his food, but there was something in his tone that made me wince.

"I know," I whispered. "Have you ever said something and wished you could take it back the second it was out of your mouth?"

Jamie laughed so hard he collapsed into a fit of coughing and I slapped at his back.

"You're ruining my apology," I informed him.

"Sorry." Jamie sniffed, his eyes watering. "Yeah, Parker. Suffice it to say I've felt like that *at least* once." There was something in the way he said it that gave me pause, but he pushed at my knee. "Please, finish your apology."

"I'm sorry," I said. "I really am. You… you made it better that night. Being there. Hugging me. Being a friend. And I… I shouldn't have said that. I never really believed it."

Jamie nodded. "I hoped it was something like that. I heard you talked to Mitch afterward and told him you'd been in shock at the time."

I drew my knees up to my chest and scratched at the fabric of my pants. "Least I could do," I said. "I *was* shocked. And angry, and… I wanted someone to blame. And I guess I was thinking that maybe I didn't really know you anymore, after the way you came to the bar all those times—"

"Acting like an idiot?" Jamie supplied. "I get it."

"You reminded me of your dad when you did that. You remember how he used to yell and throw shit at the television? And he never meant to hurt anything, but…"

"He still did? Yeah, I might possibly have a vague memory or twenty," Jamie said dryly. He sighed. "I stopped drinking. A few months ago."

"You did? Just like that?"

Jamie nodded. "I figured I should do it while I still could, before I got whacked with the Burke family curse."

"Drama king." I rolled my eyes. "It's not a curse. It's a disease."

He blew out a breath. "I know. But I can try not to let it get worse."

"And does it… is it… hard? Are you going to meetings? Or?" I had no idea how to talk about this shit, and it suddenly occurred to me that I really should.

"Surprisingly, not that hard. I went to a meeting in Camden last fall around the time when Shane…" He cleared his throat, and I nodded in understanding. "That was a mind-fuck. So I went for a few weeks then, and then again a few times around Christmas. Once last week." He shrugged.

"I think that's amazing."

"It's not."

I grabbed his chin and forced him to look at me. "I think it's fucking amazing, Jameson. And you don't get to tell me what I think. Okay?"

Jamie rolled his eyes. "Yes, sir, Parker, sir."

"Good boy." I let my fingers stroke over the rough edge of his beard before shoving his face away. "Finally showing some respect."

Jamie's eyes narrowed. "I mean, it's easier not drinking socially now that there's no bar in O'Leary anymore…" One auburn eyebrow lifted in challenge.

I gasped. "Was that… did you just make a joke about my bar burning down?"

"What? Too soon?" He grinned.

"*Forever* too soon!"

"Oops."

"*Ugh*. You're such a shit."

"Would it make you feel better if I told you that you won the Death Match?" He nodded at the chicken wings remaining on the coffee table.

"No," I said glumly. "Since we both know you won."

Jamie's lips twitched. "I really kinda did."

"Shut *up*." I grabbed a cushion from the sofa and bopped him on the head.

"I can give you the recipe if you want."

"What did I just tell you?" I whacked him with the cushion again, harder this time. "Shut it."

"I'm just trying to be *nice*, Parker. Neighborly. And you—"

I twisted to my knees and pushed him to his back. "Be. Quiet."

"I was—"

I pinched Jamie's full lips between my fingers and stared down at his eyes, which were warm and brown and... *God*.

"Are you gonna be quiet now?" I demanded. My voice was huskier than I'd intended.

Jamie's tongue darted out to lick his lips and captured my finger, sucking it into his mouth.

Fuck. My breath came out in a needy gasp.

"You could always give me something better to do with my mouth," he whispered.

This was so not good. Jamie was gorgeous, yes. I wanted him, perpetually. I could accept that. But I think somehow I'd forgotten just how much I *liked* him, in addition to all the *unrequited love* business. How he made shitty stuff—like bar fires—better, and mundane stuff—like snow storms—special. How he could make me feel like I was living life at a hundred miles an hour and make me feel absolutely safe at the same time.

I really hadn't needed to remember this part. Last night, all of it, had been more than enough.

But I knew I was never going to resist him, either, or to turn away whatever part of Jamie I could get, so…

I bent, pressed my lips to his, and let him roll me beneath him.

I skated my hands down his warm, naked back and lifted my head to taste the freckles on his shoulder with my tongue. "Wow. That flour incident really had a silver lining, huh?" I croaked. "All this handy… nakedness?"

"I'm definitely not complaining." Jamie ducked down to kiss me again. "I'm gonna taste all those sweet parts of—"

But Jamie's words were lost as the whole world exploded in a loud *crash*, like the sound of a freight train slamming into a car… or a giant tree crashing through glass.

One instant, Jamie was poised above me, and the next we were both running down the hall toward his bedroom.

"Holy shit." I peered over Jamie's bicep as he braced himself in the doorway of his bedroom. "Holy *shit*."

A giant tree branch protruded from the window above his bed in a bizarre sculpture of pine needles, glass shards, and twisted metal from the window frame. The curtains hung drunkenly, with one side of the rod dislodged by the weight of the branch.

I tried to duck under Jamie's arm to get a closer look, but he held me back.

"Glass," he said shortly, pointing at my socked feet.

I nodded in understanding.

"Fuck," he said. His shoulders slumped and he ran both hands through his hair. "I've gotta—oh."

Jamie moved me aside with a hand on each shoulder, darted to the next door down the hall, and threw the door open.

Molly's room.

"Fuck, fuck, *fuck*," Jamie said. His eyes were wide, and he looked… absolutely devastated.

"What?" I demanded, following after him, but Jamie didn't answer. He walked into Molly's room like he was locked in some kind of nightmare.

When I looked, I was horrified too, possibly for an entirely different reason.

Pine branches had broken through the window here, also, breaking the window frame almost completely, and the plaster near the ceiling was bowed, like maybe the tree outside was resting against the wall right there. But that wasn't the horrifying part.

The walls were painted bright Peace Yellow—a fact I knew since I'd been the one to help Molly pick from the paint chips—and the bedding was dark purple. Molly's paintings and photographs hung all over the walls, and her old camera sat on a shelf above her white desk, ready for her to grab, like she might walk in the door at any moment.

The room looked the same as it had the last time I'd been here. Just as the kitchen did. And the living room. And the bathroom. And Jamie's room too. The entire Burke home was like that scene from *Great Expectations*, except there was not a single speck of dust anywhere. It was like a time capsule. Like inside these walls, time had stopped.

"Jamie!" I yelled, as the man wandered toward the bed. "*Glass*," I warned him this time.

Jamie shook his head like he was coming out of a

dream and stopped by the end of the bed. "Right," he said hoarsely. "Thanks."

"Stay right there," I demanded. I ran to the kitchen and stuffed my feet into my mostly dry sneakers, grabbed Jamie's boots, and rushed back. "Here," I said, holding them out. "Put these on."

Jamie hadn't moved. He was frozen, one hand on his forehead, staring at the walls like he'd never seen them before.

"Jame?" I walked around him and stopped in front of him, grabbing his face in both hands so he looked at me. "You okay?"

"Yeah," Jamie said softly, but his eyes looked lost. "I'm fine. I—" He took the boots from me and jammed them on, then rushed to the destroyed window and looked out. "Okay," he said. "Okay. It's just a branch, I think." He looked back at me. "The rest of the tree is standing strong, so I think we're good structurally."

I nodded. "I hadn't even considered that, but that's good, right?"

"Yeah. If it was coming down on the roof, we'd have to leave."

"That's good. Good. So, now we need to… What? Call someone?"

Jamie shook his head. "I don't know. I guess. Find some wood and board it up." He swallowed. "I haven't been in here for months."

"Yeah?" I blinked. "It's really clean."

"There's a company that comes a couple times a month to keep the place tidy." He shrugged. "I mostly bother with the outside stuff. Except I forgot to cut back the trees." He stared up at the ceiling and shook his head. "*Fuck*," he said again.

"Hey," I said softly, "shit happens. But we can fix this, okay?"

Jamie's eyes came to mine, a little scared and a little hopeful, before he shut them and turned away. "Yeah. No, it's fine. I can take care of this."

I didn't miss the *I* instead of the *we*, but what the hell was I supposed to do? Insist that he let me help?

"I'm gonna take down the paintings," I told him, reaching for a landscape that had always been one of my favorites—a sunset in deep purples and orange. "And the photos. So they don't get damp or anything."

Jamie ran a hand over his face. "Yeah. Good. And, uh, maybe some of the books?"

"Her *Harry Potter*s?" I asked gently.

Jamie nodded. "Stick them in the closet in my parents'… uh. In the master bedroom, I mean… and I'll grab a tarp. And I guess I'll call the police, just in case. They can let me know when the roads might get cleared." He walked out without another word.

I gathered up a stack of artwork and brought it down the hall to the room that had once belonged to Jamie's parents. I braced myself mentally before I opened the door, but I needn't have bothered. The room wasn't another time capsule—it was nearly empty, like maybe his mom had taken all the furniture with her when she left. There was a bed in the center of the room—plain black iron—with what appeared to be a brand-new mattress on it. The rest of the room and the attached closet were empty.

Somehow, the emptiness here made my heart hurt just as much as the other rooms had.

I stacked the paintings on the floor in the little walk-in closet and made my way back down the hall to get another load.

Jamie had unearthed a bright blue tarp and a hammer from somewhere—maybe his truck—and he was standing on Molly's desk chair, tacking it to the ceiling and the wall.

I couldn't think of a single damn thing to say. Then I spotted Molly's old yoga mat standing in the corner, and realized that when bad shit happened, all *I* wanted was to have someone *be there*. To know I wasn't alone.

How much shit had Jamie been dealing with—or not dealing with—alone?

"Did you know that Molly once tried to teach me to do yoga?" I said. Jamie's only answer was a grunt, but I persevered. "It was awful. I failed. At yoga."

"How does a person fail at yoga?" Jamie demanded. "Isn't it an individual kind of thing?"

"I guess? I wasn't bendy. Not in the right way, anyway. And she kept telling me to focus on my breathing, and I kept telling her I didn't know how to do it *right*, and she kept saying there was no *right*. Frustrating as hell." I laughed. "I was more stressed when we were done."

"This surprises me not at all," Jamie declared.

"That I'm not bendy?"

"That you got competitive about yoga." I could hear the smirk in his voice.

"I'm not *competitive*," I frowned, looking up from the stack of books I was collecting.

"You are *so* competitive."

"What are you even talking about right now?" I demanded. "That's bullshit. *You* are competitive, what with your baseball and your…" I trailed off.

"Uh-huh. My what? I was competitive in baseball because that's part of the game. Otherwise?" Jamie paused to hammer in a nail, then continued, "No. Meanwhile *you* don't like not being the best at things."

I abandoned my books and stood straight, hands on

my hips, staring at Jamie's back as he worked. "That's not funny."

Jamie glanced over his shoulder. "Wasn't meant to be, Parks."

"I'm not *competitive*," I insisted. "Name one time where I—"

"Chicken Wing Death Match?"

I rolled my eyes. "Okay, besides that. That was just something I made up to pass the time."

"But you were legit unhappy when you lost."

"I… Yes, I admit that I was possibly a teensy bit peeved—"

Jamie snorted. "Uh-huh."

"But that's *one thing*," I insisted. "Cooking is something I'm good at. I'm not competitive with other things."

"Oh. Uh-huh. Like baseball, back in the day."

"Exactly!" I said triumphantly. "I didn't give a shit about baseball! I only played because—"

"Because your dad made you. I know. Everyone knows. Literally, everyone in the entire town, because you never stopped saying it."

"Because it was true!" I said, stung. "I never practiced, I never cared if we won games—"

Jamie jumped off the chair. "It ever occur to you that you might have been better at it if you *had* given a shit?"

"No! Because then…"

"You would've been sadder if you lost?"

I scowled. "That's the least-flattering interpretation of events that you could possibly—"

"Just sayin'." Jamie winked as he passed me on the way out of the room. "You don't like to do things you're not immediately good at."

"Wait!" I demanded, following after him. "That's not true. I am *not* that kind of person."

"What kind of person?" Jamie said without stopping.

"I don't know! Shitty. And lazy. And caring about my image. I mean, I don't even *have* an image."

"I didn't say you were shitty. Or lazy, either," he called over his shoulder. "You just hate admitting when you're wrong, and you hate to lose."

"I do not hate admitting I'm wrong," I insisted… possibly proving his point.

Jamie snorted. "Okay," he agreed easily.

"What does *that* mean?" I demanded, grabbing at his shoulder.

He spun around and stared down at me, surprised. "It means *okay*. If you say so, Parker. I barely know you anymore, after all. Right?"

"Right," I said immediately. Then I frowned. "Right?"

Jamie shrugged and turned back toward the kitchen. "I think I have another tarp in the garage for my room. I'm gonna look for it, then I'll call Si."

He disappeared down the hall, but I stood where I was for a minute.

Jamie Burke could cut me to the quick like no one else, and apparently he still possessed that ability, even after all this time. Why did his opinion still matter so damn much?

He was wrong, anyway. It wasn't true that I only did easy things. Not at *all*. Moving back here hadn't been easy. Leaving had been even harder.

In fact, *easy* was Jamie's MO Take, for example, this house, and… and… and… the fact that he was literally still working the same job he'd had in high school. *He* was the one who drifted along, who didn't break out of his routine until a tree literally fell through his house.

I nodded once and grabbed a chicken wing from the table as a prize for reaching this conclusion, then I went back to rescuing books.

Jamie found me a few minutes later, after I'd put the last few books in the walk-in closet. "All set?"

"Yeah," I said, straightening. "I think I got most of the big stuff. Wanna do your room next?"

Jamie shook his head. "Not much in there I care about."

"But your clothes!"

"Clothes are in the dresser on the far side of the room and in the closet. They'll be fine."

"The posters and the trophies?" I put my hands on my hips. "The books?"

"Someone recently told me that it was *pretty sad* to still have your high school trophies anyway."

"I didn't mean *you*," I gasped. "I meant *me*. I meant…"

"You didn't want any reminders of a thing you weren't good at?"

I tilted my head to one side and glared at him. "Stop."

He grinned. "Just giving you shit, Parks." He blew out a breath. "Gonna call Si now."

I nodded and grabbed the leftover wings, then followed him to the kitchen where he'd left his phone.

"Hey, Marci. How's it going?" I heard him ask. "You guys staying safe?"

"Ask her if she's gotten any sleep at all," I demanded as I wrapped the wings and put them in the fridge. "She was on last night."

Jamie rolled his eyes at me and kept talking to Marci. "Yeah, I've got a little bit of trouble. Big tree limb came crashing through a couple of windows and maybe damaged the roof. Yeah, no, I think we're safe. I was able to rig up some tarps around the branches to keep most of the snow out, but—oh." He looked at me again. "Yeah, I said *we*. Ah… Parker. Parker's here with me." He paused. "Yeah, that's right. Parker Hoffstraeder," he admitted, as though there were more than one Parker in our tiny town.

I bit my lip. In a town of inveterate gossips, Marci was possibly one of the biggest. "Think she'll guess we fucked our way through the storm?" I whispered.

Apparently not quietly enough.

I could hear Marci's screech across the kitchen as Jamie pulled the phone away from his ear and shook his head at me.

"No! Parker said we've been able to *tuck up* and keep *warm*," Jamie said firmly, glaring at me. "*No!* Warm because of the *fireplace*," he insisted.

I snickered, and Jamie shot me another look.

He sighed resignedly. "Marci, about *my house*? No, I don't think it hit any power lines, but I made sure the main breaker was turned off just in case. Uh-huh. Yeah, the food should be fine. I have a generator I've been hooking up to the fridge for a couple hours here and there since this morning. But if Si could— Uh-huh. I'd really appreciate that. Yeah, that's plenty soon enough. Thanks." He paused, rolling his eyes heavenward and shaking his head again. "Parker, Marci says hi and... *keep up the good work.*"

Oh, Lord. "Thanks, Marci!" I called.

"So helpful," Jamie said, sliding his phone onto the counter after he'd disconnected. "Remember I'm the one who's gonna have to deal with the gossip while you and your plants are winging your way to Arizona."

"Sorry," I said, chastened. "I hadn't thought." In fact, I'd actively avoided thinking of Arizona all day.

"Yeah? Shocking." Jamie blew out a breath and linked his fingers behind his neck, stretching his shoulder. It did all kinds of interesting things to his naked chest.

"Did you hurt yourself?" I asked.

"Not really. Just sore. Old injuries don't always heal the greatest."

I cleared my throat. "So. Molly's room's gonna need fixing up, huh? Have any… thoughts about that?"

Jamie rolled his eyes, and his serious brown gaze came to mine. "You are as subtle as an elephant doing the tango. Just wanna let you know that."

I shrugged, accepting the truth of this.

"I don't know what you want me to tell you, Parker," Jamie said with a sigh. "I keep the stuff in her room the way it was because I don't know what else to do with it. I'm not delusional, okay? I know nobody's coming back. It just feels like a really big deal to change it around. Like I'd be making a statement, or… I don't even know. Like I'd have to have a *purpose* for changing things. And I don't. I don't know what I'd even use that space for. So I just don't… *do* anything."

I nodded slowly. "See, I get that. I do." I hesitated, licking my lips, then said, "But maybe you could start by getting rid of the big stuff. You know? Not *all* of her things," I added quickly. "Not the important stuff we just moved out of there—the books and artwork and stuff. But the furniture, maybe? The vintage clothes and whatnot? Molly would fucking *love* to know that some other artsy teenager was using her vintage dresses, or that some little kid had inherited her bedroom furniture. She was a sucker for all that helping-the-community, hearts-and-flowers bull-shit." I winked.

Jamie snorted. "She was."

"And after that…" I shrugged. "Maybe things will become clearer. Once you clear away the stuff you don't wanna keep from the past, you'll figure out what you wanna do next."

Jamie took a step forward, closing the distance between

us, and lifted a hand to my jaw. He stroked one thick finger down the cord of my neck, pushing aside the collar of my t-shirt so he could reach my collarbone, and his eyes went molten.

"I think I have *some* idea of what I want next," he said. "We got interrupted earlier." He wrapped his other arm around my waist, pulling me against him, and I went willingly.

"But Silas and the others are coming," I reminded him.

"*Tomorrow*." He grinned. "They're coming tomorrow. We have the whole night alone."

I swallowed and nodded, but what I heard was *one more night*. The snow was nearly over, the roads would likely be cleared tomorrow or the next day, and I'd have to go. It made my heart hurt.

"You think one night is long enough?" I demanded, hoping I didn't sound as desperate as I felt. "Promises were made about *tasting*."

"I'm up for the challenge," Jamie said.

I grabbed his hand, towing him to the living room and the lingering warmth from the dying fire. "Fortunately for you, I know this is something I'm very good at, so I don't mind practicing at all." I smiled smugly. "Not that I'm competitive about it."

Jamie laughed out loud. "I don't know how you do that," he said, sounding genuinely mystified about something.

I waggled my brows. "I could show you. You could take notes if you—"

"Not *that*," he said, pushing a finger to my lips to shut me up. "I mean taking the craziest situation and making it fun. Taking all this bullshit and making it… okay."

It was so close to what I'd thought about *him* earlier

that I had to swallow again, all my words obliterated, and lift up on my toes to press my lips to his.

Fortunately, Jamie didn't seem to want to speak anymore either. He pulled my shirt off silently and let his hands cruise down my shoulders and arms, interlacing our fingers as he kissed me again.

Skin on skin, our hearts beating against each other, we generated more heat than the hottest flame, and I couldn't hold back my moan as his tongue tangled with mine. He tasted of sweetness, and spice, and something that was innately *Jamie*, both brand new and achingly familiar.

He wrapped both of our hands behind my back, grinding his hips against my abs, and my stomach swooped when I realized that he was half-hard already.

"Shit," I croaked, pushing against him again. "Home improvement projects do it for you? Nails and tarps turn your crank?"

"Must be, huh?" He bit his lip and dropped to his knees, taking my sweatpants with him. "Can't think what else could be turning me on."

He licked his lips and nuzzled his nose into the joint of my thighs. "Definitely sweet," he murmured, grazing my thigh with his teeth. "Totally bitable."

I grabbed his hair for balance, trying to rub myself against his face and step out of my pants at the same time.

"Calm down, baby. We're not in *that* much of a hurry," Jamie said, chuckling.

"And yet, I feel a very strong sense of urgency," I all but moaned. The *baby* thing totally did it for me. I could count on one hand the times he'd called me that before yesterday, and I knew it meant nothing now, but like I had for the last day, I found myself more than willing to pretend.

I probably should have been more worried by that than I was.

Jamie chuckled and nipped my hip.

I gripped his hair harder.

"I'm gonna be bald if you keep this up," he whispered, pressing open-mouthed kisses to my stomach.

"I feel like I'm going to be insane, so that's only fair." I swallowed. "You know, it might be fun if we start on the floor this time. Less falling."

"Falling's part of the fun."

"We're gonna talk about your understanding of fun," I informed him. "Right after we… *ah…* finish talking about *politeness*. Shit, Jamie!"

Jamie laughed. "Fine. Get your ass down here with me," he demanded, spreading his thighs and making room.

I sank to my knees, and then farther, until I was lying on my back with Jamie straddling me, his hands gliding up and down my thighs, getting a millimeter closer to my cock with every stroke, until I was a squirming writhing mess. "Touch me, Jamie! For God's sake!"

The sky outside had darkened, throwing the room into shadows, but Jamie's eyes caught the firelight, making them glow gold as he stared down at me. He bit his lip. "You are so…" He broke off and shook his head, like he wasn't sure how to continue.

"Impatient?" I croaked. "Fucking desperate?" I felt that way. And it was a sign of how far gone I was that I couldn't make myself care.

"Beautiful." His eyes locked on mine even as his fingers finally, *finally* closed around my cock, and I swear, I couldn't breathe, I was that overwhelmed by everything.

It wasn't the sex. Or not *just* that. I was alive to every single fiber of the worn, beige carpet at my back, every shifting shadow that moved across Jamie's cheek, every press and squeeze of his hand as he jacked me.

"Ah, *holy fucking fuck*," I breathed because I was a poet like that. "Just like that. Don't stop."

Which, of course, made the motherfucker stop.

"No, no, no," I pleaded. "Keep going. You win all the contests now until forever. I concede every argument I've ever won. Just keep going, okay?"

"Turn over, Parker."

"Turn?" I blinked in confusion. "But *no!* I thought you were gonna… you know," I croaked. "Taste."

Jamie's smile was depraved and gorgeous. "Oh, I am."

Mother. Fucker.

I turned over without another word and let him arrange me so my ass was in the air and my chest was pressed to the carpet. Jamie's hands kneaded my cheeks, pulling them apart, and his thumbs played the same game with my hole that his fingers had played with my cock, circling and circling without quite touching.

"Stop *teasing!*" I demanded. "Or I'm gonna switch places with you and show you how— *Oh, holy oatcakes!*" I yelled as his tongue swiped over me.

I could *feel* Jamie's laughter. "The things you say during sex, Parker."

"I'll be quiet," I promised fervently as he licked me again, harder this time. "So quiet. Silent, even. Not a sound. Not a peep. Not even a… *Oh fuck.*" He pushed his tongue inside me, and my words turned to needy whimpers.

"Mmm. So sweet." His thumbs pulled me apart, and he speared me with his tongue once, then again and again.

I started babbling again, because of course I did. "Yes. Please. More. This is better than anything. Better than everything. Better than—"

Except then, Jamie's spit-soaked fingers were inside me,

filling me, and I had to clutch the carpet not to come right then and there as my mind went spiraling backward.

"*Yes*," I moaned as he pumped in and out.

"You like that?" Jamie's voice was dark and low, the only real thing in the world. "I know you better than anyone else in my life, and I don't know *this* about you. How weird is that?"

"You know," I whispered. "You *do* know." Because it truly felt like he did. Like there was some kind of connection between exactly what I wanted and exactly what he did, between my brain and his hand. Like Jamie was secretly psychic.

Or maybe like the thing I wanted most of all was anything and everything Jamie wanted to give me.

"More," I begged. "More. Please."

"How much more? You want me to fuck you?" he asked hoarsely.

My eyes flew open in the dark. I hadn't been thinking that, exactly. That felt like *more*… like a lot more. Which was stupid, rationally speaking. There was no hierarchy of orgasms, and I was not gonna miss Jamie Burke more on Monday if I had his dick in my ass, and yet…

"Yes," I moaned. "I… yes."

But because Jamie *was* psychic or some shit, he heard what I was really saying, and his voice lowered even further, so he was practically growling, when he said, "Too bad. I don't have any supplies handy, and I'm not leaving you here to go find some."

I whimpered as he braced one hand on the floor while the other reached around my body and wrapped around my cock.

Jamie pushed up against me from behind, rocking his still-clothed cock against the cleft of my ass.

"We never did this," he whispered. "Isn't it crazy that we never did this?"

I swallowed, my poor blood-starved brain trying to make out his words while his thumb twisted over the head of my erection.

Jamie was right—we'd been kids the last time we were close like this, and we'd felt like we had all the time in the world… until we didn't. He'd been my first kiss, my first… almost everything. But he loomed so large in my memory, it felt like there should be nothing we hadn't done.

"We are now," I panted. "We have… hours and hours."

Jamie's hand moved away, and he flipped me to my back before lying down on top of me, fully naked this time.

He undulated once, pushing every part of his body against every part of mine.

I moaned at the sensation, and Jamie barked out a harsh laugh. "Hours and hours," he repeated, except he didn't seem quite as excited about that as I was. "Let's make them count."

He wrapped a hand around both of us and didn't stop until he'd pushed me over the edge.

Chapter Eight

JAMIE

"Bad news is, your roof's fucked," Enrique Poole said, bracing his hands on his hips and looking up at the boards he'd nailed into the ceiling above the window in Molly's room.

Parker and I had spent a couple of hours in there earlier that morning, disassembling her bed and propping her mattress against the wall to give the construction guys Marci had promised to send over some room to maneuver, but somehow that had made the damage seem even worse than it had yesterday. There was no way this room was going back to the way it had been before, even if I wanted it to.

And Parker was right—there was no reason why it *should*. But change was hard. I had no more idea what to do with this space today than I had yesterday. And tomorrow Parker would be gone.

I huffed out a breath, staring at the same spot on the ceiling. "Is there any good news?"

"Well, sure." Enrique turned and looked at me strangely. "Plenty. Nobody got hurt, for one."

I nodded. "True." And that had been more of a near-run thing than I'd thought, looking at the tree from inside yesterday. The thing was huge—way more than just the dead branches I'd forgotten to prune last year. In fact, an entire half of the trunk had sheared off with the branch and had been propped up against the roof all night long, just waiting to crumple the whole section of the roof—and any idiot sleeping beneath it—like a tin can beneath its weight.

Not that Parker and I had been in any danger, mind you. In fact, we hadn't bothered using the bedrooms last night at all. We'd fallen asleep right on the living room rug like a pair of idiots having a very grown-up sort of slumber party.

"We chopped up the tree, and I got to use a chainsaw inside the house for a minute," Enrique continued, like he was ticking blessings off for me. "Which was super fun."

"Yeah, I feel like that part was more good fortune for you than for me." I rubbed at my shoulder, which didn't seem to appreciate a night camping out on the floor.

"And you'll have some good firewood for next winter."

"Right. There's that." And I'd need it. Because there'd be no one to keep me warm next…

Wow. That was fucking pitiful. Two nights with Parker, and apparently, this was me. I refused to let myself complete that thought.

"And last but not least, no major structural damage," Enrique said with a grin. "So we should be able to get the outside part fixed up for you next week."

"The outside? What about in here?"

Enrique shrugged. "Lotsa houses got damaged, J. We're kinda triaging things right now, you know? Step one, making sure it's weathertight. Step two, making it pretty. But that's not gonna happen for a few weeks."

I nodded. That made sense. And more than that, I felt like it had bought me some time.

"Hey, Jame?"

"Yeah?"

I turned to the door, where Parker stood braced against the frame. He was wearing a pair of my sweatpants, since we'd managed to get all of his own pajamas dirty, and they hung on his hips below his t-shirt. His light hair had dried in messy waves after his shower, like someone had been running their fingers through it this morning—spoiler: it was me—and he looked gorgeous and touchable and...

I made myself look away.

"Si and his guy are here. They're waiting for you in the kitchen." Parker hooked a thumb over his shoulder.

I nodded and clapped Enrique on the shoulder. "You all set?"

"Yeah, man. I just need to finish up in the other room, and I'll see myself out."

"Yell if you need me."

"Will do."

I walked to the door, but Parker stood there watching me approach, and didn't move out of the way until our chests were nearly brushing. I lifted an eyebrow and looked down at him.

"Problem?"

Parker shook his head and blushed just a little as he backed into the hall. "Not at all. Just... admiring the view."

I had no idea how to respond to that, so I turned toward the kitchen without saying anything. I could practically sense Parker's hurt and confusion as he walked along at my side.

I mean, I knew how I *wanted* to respond. How I'd respond if all of this were real, or even if we were still alone. But it felt like the last couple of days had been spent in an alternate universe—our own personal Narnia—where, thanks to the snow and my stupid bullshit rule, the real world and our very real past hadn't intruded in any significant way.

But the snow was officially over. The rest of the town had electricity again, and we would—*I* would—too, once we—*I, goddammit*—got the all clear from the electrician who'd be coming over later. It was time to get back to reality.

As Parker had so helpfully reminded me, my dad had been an alcoholic—a pretty raging one at the end, but for a long time before that, he'd been more or less functional —and I remembered that he'd quit drinking once when I was maybe ten, just to show my mom he could. For months and months, he hadn't had a single beer, not a sip of Jim Beam, and he hadn't attended a single meeting or coun-seling session. He'd managed to convince my mom and *himself* that he could handle his shit, that it wasn't a real problem.

It had taken *one* drink, just one, celebrating his newfound control, and he'd gone right back to his old ways... except ten times as messed up as he'd been before. The next time he'd gotten clean, it had been exponentially harder and it had only lasted weeks.

And yeah, Parker wasn't alcohol... but I was my father's son, with all those same predilections to addiction. And now that I'd had Parker in my world again—his taste in my mouth, his scent in my nose, his laughter in my ear —letting him go was gonna be even harder, but that didn't mean I could keep him.

I stepped into the kitchen and found Silas wearing his outdoor gear, complete with a beanie pulled down over his forehead. He was leaning against the sink with his arms folded over his chest, watching some tall, lanky guy I'd never seen before stuff his face with leftover chicken wings.

My leftover chicken wings.

I turned to Parker, who shrugged, and then to Silas, who rolled his eyes.

"This is Marlon," Silas said. "He's from over in Camden. Mitch is looking to hire another officer, so Marlon's with us on a trial basis." His tone made it clear he had doubts that the trial would end well.

Marlon, who seemed oblivious to the subtext, gave me a cheerful wave.

"And Marlon's eating our chicken wings, why?" I asked Parker in a low voice.

"Because he said he was hungry." Parker pushed past me and watched Marlon devour wings at an astonishing speed. "It's gratifying to feed someone who so obviously appreciates good food. Speaking of… Marlon, since you're here, which wings would you say were better? The ones with the dark glaze or the lighter ones?"

"Hey!" I set my hands on my hips. "I thought the rules were that *we* would judge."

"Yeah, yeah. Officially." Parker waved a hand. "But that doesn't mean we can't solicit an unbiased opinion. And Marlon looks like a man who knows good chicken, doesn't he?"

Actually, Marlon looked like he hadn't had a good meal in years, but whatever.

"If it'll help you sleep at night, Parkie," I agreed.

Parker narrowed his eyes, and my fingers clenched as I reminded myself that grabbing him and kissing the outrage off his face would help nothing.

"Well, since you're asking…" Marlon began in a surprisingly high voice.

"Yes! Be honest. Jamie has a thick skin," Parker encouraged. "He can take it."

"I've gotta say the darker ones are better." Marlon licked his lips. "Nice and sweet."

Parker pursed his lips and immediately removed the container of wings from the counter. He wrapped the foil back around them and set them in the fridge, then shut the door firmly.

"Clearly, I was wrong," he said, all pissy and adorable. "Marlon knows *nothing*."

Marlon looked crestfallen. "But I—"

"You're fine, Marlon," I said, amused. "Parker just does that sometimes. He's very sensitive."

Parker lifted one eyebrow at me as he leaned back against the fridge. "True artists are never appreciated in their lifetimes."

Silas looked from Parker to me and back again. His lips twitched. "So, ah… how are things going, Parks?"

Parker turned his attention to Silas and shrugged. "Could be worse. My plants and I didn't freeze to death in the snow. And I heard from Joe Cross this morning. They plowed the Camden Road, so he hauled in my car. He's planning to have it fixed this week."

"That's great news," Silas agreed. He paused, then added, "Then what?"

Parker hesitated, looking at me, but I wasn't sure what the hell he expected *me* to say when he hadn't shared his plans with me. He took a deep breath. "Then… I'm leaving, I guess," he told Silas. He frowned, and said again more forcefully, "I'm definitely leaving. Heading to Arizona."

"Yeah?" Silas frowned thoughtfully. "You think that's the best idea?"

"Totally." Parker shrugged. "Nothing for me here,

right? And you know me. I hate this kinda half-assed waiting around. Time to figure out my next move so I'll be ready once my claim is finally paid."

It shouldn't have hurt as much as it did to hear him state the obvious, but it made sense.

"Yeah," I managed to say. "You've got lots of options out there. You could open another bar just about anywhere and be successful."

Silas made a thoughtful noise and both of us looked at him.

"What?" Parker demanded.

"That insurance guy was bugging Gideon. You remember Gideon, Marlon?" Silas asked. "You met him at the fire station the other day?"

Marlon nodded.

"He was asking Gideon for specifics on the samples he took and things he might have overheard the night of the fire. And he's going through the list of people on the construction crews who had access to the space."

"*Shit*. But I thought you guys already did that," Parker said a little desperately. "It was all cleared up."

Silas nodded. "We did. We found no evidence of criminal tampering. But insurance companies have their own thresholds for paying claims like this. He's not taking our word for anything, and I have no idea how long it will take for him to complete his own investigation."

From one instant to the next, Parker's face crumpled, and in less than a heartbeat, I'd moved toward him, trying to shield him from… I don't even know what. Life? Shitty, shitty reality?

I was so fucked.

Silas moved toward Parker, too, and patted him awkwardly on the shoulder. "Just hang in there, okay?"

I kept on walking, into the eating area, like that had

been my intention all along, and I spied the trio of plants Parker had left on the kitchen table. They were cheerful little things in their colored pots—cute and prickly and resilient, a lot like Parker himself. They probably weren't getting nearly as much sunlight as they needed in this shadowy corner either.

I glanced at the front window, where my mom's once-precious colored bottles were arranged on a glass shelf stretching across the middle of the sash so they could catch the light.

Perfect.

I took the bottles down, one at a time, and replaced them with the pots, before turning back around to face the others.

"Look, it's not my business to tell you what to do," Silas was telling Parker. "But if you're on the fence at all about leaving town, maybe rethink."

Parker rubbed a hand over his forehead. "For the sake of the investigation?"

Silas nodded. "Among other things. Let's just say, it can't hurt to make it clear that you're a part of this town with strong ties to the community."

Parker laughed shortly. "Like, if I stay, the investigator is less likely to realize that I lit my bar on fire so I could live out my lifelong dream of fleeing justice to a country without an extradition treaty?"

Marlon's eyes went wide. "Oh my God. Did you really?"

Silas huffed out a breath. "Jesus Christ. Of course he fucking didn't, Marlon. It's *sarcasm.*"

"Oh." Marlon frowned at Parker. "So you *didn't* burn your bar down?"

"Marlon, we came by to tell Jamie the electric crews would be coming soon just to verify that everything's all set with his utilities," Silas said, in a tone that brooked no argument. "Did you set some traffic cones outside?"

"Cones? No, sir. Why would—"

"Marlon, the streets are narrow thanks to the snow," Silas insisted. "Anything could happen. Go set some cones."

"But you didn't tell me—"

"This job is about showing initiative, Marlon!"

"But I —"

"*Now*, Marlon."

"But we don't have any cones!"

Silas sighed. "Then you need to go stand out in the street and wait for the electric crew yourself. In the interest of public safety."

"Oh. Right." Marlon blinked. "O-okay." He turned to Parker. "Um. Thanks. You know, for the chicken wings."

"Yeah," Parker said, his shoulders slumped. "You're welcome."

"A-and yours were really good too."

"Thanks." He tried summoning a smile that seemed incredibly false to me, but apparently not to Marlon.

"You know, you could maybe try adding a little honey to your—"

"*Go*, Marlon," Silas commanded, pointing toward the kitchen door.

And without another word, Marlon fled.

"I have a feeling," Silas said, rubbing the back of his neck, "that our employment search isn't over. Don't suppose you know anyone who's dreamed of being an underpaid, overworked, small-town public servant?"

Parker hoisted himself up so his ass was on the counter. "Hey, at this point, I'd consider anything that pays the bills. Does it come with accommodations?" he asked ruefully.

I walked back into the main area of the kitchen and

took up a spot as far from Parker as I could get in the small space.

"You need a place to stay?" Silas looked back and forth from me to Parker again, but this time he frowned.

"If I'm gonna stay in town for the duration of this hundred-year investigation, I do. I gave up my apartment to move into the loft over the bar, and we know how that turned out." Parker knitted his fingers together, seeming fascinated at the sight. "But apparently there's a freakin' *population boom* in O'Leary, because I can't find a new apartment either. *Aaaand* I was staying at the Crabapple, but they're overbooked. Literally no room at the inn." He glanced up at Silas. "Seemed like a sign that it was time to get out of Dodge."

"Looking for signs is a little bit like trying to pick out shapes in the clouds," Silas said. "Trust me on this. If you stare hard enough, everything looks like a bunny."

Parker laughed.

"If you need somewhere to stay, there's room at my place," Silas offered.

"Oh, I couldn't—"

"Sure you could. Ev would be ecstatic to have another cook. *Apparently*, cooking is not my forte." Silas smirked. "Fortunately, I have other talents."

Ugh. No way did I want Parker anywhere near Silas's *other talents*, whether Everett was around or not.

"He can stay here," I heard myself say. Then I repeated, looking directly at Parker, "I mean, you can stay here. If you want. There's plenty of room, clearly. And your plants are already set up... and shit."

Parker stared at me like he was trying to see through my flesh and bone and maybe figure out what I was thinking. I could have told him not to bother. Half the time I didn't know, myself, and this was most definitely one of those times.

My stomach was clenched tight with nerves—scared that he'd say no and fucking petrified that he'd accept.

"Well, I guess I'll leave you guys to sort out the details." Silas stood up straight and glanced out the window to where Marlon was standing like a sentry at the end of my half-plowed driveway. He shook his head in amused exasperation. "But look, Parker, offer's open, okay?" Silas squeezed Parker's shoulder and, I couldn't say for sure from this position, but I was pretty sure he gave him a wink also. "Pretty sure you'll find most people around here feel the same way. You'll have lots of offers right here in O'Leary."

And even though I knew better—absolutely, totally, completely knew for a *fact* that Silas was head over ass for Everett and his words had been nothing more than a friendly gesture—I found myself gritting my teeth. When Silas called out a goodbye as he walked to the door, I barely mumbled something back.

Parker had gone back to swinging his feet, but he was watching me again, and I got the feeling that I was supposed to say… *something*… but I had no fucking clue what he wanted.

It was amazing that I could read this guy like a book when I had my tongue in his mouth and my hands on his body, but when it came to anything else, anything that didn't involve sex and saliva and *fuck me harder*, it was like we spoke two wildly different dialects of the same language and were constantly misreading each other.

Parker's phone clattered on the counter near his hip, and he glanced down, breaking the stalemate. His lips twisted.

"Beatrice wants to know when I'll reschedule my

flight," he said offhandedly. He looked back at me again. "I'm not sure what to tell her."

I shrugged. "Your call, Parks." It always had been. "You wanna stick around, you've got a place."

His nostrils flared. "Yeah? For how long? Could take weeks. Could take a month or two. Who fucking knows?"

I sighed. "I know. It's not ideal, and it won't be fun." In fact, I'd bet sticking around here when he could be out in the world, making new plans and conquering new goals, was gonna suck ass for him. "But we can make it work."

Something moved over Parker's face—disappointment or maybe sadness—and I got it. I did. He wanted *out*, and he was being forced to stay.

"And how would it even work, me living here? Polite strangers indefinitely?" he demanded.

I rolled my shoulder trying to ease the tightness there. "We haven't exactly excelled at that from the first minute. We can be… friends, I guess. I mean, underneath every-thing, I never stopped caring," I admitted. "About you."

Parker peered at me. "You're serious."

"I—" I started, stopped, tried again. "Yeah. Of course."

"Because, let me just remind you that, this magical weekend of sexcapades aside, you have been an *asshole* to me for… oh, let's round up to a *year*."

"And I apologized for it."

"*Noooo*." He shook his head slowly and gripped the counter on either side of his legs so hard his knuckles turned white. "You apologized for coming into my bar and making a spectacle of yourself, knocking over chairs and yelling about the temperature of your beer."

I ran my tongue over my front teeth. I *had*. And it had made *so* much sense at the time. But right now, it was hard to remember why I'd done those things. And really fucking hard to hold the moral high ground in this conversation.

"That's not what I'm talking about," he continued. "What about all the times I tried to talk to you and you literally pretended I wasn't there? Or the time you told me this town wasn't big enough for the both of us, like we were gonna be gunfighters drawing down at high noon in the middle of Weaver Street?"

I rolled my eyes.

"Or what about the time you told me—" Parker's voice cracked just a little, and he cleared his throat before he continued, "that what we had was dead and buried?"

I watched him steadily from the other side of the kitchen. We were two islands that had once been a single continent, and now found ourselves separated by an ocean of terra-cotta tile and bad memories. And that was my doing... at least partly. Cutting him off had been my attempt at self-preservation—it wouldn't hurt as much when he inevitably left, if I didn't get close to begin with.

And look how well that turned out, you idiot.

In the end, *I'd* hurt *him*. I hadn't known I could.

So I fell back on what I knew to be true. "I've only ever wanted you to be happy and successful."

"You sound like my mother." Parker's gaze locked on mine, green like storm-tossed waves. "You might wanna watch that."

"Yeah, well. It worked out for the best in the end, right? You went off and got your degree. Got job experience. Had a good time in Boston. Saved enough to open your bar."

Parker lowered his eyes to the floor and nodded slowly. "Sure. All for the best." He took a deep breath. "And if I stay here now, we'll be... what? Friends? Or friends with benefits?" He sounded absolutely disgusted. "Because I really *hate* that shit, Jameson. Either we're friends, or we're together. All in or all out."

I swallowed. "Well, together's not an option I'm interested in." Not when he was heading for Arizona the minute he got paid. "I guess we could try to keep things platonic. I'd do that, if you wanted."

"You would?" He looked skeptical and with really good reason.

"Sure," I lied. "But it seems unnecessarily complicated, doesn't it?"

"Let me understand." Parker pursed his lips. "You think *avoiding* sex would make our being friends *more* complicated. How's that work?"

I shrugged. "I find you…" Hot as fuck? Funny as hell? You make me feel like I'm finally opening my eyes to the light after a really long, dark night? *Ugh.* "… attractive. And heat has never been a problem between us."

"Ah. So, it's basic biology," Parker huffed out a breath and it sounded like he was choking when he said, "Friends with benefits, then. For as long as I'm here."

I made myself nod. I had told myself that very thing yesterday morning, right? Basic biology? Parker didn't need to know about all the other messy, inconvenient *feelings* shit I had going on.

"Not good enough." Parker shook his head, and for a second, my breath caught, because I swear I thought he was going to say that friends with benefits wasn't enough. That he wanted *more*. But then he continued, "I need to pay rent too. I would *never* take advantage of a buddy by mooching off him." His lips edged up in a tentative smile. "And I don't consider the *with benefits* to be payment, FYI. Because that's just a little too *Pretty Woman*."

Of course.

"Don't be ridiculous," I said, more harshly than I

intended. I jumped down from the counter and jammed my hands in my pockets. "I own this place free and clear. I don't even have a mortgage. Save your money."

Parker jumped down too. "If you insist, I'll pay you in cooking," he said in an overly sweet voice. "All the chicken wings you can eat."

I bit my lip to keep from smiling. "I remember you being competitive, but I don't remember you being such a sore loser, Parkie."

Predictably, his green eyes sparked as they came to mine. "I am *not*—"

"It's okay, buddy. Nobody's perfect. You can be in charge of pancakes," I drawled, making it clear I was only humoring him. I ruffled his already messy hair and when he knocked my hand away much harder than necessary, I laughed. "As I recall, you make good burgers. Remember the ones you used to make with the white bread and excessive ketchup?"

Parker looked up at the sky. "Only *you* would remember that." He sighed. "What if I help you fix up the house? Paint and whatever?"

I frowned, looking through the doorway to the dining room. It had to be kind of a record that I hadn't thought about updating this place in a million years, and now suddenly I'd had not one but two guys offer to help me do it. But once again, it felt *right*.

And I was clearly fucked when he left anyway, right? Might as well go out with a bang.

"Yeah, okay," I said, like I was the one doing *him* a favor. "You can help paint."

One light eyebrow arched. "You promise?"

"We gonna pinkie swear? Like it's 2002 up in here?"

Parker's eyes widened along with his grin. "Did… did you just say *up in here*?"

I rolled my eyes.

"Yeah, apparently it *is* 2002." He laughed.

"Shut it."

"I'm just saying. You sound so old."

"What's that make you?" I demanded.

"Younger than *you*. By two whole years."

I backed him playfully against the counter where he'd been sitting earlier, except this time I was right next to him, pressed up against his heat. "Then respect your elders, boy."

Those gorgeous eyes lit with humor… and with something else entirely. Something that had me resting more of my weight against him and hissing when his hands came up to rest on my chest.

"If you expect me to call you *Daddy*, Jamie, you've got another think coming."

I smiled, because the words were just a little bit breathless, a little bit needy, and a whole lot turned on.

"You've already called me Jesus, Parkie. I could have you calling me Daddy in two minutes if I applied myself."

He grabbed a hank of my hair and tugged. "*Now* who's competitive?" he demanded. But he didn't deny it. He swallowed. "You do realize you're going to have to give me a key to this place, right? If I'm living here."

"Yeah."

"Because I'm just a little bit concerned. I'd hate to have you throwing spears at me if I decided to make dinner or whatever," he teased.

The thought of Parker making me a naked dinner…

"Parker?" I slid a hand up his back, feeling the ridges of his spine and the ripple of his muscles as he shivered.

"Y-yeah?"

"Shut up," I said. I lowered my mouth to slide my lips against his and tangle our tongues together.

A long minute later, he broke away with a gasp.

"Is this what I can expect from you as a roommate?" he demanded. "Ending every argument by kissing the shit out of me?"

"We weren't arguing," I countered. "But… yes, probably." I slid my mouth down to that one particular spot on his neck and grinned in satisfaction when his breath caught. "I find you particularly attractive when you're annoyed at me."

He laughed breathlessly and yanked my hair to pull me back. "Then it's gotta be a minor miracle you managed to avoid mauling me for the past year."

It was a joke, but also…

"Yeah," I agreed seriously. "I'm thinking it kinda was."

His expression softened and he ran a thumb over my bottom lip. "I thought O'Leary was driving me insane," Parker announced, apropos of nothing. "But now I'm pretty sure it was *you*."

I might have taken exception to that statement, but when he lifted himself up to kiss me and the sweet *Parker* taste of him exploded on my tongue driving every other thought from my mind, I realized that the feeling was decidedly mutual.

Chapter Nine

"Yes, Mom. I promise I'm fine," I insisted as I drove Jamie's truck toward the center of town. "I'm eating all my vegetables. I'm getting plenty of sleep. And it's gorgeous here—sixty-two degrees today and sunny."

It was *so* gorgeous, in fact, that I'd left all the windows open back at the house, to get some fresh air and vent some of the drywall dust that I was pretty sure was creeping into my pores. The sun was shining, and the breeze smelled like spring—green grass and growing things. Jamie had teased that this probably meant another blizzard was imminent, but I found that the threat of more snow didn't dampen my spirits in the slightest.

One conversation with my mother, on the other hand…

My mother made a clucking noise with her tongue. "It's eighty-two here. And sunny *every* day."

"Sounds awful," I said honestly.

"They're opening up a new strip mall right near our development. They're putting in a couple of high-end shops *and* an organic grocery store."

I stopped at the crosswalk to let Janice Turner lead a group of kids with books tucked under their arms across the street from the library to the elementary school. I waved at a couple of the kids I recognized and grinned when they waved back.

"Awesome!" I said out loud. "You love high-end kale."

"Parker, don't joke," she said severely. "Look, honey, I'm getting ready to go to lunch with your dad and a few other couples from our neighborhood. But you need to know… your poor father is having such trouble with his digestion. And his heart too. I'm really concerned—"

"Jesus Christ!" I heard my dad call from somewhere in the background. "Parker doesn't care that I needed an antacid after breakfast, Beatrice. I'm fine! Now, shake a leg, or we'll be the last ones there!"

"We're going to put that on your tombstone, Lance," my mother yelled back. "*Here lies Lance. He was fine.*" She huffed out a breath and turned her attention back to me. "I need to know when you're coming to stay with us. And," she added, as if sensing I was about to speak, "don't tell me you don't know. It's time to stop playing games in O'Leary and get a move on."

"I'm not playing games. I'm being responsible." I pulled Jamie's truck into a space in front of Fanaille bakery and cut the engine. "I told you what Silas said about the investigation."

I instinctively looked down the street to where the empty lot that had once been Hoff's Bar sat, surrounded by a chain-link fence, and rubbed at the ache in my chest.

It had been nearly three months since my bar had burned down, and Unity Financial was still investigating, still going over every scrap of non-evidence with a magnifying glass and a fine-toothed comb. A few weeks back, just when I figured they *had* to be done, some idiot teenager had spray-painted obscenities on the snow-covered empty lot, and suddenly there was a new, stupid angle they hadn't adequately explored.

This was just a teensy little bit of a sore spot for me.

Or, fine… more like a gaping, festering, aching wound in the center of my chest, if you wanted to be dramatic about the thing. I was trying to keep myself busy. I was trying to paste on a smile and make like I had all the time in the world and wasn't the slightest bit impatient, but it was wearing on me.

I wanted things *settled.*

I mean, was it too much to ask for just *one thing* in my life to be settled?

"Yes, you mentioned that. And your father has told *you* countless times that it's *nonsense.* You don't need to hang around waiting for them to finish things up, you need to hire an attorney to *force* the insurance company to pay you."

I sat back against the seat. "I don't feel comfortable having Dad get involved."

"Nonsense. He wouldn't be involved. He'd be recommending a friend. And he'd love to help, Parker. He needs a project besides endless *golf.* His heart is—"

"Mom, for real, you need to stop this shit where you complain about Dad's health, okay? He's *fine.* And so am I. I don't need or want to be Dad's new project." I paused, then added, "But thank him for me anyway."

My mom sighed in my ear, then changed tack. "Have you at least found a new place to live?" she demanded.

"Nope. I've been looking," I lied. "There's just nothing available anywhere."

"*Really?* Because I was speaking to Dana earlier in the week and she said they had rooms at the Crabapple. I'm sure she'd be happy to have you again."

Aha. I rolled my eyes and idly watched Cal and Ash laughing with a group of customers. *Here we go.*

I'd caved and told my parents I was staying at Jamie's house once I knew the situation was going to last longer than a weekend, mostly because I knew they'd hear it from someone else in town anyway. Better to control the narrative, right? Or so I'd thought.

"Jamie's doing me a favor by letting me stay with him rent-free. He's a friend. We are *friends.*"

And that wasn't a lie. We *were* friends. We hung out with Everett and Silas, Mitch and Dare Turner, and a few other folks playing darts in Silas's garage, and made a kick-ass team. We hung drywall together, and I hooked him up with a guy I knew who'd replaced his gutters at cost. I'd scouted a deal on a construction dumpster we could keep for a month, and Jamie had ordered it delivered. We'd cleaned out the furniture from Molly's room and Jamie's room, and I'd helped him move the few pieces he'd wanted to keep into the master bedroom, which he'd finally claimed as his own, then haul the remaining stuff to Goodwill. He gave me a key to his truck since I seemed to be running to O'Leary Hardware twice a week for masking tape or utility knives or something. I cooked him pasta and he bitched that there was too much sauce, then asked for seconds. He cooked me burgers and I offered to give him remedial grilling lessons, then stole the last of his burger off his plate. We watched football, and hockey, and figure skating. We talked about politics, and the latest *Doctor Who,* and books we read, and people who pissed us off…

Just a couple of buddies.

Just a pair of bros.

Totes platonic.

Except that every night, after Jamie got home from the diner, or after we'd finished working on the house, we climbed into bed together. And we didn't always end up getting off—not if he was too tired or, like one week back in February when I'd bunged up my hand, I just wasn't into it—but most nights ended with hands and mouths and skin and cocks and glorious, glorious orgasms.

Because we were friends *with benefits*.

And wasn't *that* some serious irony?

Me, who'd laid into Julian Ross about this very thing, who'd shouted from the rafters that if you weren't all in, you were out, and if you couldn't say yes, you had to say no, who'd insisted to anyone who'd listen that people who found themselves in fucked-up, half-assed relationships deserved the misery they were doomed to bring on themselves, was now smack in the middle of one.

And yeah, I could confirm, this was a solid seven out of ten on the miserable scale.

But I also got why it was so damn appealing. The same way the warm breeze blowing down Weaver Street made me want to believe spring was in the air, every day and night I spent with Jamie made me want to believe that his opinion of me, or of relationships, or of relationships *with me*, or whatever the hell he'd meant when he'd said, "Together's not an option I'm interested in," would resolve itself and he'd change his mind.

And I *knew* it was dumb. I knew, every time I caught him talking to my plants when he didn't know I could hear him, or watched him smooth my grandmother's blanket at the foot of the bed we shared, and my heart lurched one step closer to the sharp jagged cliffs of *all the way in love*, that I was actively deluding myself and setting myself up for disaster. But I'd become this creature that craved as much of Jameson Burke as I could get, and I was willing to exist in this state of half-togetherness since, honestly, it felt more *together* than I'd ever felt with anyone else.

I loved him. I always had. And I was way too chicken-shit to force his hand, when it seemed entirely probable that if I did… that would be the end of this.

It was kinda crazy to think that I'd been ready to leave him a couple months ago and now… I was willing to accept whatever scraps I could get just to keep him.

Which was super healthy behavior, obvs, and totally didn't confirm that I was the needy idiot he'd accused me of being back when he'd broken up with me a decade ago.

"You have plenty of friends, Parker. And you'll find plenty more wherever you end up. You don't need Jamie Burke. You never did."

I blew out a breath. "Mom, did you know that I didn't have a single meaningful relationship in Boston?"

"What?"

"Not one. Not any. I had acquaintances and coworkers, but not a single boyfriend for longer than a month, or even a friend I keep in close touch with other than Ethan, and I knew him before Boston. No one has ever gotten me like Jamie does. And it killed me when he broke up with me—"

"*He* broke up with *you*? But I thought it was mutual. I thought you had finally come to your senses."

"Yeah," I admitted. "I wanted you to think that. I was mortified. And hurt. We'd been planning a whole future together, you know? In the end, he didn't want it."

"Parker, honey—"

Ugh. If my *mother* gave me sympathy, I was gonna feed myself to sharks somehow.

"All over with now!" I said, forcing a smile and hoping she could hear it. But I was *such* a liar. It was *not* over. The way I felt about him now was more ridiculous than ever. "But don't talk shit about him, okay?"

I'd loved Jamie as a boy, but I *loved* him as a man. His sarcasm, his quick wit, the way his hair caught fire in sunlight, the way he'd brace his hand on the small of my back sometimes and make everything better for just a second with only that one small touch.

The door to the bakery opened and Angela Ross stepped out onto the sidewalk with a white box tucked under her arm. She saw me sitting in the truck and waved, then stopped, like she was waiting for me to emerge.

"Oh, Mom, gotta go! Angela Ross needs me."

"Angela Ross?" she demanded. "What does *she* need you for?"

I smiled to myself. Angela had been her frenemy for as long as my parents had lived in O'Leary. It was an accidentally perfect interruption.

"Well, I won't know until I talk to her, will I?" I cut the engine and the call transferred to my phone. "Gotta go, Mom. Speak to you… next week or sometime."

"But, Parker, you never said—"

I hit End and felt no remorse. Well… *almost* none.

"Morning, Angela," I said, jumping down and slamming the truck door behind me. I jammed my hands in the pockets of my sweatshirt and took a deep breath.

"Morning, Parker! Pretty day, huh?"

"It *is*," I said, returning her broad smile and feeling my good mood returning. "How are you?"

"Couldn't be better! Heading over to the flower shop for a minute. I've got a bonus son to bribe into helping me with plans for the Lilac Day festival. Fortunately, I know exactly how to do it." She shook the pastry box.

"A *bonus son*," I repeated. "You mean Micah?"

Angela grinned. "*Bonus son* sounds so much better than *my son's boyfriend*, doesn't it? Especially when the man in question is forty?" She glanced from side to side, like she was checking to make sure no one else could overhear, then lowered her voice to say, "I called him my son-in-law once.

Constantine turned five shades of red, choked on air, and told me later, in no uncertain terms, that if I gave away the proposal he was planning, he'd name his future children after my mother-in-law." Her lips twitched, and she flipped her black braid over her shoulder. "It was a darn good threat."

I laughed, because I could totally picture Con saying that.

It was kinda crazy that no one in town had known Micah and Con were even a *thing* until maybe a month ago, when Micah had gotten into some trouble around Valentine's Day and Angela had recruited us all to help him out. But since then, the two of them had become as much of a fixture around town as Cal and Ash, holding hands and generally making all of us say *awww*.

I'd even caught Jamie looking at them sappily once, but when I'd called him on it, all he'd said was, "Another happy couple. It's like there's something in the water around here."

If that was the case, I needed Jameson to drink the fuck up.

"Speaking of Lilac Day," Angela continued coyly. "You know it's one of the biggest celebrations in O'Leary."

"Oh, sure," I agreed, fighting a smile. "Along with the Light Parade, and the Pumpkin Fest, and the Fourth of July, and the Summer Picnic." Cal liked to say that if something in O'Leary stood still for two seconds, they'd build a monument to it or hold a festival for it, and I'd learned as a kid that the *biggest* and *most important* festival in town was whichever one happened to be coming up next.

Angela waved a hand in the air dismissively. "Yes, those too." Her smile turned a little cagey. "You know, your food was one of the most popular draws at *all* the festivals last year and at the farmer's markets too."

"That's, ah… nice of you to say," I mumbled. I rubbed at my shoulder, which was such a default Jamie action that I dropped my hand and shifted my weight, trying to remember how I used to stand before Jamie had come back into my life.

"I'm not trying to be *nice*, Parker. I'm trying to say that you absolutely have to claim a booth for Lilac Day," Angela said. "I won't take no for an answer."

"And yet… no." I shook my head. "I couldn't possibly. I mean, thank you. For thinking of me. But… no."

Angela frowned. "But why not? We'll find you cooking space, if that's the issue. Mari would let you use her cooking space at Burger Geek. Or, word around town is, you might have a connection at Goode's Diner." She winked and patted a hand against the side of Jamie's truck. "You could use their kitchen."

I felt my cheeks heat. It had definitely not gone unnoticed that Jamie and I were back on… somewhat better terms. We'd never talked about our relationship openly, and sure as hell never hinted we were anything more than friends in public, but I was confident that the O'Leary gossip mill was making it seem like Jamie and I were picking up our relationship where we'd left off. Love, to hate, to love again, with just a snap of the fingers.

I didn't blame them for believing it, considering how badly I wanted to believe it too.

"That's kind of you, Angela," I said. "Really. But I don't have a restaurant right now, and it wouldn't feel right."

"Ah, that's just temporary, Parker." She frowned. "Isn't it? You're going to rebuild, aren't you? I heard you were thinking of leaving town at one point over the winter, but you stayed." She nodded once, like this confirmed things for her. "O'Leary is your home."

I shrugged, thinking maybe I needed to let my mom and Angela Ross debate my future and let me know what they figured out when they were done.

"Everything feels up in the air right now," I said. "I can't even think about rebuilding until the insurance claim gets paid. *If* it gets paid."

Angela's eyes narrowed. "It's that investigator person? He's still holding things up?"

"Yeah, I guess. Him. The company." I shrugged again and pushed a hand through my hair. "I'm kinda stuck." And I hated it.

"You need an attorney," she said sagely. "I know a guy."

I snorted. She said it like some kind of mafia don, and the more I thought about it, the more I could picture Angela Ross as the mob boss of O'Leary. Literally no one else in town would do it better than she would.

"My dad said the same," I admitted. "Says I'm a fool for not getting one in the beginning. I'd already have my money and be on my way."

Angela snickered and gave me a knowing glance. "That sounds like Lance. I used to wonder how he'd ever convinced your mother to move here when she disliked it so much, but then I'd remember how convincing he could be. The man could sell ice to an Inuit."

"Salesman of the year at Felmann's for ten years running," I agreed.

Angela laughed. "And didn't we all know it?" She clapped a hand to her mouth. "Sorry, honey. I forgot who I was talking to for a second."

"It's fine," I said, waving away her apology. If anyone knew exactly how my parents had been, it was me. My mom had spent years on the town council, and my dad had coached baseball for way longer than I'd wanted to play, but they'd made it pretty clear that they only tolerated O'Leary. And they'd moved away the minute Dad retired.

"Now, you on the other hand. You belonged here from the minute you were born. O'Leary born and bred, even if you did have that little blip in Boston."

I grinned. "A ten-year blip?"

"Takes some people longer to come to their senses than others." She winked, before continuing, "I think it drove your mother crazy that you liked it so much."

"Yep. Still does. She was stunned that I ever decided to move back when Boston had so much more culture and *opportunity*." I leaned against the truck. "But yeah, she's definitely not keen on me staying."

"Ah, Beatrice." Angela shook her head. "You know, your mama and I didn't get along very well when she lived here."

I laughed. "Yeah, I'm aware."

"Two women who liked getting their own way, and we never seemed to agree on anything." She smiled, just a little. "But somehow I think we were more alike than not. We both thought our boys hung the moon. And neither of us knew when to let go."

I smiled in confusion. "I mean, maybe at first that was true. But I haven't lived near her for a while, you know? She calls and tells me what she thinks I *ought* to do, but I do what I want."

Angela blinked and her smile turned lopsided. "Take it from me, if she's still calling you and putting thoughts in your head, honey, she hasn't let go. Tell her when you want her opinion, you'll ask for it. That's what my boys did. Nicely, of course." She winked. "And believe it or not, it made our relationships stronger."

"Sure. That'll go over well." Angela had to be joking.

Beatrice Hoffstraeder firmly believed everything in the world was her business.

"You'll get to a point where it won't matter how it goes over," Angela said confidently. "With your mom or anyone else. It's the best part of getting older. Really freeing." She looked over my shoulder and waved to someone on the sidewalk. "Gotta run. See you later, honey. Remember what I said about the farmer's market, okay? O'Leary needs you." She squeezed my forearm once in goodbye, before running off.

O'Leary needed me? Ha. That was a new one.

I took a deep breath, then pushed off the truck and crossed the street to O'Leary Hardware.

The door opened with the jangle of old-fashioned bells just as my feet hit the sidewalk, and Lina Davenport walked out, clutching her purse strap.

"And I told Macarena that if he didn't stop being so naughty, he… Oh! Hello, Parker!" She stopped short and gave me a wide smile.

Theo Ross emerged from the door behind her, an enormous bag of birdseed thrown over one shoulder.

"Hey, Ms. Davenport," I said pleasantly. "Hey, Theo."

"Parks," Theo said, nodding. "How's it going?"

"I was just telling young Theodore," Ms. Davenport said, "that I'm having a little birthday party a week from Sunday, and absolutely *everyone* is invited. I'll be serving snacks and drinks."

"Oh? That sounds nice. Happy birthday!"

"It's not for me, silly! It's for Macarena. My cockatoo," she continued, when I looked at her blankly. "He loves parties! And presents. He has a gift registry set up at the pet store in Rushton."

I looked at Theo who was glancing skyward and trying not to laugh.

"Right. Yes. Of course he does," I said smoothly. I forced a smile, thinking to myself that if Jamie and I didn't have plans next Sunday, I was going to make us some real quick. "That sounds… amazing!"

"Oh, *Parker!*" she gasped, eyes widening. "I just remembered! You're a *chef!*"

"I—" I made the mistake of looking at Theo again, and found him still fighting laughter. "I suppose I am."

"You're just the person I need! What do you know about making treats with seeds?" she demanded, wide-eyed.

"Oh. Uh. Not much." I admitted.

"I'm buying forty pounds of premium birdseed, and I need hors d'oeuvres!"

I glanced at the giant bag Theo was carrying. "For… for humans? Or birds? Because I don't know if I'm qualified to make bird treats."

"Oh, Parker," she said, shaking her head in fond exasperation. "*Of course.* I'll be giving you a call later to discuss options! Toodles!" She waggled her fingers and kept walking down the sidewalk.

"Does she realize she didn't answer the question?" I whispered to Theo.

Theo snickered. "Bet you never got asked to do shit like this in Boston, huh?"

"Theodore!" Ms. Davenport called imperiously. "Come on!"

Theo settled the bag more firmly on his shoulder with a little grunt and rolled his eyes at me before following her to her car.

I shook my head as I pushed open the door to the hardware store. No, it was safe to say I'd never been asked to plan bird hors d'oeuvres in Boston. But, fucked up as it was—and it *was* fucked up—I kinda liked it. It was like being part of a very strange, very extended family, and it was as different from my existence in Boston as carrots were from carrot cake.

"Morning, Hen," I said strolling up to the counter.

Henry Lattimer, who'd been running the store longer than I'd been alive, jumped to his feet from the stool he'd been perched on, like he wanted to hide the fact that he'd been sitting. "Parker. How's that new soil working out for ya?"

I grinned. "It's only been a week, but the plants seem to enjoy it. Thanks for ordering it for me."

Henry waved away my thanks. "Never a problem. Easiest thing in the world. What can I do for ya today?"

"I'm here for some paint." I pulled a paint chip from my pocket and placed it on the countertop. "A gallon of *Pepper*."

Hen took the chip and studied it for a second. "Dark grey, eh?"

"Yep. That's what Jamie wants for the spare room."

He nodded thoughtfully. "Hmmm. How big's your spare room?"

"Not mine," I reminded him. "And it's maybe ten by twenty? I think a gallon will be more than—"

Hen leaned over the counter toward me, and looked from side to side like he wanted to be sure we wouldn't be overheard, though I was pretty sure we were alone in the store. "You ever thought about an *accent wall*?" he asked, his gray-and-white mustache twitching.

I blinked. "I… have not."

Hen sighed. "Kids today don't bother looking at the design magazines. Accent walls are all the rage."

Kids today cared about interior design? "Are they?"

He pulled a dog-eared copy of *Decor* from under the

counter and slapped it down in front of me, then pointed at the room on the cover. "See that there? *Accent wall.*"

"Wow." The picture showed a bedroom with dark-toned furniture much like Jamie's bookcases and walls almost the exact color of the paint Jamie had picked, except that the wall immediately behind the bed was a medium blue. It looked… good, actually. Really good. "That's excellent."

"Of course." Hen shrugged modestly. "I don't recommend bullshit, Parker."

"Right." I rubbed at the back of my shoulder again and forced myself to stop. *I* was not the one with an injury. "Lemme just call Jamie. Since it's his house and all."

Hen's mustache twitched. "Sure it is." But he waved a hand at me anyway. "Call him."

I turned away, then hesitated. Jamie was working at the diner, and I hated to interrupt him… But if he was busy, he just wouldn't answer, right? Friends called friends at work sometimes, didn't they?

I found his name on my contacts list and pressed it.

"Parks?" he said, answering after a single ring. "You okay?"

"Oh, yeah. Everything's fine. Sorry to worry you. I, ah, just had a question about paint."

"Paint?" He sounded a little confused, and I didn't blame him.

"You remember how I was gonna get paint for the spare room today?"

"Oh. Pepper gray," Jamie said. "Right?"

"Yeah. Well, Hen had an idea for an, um, accent wall. And I think it would look great in that space. I can just take a picture of some chips and text it to you. Or even walk the chips down, since you're like a hundred feet away. *Duh.*"

"You *could*," Jamie agreed in a low voice that did things to my belly. "Might brighten up my last hour of work."

I laughed. "Okay then."

"But just get whatever paint color you want," he said. "If you like it, that's good enough for me."

I frowned down at a display of seed packets. "You don't have a preference?" I said. "You sure? You spent like a hundred years looking at shades of gray, debating the merits of each one."

"Which is why I can say with no hesitation that I do not enjoy picking paint colors. At *all*."

I snorted. "I caught that."

"I'm happy to outsource to someone who knows what I like." His voice went even lower, and he added, "And you know what I like."

"Well." I forced a tiny laugh and felt my face go hot. "I guess that's true. But that's not… um…"

"I trust you, Parks. Just get the paint. And then meet me at *Fanaille*. I'll buy you a cupcake to thank you, and you can drive me home. The walk in to work was nice, but I'm thinking I can come up with a better form of exercise than strolling back to the house."

I barely heard the last part of his statement. My throat had gone dry at his first sentence. Because, I mean, we were talking about paint, right? But it felt like a lot more than that. Like I'd won something I hadn't even known I could win.

Or maybe this was just another way I was fooling myself.

"Parks?" Jamie asked after I'd been silent for a second. "You need anything else? 'Cause I'm kinda slammed."

"N-no," I said, but it came out all choky, so I had to try again. "No, I'm set. Thanks."

"Okay then. See you in an hour?" Jamie said briskly.

"Yeah," I agreed. "I'll be there."

I turned back around to find that—*shocker*—Hen had been avidly watching me the whole time.

"He said you could pick, right?" Hen said, nodding without even waiting for my confirmation. "Jameson knows what's what. Lemme show you some samples." He winked before limping toward the paint section.

I shook my head at his back. I was glad someone knew what was what. I, for my part, knew jack shit. There was a corner of my mind that was still stumbling over the fact that Jamie Burke was *taking my calls*, let alone meeting me for cupcakes, and flirting with me, and trusting me with *anything*.

I felt a wave of longing so strong it nearly overwhelmed me. And O'Leary Hardware might be a really strange place for a revelation, but I was having one right then and there.

I was *happy*.

Happy with Jamie. Happy in O'Leary.

And I wasn't pushing Jamie to change *friends with benefits* into one thing or another, or pushing the insurance company to settle my claim, or even rescheduling my trip to Arizona, because I knew if I moved in any direction, it could all come crashing to an end. As long as my claim went unpaid and I didn't confront Jameson, I could keep things exactly as they were.

Fuck. I had become that which I hated—someone who didn't say yes or no, who drifted along. I wasn't just stuck in the middle with Jamie, I was stuck in the middle with *everything*.

And I didn't know how to get myself out of it.

A crash of metal on metal broke into my thoughts just as Henry yelled, "Ah, damn it all!"

I hurried toward the back of the shop, where I found

Henry leaning heavily on the paint mixing counter, his face a little pale.

"Hen? What happened?"

"My damn fool leg," he muttered, glaring down at the offending limb. "Been more than half a year and it *still* isn't what it was. Just goes out from under me sometimes."

"Here, let me help," I said, pulling his arm over my shoulder and steadying him. "Let's get you back to your stool."

"Not a snowball's chance, Parker. I need to get your paint."

I wanted to tell him the paint was not *mine*, damn it, no matter how many times he conveniently forgot that, and I didn't care about the paint anymore, anyway, but then I remembered who I was dealing with. Henry was as proud as he was stubborn.

"Let me grab the stool, then," I offered. "You can direct me on how to mix the paint. Okay?"

Hen nodded once and braced himself against the paint counter. I grabbed the stool from behind the cash register and brought it back to him, then let him give me precise instructions on how to run the paint-mixing machinery.

"Not bad," Henry said approvingly when I'd finished. "You ever thought about the hardware business?"

I laughed. "You offering me a job?"

The bell over the door jangled, and Theo appeared. He took in the scene with a single glance, and his blue eyes narrowed. "Leg again?" he demanded of Henry. "I thought you agreed to take it easy."

"Parker's taking your job," Hen informed him.

"Oh, yeah?" Theo's eyebrows winged up. "Thank God. Good luck, Parks. I hope you two are very happy together." He leaned closer and stage whispered, "He gets cranky when Diane forgets he hates cherry cobbler, but you can bring him around if you buy him a donut across the street."

"She never forgets," Hen said darkly. "She does it to make a point."

I shook my head. "Not gonna touch this one. Theo, wanna ring me out for the paint?"

"No charge," Hen said, waving a hand.

"But—"

"No *buts*. Don't you have a date to get to?"

I blinked. "You heard that?"

Henry's smile turned canny. "Leg's for shit, but my hearing's as good as ever."

"Terrific." I rolled my eyes and grabbed my paint cans from the counter.

"You got rollers and whatnot?" Theo asked.

"Yeah. Plenty."

"Guess I'll see you at Macarena's birthday party, then, huh?" Theo's eyes danced.

"Probably," I admitted. "I'm kind of intrigued."

"One thing about O'Leary, it never gets boring," Theo said.

"Damn straight." Hen nodded with satisfaction. "And that's the way we like it."

He wasn't wrong.

I shook my head and walked out, letting the door jingle closed behind me. I swung the paint into the back of Jamie's truck just as the door to the bakery opened and Dennis Rodman, my nemesis, walked out.

As villains went, he was pretty lame—middle aged, medium height, medium build, with thinning black hair cut ruthlessly short and gelled into place, and a baggy suit and tie that stuck out in O'Leary like a neon sign flashing "Outsider!"—but he had these tiny, intense, brown X-ray eyes, and when he looked directly at me, it gave me an unpleasant little shiver.

He lifted a single eyebrow at me and nodded once, then turned to walk down the street toward the ruins of the bar. He lifted a hand in goodbye to someone inside the bakery, and I saw Gideon Mason from the fire station lift his chin in acknowledgment from his table by the window. As soon as Dennis moved down the street, though, Gideon visibly shook himself, like he got Dennis's creep-factor too.

I stood by the truck for a second, studying Gideon. He was older—maybe eight or ten years older than me— with close-cropped gray hair and a no-nonsense attitude. I'd spoken to him maybe a handful of times, and never about anything serious until the night of the fire. We were absolutely *not* friends, and he was the opposite of approachable. But I was dying to know if he'd talked to Dennis Rodman and, if so, what they'd discussed. I might be too chickenshit to push things with Jamie, but there was no reason I couldn't make inquiries about the fire… right?

I ran a hand through my hair to tidy it, then walked into the bakery, which was empty except for Cal and Gideon.

"Afternoon, Caelan," I said, fixing a bright smile to my face. "Large coffee, please. Extra cream, extra sugar."

Cal wiped his hands on a dish cloth hanging from his shoulder and peered over the counter with narrowed eyes. "Who are you and what have you done with Parker?"

I rolled my eyes. "Just the coffee. Keep the sass."

"There he is," Cal said approvingly. He moved to make my coffee, and I looked around the bakery, letting my eyes light on Gideon like I was just noticing him there.

I lifted a hand in greeting and Gideon frowned, which wasn't wholly unexpected, considering I didn't think we'd had more than a half dozen conversations ever, but he nodded anyway.

I grabbed my coffee from Cal without paying—he knew I was good for it—and made my way to Gideon's table.

"Hi," I said, resurrecting my grin. "How's it going?"

"Parker," Gideon allowed. "I'm doing fine. You?"

"Great. Yeah." I took a sip of coffee. "Super."

"Good to hear." Gideon glanced back down at his table, where a book of crossword puzzles sat open beside a half-eaten muffin and a half-empty cup of coffee. He picked up his pencil and tapped it against his book a few times, and I could practically *hear* him internally debating about whether he could just ignore me, but he'd lived in O'Leary long enough that good manners won out.

He threw the pencil down on top of the book and gestured at the empty chair across from him. "Wanna sit down?"

"Oh! Sure!" I said, like I hadn't been angling for exactly this. I pulled out the chair and sat. "You know, I was just thinking how funny it is that you and I don't hang out more, Gideon!"

"Yeah?" His brow lowered suspiciously. "Why's that?"

"Uh, you know. You just seem like a nice guy, that's all." I gave him a winning smile.

Gideon took a bite of his muffin and chewed it deliberately, his eyes on my face. I fought the urge to squirm.

"Parker?" he said, after he'd swallowed.

"Yeah?"

"You're cute. Really cute. Ten years ago, I would've fucked you in a heartbeat. But right now, I'm not in the market for a date. And besides, I know you and Burke are"—He waved a hand—"whatever complicated thing you are. So what exactly did you want?"

I licked my lips, my face on fire. I debated arguing about what Jamie and I were, but… it was irrelevant and dishonest to boot.

"I saw Dennis Rodman wave at you," I blurted. "I just wanted to know what you told him, unofficially, and what the heck is going on with the investigation. All I get when I call Unity Financial is a flat statement that it's still ongoing…"

"And you're getting impatient."

Actually, Gideon. Part of me would be happy to remain in this fantasyland of stasis forever, but the other part just *knows* this shit isn't gonna end well, so…

"Yeah," I admitted. "Kinda."

Gideon nodded, then he smiled, and *damn*, the dude's whole face was different when he smiled. "There. Was it so fucking hard to ask for what you needed?"

I blinked. "I guess not?"

Gideon grunted. "As it happens, I'm not allowed to comment on the investigation," he said in a measured tone. "But I could make some general comments."

"General comments?"

"Mmm. Like, for example, I could comment that if an investigation is still ongoing, and no one has been arrested or even officially questioned by law enforcement, there's probably nothing new to report."

"Oh," I said. "Yeah." I wasn't sure how to feel about that.

"I could also say that if a case of suspected arson appears to have been an isolated incident, there's nothing fucking new to dig up." Gideon rolled his eyes. "Except that someone broke in and vandalized the lot a few weeks back."

"Right."

"Which would generally point the fucking investigation

away from the owner of the bar, especially since the people who reported it—a Richard and Denise Talwood from Baldwinsville, who were staying at the Crabapple—were able to say for certain that it happened between ten p.m. and four a.m., during which time you had an alibi, provided by Jameson Burke."

I frowned. "Ricky—I mean, Richard and Denise—were the ones who reported it?"

"You know them?" he asked. Then he quickly added, "No, don't tell me."

"I don't know them," I said anyway. "I stayed in the room next door to them, though, before the blizzard." And it looked like maybe Ricky had paid me back for the sleepless nights after all.

Gideon grunted again. It seemed to be his primary language. "You just keep on keeping on, Parker. They've got nothing, and Dennis knows it. Longer he keeps this investigation going, the more important it is for him to produce some evidence of something, and if he can't figure out who might've done it, he's gonna have to close up shop here and pay your claim."

I nodded slowly. "Patience isn't my forte."

"I feel that." Gideon grinned. "So what do you think happened?"

I shook my head. "I haven't a clue. And believe me, I've spent a lot of time thinking about things when I should have been sleeping."

"You having some anxiety?" Gideon asked sharply. "PTSD? Reliving things?"

I shook my head. "I *was*. I was. But now? No."

"Good." His smile widened. "Now, *me*? I'd be spending my nights thinking about who could've done me wrong. But that's just me."

I snorted. "Yeah, well, I live in O'Leary. Nobody cares enough to be that mad at me."

"Except Jamie Burke," he reminded me.

"That was me being an idiot," I scoffed. "I never really thought that."

"Anyone else who's mad at you? Maybe carrying a grudge?"

I shook my head.

"I don't care how long I live in this town, I will never understand how all of you are like a village of cute, fluffy puppies," Gideon said, biting into the muffin with a vengeance. "Guy working at the diner turns out to be a murderer, everyone gets suspicious of everyone else for like ten minutes before you're all just smiling and singing happy songs again. How's *that* work?"

I smiled. "I don't know, exactly. But life's way better when you think like an O'Learian. Speaking of—" I grabbed his napkin and gestured toward his face, where remnants of cinnamon sugar were scattered around his mouth.

I'd intended for him to take the napkin, but instead, Gideon leaned forward, letting me mop his face for him. I shook my head and laughed as I dropped the napkin onto his empty plate. "See? You don't get service like that in the big city," I said.

"Fucking fairy-tale land." Gideon's eyes took on a faraway look. "Makes a guy wish…"

But before he finished the thought, the door to the bakery was wrenched open with a sharp jangle, and I turned around.

"Oh!" I said, jumping to my feet and giving him a big grin. "Jamie! Hey."

But Jamie didn't look happy to see me. At all.

He looked from me to Gideon, then sucked in a breath

through his nose, doing that rampaging bull thing he did when he was truly mad.

I frowned. "What the hell happened?"

"Nothing," he bit off. "Why do you assume something happened?"

I raised my brows. "Uh, because you were fine an hour ago, and now you're looking at me like you're Liam Neeson, and I'm the guy who kidnapped your daughter. What gives?"

His eyes cut to Gideon again, like he didn't wanna talk in front of the guy. Which was fine with *me*. I wasn't the one storming into the bakery and throwing a shit fit.

"I'm going home," Jamie announced. "In the truck. I'm assuming you'll catch a ride on your own."

"What the fuck? No. I want my cupcake, goddammit."

Jamie shook his head. "Get your own damn cupcake."

Then he stormed back out, nearly ripping the door off its hinges.

My body flushed hot and cold, anger warring with embarrassment. What the fuck just happened? How *dare* he? How fucking *dare he*?

Gideon made a noise that sounded almost like amusement, and I turned to pierce him with a look.

"This is not funny!" I told him. "I have no idea what his problem is or why he's taking it out on me—"

"Oh, Parker, you're precious," Cal said. He was leaning on the counter, grinning hugely. "He's jealous."

"Jealous? Jamie?" I snorted. "Of what? Of who?"

Gideon cough-laughed again. "I think I've just been insulted."

"What? Oh. *Ohhh*." I looked at the window and the diner across the street. "He saw me…" I motioned toward my mouth and then at Gideon.

Gideon nodded slowly.

"Shit. But that was…"

"Totally innocent?" Gideon said. "Yeah, well. Reality is open to interpretation, isn't it?" He lifted an eyebrow.

I shook my head again. "We don't have that kind of relationship," I insisted. "We're friends."

Cal laughed. "Bullshit. You forget I've seen you two together, right? At Ev's, playing darts, and all the times you've come into the bakery?" He looked at Gideon. "They're totally fucking. They just haven't gone public yet."

My face went red. "We… we're… friends with benefits."

"You?" Cal demanded. He snorted in disbelief. "You *hate* being friends with benefits."

"I know."

"You once told me that term needed to be stricken from pop culture vocabulary," Cal continued, his eyes narrowed.

"*I know.*"

"You once said that if two people are hooking up but claiming they're just friends, it means one or both of them lacks the balls to admit their true feelings."

I glared at my friend. "I had no idea you'd memorized our conversations."

Cal shrugged. "So what *are* your true feelings?" He raised an eyebrow. "More interestingly, what are his? Because I'm pretty sure he just showed you."

"The fucking *air* turned green," Gideon concurred. "Wonder what he would've done if I'd actually kissed you or something. *Fuck.* Missed opportunity."

I opened my mouth then shut it again. I glanced out the window and saw that Jamie's truck was gone. The fucker had actually left me stranded here.

"I'm going to kill him," I said succinctly. "That's my true feeling."

Mr. I can do platonic if you want to.

Mr. Friends with benefits.

And now he was fucking jealous over *nothing?* And he'd *left me here?*

I mean, granted it was like half a mile to his house, and a beautiful, sunny day, but I didn't care. It was the principle of the thing.

I blew out a breath. "Gideon, can you give me a ride to Jamie's house, and conveniently forget you ever saw me if the cops ask?"

"Sure," Gideon agreed easily. "But come finish your fucking coffee first." He grinned. "Let him stew, and I bet he'll realize for himself what an idiot he's been."

"Devious," Cal said, pointing at Gideon with narrowed eyes. "I like it."

Gideon snorted.

I sat, as instructed, but I was pretty sure *I* was the one stewing. If Jamie was jealous, did that mean…

Fuck. I was scared to even admit to myself what it might mean. But maybe it was time to take a stand and push things just a little because I was really tired of waiting.

Chapter Ten

JAMIE

I HEARD the kitchen door open and shut, followed by the clank of Parker's keys hitting the counter. It should have felt weirder than it did to hear those things, but I liked Parker living here. I felt like this house was more of a home with him in it.

Even when he made me lose my mind.

I heard the shuffle of footsteps through the living room, the click of a lamp followed by a bright swath of light shining down the hall, and then Parker appeared in the doorway a minute later.

He leaned against the doorjamb and looked around the room for a minute, his eyes tracking over the walls in the twilight before coming to rest on me, where I was stretched out on a drop cloth he'd spread across the floor. He lifted one eyebrow and said nothing.

I looked away. "So, how was your afternoon?"

"Oh, thrilling. Gideon is a fucking stallion. He let me wear his fire hat while we fucked."

I rolled my eyes, even as the words conjured an image that made me want to throttle something.

Parker braced one hand on his hip and looked at me steadily. "What the hell was that little display, Jameson?"

I sat up, setting my feet on the floor, and braced my forearms on my knees. "Me. Being an idiot. Surely not the first time you've seen it."

"Hmm. Heads up."

He threw a white wax paper bag at my head and I snagged it out of the air before it impacted.

"Still have those baseball reflexes, huh?" He came forward and sat cross-legged on the drop cloth so his knees were close to mine. He nodded at the bag. "It's a cupcake. For you."

I opened the bag. It was, indeed, a chocolate cupcake, the frosting slightly smashed thanks to its brief stint as a missile.

"German chocolate," Parker said sweetly. "Because you hate it, but you'll feel guilty enough to eat it anyway."

My stomach fluttered at his words, not because he was wrong but because he was so damn right... and he knew me so well. Better than anyone.

And I was *right there* on the edge of falling for him again. And when he left me this time, I didn't know how I was gonna let him go.

I peeled the paper off the cupcake and took a large bite. "Gah. Coconut."

"Yep. Enjoy every last strangely textured morsel," he said. His thumb and forefinger tapped out a little rhythm on his knee. "You wanna talk about what happened earlier?"

His tone said he definitely wanted to discuss it, but I shook my head slowly. Did I wanna talk about me being a jealous idiot? About how, when I'd seen him talking and laughing with Gideon, it had hit me like a sucker punch that sometime soon—next month or next summer or next year, it didn't matter when—he'd be gone, and all his jokes and his laughter and his smiles and his kisses would be someone else's? No, I did *not* want to fucking discuss it.

I didn't even wanna think about it.

But the door to the vault where I kept my thoughts of Parker was swinging wide open now, and suddenly, everything I didn't wanna think about was *right fucking there.*

The truth of the matter was, I wanted Parker Hoffstraeder right now more than I had ever wanted anything or anyone. More than I'd wanted a baseball scholarship. More than I'd wanted to save my dad. More than I wanted a drink—hell, I hadn't even thought about it since he'd been here. More than I wanted to fix my house. More, even, than I'd wanted Parker himself, back in the day.

I'd been without him for years now, wandering around in the darkness and wondering why I couldn't make connections the way other people did, and then, the second I'd let Parker back into my life, it was like someone had flipped on a light.

Now I realized that falling in love was the easiest thing in the universe... as long as I was falling in love with Parker.

Parker, who was gonna be leaving again.

This was what I'd been trying to insulate myself against for the past year... hell, for the past eleven years and six months, if I was being honest. I didn't know how to have Parker in my life halfway. I didn't know how to set limits and use restraint. I wanted him always, infinitely. I always had. I didn't know how to be polite strangers, or polite friends, or polite *anything*. The way I felt about Parker was not polite.

But looking at him now, in the half-shadowed light, I couldn't regret anything that had happened over the past weeks. Not one single second. Parker had shown me just how stuck I'd been—in my job, in my house, in my head. He'd changed me for the better.

Again.

And I didn't want to waste a minute of whatever time we had left.

"You know the first time I realized I wanted you?" I said.

Parker's gaze lifted to mine, his attention rapt. He shook his head.

"It was the day I hurt my arm. You remember? Coach dropped me off at the hospital after the game…"

Parker sighed angrily. "Oh, I remember alright. I remember your mom was out of town for work, and Molly was out, and your dad was wasted—"

"Probably more like mildly drunk," I corrected. "The truly *wasted* days happened after Molly died."

"Whatever. He was too inebriated to come to the hospital, even though you'd gotten hurt."

"Mmm," I agreed. "And you got your dad to take you to the ER to hang with me so I wouldn't be alone."

"Because you were practically throwing up from the pain!" he said, and it made me smile that he was still so outraged on my behalf all these years later. I swear, that man could make me smile about nearly anything. "You should never have been alone."

"I was scared to death," I continued. "Didn't wanna talk to anyone, even you."

Parker snorted. "Yeah, you've got a definite MO for dealing with unpleasant shit, don't you?"

"And you got it. You didn't make me talk. You just put your hand on my good arm. And you told me that I wasn't just good at baseball. That I could be good at whatever I put effort into being good at." I reached for his hand now, and he scooted closer so I could thread our fingers together. "I don't think I ever told you how much that meant to me, you know? That you sat there with me like that."

"Making you talk has never worked, has it?" he asked softly. "You have to get there yourself." He huffed out a frustrated breath.

"But you made it so I wasn't alone either. You made it better," I told him. "Just by being there. You always do."

It was as close as I could get to telling him how I felt about him.

Parker's fingers tightened and released, rubbing against mine, and it looked like he was fighting to say something or maybe to *not* say it. His green eyes came to mine, questioning and vulnerable, and he blurted. "I need to know, Jamie. What the hell did I do eleven years ago? How did I fuck things up?"

"What?"

"Because I would have sworn you loved me at the time," he continued in a rush. "You *told* me you loved me. And then suddenly… you didn't. And I shouldn't fucking care, because entire *oceans* of water have passed under that bridge, right? But we're doing this friends-with-benefits thing and I… I need to know why it ended before, so I don't make the same mistake again, okay? Did I break things somehow? Or were you, you know, exaggerating when you said you loved me? Because it's fine, if that's what it was. I… I mean, not fine. Definitely not *fine*. But I would get it. We were kids, and Molly had just died, and you were in a really bad place, and maybe you made our friendship into something it wasn't, and then you realized and backtracked and…" He swallowed. "I know it's breaking your damn rule to talk about this, but it's a stupid fucking rule. And I figure I've had your cock in my mouth enough times to earn this answer anyway."

It was the last thing I'd expected him to say. And it was shortsighted of me, because I *did* know Parker, and I maybe should have predicted that he'd take this on himself, but it had never occurred to me that he'd think our breakup was *his* fault. I'd said shit—the most insulting things I could think of, the things I knew would get to him most. And I wasn't proud of it, but I'd figured the end justified the means. I'd wanted him to be mad at me, mad enough to leave. Mad enough to reconsider what he wanted—whether he *really* wanted to tie himself permanently to a cranky asshole like me.

I'd regretted it almost immediately, and I'd gone to his house the next day to apologize, but it had been too late, and I'd figured that was exactly what I deserved.

But I'd never intended for him to *believe* me. Or for him to carry it this long.

And I had *sworn* to myself I would never talk about this. There was no reason to dredge up the past when it wouldn't solve anything anyway. After all, I was still the same cranky asshole who had nothing to offer him, except maybe I was worse now—working the same job, stuck in the same damn house—and Parker still had every reason to leave O'Leary.

But looking at his face, I saw the inevitability of this. There was nothing I wouldn't do for Parker. Nothing I wouldn't give up for him. My heart, my happiness… even Parker himself. And he deserved the truth.

At least, part of it.

"Jesus." I blew out a breath. "Parker… no. It was *never* about you doing something wrong. You were just… you. Brilliant and bright and curious. National Honor Society. National Merit Scholarship. Great plan to see the whole world, one country at a time." I smiled at the memory. "And I was… me. No baseball scholarship anymore. Dead-end job—that I'm still working, mind you." I laughed shortly. "Dad who was drinking way too much. Mom who had one foot out the door. Were you really gonna give all that up to stay here? No way."

Parker frowned, and his mouth opened slightly. "You said I was weak and clingy."

"I never said that."

"You implied it," he said more forcefully, snatching his hand away to run it through his hair.

I sighed. "I know."

"You told me you were tired of hearing me whine about how my parents wanted me to go to school. You said I should go. You said… you said you were done with me."

The pain in his eyes was so unmistakable, even in the dim light, that I had to shut my own to block it out… not that it worked. Even with my eyes shut, all I could see was him.

"We had plans to do things together," he said, angry now. "And you changed your mind."

"I didn't change—"

"You didn't want me."

"It had nothing to do with me not wanting you. I didn't want to *hold you back*. The guilt of it was killing me."

"So you decided *for* me?" he accused, incredulous. "You decided I should leave? And made me mad so I would?"

"I made it so you *could*. So you could leave without feeling guilty, if you wanted to. And you did."

"You manipulated me, Jamie."

"It wasn't like that," I insisted. "I did the right thing. Look at all you've accomplished! Look at all you have."

Parker scrubbed both hands over his face. "Yeah, Jamie. Look at all I have. A burned-out bar. A couple

hundred dollars in my checking account. And a friend…
with benefits."

"But that's temporary," I argued, shifting onto my
knees so I could run a hand over his head. "All of it. You're
gonna get your claim paid, Parks. You'll be back on your
feet and out of O'Leary in no time."

"Right." Parker pulled away from my hand. "You
know why I was with Gideon today? Because I was asking
him about the investigation."

"Yeah. I, ah… figured." I sat back on my heels.
"Eventually."

"Yeah, well. If your plan was to have our… *friendship
with benefits* fly under the radar until I'm gone, you fucked
yourself with that little display in the bakery. Were you
really jealous?"

"Doesn't matter." I shrugged. "It was stupid, and I'm
sorry if it made things awkward for you."

Parker blew out a breath. "You are impossible, you
know that?"

"What did Gideon say?"

"He told me to hang in there. Told me to be patient."

I snorted. "You hate being patient."

"Yeah," Parker said bitterly. "You have no idea. Must
be my competitive spirit, right?"

I bit back a retort. "Parks. I don't want to fight with
you."

"Oh, well then! I should just be quiet, shouldn't I?
Because things always have to be your way, no matter what
I want?"

"I really am sorry for being an asshole this afternoon.
But I'm not going to apologize for caring about you eleven
years ago, Parks. I'm not going to apologize for putting
your needs first."

"My needs." Parker snorted. "You're so fucking full of yourself, Jameson."

"I care about you," I told him. "I do. More than anyone in the whole damn world." I laid a hand on his cheek, feeling the rasp of his stubble. He flinched away from my touch, just a little, and it fucking killed me. "I want you to be happy," I whispered, rubbing my thumb over his mouth.

I could feel Parker's tension, the push-pull inside him, and I felt when he gave in. He let me turn his face toward mine, and his eyes, when he looked up at me, were sad.

Longing.

Parker Hoffstraeder knew me better than anyone on the planet. There was not a soul in the world who could read my thoughts, and understand my humor, and comfort me with a simple touch. But looking at him now, it occurred to me that for all the things we knew about each other, for all that we instinctively understood and always had, the most important things were still too fucking hard to discuss.

So maybe I needed to show Parker without words.

"Let me make you happy, Parks. Let me." For as long as we have left.

He closed his eyes for a second, breathing in and out, and finally nodded once.

I pulled my shirt off and threw it in the corner, then grabbed the hem of Parker's sweatshirt and dragged it up over his head. He lifted his arms without hesitation, helping me strip him so his entire torso was bare and nearly glowing in the darkness. I trailed my fingers lightly over his bare shoulders and down his arms, and he shivered in response. "Tell me what you want."

Parker laid himself down on the drop-cloth with his

hands above his head, a picture of total supplication. "Have me," he said simply. "Any way you like."

I frowned. This wasn't what I wanted at all—Parker *passive*, Parker *patient*.

"I thought I was gonna make *you* happy. Did you forget?"

Parker's lips turned up at one side in a small, sad smile. "Jamie. You being happy has always made me happy. Didn't you know?"

My breath caught.

I leaned over him, bracing my hands on the floor on either side of his head, and I leaned down to brush our lips together. It was electric—every time, always, inevitably—but there was a bittersweetness to it now. Parker wasn't leaving, and neither was I, but it almost felt like things were ending.

And maybe that had been inevitable too.

Everything good ended.

At least this time, I could say goodbye.

"You know what I want?" I said against his lips. "I want something we've never had before. Not with each other."

We'd talked around this once, weeks before, right after the storm, but neither of us had ever brought it up again. Maybe Parker, like me, had felt like it would be too much—too intimate, too final. Now, though, I craved that. Something I would remember forever.

"Yeah." Parker swallowed and nodded. "We can do that."

I pulled back a little and there was a little trepidation in his eyes, but resignation too. "You scared?"

He shook his head. "I'm not exactly a blushing virgin, Jameson. I play with a toy... kind of a lot, actually, when I jerk off."

And *holy shit*, that was enough to get my heart beating faster.

"Besides, I've bottomed before," he continued. "Topped too. I like both." He shrugged, and it made my heart squeeze with something that wasn't jealousy but deeper. More like regret. "We'll just go slow."

"Really slow." I cleared my throat. "Because I *am* a virgin. When it comes to bottoming, anyway. I'm gonna try not to blush but no promises."

Parker's eyes widened, but his gaze got more intense. "You?"

"Me."

I pushed to my feet and held out a hand so I could pull him to his feet. "But I think I'd like my first time to be in my bed. With lube." I grinned.

Parker let me pull him up, but when I tried to tow him to our... *my*... room, he resisted. "Are you sure, Jamie? This is... I mean, it's not necessarily a big deal, but..." He bit his lip. "It also is."

I nodded. "Yeah. So, come on. Show me what I've been missing."

But when I led him to the bedroom, turned on the light, and pulled down the quilt on the bed, I pushed *him* onto the mattress before he could say a word and laughed when he bounced.

I pulled each of his sneakers off and threw them over the bed in an arc so they landed on the floor.

"Hey, careful. Those are still the only shoes I own," he reminded me.

"Your side of the bed is the land where clothes go to perish." I pulled his feet apart so I could stand between his legs and stare down at him, all golden and gorgeous against the white sheets. "Shoes too."

"Not true." He pushed himself up on his elbows.

"So true. We have a hamper." I tilted my head towards the wicker basket near the door, just in case he might have missed it.

"That's your fault," Parker challenged. "I'm ordinarily a very tidy person. But *you* throw my clothes everywhere. Seems like *you* should pick them up."

"Is that so?" I leaned down to place a kiss to his stomach, feeling his muscles tense and quiver beneath my lips.

"It is. Case in point, where is my shirt? Hmm? It's been like this since I moved in. My wardrobe has suffered, but I try not to complain." He gave a put-upon sigh, and I found myself laughing.

"I see I have a lot to answer for," I agreed solemnly. I trailed my mouth up his chest, kissing a tiny birthmark, nipping at a little pink scar, licking the curve of his ribs, mapping the unique topography of Parker, committing every millimeter to memory.

"I… feel very forgiving suddenly," Parker said, and I laughed again.

It had always been this way. How had I ever forgotten? It was so easy between us—the fire and the laughter, the *love*—that I could almost believe it could be this way forever, that I could *will* it to be this way.

I unbuttoned his jeans and started to slip them down. Parker propped his feet flat on the bed and lifted his hips to help me. I got them as far as his knees before I was laughing again.

"You have Bob Ross's face on your underwear," I stated. "Why have I never seen these?"

"Oh." Parker grinned up at me. "I got a new package from Ethan yesterday. *Everyone needs a happy little friend, Jamie.*"

"So I see." I stared down at the underwear, reading the

text, then lifted my gaze to his. "I can't lie, babe. Bob Ross has never turned me on more than he is right now."

Parker snorted.

"I feel like I need a happy little friend." I skimmed my fingers over the silky fabric of the boxers, then leaned down so I could mouth his growing erection through the material.

"Take them off," Parker demanded. "You're basically frenching Bob Ross right now, Jamie. It's incredibly *not* hot."

"You think? Because my little friend seems to be enjoying himself immensely." I licked him through the slit of the boxers and he shuddered.

"If you think *my little friend* is gonna become a thing…" he began. But I pulled the waistband down so I could suck his tip into my mouth, and his threat ended with a groan.

"My little friend likes his name," I informed him. "You don't get a say."

"Your friend isn't little," he said, both breathless and cranky.

"Awww, is that the problem? You think I'm disparaging his size? Never happen. He's gonna feel fucking amazing in my ass." I licked up the underside of his cock once, braced a fist around his root, and relaxed the muscles of my throat so I could swallow him down. He was leaking already— salty and musky and sweet. Perfect.

"If you want him anywhere near your ass, you'd better stop," Parker warned, pulling at my hair a few minutes later. "I'm serious, Jamie, you've gotta—"

I let go with a pop, but his hands in my hair didn't loosen until I moved up his body to kiss him. It was wet and sloppy and tasted exactly like him.

"It's my turn," he said, pushing me to my back beside him. "That's what I want."

I nodded once, and he kicked his pants, socks, and boxers the rest of the way off without getting up. He grinned at me as he threw them in the air like confetti to land on the far side of the bed, near his shoes.

I snickered, and Parker laughed out loud.

"Also my fault?" I demanded.

"So… totally… *completely* your fault." He ran his palm over my beard and then down to grab the belt loop of my jeans and pull me toward him. "I want you so much, Jamie. It makes me crazy."

I was familiar with that feeling.

But when he kissed me, it wasn't crazed or frantic, it was slow. A nudge of his nose against mine, a brush of our lips, the slide of his fingers across my lower back, just flirting with my waistband. It was like when we were kids, when all those little touches were new and thrilling and forbidden. Like we had all the time in the world and nothing would ever come between us.

Jamie and Parker.

Parker and Jamie.

Forever and ever, amen.

I pulled him so he was lying mostly on top of me and tilted his head to the side so I could kiss his neck, loving the way he groaned and arched against me.

I'd never been a musician, but I figured making love was a lot like music. The notes were familiar, practiced, but every time you played them, you could find new meaning. Deeper meaning.

And *Jesus*. Look who was calling it *making love* all of a sudden. But it didn't feel hokey when it described what was happening between me and Parker. It felt… accurate.

Parker pushed me back with a moan and a narrow-eyed glare. "You know what that does to me."

"Yeah," I agreed. My thumb stroked over his hipbone,

just inches from his jutting erection. "And I bet I'm the only one who does. Aren't I?"

Parker narrowed his eyes but didn't answer, which was as good as confirmation. He slid off the bed and pulled open the drawer with enough force that both the drawer and its contents fell onto the ground.

"Shit," he muttered, all flustered and adorable as he bent down to retrieve it. I sat up, bracing myself on my hands to watch him. "I can do this. I have done this before. This is not a big deal."

He found the lube and tossed it on the bed, then threw everything back in the drawer, slammed it shut, and turned toward me.

"Condom?" I suggested helpfully.

"Fuck." He opened the drawer, more gently this time, and started moving shit around.

"Take your time," I told him. "We're not in any rush. And look. I can help."

I sat up all the way, unbuttoning my jeans and opening my fly to give my erection some breathing room, then pushed my jeans and underwear off completely.

Parker stopped his frantic searching so he could stare at my cock, then my face, then my cock again. He swallowed, and his eyes came to mine. "You suck," he informed me. "You suck *so* hard."

"Sometimes," I agreed. I wrapped a hand around my erection and his eyes dropped like they were guided by a homing beacon as I jacked myself slowly, more turned on by his gaze than by my own touch. "You having trouble there, Parks?"

"No," Parker said, holding up a strip of condoms triumphantly. "I've got it."

But he didn't make a move to come back on the bed.

I grinned. "What are you waiting for? I'm getting older here."

"Lie down," he said softly.

"I'm lying—"

"Down. All the way."

I frowned, still half-smiling, but complied. "I could kinda learn to get off on you being boss—Parker?"

He kissed my hip, right near my cock, but not nearly close enough. Then his lips wandered up my torso, kissing every freckle—and God knew I had plenty—along the way. It was the exact same thing I'd done to him earlier and I wondered if he knew what I'd been trying to convey with the gesture. I wondered if he was trying to convey the same thing.

"You are gorgeous," he whispered between kisses. "And talented. And funny. And smart. And generous. And good."

"Did it seem like I needed a pep talk?" I teased, when his lips hit my collar bone, but it came out like a whisper because I couldn't hide how much his words meant.

"Maybe a little," Parker agreed. "And maybe I just felt like it was something I wanted to say. Something you ought to know."

He kissed my shoulder, my bicep, the scars from the operations that had made it so I could still use my arm, though never well enough for baseball again, and I swallowed against the lump in my throat. And it shouldn't have been *sexy* that he was getting all sappy, but it was. I wanted his skin on my skin. I wanted him inside me. "Parker, I—"

"Turn over," he said, like he could read my mind. And about this stuff, I was kinda convinced he could.

He arranged a pillow beneath my hips and straddled my legs from behind before running both hands over my ass, stroking the muscles there.

I took a sharp breath because *holy fuck*. It felt momentous and hot as sin and a little scary, the way the unknown is always scary. But I wanted it. No doubt about that. I wanted Parker to take me. Wanted to give this to him.

Parker's hands stilled, and he grabbed the bottle of lube from somewhere near my elbow. I heard the cap crack open, felt the cool liquid slide between my legs, and heard Parker's breath go ragged as he ran his finger over my hole... and that was when I realized I'd closed my eyes. Because there was nothing to see from this angle—everything I cared about was happening behind me, and I didn't want to miss a single second of it.

And God, that was even worse than *making love*.

I was turning this into something it wasn't. A religious experience. A consummation. A promise, when that wasn't—

"Oh fuck yes," I groaned, as his finger pushed inside me slowly. It burned, yeah, but in the best possible way. The brand of ownership I'd been craving. "More."

"We're going slow," Parker said. "Nice and slow."

"I thought you hated being patient," I insisted. "Give me another."

"For you, Jamie?" Parker whispered. "It looks like I've got all kinds of patience."

I tried to lift myself up, to push myself back, to *take* more when he wouldn't give it, but he pushed between my shoulder blades and forced me down. "For once, you'll take what *I* give you," he said. "See how it feels to have someone else in control."

I was pretty sure he meant that as a warning, but to me, it sounded pretty damn good. I didn't trust the world farther than I could throw it, and I wouldn't trust *myself* for one second, but Parker? Parker, apparently, I trusted.

So I tried to make myself patient as he rocked against me, as he opened me slowly and the single finger inside me became two and then three. I squeezed my eyes shut and listened for the tiny sounds—the slick of the lube and the rasp of my beard against the sheet beneath us. I savored the feel of my erection sliding against the pillowcase and the way Parker's breathing hitched every time his fingers sank into my ass. I knew without knowing that he was picturing his cock owning me, and that he was every bit as excited about it as I was, which made me want it even more.

I banged the side of my fist against the mattress. "Parker, please, baby."

Finally, *finally*, he withdrew his fingers. "Okay," he said, leaning forward to sink his teeth into my shoulder. His cock —the hard, smooth length of it—left precum where it rubbed against my back, and I groaned, hanging my head. "Are you sure you want this, Jamie? Are you a hundred percent sure?"

I pushed up on both hands and turned to look at him over my shoulder. "How could I be anything but a thousand percent positive, Parker? Do it now."

Parker bit his lip and pushed himself up onto his knees. He grabbed one of the condom packets, fumbled it slightly, and stopped to settle himself, one hand wrapped around the base of his dick like he was in danger of coming.

I dropped my head.

"Please, baby," I said again, knowing that it would spur him on. "Please."

Parker inhaled sharply and a second later, he was sinking inside me.

"This… it's…" Fuck. The fullness, the slide, the fact that it was Parker… it was incredible.

"Good?" Parker sounded drunk. "Because you are so tight, Jameson. And I am trying to be patient, but I think…"

"You're tired of waiting?" I demanded breathlessly. "Do it. Move."

He pushed back and surged forward and… holy fucking hell. "Jesus Christ."

Parker laughed—I didn't know where he got the oxygen. "If I were you, I'd be making a joke right now about names."

"If you were me, you'd be getting… Oh, *shit!*" I said as he tagged my prostate. "It feels like I'm being jerked from inside." It was so much better than anything I'd ever accomplished with my own fingers.

Parker huffed again. "You're like a poet." But his hips sped up and he demanded, "Tell me more. Tell me exactly what it's doing to you."

He wanted dirty talk? I could give Parker dirty talk.

"It feels like you're fucking huge," I told him honestly. "Like, *I will never make a little joke again* huge."

He snorted. "What else?"

"It feels like… *ah*, fuck. Like this is exactly what I've been missing." The words came tumbling from my lips like he'd fucked the honesty out of me. *Shit.* "It feels like you're exactly where you're supposed to be."

"My dick?"

"Yeah, Parks," I lied. "Obviously your giant dick. *Harder.*"

"Tell me what you missed," he demanded. "Tell me. Did you miss *me?*"

"*Every damn day*," I growled. "Every day. While you were gone, when you were back. I have missed you every day that we weren't doing this."

"You could've been fucked anytime, by anyone. Why *me*, Jamie?" He pistoned his hips harder so the smacking sound of skin on skin reverberated around the room. "Why did you wait for me?"

"Because." I slid one hand out from under me and down between the pillow and my cock. Parker grabbed my arm and pulled my hand away.

"Not yet," he demanded. "Because *why*?"

Fuck. Fuck, it was so good. I couldn't last. I could feel my orgasm coming, all I needed was the tiniest bit of friction.

"Parker!"

Parker's voice was breathless. "Answer me, goddammit."

"Because it had to be you." Shit.

"But *why*, Jameson. Tell me!"

It didn't even matter anymore. This was Parker, after all, so why not?

"Because I love you. Because I have loved you forever. Because it's never been right with anyone else. And it never will be."

Parker pulled me up onto my hands and knees, sliding the pillow away so he could wrap his hand around me, jerking me in time with his thrusts. It took two thrusts, three, four, and that was it. I was coming all over the sheets, all over myself, arching my neck back and screaming at the ceiling because nothing had ever felt so good.

Parker grabbed my shoulders and thrust harder, working himself into me with abandon, like he was as eager to mark me as I was to be marked, like he wanted to ruin me as much as I wanted to be ruined. And then he came with a shout also, filling the condom inside me, completing the connection, because nothing made me happier than knowing Parker was happy…

Especially when he wrapped his arms around my chest from behind and whispered in my ear, "I love you too, Jamie. I always have."

Chapter Eleven

I woke up grinning.

The sun was shining in the window, Jamie Burke was wrapped around me from behind and snoring lightly in my ear, and I couldn't imagine wanting anything beyond what I had right then and there.

Money? A job? *Pfft.* That shit would sort itself out.

I was in love. I was well rested. And, in probably related news, Jamie Burke loved me too.

I couldn't remember the last time I hadn't tossed and turned for hours every night, waking up at three and four and five before forcing myself out of bed. Even staying here at Jamie's, even sleeping in his bed, hadn't entirely rid me of my nightmares. But last night... last night was different.

Apparently love did that to a person.

I threaded my fingers with Jamie's where they lay against my stomach, and stretched just a little. Jamie's snoring cut off, and he pushed his morning erection against my ass.

Okay, maybe I could think of *something* else to wish for.

"Morning," Jamie said, his voice a sleepy growl that had my dick immediately perking up. He scooted his head closer and pressed a kiss to my neck. "Sleep well?"

I twisted my head to smile at him.

"I don't think I've ever slept better in my life."

"Is that so?" Jamie slipped his hand from mine and slid his fingers down to wrap around my cock. "Parts of you do seem very perky this morning."

"Please," I scoffed. "That's not *this* morning; it's every morning. That's you looking at me. Or touching me. Or existing in my vicinity."

"Sounds uncomfortable," Jamie said sympathetically, stroking me lightly.

"You have no idea."

"Have you thought about having this problem checked out?"

Jamie's phone vibrated on his nightstand, but he ignored the clatter, and I sure as fuck couldn't care less, not while he was jacking me so nicely.

I bit my lip and groaned, turning my head into the pillow. "Nah. I've, ah… been managing the symptoms on my own."

Jamie *tsked* and his hand tightened around me. "That's never good, Parks. You should be seen by a professional."

"Yeah?" I breathed. "You know anyone?"

"Just so happens," Jamie said, "that I am *kind of* an expert at this. I could help you out. For a price."

"Wow! How… lucky." I pushed my hips forward, thrusting against his hand, and it felt so good my toes curled. "What kind of fees do you charge? Because I'm concerned that my insurance won't cover this kind of procedure."

Jamie snorted and buried his nose against my neck. "That's why I only bill directly."

His phone clattered on the nightstand again, and he huffed a breath that warmed my skin. "People need to get a life. It's barely seven thirty," he muttered. But his hand didn't stop moving, which I took to be a very good sign that he wasn't going to let anyone distract us.

"I don't have much money to pay you," I said sadly, getting us back on track. "I'd imagine a professional like yourself could command a really high price."

"It's true," Jamie growled. He nudged his cock against my ass again. "But I have a whole different pay scale in mind for you."

"*Shit.*" I reached back and gripped his hip, pulling him more tightly against me.

Jamie hissed slightly, and I turned my head, not understanding… until suddenly I did.

"Sore?"

Jamie grunted an affirmative, but that didn't stop him from nudging against me again.

"Poor thing."

"I'm definitely not complaining," Jamie said. "More like, wondering how many more times we can do that before you go…"

Jamie's doorbell rang, and I felt him tense behind me.

"Are you fucking kidding me?" he demanded of no one in particular. "Who rings someone's doorbell unannounced?"

"Girl Scouts with cookies?" I suggested. "Missionaries? Gutter salesmen? Sexy, twinky bottoms who get lost in the rain and break down on a deserted road right in front of a sex club full of horny tops?"

Jamie relaxed against me again. "Parker, why does this stuff never come up on *my* porn searches?"

"Porn with plot subreddit," I said solemnly. "It'll change your life."

"I think I'd prefer to— *Shit.*" The doorbell became insistent knocking on the front door.

"You could ignore them," I suggested. "It'd be kinda unprofessional of you to leave a patient in this condition. Your reputation might suffer."

Jamie laughed. But when the doorbell ringing started again, he groaned against my neck. "They're not going away, are they?"

"Go." I pulled his hand off me and pressed a kiss to his palm. "Just fucking get rid of them."

"I'm gonna kill whoever it is," Jamie said, rolling over and grabbing his jeans from the floor. "What do we know about hiding bodies?"

I laughed. "I'll google it. Hey!" I demanded, when he started for the hall still naked from the waist up. "Shirt?"

"Right." He went to the closet and grabbed a sweat-shirt blindly from the shelf. It happened to be one of mine, and no lie, seeing the Boston logo across his broad chest did *nothing* to make my erection go away.

"If it *is* Girl Scouts, buy out their entire stock first!" I called. "I like the mint ones! And if it's a twinky bottom—"

Jamie tossed me a look over his shoulder.

"Tell him we're busy," I finished meekly.

He grinned and pulled the door closed.

"Ugh." I flopped back against the pillows and smiled up at the ceiling.

It was fine. Totally fine.

Jamie would come back to bed and we'd finish. And if it was someone important at the door, we'd have another chance to finish tomorrow. And the next day. And the day after that. Little bubbles of excitement popped and fizzed in my stomach like champagne.

I was going to live in O'Leary. I was going to live with

Jameson Burke. And we were finally, finally going to have that future I'd dreamed of.

We hadn't talked about things yet, but that was just a formality after everything that had happened yesterday.

Jamie's voice floated in from down the hall, loud and insistent. I grinned to myself. If my guy assaulted a gutter salesman, I'd totally bail him out… but maybe it'd be better if it didn't come to that. I pulled on a pair of clean underwear and jeans, then grabbed one of Jamie's shirts— an old yellow t-shirt that said "O'Leary Summer Picnic 2014" in a circle around a cartoon sun—because it was only fair to steal his clothes back. Then I padded barefoot down the hall to find some coffee.

The voices were coming from the kitchen, indicating that this wasn't a stray salesman or missionary, and I sighed. I didn't want to invade Jamie's privacy, but the coffee was in that direction, and if I was going to be upright, I needed some.

"Look, it's not a big deal, Jameson, I'm just returning your stuff."

I hesitated outside the kitchen doorway and frowned, unable to place the voice.

"I'm not sure how you got this stuff to begin with." Jamie sounded bewildered. "I didn't give you any of these things, Brian."

Brian. I inhaled sharply.

You have no reason to be jealous, I reminded myself.

I was the one in Jamie's bed, after all. The one in his house, the one in his life, the one in his heart.

But I was starting to get what Jamie must've been feeling when he saw me with Gideon yesterday, because I knew if I walked into the kitchen right then, I'd grab the asshole by the elbow and bodily eject him from the house. Logic played no part in it.

"We were together a long time," Brian continued. "I must have borrowed them and not remembered."

"It wasn't that long," Jamie began. He stopped and blew out a breath. "You know what? *Whatever.* Thanks for returning them. I appreciate it." His voice had an unmistakable edge of *and now you should leave* that somewhat appeased me.

"I, um, also brought you some of that coffee you like," Brian said. "You know, the expensive Hawaiian kind."

Jamie sighed. "I wish you hadn't done that."

"But it was on sale, and you said it was *orgasmic.*"

What the fuck coffee was this? Why had I never heard of it? Why did I not know Jamie had a particular coffee he orgasmed over?

"I've never used that word in my life," Jamie said wryly. "But I did like it a lot." He hesitated. "Thank you. That was really sweet."

"Because I'm a sweet sort of person. You could make me some," Brian suggested. "We could talk."

"Brian." Jamie blew out a breath. "I think we've said all we need to say to each other."

"Now, that's not true," Brian said. "Remember, we were friends before we were anything else."

Jamie said nothing, and I found myself scowling. He and Brian had been *friends*?

"Which is why I was kind of upset that I had to hear about the damage to your house from Enrique Poole. You know I would have done the work for you *gratis.* And I would've finished it faster than Riq did too."

"I'm not using a contractor," Jamie said. "And it's going fine. But thank you."

"You? Are doing it yourself?" Brian was openly skeptical.

I waited for Jamie to explain that I'd been doing most

of the work. That I'd been helping him, at least, but all he said was, "I'm capable of painting and… stuff."

"Right. Remember a couple years ago when you tried to replace the outlet in your bedroom and ended up frying your whole electrical panel? And you were all, '*But I swear I turned it off.*'" He laughed, and to my horror, Jamie laughed too.

"That was a long time ago," Jamie said. "And painting is a lot easier than electrical anyway."

"But drywalling? Do I even wanna see what it looks like?"

Brian's voice came closer, and before I could move—though, like, where the fuck was I gonna go? And why should I have had to move anyway?—he stepped out of the kitchen and spotted me.

"Oh," he said. Then he spotted my shirt, which was obviously Jamie's shirt, and said again, more loudly, "*Oh.*"

"Fuck." Jamie stopped in the doorway and hung his head, rubbing a hand over his forehead. With the other hand, he gestured between me and Brian. "Uh, Brian, this is Parker. Parker, Brian."

"I know," Brian and I said at the same time… which could have been funny, but wasn't.

Not even a little.

"Well, isn't this cozy?" Brian said, folding his arms over his chest. "So many things are suddenly crystal clear. Like, why you suddenly broke up with me when things between us had never been better."

"Brian," Jamie said, shaking his head. "That's just not true. None of it."

Brian narrowed his eyes at Jamie. "You're saying you didn't have feelings for him while we were together?"

"I… no," Jamie said, darting a glance at me. "No. This all started after we broke up."

I snorted. *Like, ten minutes after.*

Jamie gave me a look that said I wasn't helping. "Parker and I… We have history. You know this."

"Of course I know about your *history*," Brian put his fingers up in air quotes. "The whole town knows about your history. But *you* told me two years ago that you and Parker were done. That you'd been kids. That you didn't love him anymore! Was that a lie?"

I turned to Jamie and tilted my head to the side. *Tell him,* I tried to tell Jamie telepathically. *Tell him it's always been me. Tell him.*

"It wasn't a *lie*," Jamie said instead, and I tried to tell myself I wasn't disappointed. "I didn't… I just… I was angry at Parker for a long time, and—"

"Angry?" Brian demanded. "Why, if you were done with him? If you were just kids?"

"Yeah, good question, Brian." And one Jamie really hadn't answered. "You wanted me to leave town. You *told* me to go. For altruistic purposes," I explained to Brian. "So I could be *free*."

Brian rolled his eyes, and I nodded. He got me.

"Yeah, I did," Jamie allowed. "But—"

"But?"

Jamie hesitated. "Forget it."

"Forget it?" I exchanged an incredulous glance with Brian. "It's like you don't know me at all," I told Jamie.

"Seriously," Brian said. "When, in the history of forgetting things, has anyone ever told someone to forget something and had them forget it? How would that even work?"

"Thank you." I pointed at Brian and nodded, then glared at Jamie. "Why the fuck were you angry at me?"

"I wasn't angry."

"You just said you were," Brian pointed out.

"Damn it." Jamie searched the ceiling for patience. "Angry's not the right word. I was… upset. Because—"

"Yes?" I encouraged.

"Because—"

"We're waiting," Brian said.

"For fuck's sake! I was upset because you *went*," Jamie finally exploded.

"You told me—"

"I know! I know, Parker. I told you to go. But I didn't totally expect that you *would*. Like, it was just that easy. Like you'd already had one foot out the door and were just waiting for a push." He shook his head. "I expected you to protest. I expected that you'd come back at some point, after the first year, and… you didn't."

"Why the hell would I?" I demanded. "Why would I come back when there was nothing here for me but my parents, who saw me plenty whenever they came to Boston for holidays, and when every fucking second in this town would remind me that you and I weren't together?"

Jamie blinked.

"And why," I demanded, "didn't you fucking call me? Why didn't you email? Or send a… a… what do you call those things with the Morse code?"

"Telegram," my new best friend Brian supplied. "*Yeah*. Come on, Jamie. You could even have sent a gorilla-gram."

I swung my gaze to Brian, who shrugged. "I once dressed up like a gorilla to ask Jamie to move in with me," he explained. "It was mildly mortifying and not at all effective. Do not recommend."

Oh. Shit. I had heard this story a couple months back from Julian Ross, and at the time, I'd laughed my ass off imagining Jamie, who'd always hated public displays, being accosted by this guy in a gorilla suit professing his love.

Now, though, it seemed really sweet, if somewhat misguided.

"That sounds *lovely*," I told Brian. "Except Jamie hates PDA and doesn't like O'Leary knowing his business. *Apparently*, he doesn't like the guys he's dating knowing his business either. We're supposed to *guess*."

Jamie rolled his eyes and huffed. "Why would I have called you when you were clearly doing well in Boston, Parker? I figured if you needed me or... or *wanted* me, you would've gotten in touch."

"After *you* broke up with *me*," I clarified. "After you called me weak and told me you were tired of my shit, you thought I should just call you. To, what? Take your temperature? See if you'd been *joking* or *testing me* when you broke up with me, and actually wanted to get back together? That's the stupidest—" I glanced at Brian. "Uh."

Brian waved a hand. "No, you're right. It *is* stupid. Learned *that* lesson." He glared at Jamie now too.

"You claim you broke up with me because you were being all noble and concerned about my needs." I took a step closer to Jamie and his gaze grew wary. "*Fuck that.* If you were concerned about *my* needs, you wouldn't have said the shit you said." I shook my head. "This was about *you* not wanting to do the work of being in a relationship. Wasn't it? Do you even consider us in a relationship *now*?"

Jamie's mouth opened and closed, but he didn't answer.

"Preach, sister," Brian said. "The man has no concept of how to communicate."

"You told me you loved me, Jameson, but you didn't love me enough to keep me. And even now? You wanna be friends with benefits so we can fuck and flirt and be *in love*, but you still don't have to risk anything. It's easy, isn't it, to just drift along? To never make a decision, or clean out a room, or go after something you want?"

"It is *not* easy!" Jamie's eyes were all-the-way dark, and the pain I read there almost made me want to back down, to pause and reconsider.

Almost.

Because I was hurting too. And it sucked.

"If you love me, Jamie—"

"You know I do," he shot back. Brian gasped. "But what does it matter when you're *leaving*? When everything you want is out there waiting for you?" He waved a hand in the direction of everything that wasn't O'Leary.

"If you love me," I repeated, "then tell me not to leave. Tell me to stay."

Jamie stared at me and his throat worked, like the words were stuck there.

"Just fucking *say* it," I demanded, and *of course* there were tears in my eyes because *of course* I had to make a mess of myself in front of Jamie. "Three words. Stay. Here. Parker. That's it. I'm waiting."

"Uh, Parker—" Brian started, but I made a cutting motion with my hand. This was between me and Jamie, and I needed him to say the damn words.

To tell me that the fucking pipe dream I'd been deluding myself into believing was *real.*

To tell me that we were gonna be together this time.

That he'd fight for me.

That I wasn't gonna end up getting hurt again.

But Jamie said nothing. Not a single word.

And my heart cracked right down the center.

I forced myself to nod. "Okay. Alright, then. Good to know. I'm gonna go... shower. I think." I turned away, but Jamie stepped forward and grabbed my wrist.

"Parker." His voice was wrecked. "I need to talk to you. Privately. To explain. I…"

"There's nothing to explain, Jamie. Really."

Okay, there were epic mountains of things I'd love for him to explain, but I didn't think I could stand to hear any of it right then.

"I love you," he repeated.

I nodded again. It was apparently possible to feel completely hollow and heavy as lead at the same time. *How interesting*.

"I love you too," I said, smiling just a little. "A lot. Love's never been our problem, though, has it? We spark like a flame to paper and always have. Trouble is, it takes more than a spark to build a fire and keep it going. We're basically a pair of toddlers playing with matches. We keep hurting ourselves and each other. It's better if I go."

"Parks, please," Jamie said. "Don't leave like this."

"Like this." I smiled. "So close to what I need you to say, but so far."

I turned and walked down the hall to our… no, *Jamie's* room. The bed looked so freakin' comfortable, still warm from our bodies and the closeness that we'd shared literal *minutes* ago. I wanted so badly to just crawl back in there and pull the covers up.

Because ignoring shit had worked so well for me up until now.

Fuck the shower. I needed to get away. I grabbed my backpack from the closet and started randomly throwing in shirts and jeans—mine, Jamie's, I didn't even care, I just wanted to get some stuff together and leave the house before I lost my composure entirely.

I felt it when Jamie came into the room. The sadness and confusion were coming off him in waves and I got it. I *so* got it. Being with him last night had started out like goodbye, but by the end, it felt like we'd reached a turning point. Figured that we'd managed to turn ourselves around a full three hundred and sixty degrees, so we were back at The End.

"Brian's waiting for you," I said. "Don't be rude."

"Brian can go fuck himself. Were you serious? Are you leaving?"

I turned and found him standing by the bed, watching me intently. The look on his face would have broken my heart if it weren't already broken.

"Why should I stay, Jamie?"

He ran a hand over his mouth. "If you don't know… I guess I don't know either."

"Yeah." I slung my backpack over my shoulder. "Take care of yourself, okay?"

I pressed a kiss to his cheek and walked around him out the door. Jamie made no move to stop me.

———

"So you just *left*?" Cal demanded. "Just grabbed your bag and flounced?"

"I did not *flounce*!" I informed him. "I walked. Slowly. Deliberately. *Maturely*."

"You flounced," Cal repeated, not a question this time.

"Babe." Ash gave Cal a secret smile and put a hand on his upper back in a half-restraining, half-supportive, totally loving gesture that made me wanna stab someone.

I made a disgusted noise and reached for the bottle of whiskey in the center of their little dining table. My mug already contained more Irish than coffee, but it wasn't enough.

I'd known from the minute I walked into the bakery this morning, not sure if I wanted to cry or get drunk or find a yurt someplace in Mongolia where I could be alone, that I'd picked the wrong place to turn for sympathy and commiseration. Sure, Cal and Ash had immediately taken me upstairs to their apartment, leaving Moira to run the bakery, and they'd plied me with caffeine and alcohol until I'd spewed the whole sorry story to them, but they'd also sat next to each other the whole time, and the aura of *couple* in the air was thicker than syrup.

Vomit.

Cal and Ash had gotten engaged over Valentine's Day. Now the pair sported matching platinum rings that caught the light and identical sappy expressions every time they looked at one another, which was approximately every four seconds. When one of them moved, the other moved too in a kind of instinctive harmony that reminded me of me and Jamie, except that with Cal and Ash it was *real*. They'd always been rock-solid and schmoopy as hell—but now they were even solid-er. Like concrete. Or granite. Or something.

"Whass harder than granite?" I demanded.

Cal and Ash stopped eye-fucking each other and turned to me. Cal rolled his eyes, but Ash's widened with worry. "Parker, maybe that's enough whiskey," he suggested. "Maybe I could make you a sandwich? Or I've got some leftover chana masala? It's almost lunch time."

"Is your leftover chana masala going to make me feel less shitty about the fact that Jameson Burke, who I have loved since I was a teeny, tiny baby, doesn't love me enough to want me to stay in O'Leary and build a life with him?" I demanded, and the whine in my own voice made me cringe.

I tried to dig deep for some reserve of strength or pride, to put a happy smile on my face, but I came up empty. I *wasn't* fine. I couldn't pretend this was fine. My dad would be horrified, but I couldn't make myself care.

I'd let myself fall into the trap of *friends with benefits*, with Jameson Burke no less, and the whole situation had exploded in my face, as any idiot could have predicted.

Any idiot but me.

I took another gulp of coffee, enjoying the dual burn of the heat and the alcohol.

"Yes," Cal said, getting to his feet. "Yes, it will make you feel better. Because while Ash heats it up, you're gonna go take a shower." He took the coffee mug from my hand and gave it to Ash, who brought it to the sink and dumped it out without a word.

"Hey! I was enjoying that!"

"But it's hard to drink in the shower," Cal said reasonably, pulling me out of the chair by my elbow. He grabbed my bag from the sofa, where he'd tossed it earlier, and shoved me toward their bathroom. "And I have things to tell you that you're gonna need to sober up to really hear."

I stopped in the hall. "I don't want to shower. Couldn't we go key someone's car?"

From the kitchen, I heard Ash huff out a laugh.

"Key someone's car," Cal repeated dryly. "Sure, Parks. Anyone in particular?"

I frowned. "I dunno. Jamie's probably. Except I really like his truck. I have a key to his truck. Did you know?"

Cal sighed. "Shower, Parker."

"And I have a key to his house too. He gave me those things. And I thought they meant something." I sniffed. "But they didn't."

"So you said."

"And I fell in love with him again. But that's not a shock because I loved him all along, really. And I *never* just wanted to be friends with benefits." I grabbed Cal's hand because it was important that he understand. "I *never* did. But I did it anyway. For him. Because I love him." I sniffed. "But it wasn't good enough. *Love* isn't good enough."

"Shit, Parker." Cal shoved my shoulder toward the bathroom. "You do like to create problems for yourself, don't you, buddy?"

"What? No! That's the *trouble*, Caelan!" I spun to face him, then threw a hand out to catch myself against the bathroom door when the world suddenly tilted too fast. "I didn't make problems or make waves or make *any fucking thing*. I just… I sat. I… was patient." I leaned against the wall. "I waited for other people to sort their shit so I could sort mine. And I… I don't wanna wait for shit to be sorted anymore. You get me? *I* am going to sort *my own* shit."

"Oh, I get you," Cal agreed. He reached behind me to turn the knob, and the door gave way beneath my hand, causing me to stumble into the tiny room. "And you *are* gonna sort your shit. I'm gonna help you."

"I am going to be a man of action!" I proclaimed, propping my ass against the vanity. "I'm going to make plans, and I'm going to *do the plans*."

"Do all the plans. Yup." Cal moved to turn on the water.

"And no one will stop me. *Jamie Burke* will not stop me!"

"Jesus Christ," Cal muttered under his breath. "How much whiskey did Ash put in that drink?"

"Not enough, so I added more."

"Of course you did. Okay, get in there. Wash off the Jameson." Cal snorted to himself. "Best joke I'll make all year and you're too drunk to appreciate it."

"That's not true," I said solemnly. "I appreciate you very much, Cal."

Cal rolled his eyes. "Good. I hope you appreciate it when I explain how this situation is mostly your fault."

"*My* fault?" I leaned toward him. "Perhaps you haven't heard my *words*, Caelan."

"Dear God, you've been talking at me for two hours, Parks. I've heard *all* your words. And all about Jamie's words. And about your strange fascination with yurts, and how Brian Carr is actually a really decent guy, and how competitive yoga should be a *very real, very serious* thing." He rolled his eyes as the room began to fill with steam. "And as your friend, I'm about to give you what my grandmother likes to call a Come to Jesus. You ready?"

"Maybe?"

Cal nodded. "Ya fucked up."

"No!" I shook my head. "Cal! Cal, Cal, Cal. How can you fuck up when you haven't done anything? When you let other people call the shots and you just… you just… *smile through* and *be strong*? You see?" I said patiently. "When I don't *do* things, I can't be at fault."

"Oh, I see. You're good at anything if you don't try. Everyone's a winner until they play their cards. But you're missing the—" He broke off and shook his head. "Nope. *Nope*. Shower first. Then chana masala. And when you're a little more sober, I'll explain how your mind is a logical wasteland." He grabbed a towel from under the sink and hung it on a hook for me. "But don't worry, Parks. This is a good thing. This means *you* can fix it."

He winked, then pulled the door shut behind him.

I found I had to sit on the toilet lid to get my jeans all the way off, which suggested that Cal might have had a point about the whiskey, but about the rest? Not a chance. If Cal thought that running water was going to somehow change the basic facts of the situation, then love had damaged his brain.

I stood under the hot spray for a while, trying to decide where to go from here. What came next? If my lack of money and my lack of job weren't factors, I asked myself, what would I want to do?

But the only thing I could picture when I closed my eyes was Jamie's face when I'd left the house earlier… and the memory made me want to vomit even more than Cal and Ash's schmoopiness had.

How the hell were you supposed to walk away from someone you cared about, even when they hurt you? Even when they were a stupid, dumb, idiotic… *idiot*, who refused to go all in and take the risk of being in a real relationship?

I shut off the water and wrapped up in the towel, then propped my backpack on the vanity to take stock of my clothing choices. Two pairs of Jamie's jeans that were too big for me, a bunch of his t-shirts, a pair of rainbow polka dot underwear, and no socks.

Jesus. Five-year-olds packed to run away from home with more efficiency than this. *Mostly because they know they won't actually leave*, a voice in my head whispered, but I tried to tune it out.

I pulled on the underwear and jeans, taking a second to cuff them first, and then grabbed a shirt randomly and pulled it on. It smelled like Jamie—like the lemon-lavender laundry detergent he loved—and my stomach clenched.

"You done?" Cal called. "Food's ready."

I swiped my towel across the condensation on the mirror and took stock of my reflection. My eyes were red, my cheeks were bristly, and my hair was a mess. I looked… fragile. I looked like a guy who sat around waiting for other people to decide his fate, because that's exactly what I'd been doing.

I shoved my pajamas into my bag, then tossed the bag onto the sofa in the living room before heading back to the kitchen. There was a steaming plate of food and a glass of water where my Irish coffee had been, and Cal was sitting in the seat opposite mine with his hands folded on the table.

"Better?" Cal asked as I sat down. "Clear head?"

"Maybe a little," I allowed. "Food smells incredible." I took note of his posture. "Is this an intervention?"

Ash, who was leaning against the wall by the kitchen door, smiled, but Cal raised an eyebrow. "Do you *need* an intervention?"

I picked up my fork. "Definitely not."

"Nice shirt," Cal commented, nodding toward my chest. "I had no idea you were on the Camden-O'Leary Varsity Baseball Team in 2005."

I took a bite of the fragrant food in front of me and realized I hadn't eaten all day. "Jameson never throws away a shirt." I rolled my eyes. "Or a piece of furniture. Or a book. Or a trophy. Or *any damn thing*."

Cal and Ash exchanged another of their looks, and I tried not to notice.

"Then do you think it's likely he just throws away guys he's in love with?" Ash said gently.

I paused with my fork halfway to my mouth. I'd sort of expected Cal to be the one making pointed comments. Ash was usually the quiet one.

"I don't think he's throwing me away," I said, setting my fork down. "He's just… not interested enough in keeping me."

"See, the law frowns on keeping people against their will." Cal folded his arms across his chest. "And you're a legal adult, Parker."

I narrowed my eyes and reached for my fork again.

"So, what? I'm just supposed to decide to stay? '*Hey, Jamie, guess what? We're in a relationship now, whether you like it or not!*'" I snorted. "Pretty sure the law frowns on that too."

Cal leaned back in his seat. "Did you or did you not tell me that Jamie admitted he broke up with you back in the day because he wanted you to have a better life than he thought you could have in O'Leary?"

"Oh, that's what he said," I agreed around a mouthful of chickpeas. "Like he's my mother, tryna make decisions for me. Can you even believe it?" I shook my head. "The guy's scared as fuck and trying to pretend it was all some kind of '*if you love it, set it free*' bullshit. And then he tells *me* I don't understand that actions have consequences! The man is—"

"Scared of what?"

"Huh?"

"Jamie's scared, you said. Scared of what?"

"Well… of relationships, obviously. Of commitment." But it didn't ring true, even as I said it. He loved me. I believed that. And if anything, he was too committed to things. To his job, to his house, to Diane down at Goode's.

"Yeah? Why, Parks? Why's he scared?"

"I guess because…" I trailed off.

"Because why?" Cal insisted.

"I don't know why! He doesn't want to risk… things."

"Parker." Cal leaned forward. "I know there's one tiny seed of logic floating around in that brain along with the whiskey. Find it and plant it."

"What?"

"What Cal's *trying* to say," Ash interjected, "is that if Jamie broke up with you last time because he didn't think O'Leary was good enough for you, or didn't think *he* was good enough for you, or whatever… isn't it likely he's still concerned about those very same things? That the thing he doesn't want to risk is your happiness?'"

I frowned. "That's… that's not what's happening here. And it's not his business to make choices for me."

"He's not making *any* choices, Parks," Cal said. "He's doing what he did last time, which is removing himself from the equation so you can decide what *you* need to do. Remember, Parker, you left town. You moved back. You decided to leave again this morning. Jamie didn't make any of those decisions for you."

"But all of that was *because* of Jamie," I insisted. "All of it. I think I've made every decision since I was seventeen based on Jamie Burke." I dragged my fork through the food, dividing it into sections and those sections into sections. "Deep down, it's all been about him. Always."

And look where that had gotten me.

"No," Cal said, shaking his head. "It's been about *you*. Because *you* were scared. You remember what you told me a minute ago? You were waiting for Jamie to tell you to stay, because if you don't make the decision yourself, you'll never get anything wrong. Life doesn't work that way. You *know* life doesn't work that way. You're the one who goes around saying '*If you can't say yes, you have to say no,*' right? Well, guess what? Not deciding is a decision too, Parks. It's just a really crappy one."

I put my fork down again with a clack and stared at Cal's face as I swallowed. "But—"

"And just to say," Ash interrupted, "if he *is* protecting himself, Parker—if he *doesn't* wanna take a risk—can you really blame him? Hasn't Jamie lost pretty much everyone in his entire life? His sister, his dad, his mom… you? Doesn't it kinda make sense that you wouldn't want to try to hold onto anything too hard, since it all seems to go away anyway?"

"No," I argued, shaking my head. "No, come on. I would stay! I would stay in a fucking *heartbeat*. Stay *forever*. He doesn't have to lose anything! He just has to… tell me. To fight for me."

"Uh-huh," Cal said. "But does Jamie know that? Have you said that to him? 'This is forever, Jamie. This is what I want. I'm not leaving.' Have you said *any* of that?"

"No! *He* broke up with *me*."

"You keep saying that, precious. Will it keep you warm at night?"

I gaped at Cal.

"I think, to, um… expound on Cal's point there," Ash the peacemaker said, "yes, you might have a valid reason for being scared too. But you're the one who keeps walking away, Parks. And you're pissed at Jamie for not taking a risk, but you're really not taking a risk either."

"When Jamie gave you an out, you took it, instead of staying to fight for *him*." Cal shook his head. "You know, the bravest person in this whole mess is Brian *fucking* Carr. How sad is that? He wanted Jamie, and he gave it his best shot. He didn't let his pride get in the way. And it didn't work out for him, yeah. But he didn't faint at the first hurdle. He didn't quit when things went bad."

I squeezed my eyes shut. Brian didn't quit things because he wasn't immediately good at them. He tried to make them better.

Goddammit.

"Have you ever read 'The Gift of the Magi'?" Ash asked, seemingly out of nowhere.

Cal and I turned to look at him.

"You know, Christmas story? With the hair and the pocket watch? No?" He waved a hand through the air when we both continued to look at him blankly. "Whatever. The point is, you and Jamie are so busy giving each other what you think the other one wants, you're both sacrificing the things that are most important to you. You need to *talk*."

"We talk all the time."

Ash's lips twisted in sympathy. "Talk harder."

Talk harder. *Try* harder. Do better. Don't walk away.

I scrubbed a hand over my face as certain things came sharply into focus. Jamie talking about his mom leaving. "*Why would she stay?*" Jamie talking about me having so many options out there, so many places I could be successful… not because he didn't want me, but because he thought he wasn't enough.

"I wanted a sign that I should stay," I whispered. "I'm such an idiot."

"Parker." Cal leaned forward and clapped a sympathetic hand on my shoulder. "You really *are*. I mean, you were living with him and sleeping beside him. You're wearing a t-shirt right this minute that has Jamie Burke's name on the back."

"I am?" I craned my neck to look behind me.

"You are," Cal confirmed. "And he came into the bakery yesterday, so jealous his hair was practically on fire, and then *told you* he loved you. Are you waiting for skywriting? For a parade of Oompa-Loompas to come dancing through the door and sing you a song?"

Ash snorted, but his smile was sympathetic. "You ever notice that we spend our time looking for a deeper meaning in the *bad* things that happen, but when things are going well, we hardly notice it at all? Like, you spill your coffee or burn your toast, and you're convinced that it's gonna be a bad day, right? But how often do you say, 'Look at that perfectly cooked toast! Today's gonna be amazing!'" Ash shrugged. "Secret to being happy is seeing the signs in the good stuff, I think."

Cal gave Ash another one of those sappy looks, like he couldn't quite believe anyone that amazing could be real, but this time it didn't bother me at all since I was pretty sure I was giving Ash that same look myself.

"Wow. That's… wow," I repeated. "Damn, Ash. They teach you this stuff in the navy?"

Ash blushed. "Finish your food, Parker. Apologizing's gonna be easier on a full stomach."

"You sure? It might be easier with a little more whiskey."

Ash shook his head and I sighed. "Jamie and I know each other *so* well, but… I'm thinking maybe that's kind of a blessing and a curse. We both made assumptions. We didn't communicate."

"Nope. You really didn't," Cal said, studying his fingernails with no sympathy whatsoever.

"But that's something that happens to the best of us," Ash said pointedly, batting his long eyelashes at his fiancé. "Isn't that right, Caelan?"

"What? Oh, come on. That was one time, before I really even knew you," Cal said. But he was blushing, which cemented Ash's superhero status, as far as I was concerned.

"And what about that other time last summer?" Ash asked, grinning.

"Alright, fine." Cal blew out a breath. "Happens to the best of us," he told me grudgingly. "The important thing is what you do to fix it."

"How'd *you* fix it?" I demanded.

Cal grinned. "Pretty sure I gave Ash a…"

"Discussion," Ash interrupted, giving Cal a quelling look. "A lovely, lovely discussion."

"A discussion, huh?" I snorted.

"Yep. In the woods, if I recall correctly." Cal grinned at Ash. "I'm very good at… discussions."

Ash smirked. "You *are*, baby. Very good."

"I need to talk to Jamie," I said, pushing my chair back to stand.

"Hallelujah," Cal said, smacking his palm on the table. "Yes, you do. *Now.*"

"I'll even drive you," Ash offered. "And walk home."

My phone rang from the kitchen counter and I leaped up to grab it, hoping that somehow it would be Jamie.

Alas, no.

"It's my mother," I said, glancing at the ceiling. "Probably calling to find out when I'm leaving. *Again.* I don't have time for this right now."

"Maybe you should answer and tell her you aren't leaving, once and for all," Ash suggested. "Might be good practice."

I huffed out a laugh. "Yeah, maybe so." I hit accept. "Morning, Mom."

"Oh, Parker! Thank goodness you answered. How soon can you be in Arizona?" she cried.

"Actually"—I swallowed—"I'm not leaving O'Leary at all. I'm staying here. And I—"

"Parker!" she interrupted. "It's your father. He was playing golf with his friends earlier today, and he collapsed."

"Collapsed?" I demanded, my heart beating faster. "Dad did? But he's so…" Strong? Healthy? Never showing weakness? Like a fucking Hoffstraeder man? *Shit.* She'd been the mother who'd cried wolf for months and months, complaining about his ailments, and I hadn't believed her.

"I just knew it was going to end this way, Parker. I just knew it." She sounded near tears. "They took him to the hospital in an ambulance, and Gary and Stu went with him. Gary said to ask his wife to drive me, but Virginia is the one I told you about, with the Pomeranian? Remember? There's going to be dog hair all *over* her car, so I don't know *what* to do! Can you come and get me?"

"Parks?" Cal said softly, rising to stand beside me. "What's going on?"

"It's my dad," I whispered. "They're taking him to the hospital. I've got to get there." To my mom, I said, "Focus, Mom. Let Virginia drive you and screw the dog hair. I'll meet you there. What hospital are they taking him to?"

"Shea Medical! I think? They'd better have! That's where his primary care *and* his podiatrist are. Do you think I should call and make sure they took him there, Parker? He'll just *hate* it if they took him someplace with fewer amenities!"

I could practically picture her wringing her hands.

"I think the ambulance is going to take him to the closest place, and that's fine," I soothed. "I'm gonna call and get a flight, okay? Just keep me posted on his condition."

"There's one leaving from Syracuse at two." Ash held up his phone. "I'll book it now."

I nodded and dug out my credit card.

"I'll ask Moira to stay late," Cal called, already on his way downstairs. "We'll drive you."

"Just hurry, Parker, please," my mother said.

I hung up and grabbed my bag from the sofa, then made to follow Cal down the stairs to the back alley off the kitchen. "You guys don't have to take me. I've got my car."

Ash put his hands on my shoulders. "Parks, half an hour ago, you were drunk off your ass, slurring your words, and talking about Mongolia. You might feel okay now, but once the adrenaline wears off, you'll be in even worse shape."

"But it's gonna take you hours—"

"We got this," Ash said. "Now come on. I'll grab you a coffee on the way out."

I nodded and followed him, then stopped. "Shit. Jamie! I can't just leave things the way they are."

"You've waited eleven and a half years, Parker," Ash said, taking the backpack from my shoulder and ushering me down the stairs. "You can wait a couple more days."

I guessed I didn't really have much choice.

Chapter Twelve

JAMIE

Lift… and drop. Lift… and drop. My muscles burned, my lungs heaved, and my shoulder threatened to rebel completely, but I kept breathing, kept working, kept going, letting the pain in my body drown out the pain in my heart.

One foot in front of the other.

Get by.

Get through.

Keep going.

It had worked before. It would work again.

"Jamie?" a voice called through the open kitchen window. "You here?"

There was one tiny moment when I thought the voice was Parker's… that he'd come back.

But then I realized Parker wouldn't ask for permission, because this was his home too.

And then I remembered that it wasn't anymore.

So I answered whoever it was by slamming my sledgehammer against the countertop with another satisfying *crunch*.

"Holy shit." Everett walked through the door from the breezeway carrying a pizza and a six-pack of soda, but stopped dead when he saw the state of the room. "What the hell happened?" He looked up at me, sweating through my t-shirt and covered in plaster dust, and his eyes went wide. "Was there a leak? Did you find that the tree caused more damage than you'd thought?"

I swiped my sweaty forearm over my equally sweaty face and made a gimme motion toward the soda. "Nope. Just ready for a change."

"For a change," Ev repeated, passing me a can and then looking around again. "A spur of the moment change. Of your entire kitchen. Sure. That's a reasonable thing people do."

I drank half the can in one go, then belched. "You need something, Ev?"

"Nope. Not a thing. Just came by to hang out." He looked around for a place to set the pizza and found that I'd already demolished the kitchen table and all but one counter. He ended up setting the pizza on top of the refrigerator, which I'd moved to the eating area, and put the rest of the soda inside. He wiped his hands on his jeans. "What, ah… prompted all this?" he asked as he closed the fridge door. But the tone of his voice—a little too careful, a little too sympathetic—said he already knew.

I finished my soda and threw the can in the sink. "Word spread that fast, huh? Everyone knows Parker and I —" I couldn't finish the sentence.

We hadn't broken up if we'd never been together, right?

He hadn't moved out if he'd never officially lived here.

He hadn't hurt me if I'd never let myself believe this was anything but temporary.

Ev's mouth twisted to one side. "You wanna talk about it?"

I chuckled once, with zero humor. "Does it look like I wanna talk about it?" I grabbed two splintered pieces of countertop and threw them in a huge rolling bin I could transport out to the dumpster in the driveway.

"I feel like I'm missing whatever gene lets guys deal with shit through physical labor," Ev mused. "You do it. Silas does it. It looks… uncomfortable."

"Destroying things?" I looked at him, amused against my will. "It's fun."

"Is it?"

"No," I admitted. "Not fun. But tiring. Numbing, I guess." I shrugged. "I thought about drinking. Thought about it a lot actually. And then I thought about going to a meeting. AA," I added, when Ev looked confused. "I go sometimes."

"Ah. Cool. And then you decided to destroy your kitchen," Ev said. "I mean, it's not the worst choice of the three. Possibly not the best either."

"So, um…" I blew out a breath. *Don't ask. Don't ask. Don't ask.* "Did you see him?" I asked.

"Who, Parker?"

"No, Michael Flatley, Lord of the Dance. *Of course* Parker."

Ev burst out laughing. "That might be the gayest thing you've ever said to me, Jameson."

I rolled my eyes. "Whatever that means."

"Nothing." Ev waved a hand. "Just glad to know I'm not the only one with a *Riverdance* fetish."

"Pretty sure you are," I returned. I swallowed. "So… did you?"

Everett shook his head. "I heard from Cal. He called an hour or so ago. Ash got Parker liquored up on Irish coffee, and Cal put him in the shower to sober up. From what Cal said, he was pretty upset."

I winced, remembering how devastated he'd looked when he'd left. I fucking hated that he was in pain—hated that I was the one who'd hurt him. But it was probably for the best.

"So what happened?"

I shook my head. "Buncha shit. Doesn't matter."

"Clearly," Ev agreed, looking around at the wreck of my kitchen. "Doesn't matter at all."

"We broke up," I said. "That's the short version."

"Well, maybe you'd better give me the long version and catch me up." Ev leaned against the wall and folded his arms over his chest. "Since I wasn't aware the two of you were actually *together*."

I ran a hand over my face. "We weren't. Officially."

"But you wanted to be," Ev prompted.

Another humorless laugh. "Since I was seventeen. That's not new."

"And Parker didn't want to be?"

"No, he… I don't know. Yes. Maybe." I shrugged. "He says he loves me."

"Parker *loves* you. Okay, clearly I'm more than a couple of episodes behind here," Ev grumbled. "More like a couple of *seasons*. Why don't we have one of those friendships where you *tell* me things?"

I rolled my shoulder, which was really starting to ache now that I'd stopped moving. "I feel like I'm missing whatever gene it is that lets guys deal with shit by talking. It seems… uncomfortable."

Ev laughed. "Touché. So… love, huh."

"Things change fast around here, Ev." I looked around at the kitchen's yellow walls, which looked particularly dingy and old now that the rest of the kitchen was gone. "Except when they don't change at all."

"Come on." Ev tugged on the sleeve of my shirt and tried to pull me toward the living room. "Surely you have some furniture in this place where I can sit my ass down and hear this story."

I laughed as he took stock of the empty living room with its newly refinished floors and fresh, cream-colored walls. "I'm kinda low on furniture, to be honest."

"Shit," Ev said, looking around at the transformed space. "No carpet? No little tchotchkes on the shelves?"

"Not a dust catcher in sight," I agreed.

He wandered down the hall, past the bathroom—which hadn't changed at all—to Molly's room. The walls were covered in primer and the drop cloth on the floor was covered with boxes and containers of dishes and other kitchen stuff. On a table by the window sat Parker's plants in their little pots.

Of course, Everett noticed them immediately.

"These are new," he said, touching one of the succulents' spiny leaves and giving me a *significant* sort of look.

"They're Parker's. He left them behind." I shrugged.

"And you're taking care of them."

"I wouldn't say *taking care*. I moved them in here so they wouldn't get destroyed. Least I could do."

"Right. Least you could do, while you were destroying your kitchen, was to set up a cute little table by the window where the plants could be happy."

I ran my tongue over my teeth and said nothing.

Ev shook his head. "You and Parker, man. I have never seen two guys who needed to *love something* as much as you guys do. A bar, a plant, a house full of memories. Too bad you couldn't just figure out how to love each other, huh?"

I turned Everett around by the shoulder and shoved

him gently into the hall, then closed the bedroom door behind me.

Ev turned around once he'd reached the hall and set his hands on his hips. "What happened with Parker, Jamie?"

I rolled my shoulder again and contemplated how much to say, but… fuck it. What the hell did I have to lose anymore?

"We had a fight. Brian came over this morning—"

"Jesus. *Brian*? He's like a bad penny." Ev's voice promised retribution.

"Yeah, well, think twice before you say shit, because apparently he and Parker are best friends all of a sudden." I grimaced. "I got to stand in the living room for ten minutes while they tag-teamed me about how I can't communicate and don't like to risk anything in relationships, when I bother to admit that relationships even exist."

Ev winced. "Ouch?"

"Yeah. Shit was falling down around my ears *before* I ever got the bright idea to attack the kitchen."

"And what, um, prompted that little conversation?" Ev asked.

I sighed. "Honestly? I hardly even know. Everything was *fine*. Better than fine. And then suddenly, we were talking about how I was upset when Parker left—I mean, the *last* time Parker left. For college."

Ev nodded.

"And how I didn't have any right to be upset, since it was my own fault. And how I was an asshole to him when he came back and gave him shit for months—which I *was*, and I *did*, and I'd already apologized for it. And then that somehow became Parker demanding that I tell him to stay in O'Leary. As in, permanently." I laughed hollowly. "And obviously, I wasn't gonna do that."

"Obviously," Ev echoed, frowning.

"And then he left, and I decided to sublimate my feelings of hurt and frustration into kitchen demolition because I *still* don't know how to communicate. Shit, where'd you leave that pizza?" I headed for the kitchen. "I'm suddenly ravenous."

"Um. Wait," Ev said, following behind me. "*Why* didn't you tell him you wanted him to stay when he asked you to? When you clearly wanted him to?"

I took the pizza down from the top of the fridge and held the open box in my hand like a giant plate as I took a slice. "Come on, Ev." I took a bite of cheesy goodness and didn't even care that it was burning the roof of my mouth. "What would he want to stay here for?"

Ev ran a hand over his forehead. "Oh, my God. I'm so confused."

"Yep. Well, join the club." I stuffed most of the rest of the slice in my mouth and put the box back on top of the fridge. "Listen," I said around the pizza. "Nice of you to come by but I kinda wanna finish this tonight, so…"

"Stop! Stop right there!" Ev set his hands on his hips again and gave me a narrow-eyed glare. "Find me furniture, or I'm dragging you out to my car, but we are *going* to sit down, and we are *going* to talk about this. Right now."

"I'd rather not."

"And I'd rather be naked on a beach while my boyfriend feeds me tropical fruit. But here *I* am." We stood staring at each other for half a minute before he added, "And I brought you pizza."

I sighed and ran a hand through my damp hair.

"The faster you tell me, the faster I'll get gone," he prompted.

"Fine. *Fine.* We can sit on the floor in the living room," I agreed grudgingly.

Ev sat in the center of the floor with his legs drawn up like a pretzel and watched me expectantly. But when I sat down, I couldn't help but slide my hand over the smooth wood and remember how Parker had cursed and laughed while we refinished it last month, and I couldn't think of a damn thing to say.

When I'd broken up with Brian, it had felt like things were realigning the right way. I'd felt kinda weightless and free.

Parker left, and not a damn thing seemed right. Pizza tasted like cardboard. Soda didn't soothe the ache in my throat. I didn't want to be in the rooms Parker and I had redecorated, and I couldn't stand the sight of the rooms we hadn't worked on yet. Everything was too quiet. Even my clothes felt uncomfortable against my skin. And I couldn't settle to anything. I felt… rudderless.

"So." I said, once it became clear that Ev was waiting for me to speak. "I think my problems began when I was a tiny embryo, doctor."

Ev smiled. "Same, honestly. Then I turned into a scrawny, sensitive, artistic little kid with big eyes. Got picked on constantly."

"Yeah?" I could see that. Everett was a little like Parker that way. "Not me. I was taller than everyone from preschool on up. And I was *popular*."

Ev's eyebrows went up at that and I grinned. "I know, right? Hard to believe. Ginger-haired giant, freckled as fuck, but I played baseball, and kids around here have low standards for what's impressive, I guess."

"Or they have normal standards. And you met them. Because you're a decent human."

I shrugged. "If you say so. You know, it's funny. I had a ton of friends, but I didn't have anyone I could talk to about anything *real*. My sister Molly, a bit, but that was different. And then I met Parker." I smiled at the memory. "He was two years younger than me, a year younger than Molls, but he stood up for her when this little punk was saying shit and got himself knocked down for his trouble." I shook my head. "He was never one to start a fight, you know? But once he was in it, he was *in it*."

"And let me guess. You beat up the kid who knocked Parker down?"

"Not exactly. But… kinda." I pulled my knees up to my chest and looped my arms around them.

"You protected him."

"I tried."

"And you were best friends ever after."

I nodded. "Until we weren't. We, ah, started dating a couple weeks after my sister died." I looked at Ev, and he nodded. He was a little too familiar with the details of my sister's death.

"I'd already graduated, oh… a year and a bit before that, I guess. I was working at the diner, saving pennies, taking care of my dad. He'd gotten hurt at work a year or so before, and he lost his job," I explained. "And Parker… he was my lifeline. He got me thinking about the future again when I'd kinda stopped caring. He'd always liked cooking and so had I, and we were gonna open a restaurant someday. Together."

"*Reeeally.*"

I gave him a small smile. "Anyway, we started dating, and his parents were *not* happy."

"Yeah, I've heard this. They didn't like O'Leary?"

"They thought Parker deserved more than he could have here. Small restaurant, small town, small life. Did you know that with his test scores, he could have gotten into nearly *any* school? I'm talking Ivy League here. And he could've studied just about anything he wanted. Business.

Pre-med. Anything. But he kept saying he just wanted to be here. With me. And run a restaurant. Like he owed it to me."

"I do *not* like where this story is going, Jameson." Everett's voice held a warning note. "Tell me you did *not*—"

"Oh, I did. Yep. His mom came into the diner one day. *Beatrice.* She told me she knew I loved Parker, but really, was love *enough?* How long would it last? And we were both *so* young. *Too* young, really. We were making decisions before we gave ourselves a chance to figure out what we wanted."

"And you told her, 'Fuck you, lady. Parker and I know what we're doing, so mind your own damn business.' Right?"

"Actually… yeah. I kinda did. But then I got to thinking about it. And, you know, she had a point, Ev. She did. We were kids. Small-town kids, at that. What the hell did we know about what else there was out there? And I knew *I* couldn't leave here. Not with my dad so sick, so I thought… what would happen if we broke up? Would Parker still want to live in this small town, running a restaurant? Or would he go off to Boston?"

"Jameson," Everett groaned. "You're like every sappy movie I have ever *hated* all rolled into one. *If I love it, I'll set it free.*" He made a gagging noise.

"Yep. Yeah. That's what Parker said too, when he found out. Which was yesterday, by the way." I cut my eyes to him.

"*God.*" Ev looked at the ceiling. "Of course it was. *Of course.* You couldn't have told him about this *right away*, like a normal human? Or even when he came back to O'Leary? You couldn't have engaged in dialogue? Trusted what he said? None of that? No? You had to be all strong and silent? Didn't this happen in *Twilight?*"

"How the hell would I know?" I gave him a look. "For that matter, how the hell do *you* know?"

Ev lifted one slim shoulder. "Pop culture exists, Jameson. It's a *thing.*"

"If you say so. Did *Twilight* end with the guy running off to Boston?"

"Mmm. No, pretty sure she became a vampire."

"So what you're saying is that this is in no way similar to *Twilight?*"

"Alright, alright." Ev waved this away. "So you were being all stupidly noble, *and?*"

I sighed. "And it seemed like the right idea, Everett. It did. Even now… I dunno. It doesn't seem entirely *wrong.* Except…"

"Except?"

"I said some truly deplorable shit. Shit I couldn't believe he would ever believe, you know? *I don't love you,* blah blah blah. I was trying to be extreme. I was trying to shake him up. Make him… think. But the *second* he left, I knew I'd gone about it wrong. Like, the minute he drove away. Parker and I loved each other, and I'd hurt his feelings for nothing, because clearly one little fight wasn't gonna change his mind, right? So I went to his house." I could smell the freshly cut grass when I thought of that day. I could hear the cicadas buzzing in the heat.

"And?" Ev prompted. "Just finish it. My heart can't take much more."

"And nothing. He'd already gone, his mom told me. *That morning.* His dad took him to Boston, got a meeting with some friend of his who worked at BU, and Parker never bothered to come back. That was that."

Ev shook his head in silent sympathy.

"I wasn't *angry*," I said. "Not angry-angry. Just… hurt, I guess. And maybe Parker's got a point, that I didn't have any right to be hurt either. I'd told him to go. I'd broken up with him, and he'd taken me at my word, so that's on me. But it sucked. And I… I guess it was easier being mad than hurt. Definitely easier being mad than getting close to him again and getting hurt again, I can tell you that *for damn sure*." I blew out a breath. "And that's it. End of story."

"Mmm, no. Couple pieces of crucial information missing," Ev argued. "Like, why couldn't you tell Parker to stay? He's in love with you, you said. You're in love with him, *clearly*."

"Because I'd be doing the same thing I didn't wanna do before. *Duh*. Holding him back, when his real dream was out there." I waved a hand toward… the world.

Everett blinked at me. "You… you realize that you were wrong the first time you broke up with him, though, yes? His mom was *completely wrong*. And she put an idea in your head, and then you were completely wrong too?"

"No. Not completely. Yes, I shouldn't have done it the way I did, but… He got his degree, Ev. He made something of himself."

"He made himself *miserable*, Jamie. Take it from me, Boston's a really nice town, but it's not a magical land of hopes and dreams. No manna from heaven. Parker knows that. He left, of his own free will, as soon as he could."

I frowned.

"And why do you think he came back here?" Ev persisted. "Why'd he come directly to O'Leary, and not head to Dublin, or Dallas, or any of the hundreds of towns in between? Why'd he start a business in the smallest, nowhere-est town east of the Mississippi, and never say a single word about leaving again until his bar burned down and he felt like he had no choice?"

"I guess… I dunno. To prove a point, maybe. To show us all what a success he'd made of himself."

"Maybe the point he wanted to prove was that he wanted to be here all along. Because when he's in it, he's *in it*, like you said."

I lay down on my back on the hard floor and stared up at the ceiling. It was freshly painted, but the old whorled pattern was still easily visible—an endless tangle that was eerily similar to my own thoughts.

"Parker's an adult," Everett continued. "He makes his own choices. He doesn't need you to protect him anymore, Jamie. Not from shit like that, anyway. He asked you a question. He asked you to tell him you wanted him to stay. The only thing you owed him was an honest answer and the space to make his own decision."

I rolled my head against the hard wood. "It's not that easy. Of course I wanted him here. Jesus, I wanted to tell him he wasn't *allowed* to leave. I wanted to slam the door and lock him in. But it wasn't fair of him to ask me. Not without telling me what he wanted first."

"Oh, right! He should just keep throwing himself at you and giving you chances to shut him down. I see. Well, that makes sense."

I ran a hand over my face and said nothing.

"When Adrian died," Ev said softly, "I felt like I'd put all my faith in something that didn't pan out, and I never, never wanted to risk myself again. It hurt too damn much. So, I told myself I couldn't fall for Silas. That it would be cheating on Adrian to feel that way." He snorted. "It was literally the stupidest, unkindest thought that's ever taken up residence in my brain, because my husband *loved me*, and if there's an afterlife? If he's watching over me? He's feeling nothing but pure joy. He's beyond jealousy. You know? But it was easier to tell myself I was doing it for him, that I was sacrificing my happiness for *him*, than to admit that I was scared."

I sucked in a breath through my nose. "And what changed?"

"I got a handy reminder that life was short, and pain was a part of the process. There are no guarantees in love, but you're guaranteed to be miserable if you cut yourself off from it." Ev shook his head. "So if you *really* love him, Jamie—if you love him enough to let him go and doom yourself to misery for the rest of your natural life—then love him enough to be vulnerable with him, and honest with him, and believe him when he tells you he loves you too. Learn from the past, man. Don't cut yourself off from it. And for fuck's sake, don't relive it."

I pushed myself to sitting and felt a little light-headed.

All this time, I'd been trying not to let the past define me. I hadn't wanted to talk about it; I hadn't wanted to think about the good times because they reminded me of what I missed or the sad times because they reminded me of how badly I'd fucked up. But Ev was right. You couldn't just cut yourself off from the past like that.

The past was the fire that forged you, that strengthened and weakened you, that molded and shaped you. It formed the magnetic core at the center of your being that meant some people wandered into your orbit and *stuck* there, like Ev and me, while other people, like Brian, got repelled time and again, no matter how sweet and on-paper-perfect they might seem.

The past was all the missing pieces, all the jagged cracks and rounded edges, all the tiny earthquakes, and volcanic eruptions, and slow-but-steady erosion that had created your personal topography.

No *one part* of it had to define me. But, like Everett had

said, I had to learn from it. I had to try not to make the same mistakes twice.

"You're a really good friend, Everett. I haven't told you that, I don't think."

Ev smiled, clearly pleased. "Yeah? Back atcha."

"And you are definitely qualified to dispense wisdom to me, whenever you think I need it."

Ev let his head fall back and spread his arms wide. "Ah, finally. Official authorization to do what I've already been doing for months." He laughed. "So now that we've established that I'm right and you're wrong, pretty much always…"

"Yeah."

"What are you gonna do?"

"I'm gonna talk to Parker," I repeated obediently.

"Excellent! Call him. Do it *now*. Before I leave and you decide to destroy your bathroom instead."

"I'm gonna do better," I said, pushing to my feet. "I'm gonna go to Cal's in person, and I'm gonna tell Parker that he's staying here with me. I'll pitch a tent in the alley behind Fanaille until he comes home."

"Oh, praise Jesus," Ev said in a rush.

I laughed once. "You having a religious moment over there, Everett? I didn't think you were the type."

"Witnessing a miracle changes a man," Everett said dryly. He stood also. "And… just to be sure… what happens when you hit a wall? What happens when you assume Parker feels a certain way and he assumes you feel something else?"

"I will talk to him. I promise. Every single time. And I won't let him leave again, unless I'm leaving with him."

"Excellent." Everett clapped his hands. "Now, take a damn shower, before you scare the man, and I'll drive you to Cal's." He winked. "That way you can at least make sure Parker drives you home."

———

I JAMMED myself into Everett's tiny car maybe seven minutes later, and I nearly exploded onto the pavement when he finally pulled up to Fanaille. Parker's car was parked at the curb, and I was suddenly dying to see him, to touch him, to reassure him, and to reassure *myself* that I hadn't broken everything because of my stupid fear. I couldn't believe I'd nearly let Parker slip away from me *again*.

I threw open the door to the bakery, without even waiting to see if Everett was behind me, and strode in only to pull up short. The place was packed with customers. Mitch and Marci were sitting at one table, Henry and Diane at another. Theo Ross and a pack of his friends were taking up two entire tables by the window. Lisa Dorian and Quinn Tierney were standing and chatting by the door. At least six people were standing in line, and I didn't even recognize two of them.

Cal and Ash were both behind the counter, but there was no Parker in sight. And I tried to be patient, I did, and to wait my turn, but Jesus Christ, did Suzanne O'Deigh really need to have a fucking discussion about the ingredients of the muffins when I had revelations to share and a real live, actual *relationship* to start?

I started tapping my foot when the line shuffled forward and finally lost my patience entirely when Cal started having a protracted conversation with his soon-to-be sister-in-law, who was heavily pregnant and clearly displeased by this fact.

"Hey, Cal!" I called from the back of the line. "Parker upstairs?"

Cal glanced over at me, looking a little tired and distinctly unimpressed by my presence. "Parker? What would he be doing here?"

What? "Everett said he was here." I looked around to find Ev for confirmation, but he'd apparently decided not to come inside.

"He was," Cal confirmed. "He's not now."

Cal smiled at his sister-in-law. "Sorry about that interruption, Karen. Now, what were you saying about your back spasms? Don't leave out a single detail."

I huffed out a breath.

Ash was turned around, preparing coffee at the little espresso machine on the back counter, so I tried him instead. "Ash! Do you know where Parker went?"

Ash turned around and surveyed me. He took a deep breath, but before he could answer, Cal interjected.

"Not sure why you wanna know, Jameson."

I blinked at the hostility. "Because I need to talk to him, obviously."

"Have you tried his phone?" Cal shot back.

I swallowed. "No, I haven't. I need to speak to him in person."

"Hmm. Well, that's gonna be tricky."

He smiled at Karen again and handed over a white box of treats. "Lavender vanilla cupcakes. For little Bronwyn."

Karen smiled at Cal, which was kind of a minor miracle in and of itself, since she was generally even crankier than he was, but I couldn't bring myself to care.

I gritted my teeth impatiently. "*Why* will it be tricky? Where is he?"

"Hard to say," Cal said. He glanced at the ceiling and

then out the window at the sky. "What with the time change and all."

My heart sank, and I put out a hand to brace myself against the display case. "The what?" I whispered.

Cal's eyes narrowed on my face. "We drove him to the airport earlier so he could catch a flight to Arizona."

"No," I whispered. This could not possibly be happening again. Not *again*.

"'Fraid so," Cal said. "He should've just had us drive him the first time. Would've made a lot of things easier, huh?"

I was too stunned to move at first, too stunned to reply. I wasn't sure how I was remembering to breathe. Then his words finally penetrated.

"No," I told him. "It wouldn't have been easier. That was our do-over. It was supposed to be, anyway." I ran a hand through my hair. "He didn't even take his stuff. His car's out there, and I have his plants. His memory box. Half his clothes."

"I don't know what to tell you." Cal shrugged. "He was pretty upset."

"Well, and he was in kind of a hurry too," Ash added. "His mom…"

Cal cut him off with an elbow to the side, and Ash looked down at him curiously. They exchanged some kind of telepathic conversation that had Ash saying, "What? *Ohhhh!*"

Ash turned back to me. "Yep. Yeah, what Cal said. Parks was just… super upset. *So* upset. Ran off. Couldn't stop him. He's gone. *So* gone." He made a whistling noise and waved his hand in the general direction of Arizona.

I buried both hands in my hair and groaned. "I need to talk to him. I need to see him. I have to explain… He doesn't have all the facts."

"Oh, really. What facts?" Cal demanded.

I dropped my hands. "That I love him. That I want him to stay in O'Leary. That I'm tired of being scared. That we are meant to be together."

"That's so beautiful," Marci sniffled, and I remembered suddenly that I had an audience.

"You bring him back here, Jameson!" Hen Lattimer said.

"Oops," Cal said, like he could read my mind. But his grin suggested he'd gotten exactly what he wanted out of our conversation.

I rolled my eyes. "I'm going after him."

"Thank God," Ash said. He held out a set of car keys and nodded at Parker's car. "It's got a full tank. And I happen to know there's a flight leaving at six."

Chapter Thirteen

"I TOLD YOU GOLF WAS DANGEROUS!" The only thing higher than the pitch of my mother's voice was the decibel level she insisted on using, despite the fact that no one in the car was arguing… or even speaking at all.

My head was aching violently, reminding me that I was too old to drink whiskey before noon, I hadn't eaten anything all day except some exceptional chana masala, and I'd been an idiot to ever think I could stay with my parents in Arizona for even a *week* let alone some indefinite span of time. I'd literally hemorrhage my brains from my ears if I had to listen to my mother for much longer.

I pulled my parents' Acura into the driveway of their house and sighed tiredly. The sun had set while we were on our way home from the hospital, but it was still light out enough for me to make out the lines of their new place which, as my mother had reminded me no less than twelve times in four hours, I had never bothered to come see before.

It looked like a very tiny, very exclusive prison. A tall black gate topped with spikes guarded the entrance to the community and bright lights shone on nearly every public space, from the little pool—which was behind a second gate—to the long, winding road that led to my parents' house. And the house itself? It looked like a long, grayish-brown cinderblock sitting on top of a grayish-brown driveway, set in an entire landscape of grayish-brown. There was a single spindly tree poised next to the house and a few succulents lining the driveway, but they did almost nothing to lessen the severity of the lines and angles. I felt like I'd landed on an alien planet, and I missed the lush landscape of O'Leary, with all its hairpin-curved roads and muddy imperfections and the promise that even under its winter-brown covering, things were waiting to bloom.

But more than that, *so* much more than that, I missed Jamie. I missed the awareness that buzzed and crackled between us when we were together, the ever-present air of *challenge* that made everything interesting and fun when he was around. I missed the way he could make terrible things better. I missed his arms around me, and even though it had only been half a day since we'd been together… it was half a day too long.

I put the car in park and stepped out, taking a minute to stretch my back. The night air was cool and fresh and blessedly silent… for the two seconds before my mother got out of the back seat.

"Lance! Lance, don't you try to get out of the car by yourself, you hear me? You'll fall and crack your head, and if I have to spend another minute breathing the nasty air of that hospital, I'm going to scream. Parker! Parker, grab the crutches!"

I took another breath and closed my eyes for a second.

"Mom, he's fine. The crutches are just a precaution," I reminded her.

"If you trust *that* doctor," she muttered. "He wouldn't even admit your father, despite how pale he looked."

"You'd look pale too, if you'd taken a golf ball to the back of your leg," my father grumbled, throwing open the passenger's side door. "Damn thing knocked out my knee and had me sprawled on the grass."

I rolled my eyes and went around the back of the car to get the crutches from the trunk along with my backpack. "You know," I told my mother, "you had me believing Dad was dying."

"Well, how was I supposed to know? Gerry said he collapsed on the golf course!"

"And of course you believed the worst," I said. *Of course.*

"Still can't believe how badly Stu fucked up that shot." My father snorted. "Wait until I see him."

"I thought he told the doctor that *you* wandered into his shot."

"Please," my father scoffed. "His shot went wide. And it barely even *bruised* me. No power behind the drive *at all*. I'm never gonna let him live this down."

"I'm so glad I've never taken up golf," I muttered. I brought the crutches to my dad and held out a hand to help him from the car, but once he was up, he waved the crutches off and limped toward the house on his own.

I rolled my eyes. Lance Hoffstraeder on crutches? Never gonna happen.

"But you'll take it up now!" my mother said. She smoothed my t-shirt across my shoulders and sighed in satisfaction, then looped her arm through mine and led me around my limping father toward the front door. "Now that you're here, we'll finally get you out on the course. After we get you some new shirts, of course. And pants."

She patted my arm and moved ahead of me with her key out.

I smoothed a hand over the soft thigh of Jamie's jeans, which were hanging from my hips. "I like my pants just fine," I said softly. The only thing I would have liked better was if Jamie was here wearing them, because that would mean...

"Oh, Holy Mary!" my mother screeched, jumping back and nearly knocking me over until I caught her shoulders and set her back on her feet.

A tall, broad-shouldered figure emerged from the shadows next to the door, and at first I thought I must be imagining him—conjuring his features or something, because I wanted him to be there so badly.

"Jamie?" I whispered, hardly daring to hope.

But then he said, "Hey, Parks," in his deep, soft voice and... fuck. I felt like kneeling down and crying, no lie. And my dad could think what he liked.

"Jameson Burke?" my mother gasped.

"Beatrice," he returned, his eyes never leaving mine.

"How in God's name did you get here?" she demanded.

Jamie scratched his head like the question confused him, and I had to stop myself from reaching for him and kissing him right there and then.

"Well," Jamie said. "There was a plane. And then a Lyft. Before that, I borrowed Parker's car to get to the airport."

"We *live* in a *gated community*," my mother informed him.

"Yeah," he said, looking at her for the first time. "You might wanna be careful about that. The driver knew the code 'cause he's been here a few times." He shrugged. "And when I got to your house, your neighbor told me you were at the hospital, so I decided to wait. She's got the cutest little dog. Pomeranian, I think."

My mother sucked in a gasping breath, but before she could say a word, Jamie's gaze swung back to me, and then beyond, to my dad, who'd finally hobbled his way up the path.

"Everything okay?" Jamie asked me softly.

And just like that, it *was* okay. Because Jamie was *there*.

So, it was the easiest thing in the world to take the two steps that separated us, to grab his head in my hands and yank him down to me, to press our lips together with absolutely no finesse whatsoever, and show him how fucking glad and relieved I was.

"I was going to call you, but my phone died," I said, pulling back. "And I left my charger behind."

"You left a lot of things behind," Jamie whispered, his hands locked on my waist. "Like me."

I swallowed. "Did I?"

"You did. So I decided to come to you."

"You didn't have to. I told Cal there was a misunderstanding as soon as I got here, and that I'd be back as soon as I could."

Jamie's eyes narrowed. "Is that so?" He shook his head once. "Because Cal *and* Ash led *me* to believe you were gone for good."

"Oh." I blinked. "And… that's why you came?"

Jamie nodded. "This was supposed to be my dramatic gesture."

My stomach swooped, and I was pretty sure I owed Cal a fruit basket. Or a bottle of whiskey. Maybe a car.

What *was* the appropriate gift when your friend provoked the love of your life into flying halfway across the country to prove he loved you?

"I'm glad you're here," I whispered. "So, so glad."

"And I'm glad you were coming back," he said softly. "Even if it does mean that the whole speech I've been delivering to that plant over there for the last half hour is useless." He smiled wryly. "Apparently talking to succulents is kind of my thing now."

"I know," I crowed. "And I love you for it. But I definitely want the speech, please and thank you."

Jamie's hands tensed on my waist. "Parker Hoffstraeder, I want you to come back to O'Leary with me..." He took a deep breath. "Or not."

"Wow." I raised an eyebrow. "That was the speech? Because the beginning was good, but the end could use some—"

Jamie put a hand over my mouth. "In my rehearsals, there were fewer interruptions."

"Because it's a plant, Jamie," I said patiently. "Plants don't talk back."

Jamie looked behind me at my mom and dad. I could imagine what he saw: a one-two punch of breathless outrage and stoic skepticism. They were definitely finding no joy in this. But I was.

Oh, I *so* was.

Jamie swallowed and squared his shoulders before he continued, "I didn't want to tie you down, and I still don't. But I want you. I want to be with you. Forever. Because nothing feels right when you're not around. And I should've learned that lesson eleven years ago, but I didn't. I can survive without you, but it's not really living when you're not there. So..." He swallowed again. "So, I'm here to say... whatever you want, Parks, you can have it. You want O'Leary? We'll have it. We'll rebuild your bar. Or build something else. A restaurant. A skyscraper. A botanical garden with thousands of tiny succulents in little colored, labeled pots. O-or if you want something different, something bigger? We'll make that happen instead. Boston. New York. Or Arizona... I guess." He looked around at the house, with all its harsh angles and glass, looking sort of bewildered. "Or we could travel like Ethan. Wherever you wanna go, whatever you wanna do, we can do it... I just... would really like... if we could... go... together."

He sucked in a deep breath, like he'd exhausted all the oxygen in his lungs, and rolled his shoulder to ease the tension there. Then he nodded once, like he was putting the period at the end of a sentence.

Fucking adorable.

Holy shit. How was it possible to love someone this much? How was it possible to go from happy to miserable to worried to annoyed to happy, all in sixteen hours? I'd gone over a decade without feeling half as much as I felt with Jamie every single day.

"Be good if you'd say something right about now, Parks," Jamie said.

From somewhere behind me, my dad snorted.

"Oh, right," I muttered. "Well, I don't have a speech because I've been at the hospital watching my dad eat Jell-O and watch the same stories on the news, over and over and over. But... I was gonna come back, Jamie. And I *am* going to rebuild. Eventually. I already got the number of my dad's lawyer friend, so I can push my claim with Unity Financial. And I was gonna talk to Dana about renting a place at the Crabapple for a while, in case I needed a place to stay while I convinced you to give us a shot. But I'm not going anywhere. I belong in O'Leary," I told him. "And with you."

Jamie sucked in a breath, then wrapped his arms around my waist and huffed in relief a second before his lips hit my forehead. "Okay, then. Okay."

Behind me, I heard my mother huff *unhappily*. It wasn't enough to kill the mood, but she was trying.

I turned within the circle of Jamie's arms and narrowed my eyes at her. "Enough. This is what I want."

"I promise, Beatrice, I will do anything to make him happy. You know I love him, and that I always have," Jamie said over my head.

It was beautiful.

It also sounded like something they'd discussed before, and the resignation on my mother's face clinched it.

"Did you know?" I demanded. "Did you know Jamie broke up with me so I could go to college, in a very sweet but incredibly, unbelievably misguided attempt to ensure I was happy?"

"I… no!" Beatrice insisted, slapping a hand on her chest. "I may have mentioned to Jameson that your father and I were… disappointed… in your decision not to go to college, but I had no idea what he planned. When you broke up, I assumed you'd come to your senses and ended things yourself so you could go to school. Which is exactly what I told him." She nodded once. "When he came to talk to you."

I looked at Jamie, who winced, and then back to my mother. "When he came to talk to me?"

My mother pushed back a stray strand of blonde hair from her temple. "You and your father were already on your way to Boston," she said. "I thought you'd broken things off, and you didn't say any differently. I didn't want to… trouble you."

I shook my head, momentarily speechless, and Jamie's hand rubbed up and down my back, reminding me that whatever had happened to get us where we were, he was here with me now. And maybe that was all that mattered.

But Angela Ross's words came floating back to me too.

There was a point where you didn't care how things went over, and I was at that point.

"Let me be clear," I told my mother. "We—that is to say, my boyfriend Jamie and I—are going inside in a minute. We're going to sleep in the guest room with the memory foam bed you keep telling me about. And then tomorrow, we're going back to O'Leary. Because I've got a bar to run."

She shook her head minutely. "Fine. Do as you like. But I'm afraid you'll regret this someday. Tell him, Lance."

My dad laughed. "I'm not telling him shit, Beatrice. Now would somebody open the damn door? Judge Jeanine's gonna be on soon and I'm hungry as hell." He clapped me on the shoulder—*hard*—as he passed me and winked at me. "Proud of you, Parks."

"That… was weird," I told Jamie after they'd gone inside and left us wrapped together in the gathering darkness. "Pretty sure my dad never told me he was proud of me before."

"He should have," Jamie said against my neck. "You've done a lot to be proud of, Parker."

"Yeah? I don't know." I mapped the planes of his back with my hands, fucking thrilled that the universe had given me another chance to do this. I wouldn't waste it.

"You had the best bar in town."

"I had the *only* bar in town." I snorted.

"And now you'll have an even better one." Jamie brushed his hand through my hair.

"*We* will. That is, if you're interested in doing this with me. There's no pressure, okay? I know you already have a job you like. And maybe running a bar isn't the best choice for you, and that's okay. You just have to tell me and—"

"Parker," he whispered. "What part of '*We'll rebuild your bar*' was unclear?"

I grinned. I couldn't help it. "Well, then it won't *be* my bar. It'll be ours. Not Hoff's, but something else. Maybe we can call it… Lucille's."

"After your plant?" Jamie pulled back just enough to see my face, and his lips twitched. "Nah nah nah. How about Burke's Beer and Chicken Wing Emporium?" He wiggled his eyebrows playfully.

"Oh, wow. An *emporium*." I wrapped my arms around his neck. "Impressive. And will you be the one cooking the wings?"

"Parker," he chided. "Of course not. We'll have both our recipes on the menu."

"Aw." I reached up to peck his lips. "See? That's really—"

"I mean, mine will get top billing. Naturally."

I narrowed my eyes.

"Parks, they've won *awards*."

"*One* award," I argued. "*One*. And it was awarded by *me* under what were, quite frankly, extremely challenging circumstances."

"The blizzard?"

"The sugar in my pants!"

Jamie laughed. "So you want a do-over, huh? Chicken Wing Death Match, Part Deux?" He raised one eyebrow.

"Yep. And the winner gets to name our bar."

"Oh ho. That confident? Alrighty, then. Let's raise the stakes. Winner gets to name the bar, and the loser—" Jamie rubbed the inside of his cheek with his tongue. "—gets on his knees."

I laughed. "That sounds like the kind of challenge I win either way."

"Which makes it the best kind of challenge," Jamie agreed.

"I'm still gonna win," I insisted. "Only now you'll be

going down *literally*." I snorted at my own joke. "See what I did there?"

"Oh, I see," Jamie said dryly. "You're delusional." He grabbed both of my hands and laced our fingers together, then drew my hands up to his lips so he could kiss them one at a time. His eyes were like melted chocolate in the dim light as he gazed down at me lovingly. "But it's cute."

"You sound scared, Jameson!"

"Of your chicken wings?" he scoffed. "Not even a little. Of other stuff…" He glanced up at the wide-open sky. "Maybe a little. That I'm gonna fuck things up again. That I'm gonna forget to talk. That I'm gonna require do-overs for things that don't involve chicken."

"Me too," I admitted. "But it's a shit-ton easier being scared *with* you than it was being scared *without* you. And that's one thing I promise I'm never gonna forget again."

Chapter Fourteen

THE ROAD to O'Leary was long and winding—the kind of road that prevented outsiders from getting in, and insiders from getting out... especially in snowstorms. There were times, when the weather was perfect and the sun was shining down through the trees, that the Camden Road seemed like the doorway to a beautiful, enchanted land.

Today was not one of those days.

The windshield wipers on Parker's little Prius were going as fast as they could, but they could barely keep up with the heavy March rain that poured down on us as we made our way home from the airport.

"I'll say one thing about Arizona," I said, as I adjusted the blower for the seventh time. "It was dry."

"Eh." Parker shrugged. "I missed the humidity."

I glanced over at him. "You miss the weirdest things, Parks."

Parker picked my hand up off the steering wheel and brought it to his lips for a quick kiss. "I know," he said, and when he smiled at me, I couldn't help but laugh.

He kept holding my hand as we drove down Weaver

Street, and while it sounded ridiculous even in my own head to say that his hand in mine improved the view, it kinda did. And for once I didn't mind being ridiculous. I even kinda wished the weather were better so that people could see us driving through town.

Yeah, that's right, I *wanted* O'Leary up in my business. I wanted them to know Parker Hoffstraeder and I were together. That we were in love. Because I *believed*—truly believed—that it would last forever, not because it felt right, even though it did, or because I believed in fate, although I was starting to, or even because I thought I deserved him, because I didn't, but because I knew I'd be willing to do the work to make sure it lasted. And so would the man beside me.

"Oh, hey!" I pulled my hand away from his and fished in the pocket of my sweatshirt. "Got you a present."

"You did?" he demanded. "How? We spent all day yesterday with my mother, so she could try to get back in your good graces—"

"I don't think it's *my* good graces she cared about, *Parkie-kins.*"

"Shut up," he said, whacking me lightly on the arm. "She knows she needs to get in your good graces if she wants to get in mine. And you enjoyed the snickerdoodles."

"True," I admitted. I'd enjoyed watching Beatrice try to be polite to me even more. It had been worth the extra day delay in getting home.

Almost.

"So where'd you have a chance to get the present?"

"Airport gift shop. I wanted you to have an Arizona memento to add to your box." I pressed a tiny wooden magnet into his hand. "Something to add to… whatever else you've got in there now. All your little Boston treasures."

"Oh my God."

I grinned. "You might hate Arizona, but I've got a certain fondness for it. Though, if we ever go back to visit, we are staying at a hotel. I've been dying to get close to you for two days, and the guest room is way too close to your mother's... uh, Parker?" I glanced over and found him staring down at the little magnet, tracing the contours with his fingertip. "Everything okay?"

"It's a cactus," Parker said, sounding stupefied. "A little cactus magnet."

"Yeah," I agreed. "Because it looked like Lucille. No?"

"It says, 'I'll never *desert* you.'"

"It's a pun," I explained, glancing over at him again. "Get it?"

Parker sucked in a breath through his nose and clasped the little magnet tightly in his hand.

"Babe, it's only a magnet."

"A magnet with a *cactus-based pun*. For my memory box."

"*Riiiight*," I agreed, stretching the word out. "Because it's a happy memory. Isn't it?"

"Very," Parker said, but he didn't explain further, or look at me, or even smile, and I was totally missing something.

"Parks, you remember we're doing the talking thing now, yes? Where we explain our emotions and don't make assumptions?"

"I remember," Parker said. "But this is a case where explaining might not work. I think maybe I need to *show* you instead. When we get home."

I sucked in a breath at that, because even though I'd lived in that house my whole life, it had never felt as much like a home as it did now that Parker would be living there with me...

And also because, when my boyfriend offered to *show me something at home*, it reminded me that it had been a very long, very sexless two days.

We pulled into the driveway, where I parked behind the construction dumpster and reached for the door handle. "I'll grab your backpack," I said. "You get ready for show-and-tell."

But Parker didn't move.

"Um. Jameson? Why does it look like there's a section of the kitchen counter poking out of the dumpster?"

"Oh." I bit my lip and winced. "That."

"Do I want to know?"

"Well"—I cleared my throat—"you know how you dealt with our argument by going to Cal's and drinking Irish coffee?"

Parker looked at me.

"Well, whiskey isn't a good option for me. And I needed to blow off steam."

"By ripping out the countertops?" he demanded.

I bit my lip as I remembered the state of the kitchen when Ev and I had left the house. "Possibly the cabinets too. And the table."

"What?" Parker gaped at me. Then he threw open the door and ran for the house through the rain, like he needed to see for himself. I grabbed his bag and followed more reluctantly.

The room looked even rougher than I remembered. I noticed I hadn't been particularly careful when taking the cabinets off the walls, and there was a heap of debris thrown in the corner next to the fridge where the table used to be. It looked a lot like the nightly news footage of a house ravaged by a natural disaster.

Parker stood in the middle of the room and turned in a

slow circle. He let out a low, keening moan. "You Hulk-smashed our kitchen?"

I pushed my lips together. "This… would not be a good time to tell you how much I love hearing you call it *our* kitchen, right?"

Parker turned to me with wide eyes. "I want to see the humor here, Jamie. But this isn't gonna be just joint compound and paint, babe. Cabinets are expensive. And counters." He ran a hand through his hair. "It'll be fine. We'll make it fine. But… shit." He drew a deep breath. "It's a lot."

"Parks," I said, grabbing him by the belt loops—which happened to be *my* belt loops, since he was still wearing my pants—and pulling him against me. "I admit I wasn't at my most rational when I did this—"

Parker hooted in agreement.

"But I promise, I'm not *quite* stupid enough to destroy my kitchen without knowing how I was gonna pay to reno-vate it."

Parker's fingers traced the collar of my shirt. "Yeah? Where are you getting the money, sugar daddy? It's gonna cost a shit-ton."

"I'm aware. I told you before that I don't have a mort-gage on this place. My dad's life insurance covered it with a good bit left over. And I mostly bank my paychecks too, so…" I shrugged. "It's covered."

Parker raised one eyebrow. "Covered? Everything?"

"I mean… within reason, yes. Everything."

"So… what are we talking here? Industrial stove?" Parker asked in a hushed voice. "Soapstone counters?"

I snorted. "You're getting hard right now, aren't you?"

"No!" Parker toyed with my collar again. "That would be weird."

"Parks?" I walked him backward until his back was flat against the fridge, and his eyes sparkled up at me.

"Yeah?"

"I think I like you weird," I whispered. "I kinda always have."

"I really love you, you know?" Parker said, thrusting his hands up into my hair.

"Yeah?" I lowered my head to nip at his bottom lip. "How much? Is it time for show-and-tell?"

Parker lifted up on his toes, rubbing himself against me, and pressed our lips together. His taste was familiar— we'd spent the last two nights talking and kissing, and while it wasn't a new sensation, I'd loved the way it had felt knowing both of us had laid our cards on the table. Every touch of our lips had felt like a promise.

Kissing him here, in our home, was something different again. We were building something here, Parker and me. Something strong and special and *real*. Not just a flash of passion, but something nurturing and sustaining.

Parker made a little sighing noise as he broke away.

"Go lie on the bed," he said softly.

"It *is* that kind of show-and-tell." I grinned. "Excellent."

Parker rolled his eyes. "Believe it or not, I have no idea what you're picturing in your head right now, but I can almost guarantee that's not the kind of show-and-tell I mean." He paused. "At least not right now."

"I'm intrigued."

"And I'm waiting. *Go*."

I saluted him sharply and hefted his backpack more firmly on my shoulder as I went down the hall.

Our bedroom looked exactly the way we'd left it—sheets rumpled and pushed to the foot of the mattress, dents in the pillows where our heads had been. I tossed the bag on the floor on Parker's side of the bed and couldn't help but think about how close I'd thought I'd come to having nothing left of Parker but this impression of his head on my pillow.

And clearly this relationship stuff was turning me into a sap, because I *felt* the pang of that hopelessness as I plumped the pillows and straightened the blankets, followed by a wave of intense gratitude as I took off my shirt and threw *it* on Parker's side of the bed too.

He was gonna give me so much shit for the clothes on the floor. Which meant he'd be *here* to give me shit.

I lay down on the bed, reclining against the pillows, and propped my hands behind my head. My shoulder twinged a little at the motion, but I ignored it in antic-ipation.

When Parker opened the door, though, he looked the same as he had in the kitchen—still fully dressed, down to his shoes.

I lifted an inquisitive eyebrow, and he threw out his arms. "Ta da! Not quite the show you'd expected?"

"You *did* once promise to answer my questions in inter-pretive dance. I can work with this."

Parker rolled his eyes and grinned. "I sent you ahead so I could get a glass of water. Which became extremely complicated when I had to go searching for both the glass *and* the water."

"How did either of us survive for the last eleven and a half boring years without this kind of excitement?" I wondered.

"Eleven years, seven months on Tuesday," Parker corrected, moving toward the walk-in closet. Then he stopped and turned back to flash me a wide smile. "You know what? We can stop counting now."

I grinned up at the ceiling as he rummaged in the

closet and came out triumphantly brandishing his little red tin memento box.

I widened my eyes. "*This* is show-and-tell?"

"Disappointed?"

"Not even a little. Show me."

I wanted to know everything about Parker's life in Boston, about all the important things I'd missed. But more than that, I got that this was an expression of trust, another sign that there were no more walls between us, and that was something I craved.

"'Kay." Parker hopped up on the bed and sat cross-legged with his back against my hip and the box in front of him. He paused with his hands on the lid and drummed his fingers impatiently. "I feel like there's going to be a let-down here," he admitted. "Like, if you think there's *actually* gonna be pictures of me with Mark Wahlberg, you're gonna be——"

I leaned up and kissed him, hating that he felt vulnerable sharing this with me and loving that he was telling me anyway. "I love you," I reminded him. "I have always loved you. Show me."

Parker nodded and pried off the lid, then smiled softly down at what he saw.

He handed me a pasteboard coaster, bearing the green and gold Hoff's bar logo.

"Okay, that's not a surprise," I said, smiling. "First coaster out of the pack?"

He nodded. "I helped design the logo too." He pulled out the next item from the tin.

"Oh, look at you and Ethan," I said, glancing over his shoulder at the framed picture in his hand. "College graduation? Ethan looks exactly the same."

"He does," Parker agreed. "But then, blonds get better

looking with age." He ran a hand through his own light hair and batted his eyelashes.

"I won't argue with that," I said softly, and he leaned down to brush an appreciative kiss over my lips… which turned into something else entirely when I grabbed him by the back of the neck and licked my way into his mouth. He dropped the picture somewhere on the bed and leaned over me, coasting his hand up my flank as he moaned.

"*Fuck*," he breathed. "Okay, maybe this was a bad idea. It's been two days and we haven't even had makeup sex yet. Show-and-tell can wait." He bent to kiss me again.

"No," I insisted, pushing at his shoulder even as my cock strained insistently against my jeans in protest. "No, this is good. Makeup sex can wait a few more minutes. Waiting'll be fun. It'll make it even better."

Parker laughed. "You have a strange idea of fun, Jameson. You're at least as weird as I am."

"Which is why we're perfect together," I said serenely. "We get each other."

Parker grinned. "And always have. See?" He took the next item out of the box and handed it to me.

"Oh, shit," I said, sitting up straighter. "What the hell?"

It was a wooden block with the letters P-A-R-K-E-R carved out on each side, each one showcasing a different staining technique I'd learned in wood shop.

"You kept this thing?" I demanded, stroking a finger over the wood I'd spent what felt like decades of my life sanding to perfect smoothness.

"Uh, this *thing* was my fifteenth birthday present," he scoffed. "And it's *beautiful*. And you made it for me. Of course I kept it."

"Even after—" I began.

"Even after," he said, nodding once. "Here." He

handed me a stack of pictures, and I leafed through them slowly.

One was from his homecoming dance senior year—our first "outing" as a couple, *literally*—where we posed with our arms around each other's waists in matching dark blue suits and matching slicked-down hair.

Another was of me from that ridiculous *Harry Potter* release party the following summer, where I sported a "Muggle" t-shirt he'd bought me. One of my eyebrows was raised, like I recognized I was way too cool to be in this picture, but the grin on my face said I'd have done just about any un-cool thing Parker asked of me.

Another was of Molly on Parker's shoulders as they tried to recreate some abstract, artsy pose up on Jane's Peak during the golden hour. I remembered the day clearly, since I'd been the one taking the shot.

Another was of me, leaning on my old, green car in my baseball jacket.

The last was a shot of me that I didn't remember at all. It was wintertime, I gathered, since I had a beanie pulled low on my forehead, and I was talking to Diane and rubbing at my injured shoulder. I looked tired as hell, and I was smiling without really smiling.

"When was this?" I asked, tapping the picture with the back of my finger. "Doesn't look familiar."

"Parade of Lights here in O'Leary. Nine years ago, now, I think? Ethan took it when he was home on break." Parker took the picture from my hand and studied it, then bit the inside corner of his mouth. "He'd done a photography class the semester before, and he was all about taking candid shots on an old-school camera. When he came back to school, he insisted on developing them in our one *tiny* bathroom, so I figured he deserved to have me steal it." He traced the curve of my half smile in the picture. "I liked to imagine you were missing me."

"I was," I said thickly.

"Yeah? You think?" Parker smiled sadly. "I mean, not like you even remember this particular day or anything, but it's nice to think maybe—"

"I can guarantee it. There wasn't a day I didn't. Even when I told myself not to think of you, it was like not thinking about elephants, babe. But at times like this? Festivals and stuff? Yeah. You can bet I was missing you."

Parker leaned more heavily against me, like maybe he wanted to feel the solid weight of me as much as I needed to feel him. I ran a fingertip over the curl of his ear.

"I've got more stuff," he said with a little sniff, getting back to business.

He took out a baseball—"From that no-hitter game you pitched, remember?"—and a sketch Molly had done of him. A bunch of Magic: The Gathering cards—"They don't make *Forcefield* cards anymore. That's worth money." —and a picture of baby Parker on his grandmother's lap, all wrapped up in the blanket she'd made him. A quote from a Jane Austen book written on notebook paper. A recipe for his aunt's cookies. An old business card of his father's. A graduation card from his mom. A *Harry Potter* wand. A newspaper clipping of his birth announcement.

"And that's it, really," he said, piling his treasures back into the tin. "I try to keep it down to the most essential things. The things that mean the most. The things I never, never want to forget." He shifted up on one hip so he could reach into his pocket and pulled out the cactus magnet. He carefully stuck it to the inside of the lid before putting the lid back on the tin. "Like people who understand that cactus-based puns are a thing and come to Arizona to fetch me, even when I've been an idiot."

I swallowed past a lump in my throat.

"Do you see now? Do you get it?" Parker demanded, setting the box on the floor. His eyes were wide and earnest and maybe a little bit shiny.

"I get it," I said softly.

"There's hardly anything from Boston," he said, like he needed to *make sure* I understood, and I got that too. No more assumptions. "I'm not gonna tell you I cried every day, Jamie. I didn't. Or that I never enjoyed myself in the city, because I definitely did. But the most important things? The things that touched my heart? They're all from O'Leary. They're *almost* all about *you.* So it was a given that I was gonna end up back here... *both* times I left."

And that was when it clicked, when I *finally* understood on a soul-deep level that Parker really was mine the same way I was his. We'd just been marking time in our lives while we were apart.

"Have I ever mentioned how glad I am that you came back to O'Leary, and how very glad I am that you *stayed,* even though I was an asshole?"

"You can always mention it again," Parker teased. He drew his finger in a line across my stomach, just above my waistband, and then circled my navel.

"It kinda sucks, doesn't it?" I said suddenly. "We could have been together all these years if I hadn't—"

"Been the protective, loving person you are? Nah. I mean, you were totally misguided and wrong. Intensely wrong. *Incredibly* wrong."

"Thank you."

"But still. We had to change and grow and... maybe even lose each other so we could really appreciate how important it is to have each other. We had to have the big stupid misunderstanding so we could realize that for all that we know about one another, we've been shit at communicating."

"We needed to mess up to figure out how to do it right?"

Parker nodded.

"And you think we've got it now?"

"I think I'm not letting you go again. Not for anyone or anything," he said.

I pulled him down and rolled him underneath me. "That's a pretty serious statement," I warned, hovering over him. "You sure?"

Parker solemnly held up one crooked pinkie finger, and I burst out laughing before I captured his pinkie with my own and then kissed him with my heart on my lips.

There was nothing in the world but Parker and me. The rain beat insistently against the window, and the kitchen was an empty wreck just waiting for us to set it right, and O'Leary still needed a brand-new bar, but none of that felt important just then. A marching band could have tramped through the room, a dozen gutter salesmen or needy ex-boyfriends could have knocked on the door, and I wouldn't have noticed. I was focused on the only thing in the world that really, truly mattered.

We lay like that for the longest time, just kissing. I slid off his shirt just for the pleasure of feeling his skin against mine, and he kicked off his sneakers so he could brace his feet on the bed and cradle me between his legs. We stood up at one point to shed our jeans and then went right back to where we'd been, totally unhurried—because *Jesus*, why would I have hurried when there was no one I wanted to be with more than him and no opportunity in the world more important than this one I'd been given?

My hand trailed down to wrap around his cock, and Parker's head went back on a gasp.

"Yeah," he breathed. "Just like that, Jamie. Oh, fuck. I want…"

"What do you want, love? Faster? Harder?"

He slid his knees up to lock his feet behind my waist. "I want you. Inside me."

I slid a little lower on the bed and rocked again so my cock slid against the cleft of his ass. "Like this?"

He sucked in a breath through his nose, and his hand gripped my shoulder with bruising intensity. "Do you feel that?" he demanded. "It was always supposed to be this way between us, Jamie. Always. And now it can be."

I shifted up to press our kiss-swollen lips together one more time, then I fished the lube and a condom out of the nightstand drawer.

"No prep," he demanded, eyes shut, as I flipped the cap open and squeezed the lube onto my fingers. "Just you."

"Parker…"

His eyes flew open. "Just you, Jame. Slowly. I want to feel it."

Just me… and sixty-seven tons of lube, I thought grimly, because there was no way in hell I'd chance hurting him. But he shivered when I rubbed the cool liquid over his hole, and I lost any desire to protest. I wanted to be inside him as much as he wanted me there.

I ripped open the condom with my teeth and rolled it on, then squeezed more lube out of the tube, coating my cock and my hand, then I spread Parker's cheeks and coated him too.

Part of me couldn't believe this was finally happening. That Parker was underneath me, his eyes shining up at me with love and trust. Part of me felt how inevitable it was, like stars finally coming into alignment or something. Part of my brain—probably that stupid, self-sabotaging part—

was rolling its eyes at how I'd become a poet all of a sudden, when I'd fucking hated stuff like this before, but the rest of me knew that this was inevitable too. And *right*. Because it was Parker.

I braced one hand on the bed, wrapped the other around the base of my cock, and pushed against him. Parker pushed back, and then suddenly the tip of my erection was inside him. It felt like the most serious, solemn thing I'd ever done—

"Oh holy *mother* of a fucking *duck*," Parker yelled, his eyes popping open. "Do we need to talk about the definition of *slow* when we finally have that discussion about being *polite*?"

And just like that, I was laughing. Propped above Parker, looking down at the man I never wanted to be without, and laughing my head off, because no matter how well we knew each other, he would always surprise me and keep me on my toes.

"I love you," I told him, and his outraged face softened as he smiled up at me.

"I love you too," he said. "Just give me one teeny, tiny minute."

But it didn't even take that long before he was pushing against me, silently demanding more, and I was sliding inside him fully. It felt so good, I pulled out and sank back in again just to see if it was as good the second time, but it was even *better*, especially with Parker's moans in my ear, and his hands clutching my hair, and the look of frozen shock on his face when my cock tagged his prostate.

"You are so fucking *tight*, Parker."

"*Touch me!*" he demanded. "Please, please, please…"

I levered myself up farther and reached a hand between us so I could jack him in time to my thrusts.

One of his hands landed on my bicep—the one

supporting all these antics, the one I'd injured years before —and he trailed his fingers over the muscle slowly, his eyes hot and wild.

"You're so damn strong, Jameson. You always have been."

I moved my hand faster because the rasp of his voice and the heat in his eyes made my balls draw up tight, and I could practically feel my orgasm coming, like a line of wildfire running down my back.

"Come on, Parker. Come for me, baby."

"Coming. Fucking coming! I—Oh, shit. Jamie!" Ropes of cum shot out of his dick and up onto my chest and abs, and the sight of it, the sticky *heat* of it, was enough to over-power my resistance.

I thrust inside him once, twice, and then I was coming too, harder than I ever had in my life, throwing my head back to the ceiling and positively roaring because it felt that damn good.

We lay together for a minute—glued together more like —while I tried to catch my breath and my heart resumed its normal rhythm. I finally pulled out a few minutes later, but Parker didn't let me pull away.

"I like you right on top of me," he said, his words slurred. "This way I can keep an eye on you. Make sure you don't wander off while I'm sleeping."

He patted my ass firmly, his eyes closed.

"I'm not the one who left," I reminded him, bracing on my forearms so he wouldn't have to take all my weight.

"Fine, then." Parker waved a hand in the air. "So *I* don't wander off. Whichever. *Shhh.* Sleepy time now."

I snorted, then very deliberately leaned forward to suck his neck. His eyes flew open.

"Wait. What are you doing?" he demanded. "Jamie! We just... *ungh...*" He tilted his head so I could have better access. "Jameson, seriously. It's been like ten minutes," he moaned. But I could feel him hardening against my stomach already. "Oh, fuck. I get it now. I so, totally get it."

"Get what?" I asked, sucking harder.

"So, so many things," he sighed biting his lip. "Remind me to tell you a story about Ricky and his wife… sometime. A time that's… not now."

"You sure? Because I can stop if you want," I teased.

Parker grinned up at me, a devilish light in his eyes, and laughed. "Fuck me forever, Jamie. Don't ever stop."

Epilogue

PARKER

"Good morning, O'Leary!" Pete Daley yelled. "Happy Lilac Day to all of you! Here's a brand-new song we've been working on for ya!"

I snorted as I flipped burgers on the portable grill Jamie and I had set up on the fairgrounds sometime just after dawn that morning. It was barely eleven, but the heat and humidity had already reached what the weatherperson had called "unseasonable warmth" and what I called the eighty-seventh layer of hell. And that was *before* my boyfriend plastered himself to my back with his hands at my waist and whispered, "You think Pete knows Lilac Day isn't really a holiday?"

I laughed out loud, not even caring about the way our combined sweat glued us together, because there'd never again be a time when I didn't want every part of Jamie pressed against every part of me, even if it meant we were gonna melt into a puddle right there and then.

And then Pete's band launched into their song.

"Did... did Pete just Rick-roll us?" I demanded, as a country version of "Never Gonna Give You Up" began playing over the speakers. "Pete's gotten taller since middle school, but not a lot brighter," I muttered.

"Eh, he's a decent guy these days. Since Dex left town."

"If you say so," I allowed.

Jamie put his lips to my neck—to that *one particular spot*—and breathed, "I do."

"Hey, unfair," I said, spinning around and brandishing my metal spatula at him. "You can't use that move outside the house." Otherwise I'd never utter a cogent sentence in public again.

"Is that a new rule?" my boyfriend demanded innocently, hands up and grin spreading across his gorgeous face.

"No, it's not new, as you very well know. Also? Stop with the… hotness." I moved my spatula up and down in front of his body, gesturing from his booted feet, up his muscular, hairy legs, past the shorts that showed off the curve of his ass and the t-shirt that clung to his broad chest, to his hair, which glowed bright copper in the sunshine. "It's very distracting, and I have wings to prepare. Soon-to-be-award-winning wings."

Jamie braced his hands on his hips, and his smile somehow got even wider. "And you're *sure* you wanna do this *here*?" He waved a hand in the air, indicating the already crowded fairgrounds. "Now?"

I narrowed my eyes. "I am very extremely positive. Our bar shall be called ALL HAIL PARKER'S AMAZING WING BAR." I moved a hand through the air in a half circle, like I was spelling it out on an imaginary sign.

Jamie scratched a hand over his chest, and his mouth twitched beneath his beard. "Not even Jamie and Parker's, huh?"

I glanced up at the corner of the tent like I was

thinking about it and allowed, "We can put 'now featuring Parker's boyfriend Jamie' at the bottom."

Jamie stepped closer again and grabbed me by the waistband of my jeans, pulling me into him again. "Thoughtful of you."

"In smaller print, of course," I warned.

"Of course," he agreed solemnly, pressing a kiss to my lips.

But before I had a chance to sink into it, one of Jamie's hands moved around to the small of my back, while the other wrapped around my hand on the spatula, and the next thing I knew, we were dancing around our tiny booth, right there at the fairgrounds, to fucking Rick Astley.

Only with Jamie.

"You're an idiot," I said, but what I meant was, *I love you*.

"I know, baby," Jamie said softly, and the look he gave me said he understood the words I didn't say.

"Morning, boys!" Angela Ross said, walking up to the front of our booth wearing a summery smile along with her trademark black braid. She had a large empty flowerpot in her hand. "Such a perfect day for the celebration!"

Jamie stopped twirling me, but he didn't let me go, and that was fine by me.

"A perfect day for O'Leary's most important festival of all," I agreed.

"Exactly." Angela laughed. "Although, remind me that later this week we need to chat about the Fourth of July. Think you two will have your place up and running by then?"

Jamie and I exchanged a look, and he shrugged.

"We're working on it," I said. "I've got a lawyer friend of my dad's on the case. Skip's semi-retired now, and he's kind of a bulldog. He's been on Unity Financial like a bad rash. So… we'll see."

Jamie and I had been working on our finances—when we weren't outfitting our kitchen with an embarrassing amount of stainless steel and custom cabinetry—and while Jamie had a good amount of savings even after the kitchen reno, it wasn't nearly enough to get us up and running. Yet.

But that was okay. I was finding it remarkably easy to be patient these days.

"Well, I thought I might be able to help out with that." She set the flowerpot down on the front counter and turned it to show us the painted front.

"Official O'Leary Bar Fund," I read. I looked back up at Angela, whose eyes were sparkling. "What's this?"

"Some folks around town have mentioned throwing a fundraiser for you two. But we figured this would be easier."

"Nah," I said, shaking my head. "Thanks anyway, but there are plenty of more worthy causes where people could donate their money."

"I think you're underestimating just how much O'Learians miss your place, Parks," Angela said, stepping away from the counter. "And how important you are to our community. Both of you." She winked at Jamie.

"That's sweet," Jamie said. "Really. But Parker's right. I wouldn't feel comfortable…"

"What? Letting people help you the way you help them?" She shook her head. "It's like you boys don't even know how life in O'Leary works, even after all this time. Every once in a while there's a silver lining to having everybody know your business." She tapped the container. "Enjoy yours."

Jamie and I shared a look. Arguing was pointless.

Besides, if we earned a few dollars in tips, I'd just donate them somewhere.

"Thank you," I said. "Sincerely. For thinking of us."

"We love you," she said simply. "Now, give me one of those burgers before my stomach eats itself."

I laughed and broke away from Jamie to get Angela her food while Jamie got busy making up chicken wings.

Angela paid for her burger, then took a white paper from her pocket and tucked it into the flowerpot. "Consider this a small business grant from the town council," she said. "To thank you for going to all this trouble for the festival."

I frowned at Jamie and made a move to look at the paper, which seemed to be a check, but before I could pull it out, Hen Lattimer and Diane Perkins walked up.

Hen took a spot at the counter next to Angela, but Diane walked right into our booth and threw her arms around Jamie like she hadn't seen him in years, when I knew for a fact they'd just worked the closing shift at the diner together the night before.

"Jameson, I'm *so proud*!" she exclaimed, patting Jamie's chest like a fond parent. "You and Parker working your own booth!"

It was adorable… especially when Jamie blushed and rolled his shoulder like he wasn't sure what to do with her approval.

"I'll take one of them burgers, Parker," Henry said, watching Angela devour hers. "And some wings."

Jamie and I exchanged a glance that had me fighting a smile.

"Which kind, Hen?" Jamie asked. "We have two varieties today."

"Two, huh?"

"Jamie and I are trying out a couple of sauce flavors," I

interjected quickly. No one needed to know the details of Chicken Wing Death Match, Part Deux. "To see which one ends up on the menu. When we have a menu."

Hen frowned and nodded. "Gimme a couple of each."

Jamie put the wings together in a cardboard container while I got Hen's burger, then I watched with my arm wrapped around Jamie's waist while Hen took a bite of each chicken wing.

"Oh, this is good," Hen said, taking a bite from a wing with Jamie's darker sauce, and I could practically feel the smugness emanating from my boyfriend, even though he didn't say a word.

"I refuse to open a Chicken Emporium," I said under my breath.

Jamie's whole body shook with his laughter, and I buried my face in his bicep to hide my smile.

"Oh, but this one," Hen said, eyes widening as he bit into one of the chicken wings I'd made. "It's got a little bite to it, don't it? Yeah, this one's *real* good."

"Ha *ha!*" I gloated.

"Can we at least call it All Hail Parker *and Jamie?*" Jamie muttered.

"Sure," I agreed. "As long as your name…"

"Is in smaller print," Jamie and I finished together. Then the two of us collapsed into giggles.

"I dunno boys," Hen said, sucking on his fingers. "I'm thinking your best option is to include both."

"Two wing options on the menu," Jamie said, taking a deep breath to control his laughter. "Yeah, we've thought of that."

"Nah, both in one order. You know? Little of this, little of that. Like a… whatchamacallit, Diane?"

Diane leaned over Henry to scoop up some of the sauce on her finger.

"A variety pack?" she said. She popped her finger into her mouth, and her eyes opened wide. "Oh, I agree. Tangy and spicy and sweet all at once. I'd order both together. I don't think either one is better than the other."

"And I'm gonna need these in my life at least once a week," Henry said.

Diane rolled her eyes but grinned too. "Speaking of which," she prompted. "Don't you have something for the boys?"

"Oh, right. I'd forget my head without you, Diane." Hen dug in his pocket and produced a white envelope that he placed in the flowerpot. "Little thank you for Jamie being so good to Diane over the years and a little incentive too, in case Parker decides the hardware business is more his speed." He winked, and they moved to one side to finish their food.

"Hey, Parks, I'd like an order of both wings," Angela said, before I could pull that paper out either.

And as soon as I'd gotten her order up, Lina Davenport, Daniel Michaelson, and Julian Ross were standing in line waiting to order.

I handed Lina her burger and a soda, and she thanked me profusely, then put a blue envelope into the pot. "A little something from Macarena and me," she said happily. "A little thank you for the birthday party birdseed treats."

I laughed. "It was no big deal."

Jamie finished Julian and Daniel's order, and then Julian nudged his boyfriend. Daniel fished a paper from his pocket and dropped it into the pot too.

"From Jules and me. Apparently I have you to thank for a lot of things, Parker." He put an arm around Julian's waist, and Julian looked up at him adoringly.

I shook my head. "That's not——"

"Mostly, we really miss having a place to watch football," Julian interrupted. "Daniel doesn't have a television."

"Besides, Angela told us what was going on… and I try to always do what Angela tells me," Daniel said, winking at Julian's mom.

"Not nearly often enough," Angela said, wagging a playful finger at him.

I frowned at Jamie, honestly bewildered, and he shrugged back, equally stunned.

And that was just the beginning. Cal and Ash came by, dropping something into the flowerpot that they called a "down payment on their wedding venue."

The Turner brothers came by, and while Mitch and Jamie discussed the ingredients in Jamie's special ketchup, Dare deposited an envelope he called, "a donation from the darts club, because playing in Si's garage is getting old."

Everett and Silas came by, and Ev left an envelope he told Jamie was his "friendship tax, because if Jamie leaves I'll officially be the crankiest person under forty in this town."

Bill Nickerson and his pretty wife came by for wings, and Dhann dropped some cash into the pot. So did Theo Ross, when he collected his burger, because he'd "be able to drink legally soon, Parks, just FYI," and Rae Martin, when they came by for a soda, because they'd loved working for me and "I'm basically paying you to give me my bar-back job again."

Even *Brian Carr* came by and dropped in a twenty, thanking me for showing him the error of his ways and offering to help out for free if we needed him.

Constantine and Micah came over later, along with Micah's little brother Mason—a younger, cuter version of Micah who worked as a doctor over in Baxter. While Con was moaning over the wings, Micah gave us something on behalf of his flower shop, Blooms, because he knew how hard it was to start his own business, and he wanted to pay it forward. And even *Mason* got in on the action, putting a wad of cash in the pot with a sad little smile because, "money's just a tool, and you two have something money can't buy," which was kinda cute and made me feel bad for him at the same time.

Then Dana and Rena Cobb strolled up hand-in-hand, and while Rena collected their food, Dana produced two pieces of paper from her pocket.

"This is a check from O'Leary's newest residents, the Talwoods."

"Who?" I demanded. "I don't know them at all!"

"Denise and *Ricky* Talwood," she said, wiggling her eyebrows.

"No way! Ricky and Mrs. Ricky are moving to O'Leary?"

Dana nodded. "We've kept in touch since they were here over the winter. They loved the small-town aesthetic, so they're moving once their kids are out of school. And when I told them about you and your bar, they agreed that community spaces like that are important." She dropped the check into the pot and leaned over the counter. "I've also got Ricky's business card. Have I mentioned he's a venture capitalist?"

"A venture capitalist," I repeated dumbly. "Are you serious?"

"As a heart attack. And looking for local investment opportunities. But I've got something even better." She waved the second check, and I grabbed it from her hand before she could put it in the pot.

"This… is from my parents," I said, glancing over my shoulder at Jamie, who handed Rena a container of wings and then came to stand behind me to look at the check in my hand.

"It's for *twenty thousand dollars.*" Jamie sounded as stunned as I felt.

"Beatrice says she's glad you finally found the *right* opportunity, even if it is in O'Leary." Dana grinned. "Lance says, '*Tell Parker not to expect a wedding present.*' And also that he's proud of you."

"And here's a little something from Dana and me," Rena said, putting her own check in, as well. "If you need some artwork once you're up and running, you just let me know," she added.

"Paul and I didn't wanna be left out," Quinn Tierney said, striding up with his little dog Emmylou in his arms and dropping in his own contribution.

My hand started shaking a little, making the check flutter like there was a dry monsoon hitting Upstate New York, and Jamie slid the paper from my hand. He took the other checks and envelopes from the pot and started rifling through them, then his hands started shaking too.

"Parker. *Babe.*" He swallowed and ran a hand over his mouth and beard. "There are *thousands* here. Jesus Christ." His brown eyes were liquid gold as he stared at me. "Thousands."

I blew out a breath and looked at the smiling faces all around us. Our neighbors. Our family, in a really weird way.

I'd thought there wasn't a Parker-shaped hole in O'Leary. Clearly, I'd been wrong.

"I don't know what to say," I said honestly. "This is so far beyond…" I sniffled in a totally unmanly way.

Jamie's hand came to the back of my neck and pulled my face into his shoulder, likely sensing I was about to lose my shit.

"Thank you," he spoke over my head. "You have no idea what this means to us."

"I'm guessing it's just about what you mean to us," Quinn said.

"O'Learians stick together, son," Hen said. Then he clapped his hands together once. "Hot damn! I feel like Santa Claus! Who else can we help out, Diane?"

Diane laughed and smacked him lightly in the stomach. "I'm sure an opportunity will present itself soon enough, honey. Now, I've got pies to sell, and you promised to help me out."

"She's a slave driver," Hen told no one in particular, but everyone laughed, which was probably what he'd intended, and the crowd dispersed with calls of congratulations and sincere offers of help, leaving Jamie and me alone for a second.

"You okay?" Jamie asked, rubbing my shoulder.

I turned to brace my hands on his waist and ground myself in his steady presence. "I'm having a moment," I told him. "What the actual fuck just happened to us, Jameson?"

Jamie huffed out a laugh, but he was clearly as surprised as I was. "I think they call this… *luck*?"

"Pardon?" a high-pitched voice called. "Mr. Hoffstraeder?"

I turned, wiping my face a little against Jamie's shirt as I did, and found a small man with beady eyes, wearing a full suit and tie.

"Dennis Rodman," I gasped. "What do *you* want?"

The insurance investigator rolled his eyes and sighed.

"I just wanted to let you know your investigation is officially closed. There's no evidence of arson." He sounded almost disappointed, the way the weathermen sounded when a monster storm passed just to the south of us.

"As every single person in this town has been trying to tell you since December?" Jamie said heatedly. "Imagine my surprise."

"I keep telling my wife, this job's not worth it," Dennis muttered in that same high voice. "Nobody's ever happy to see me. People look at me like I'm the Grim Reaper."

I lifted an eyebrow. "Uh, sorry?" Then I frowned. "Wait, you have a wife?" He'd been in O'Leary for months, and I hadn't seen her.

He nodded and said sourly, "She's never happy to see me either." He lifted a hand to slick his thinning hair to his head. "You'll be hearing from our office on Monday," he said as he walked away.

"This is… a little scary," I told Jamie, turning to look at him with wide eyes. "I don't know how to be this happy. What will I do with myself? What will keep me up at night?"

"There are still the plants," Jamie said comfortingly. "Lucille's gonna need to be repotted soon."

I laughed and shook my head. "But I already even have a *pot*," I whined, throwing out a hand to the pot on the counter.

"If you really need something to keep you up at night," Jamie said, drawing me into the circle of his arms again. "I'm sure I could find something." His voice was a husky promise, and I let myself relax against him… only to have him slap my ass through my jeans *hard*. "But in the meantime, baby… don't you have a Death Match to win?"

I laughed and glanced at the pot on the counter, then blinked and looked at the pot again. "Jame?" I said, pointing. "I think I have a better idea for the bar's name than Jamie and Parker's Amazing Chicken Emporium."

Jamie looked at the pot too, and a slow, beautiful smile

broke out across his face. "You thinking what I'm thinking?"

"The O'Leary Bar…"

"…and Grill," Jamie finished. He shook his head and laughed. "It fits."

"Yeah," I agreed softly. "It really does. But this doesn't mean I'm forfeiting the Death Match," I warned. "We still have a debt of honor to settle at home later."

"I wouldn't dream of giving up on it, Parks. Not giving up on anything anymore." He winked and gave me a quick kiss before going back to work.

I stood there for a minute, drinking everything in—the warmth of spring, the beauty of the town, and the knowledge that this one moment, this pure happiness was *mine.*

I didn't delude myself into thinking the rest of our life together was going to be idyllic, that bad things wouldn't happen—hell, I was about to lose a Death Match, and I knew it—but I wasn't scared of what the future had in store.

I'd spent years trying to figure out what was going to happen next in my life so I could plan for it. Brace for it. Mitigate it.

But the truth was, you couldn't plan. *And that was okay.*

I couldn't have planned for my bar to burn down. Or to lose my home.

But I also couldn't have planned for Jamie to come back into my life in a fucking *blizzard.* I could never, ever have planned for what had just happened at the Lilac Festival, of all places.

Sometimes bad shit had to happen to lead you to even better things farther down the road.

Sometimes you needed a fire to burn away what *was* to make room for whatever would come next.

And looking at Jamie in that moment, I knew whatever came next, good or bad, it was going to be beautiful.

———

Don't miss the next Love in O'Leary novel, *The Night*, available here → https://readerlinks.com/l/1570170

And if you want to see Brian find his happily ever after, check out *The Castle*, a Love in O'Leary novella, available here → https://readerlinks.com/l/1570173

www.ingramcontent.com/pod-product-compliance
Lightning Source LLC
Chambersburg PA
CBHW032340310726
48973CB00007B/1778